THE RECONSTRUCTION OF CYPRIAN

A BAD BOY BILLIONAIRE ROMANCE

MICHELLE LOVE

CONTENTS

Made in "The United States" by:

Michelle Love

© Copyright 2021

ISBN: 978-1-64808-851-3

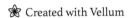 Created with Vellum

BLURB

Cyprian Girard is a 35-year-old billionaire investor who works like hell all week, making himself (and others) tons of money.
On the weekends, he parties like there's no tomorrow. Being a confirmed bachelor, who's looking to score all the tail he can possibly get, has him making his move on a certain convenient store cashier, who ignites something in him as she's not about to give into his charming ways.
Camilla Petit is a 25-year-old Science Major at Clemson University in Clemson, South Carolina. She's working as a cashier at a convenience store to help her makes ends meet while she goes to college. She works the night shift and every weekend, she sees the driver of the ultra-rich Cyprian come in and purchase condoms along with other things. One fateful night, Cyprian himself gets out of the car to make his own purchases and sets his sights on her.
Camilla is nobody's fool. She's on the verge of starting her career as a lab technician and womanizing men have no place in her life. But Cyprian is no ordinary man. He's been constructed, nearly from birth, to charm women into his bed and then leave them wanting more.

With a lifetime of kudos from his father on his romantic endeavors, can Camilla, who he affectionately calls Cami, reconstruct him to fit into her world? Or will it be the other way around? Will Cyprian mold her to his specifications, making her just another notch on his bed post? Can Christmas give them both a miracle?

BOOK 1: THE FLIRT

A Bad Boy Billionaire Romance

By Michelle Love

1

CYPRIAN

A golden hue falls over the crowd of people who dance under the disco ball as yellow lights shoot up at it and bounce off the millions of mirrors used to create the magical ball. Loud music vibrates my body as I sit, unseen, at the top of the spiral staircase which leads down to the ballroom of my father's mansion.

He's having another party, the way he does each and every Friday and Saturday night. Sunday is reserved for other social functions. On Sundays, we go to watch horses run around a track while my father trades money with the people around him. On occasion, we get onto the jet and go to other places where my father bets with other people about various things.

Once we watched dogs run around a track and that was cool, because he took me to look at them before they raced and I was allowed to pet a couple of them. The horses are always too high-spirited. I'm never allowed to touch them.

I am, what my parents call, a happy mishap. My mother left me with my father when I started kindergarten a year ago. Up until then, she and I lived in Los Angeles. We lived in a small home and she stayed with me.

She decided, since I was going to start school, she could go back to her job. So, I came to live with my father in Clemson, South Carolina. I am what they call a child prodigy.

I was reading and writing at 3-years-old. I was drawing pictures which won awards at 5-years-old. Now, at 6-years-old, I've skipped a couple of grades. I'm in third grade now and my teachers believe I will continue to skip grades.

My father owns a company that makes investments for people. He's already tutoring me on what types of things make good investments. He tells me often we are a family who works hard and plays harder.

Looking down at the men and women who are dancing, hugging, kissing, and drinking things that make them stagger at times and slur their words, I find my father out of the crowd and see him with a woman on each arm.

He must sense me looking at him, as his dark eyes scan the staircase until they meet mine. He smiles and tips his tall hat at me. The women wave at me and blow me kisses.

I blow them back and they act as if they catch them and hold their hands to their hearts. With a sigh, I get up and make my way to my bedroom to study some more before I go to bed.

My life is full, not the way most children's are. In other ways. I spend the school days having breakfast with my father, then his driver takes me to school. I stay there for a long time and then the driver brings me home. My nanny makes sure I eat dinner and bathe then I get into bed and go to sleep.

Only in the mornings, do I see my father. We go over the newspaper to see what the stock market is doing. Then we head off to do work, as he calls it.

ON THE WEEKENDS, I do not see him at breakfast. My nanny makes sure I have my breakfast and maybe at lunch, my father will come out of his bedroom. He always has different women with him when he does. Sometimes there are two or even three women who come out of it with him.

I don't know what they do when he has his sleepovers. I just know I'm not invited to join them. And I'm not to get to know the women. I am to exchange polite hello's and goodbye's but that's all.

My father makes it crystal clear, none of the women have a place in our little family. He and I are a family and my mother and I are a separate family.

I asked my father one time about love. A friend from school told me his mother and father are in love and they are married and live together. He told me he has brothers and sisters and a real family. Not like mine.

When I asked my father about that, he said some like to live life that way, but he doesn't. He has little time for relationships. His time is better spent on making him and other people money. And when he's not doing that, he wants no fussing and fighting. He says those things come along with love and marriage.

I SUPPOSE HE'S RIGHT. I saw one of my teachers arguing with a man in the hallway once. When I asked her if she was okay because she was crying, she told me the man I saw her with was her husband and they'd had a disagreement.

If a mere disagreement can make a person, who is in love, cry then I too want no part of that either. Just like my mother and father. I've never seen either of them cry and I also have never cried unless I was in physical pain.

I did cry a little when my mother left me here with my father and a nanny. But she told me that I'd be fine and she'd see me when she could. I see her once a month. She comes to my father's parties for the weekend at the end of every month and I see her some while she's here. She was right, I was fine, eventually.

I saw her dance one time at one of the first parties she came to. That's when I found out what the job was she wanted to get back to. She is, what my father calls, an exotic dancer.

At one of my father's parties, I sat on the stairs, watching my mother dance and toss away her clothes, my nanny found me and scooped me up and took me back to my bedroom where she sat outside my door in a chair to make sure I stayed in my room. She told me I shouldn't see my mother doing that.

I ASKED her if what my mother was doing was considered wrong. She told me there is no wrong or right. But some things should go unseen by one's children.

With no wrong or right in this world, I suppose it is my destiny to follow in my parents' footsteps. Love may be what some people fall into. I am not like those people. I am like the one's I came from.

My father told me I was not planned. He wasn't sorry that I came along but he wasn't happy with something called the condom that gave me to him and my mother.

Apparently, this thing called a condom has the power to stop an egg from becoming a baby. The one he said he was using must have had a hole in it. He told me never to skimp on condoms and always make sure I had plenty of them when my time comes.

I don't know when or why my time will come to use condoms but I will remember my father's advice on them. He must know what he's talking about since he's never had any other happy mishaps. My mother hasn't either.

Laughter fills the hallway outside my bedroom and I get off my bed and sneak to the door, pulling it open only a tiny crack to see who's coming upstairs.

My father has the same two women under each arm as he did when I saw him downstairs. They're taking turns kissing his cheeks and he looks very happy and relaxed. Not the way he looked when he got home from work, earlier this evening.

"GOODNIGHT, PAPA," I call out as I open the door a bit more.

All three of their heads turn my way. "Hey, cutie," the woman with red hair says to me. "Aren't those pajamas the cat's meow?"

My father jostles her a bit to get her to look at him. "No talking to the kid, Bonnie." He looks at me and gives me a grin. "Goodnight, son. I'll see you for lunch tomorrow. You get some rest now."

"You too, Papa," I say and close my door.

Going back to my bed, I have to admit my father looks way happier than my married teacher ever does. His way has to be the best way. He and my mother are happy people. I want to be happy too.

My friend from school will most likely follow how his parents live and I find myself feeling sorry for him and how his life will certainly turn out.

Poor kid...

2

CYPRIAN

The disco ball is reflecting purples and pinks as I walk down the spiral staircase to go to my graduation party. I've finally earned my Bachelor's Degree in Investment. I still have to get my Master's in Finance, I'm not quite ready to become the CEO of Papa's company just yet. But I am working at Libertine Investments as an assistant to the CLO, Stan Franco. He oversees all the legal affairs of the company.

At 16-years-old, I am the youngest person who works at my father's company. No one treats me like a kid, though. Not when I can handle myself like an adult. And being the boss' son doesn't hurt either.

As I hit the last step, I am met by a couple of beauties. "I'm Roxanna," the brunette tells me. Her arm moves around my waist as she leans in and kisses my cheek, purposely rubbing her breast against my arm.

"Hello, Roxanna," I say and turn my head to catch her lips with mine. She tastes like rum and coke as our tongues move around together.

A touch on my ass has me pulling away and looking at the skinny blonde who's also waiting for my attention. "I'm Bambi. I work at your mother's club in L.A." Her breasts are nearly popping out of the tight dress she has on. The silver beads on it catch the strobe lights, just like the disco ball does, making her light up.

"Nice to meet you, Bambi," I say and take her waiting red lips and kiss her too.

She's a smoother kisser than the other woman. But the other woman has the curves I like.

I guess I'll have to keep them both for the night!

The music goes down and I hear a clanking sound. Both women wrap themselves around me and I wrap my arms around them as my father calls everyone's attention to him as he walks up on the stage.

His temples are going gray in his otherwise dark hair, he's growing older, a thing he reminds me of often as he seems to be hurrying me along to take over his position as CEO of Libertine Investments. He looks out at the crowd of people who've come to my party.

None of my schoolmates were invited. I never made any friends while in college. I wasn't there to make friendships, my father told me. School was work and not a place to fraternize.

He took care of filling his parties with people. I found out almost every woman who comes to them are escorts, provided by several adult clubs around the nation. And at times, they come from around the world.

My father calls himself a connoisseur of fine women. He likes to taste them all. And escorts are liberal with their bodies. The men who fill his parties are business associates. Some of whom I know are married men but they come to enjoy the buffet of beauties who don't mind at all showing a man a good time.

I find my father holding up my degree and a smile fills his face.

"Tonight we're here to celebrate my son, Cyprian Girard's, achievement. He's earned his Bachelor's Degree in Investment. He has a Master's Degree to get before he can take over my role at Libertine Investments but I have no doubt he'll make quick work of that.

The way he's done with everything else, academically speaking. And sexually speaking as well! Am I right, ladies?"

Cheers go up as women hoot and holler. I smile and wave then give them a bow. I am my father's son, after all. I have learned from the most sexually advanced women on the planet, thanks to my father's generosity when it comes to bringing in women for his parties.

The two, who have claimed me for the night, hold tight to their prize and I have to smile as I find other women looking at me with lusty gazes and some flat-out show me parts of themselves to entice me.

I FOUND OUT, when I first started my sexual endeavors, when I was thirteen, not to go overboard with too many women at one time. My father caught up with me after an all-nighter with seven women. He told me, just like candy, whiskey, or food, you have to allow yourself to have only what you can handle. Moderation is what he taught me, in all things.

So, now I limit my women to three, tops. I find a feisty woman, with pink hair, looking at me with a raw hunger I think this current threesome could use.

My father goes on as I wiggle my finger at the vixen who is salivating over me. She comes to me as my father continues his speech. "Cyprian is the only fruit to have fallen from these loins." He gyrates his pelvis, making the women scream. "My happy mishap has made me very proud of him on this day, and all days, for that matter. So, please join me in letting him know he's appreciated by us all." More cheers ring out by all the attendees as the pink-haired girl drops to her knees in front of me.

I look back and forth at the women on each side of me.

"I'll let you two decide. Can Pinky, here, join us this evening for some fun?"

Roxanna asks the new woman, "Do you mind kissing another woman?"

"Excellent question, Roxanna," I say and give her cheek a quick peck.

Pinky, as I've dubbed her, shakes her head. I look at Bambi. "Do you have any questions for her?"

She looks Pinky over then asks, "Do you have any piercings that might add to the night's activities?"

HER MOUTH OPENS and I find a silver stud on the tip of her tongue. Bambi and Roxanna both gasp then Roxanna says, "We'd love to add her to tonight's activities, Cyprian. Please add her in for our complete enjoyment."

"Seems, you're in, Pinky," I say as she gets up and runs her hands over my chest.

"My name is Paula but Pinky will do," she says then kisses me, using that little bead on her tongue to run over the roof of my mouth.

I'm happy with the addition to the pack and find myself ready to dance a bit, drink a little, and then fornicate like animals for the rest of the night.

Life is good...

3

CYPRIAN

It's Friday and my nerves are frazzled as the board meeting has gone on longer than expected. "Iran is a no go," I say as I slam my fist on top of the huge, dark oak table. "I will never budge on that! I am not my father. I will do no business with countries who are terroristic."

"But their money is as good as anyone's, Cyprian," the CFO, Bob Steward, argues.

"Not to me, it's not. Can we end this now?" I ask as I look wearily at the board. "I will not cave to you people. I am the CEO now. My father, Corbin Gerard, has entrusted this company to me and I have gone to school for a long time to get to where I am. I've studied the outcomes of such investments. Something like that, in a time of war, could end any political plans anyone of you may have."

"How are you so sure?" Claudette, an elderly board member, who's been here forever and three days, asks as she looks at me as if I'm a stupid child.

I TURNED TWENTY-SIX LAST WEEK. I am far from a stupid child and have more education than any of these people have. I earned my

Master a few years ago and am finally through with school and ready to move on to running the company my father started and has entrusted to me. But this, old as hell, board fights me on every last thing I want to change.

Standing up and picking up my briefcase, I answer her, "Claudette, you may not have aspirations for political greatness but some in this room do. While I don't care for politics, per say, I am a true American who has tremendous respect for those who have fought a war that's gone on far too long. I will not make money for or take money from any enemy of the United States. That said, I will be ending this week's meeting as it's eight in the evening and my father is hosting a lovely party you are all invited to."

Claudette looks at me as I walk out of the board room. Her frown is evidence she's unhappy with me cutting the meeting short, in her opinion. But I am the CEO and I can do such a thing.

My body is weary from the many struggles I've gone through this week. It's been past eleven each night before I've seen the comfort of my bed. I have worked so hard and the knowledge pretty girls are waiting in the ballroom at the mansion is just too enticing for me to stay and argue with the old battle-axe any longer.

A chill runs through me as I hear the click of her one-inch heels as she comes up behind me.

"Cyprian, this is not over."

"Oh, but it is, Claudette. How I wish you could join us over here in the real world. You are from an ancient way of thinking. One that's dangerous now," I let her know. "In this time of such upheaval, we need to form a solid stand to make sure we remain the country we've always been. Helping that Iranian company make more money is a crime, in my opinion. Let it go. Next week, I've got a fantastic company in Hawaii to look at. And we'll all get to go to the resort owned by the huge company. It'll be fun, relaxing, all expenses paid, you'll love it. You should bring that granddaughter of yours along. What is her name again?"

Suddenly, her icy demeanor changes. "Margie is a wonderful young woman. She's your age and such a prize. The right kind of women to marry such an eligible bachelor as yourself. She's well-educated and helps out at all of the church functions. She's a great young woman!"

I'm afraid she lost me at the word, marry.

"Send her to the party tonight."

"Heaven's no!" she says as she shakes her head. "Cyprian, she's a nice young woman. But I could give you her phone number and you could take her on a nice date. A fancy restaurant, some wine, and good conversation. Doesn't that sound lovely?"

IT SOUNDS LIKE PURE HELL. "Maybe another time. I'm really wrung out from work this week. I need to relax and I'd make awful company for such a nice young woman. Another time perhaps." I hurry to get on the elevator and find Claudette right at my side.

She's rubbing her palms together, quite obviously trying her best to come up with another wonderful date idea. "Our church is having a social after the morning services. You two could meet there. It would be fun. You're such a patriot, aren't you a God-fearing man as well?"

"Church? I've never gone. We go to the track on Sundays. You know that," I say and find myself relieved when the elevator doors open and I can finally get rid of the old woman.

It's my fault and I know it, that she's hooked onto me, as I've made the mistake of asking about the woman I've seen in pictures around her home when I've been there on other occasions.

"WHICH ONE WILL you be at this Sunday?" she asks and I see it all there in her beady little eyes. She'll bring the good woman there and expect me to court her.

"You know what," I say as I act as if I just recalled something. "We aren't going to the track at all. I'm going to my mother's club in L.A. for a visit. I completely forgot. Some other time, Claudette."

My driver pulls the car to the curb and hops out to open the back door for me. My long black limousine is spacious, with a full bar, and lots of seating. Tons of room to have fun while getting to another place to have more fun.

I find a flashy platinum blonde with her long legs stretched out, waiting inside of it for me. Claudette does too. "Who is this?" she asks.

With a shrug of my shoulders, I ask, "What's your name?"

"Lola," she answers. "Your father sent me to accompany you home after a hard week of work, Cyprian."

"How, lovely," I say as I slip into the black-cherry leather seat. "See you next Friday, Claudette." My driver closes the door as Lola finds a sweet spot on my neck to nibble as she rubs me in all the right places.

I love my life...

4

CYPRIAN

"The walls in here are a decadent shade of yellow," the real estate agent tells me as I follow her through the home on the estate I'm looking to buy.

"I've never heard yellow called decadent before," I say as I look at the walls I would describe as canary yellow. "Good try, though. I do like the ten bedrooms and the theater room that's in the basement. I bet the sound would be amazing down there."

"I'm sure it is. Would you care for a demonstration, Mr. Girard?" she asks as she seems about to bend over backward to make this sale to me.

Her commission will probably be more than most people make in a year. Time to haggle a bit, I think. "My father said I needed to get myself a home. It's a good investment. I'm looking for a place that needs some help getting back up and going. I can use the repairs and reconstructions as write-offs. But I'll pay no more than what I believe this place is worth right now."

"Understood. This is an excellent property for you, Mr. Girard," the woman says as she points out how out of date the crown molding is. "All of this should be replaced."

. . .

As I LOOK around at the massive home that sits on one hundred acres, I contemplate all the people I'd need to hire and the money I'd have to pay them to take care of the place. I'd also have to hire contractors to make the renovations. With the work it needs and the write-offs I can take, it seems like the perfect home for me.

It sits just outside of Clemons, South Carolina. The office is only thirty minutes away on the other side of town. The drive out each night might be relaxing.

I open the door off the kitchen and listen to the crickets chirp in the cool evening air. "Nice, peaceful, relaxing. This will be perfect for me."

"And all this room is great for a man who's thinking about marriage and family soon," she says as she looks past me, at the vast backyard.

I laugh at her idea. "I'm not about to get married. Ever."

"I'm sorry," she says as she looks down at the clipboard in her hand. "Your birthday shows me you're 35. Surely, you want to settle down pretty soon. I mean, you can't wait forever."

"I can and I will. I'm not the marrying type. I work hard. I have no time for the bickering that goes along with having a wife and kids. No, thank you!" I step outside and smell the fresh air and look up at the sky where stars are already beginning to show with no city lights around to hide them. "This is great. I'll take it."

Her words of marriage and kids are put behind her as she sees dollar signs and hops up and down with excitement. "Fantastic!"

I am about to become a homeowner. A thing I've never been. I will be the lord of this castle. Ruler of the many it will take to keep this place running like a well-oiled machine.

TURNING around to go back inside, I find myself laughing. "I've never overseen servants and groundskeepers and people like that. I hope I'm good at it."

"I'm sure you will be, Mr. Girard. Now, when would you like to meet to sign the papers and set up financing?" she asks as we walk toward the front door.

"I'll be paying in cash. If the seller accepts my offer." I take her clipboard and write in the amount I'm willing to pay for the place. "I've managed to squirrel away a few dollars."

The fact is, with no bills, and making the money I make as CEO now, I'm a multi-billionaire. There never was any doubt I'd meet my goal to become one. I set that goal when I was a child and it took a little over twenty-five years for that to come to fruition but I made it happen.

The other goal I have is to make sure my life stays happy and carefree. Well, carefree as far as women go. Women and children have limited roles in my life.

Do I like kids?

Sure, but on a limited basis.

Do I like women?

Again, sure, but on a limited basis.

I don't consider myself a user of women. I do consider myself a man who knows himself and knows what he wants. Am I capable of having a real relationship?

Of course, I am.

Do I want one?

Of course, I don't!

Women are beautiful creatures. Their bodies come in all shapes and sizes and that's wonderful to me. Why settle on one when you can have so many?

My father is still reaping the benefits of bachelorhood. My mother is a very happy single woman. I think I'll be fine as a single man who has fantastic weekends with women who expect nothing from me, other than amazing sex.

I can deliver that two nights a week. Work has me exhausted the other five, anyway. I never realized how hard my father actually worked until I took over his role in the company. It's a huge job. It takes forever. And so many people depend on me now.

With all that responsibility, why on Earth would I add in a wife and kids?

Why would anyone?

IT MAKES no sense to me. I have tons of beautiful women at my fingertips two nights a week and all day on Sunday. Who could ask for more?

I'm not greedy. I've seen men who are married and have families and still dabble with the women at my father's parties. They're walking a tightrope. If they ever got caught, they'd lose half of everything they've managed to gain.

I, on the other hand, have nothing to fear. I've watched men run and hide when their wives have shown up, unexpectedly. I've helped many to dash out secret doors and get to cars their wives knew nothing about while making sure those women were treated well while they looked for their errant husbands.

I don't want that. I don't want to look over my shoulder for the one woman who wants to hold me down. I don't want to change into a man who is a hypocrite. Telling the woman, he's made a life with, to be faithful, while he whores around.

That's just mean. Why do that to another person? Why hurt people like that?

You don't have to if you keep it all real. Don't make false promises, like I love you and I will always love only you.

If it's not even possible!

I SEE no reason to lie to a woman. I see no reason to lie to myself. I like women. I always will. But I will never see fit to cage myself or any woman into a life of dread, deceit, and anarchy.

Yes, some call it love. Is it really something so easily captured with one word, though? Is it really so easily done?

'I do' can turn into, 'I can't' in the blink of an eye. Why put myself or some poor woman through that torture?

Not a thing I'd like to do. Not a thing I have a goal to do.

Not a thing I want!

"I know the owners will go for this amount. So, how about tomorrow then?" the real estate lady asks me. "I can have you and this house together before you know it. I just know you'll treat her well, Mr. Girard. Give her that tender loving care, she's been needing. You'll have this estate blossoming in no time. I can't wait to see her with your hand on her."

Staring at the woman, blankly, I shudder as she sounds as if she's talking about a woman. Suddenly, owning a house sounds like a huge commitment.

"I'm going to think on it," I say as I walk out the front door.

"I thought we had a deal," she calls out to me, waving her hand, frantically.

Ducking into the back of my car, I slam the door. "Drive away, Beau. That woman is trying to tie me down!"

As he speeds away, I turn back and see her slumping as she walks to her car. I may have just cost her some of her time but she was about to trap my ass with that house.

And I cannot have that...

5

CYPRIAN

"What do you mean, you don't want to be tied down to a house, Cyprian?" my father asks me as he looks at me over his morning cup of coffee.

"It sounds awful," I say as I look over the stock report in the New York Times. "Have you seen the price of pork bellies, it's atrocious?"

"I have," he says as he pushes the paper, gently down and looks over it at me. "You should stay away from them. About the house. You need one, Cyprian. Every man needs a castle to call their own."

"This place is great. Why move away?" I ask as I fold the paper and put it aside.

"It's not that I want you to move away," he says as he taps the cherry wood table we eat breakfast at on the weekdays in the small breakfast nook just off the main kitchen. "It's just that you seem a bit stifled. You haven't made much progress in the last, say ten years. You took over my position and that's where you've stopped. I love to watch you progress. You're so good at it."

"I don't know what you mean. I've made Libertine Investments billions in that amount of time. What's not progressive about that?" I ask as I watch his eyebrows dance as he thinks about what I've said.

"I mean you, personally, son," he says then places his hand on top of mine as he looks into my eyes. "You have been a person who has moved rapidly through life. You make goals and meet them and then you make new ones. You haven't made a new goal since taking the CEO position at the company. That's what I mean by progressing. I think a home of your own and building it up to be what you want it to be should be your next goal. You're so much happier when you have a goal to work on."

Looking away from him, out the window that looks over the large swimming pool in the back of the mansion, I think about what he's said. "Papa, I have only had one final goal this whole time. It was to take over your position, so you could take an early retirement. And I've met that goal. I've seen that you have more money than you could spend in a lifetime and watch you enjoy your free time. And that's my prize at the end of all of my hard work."

"Cyprian, while that is very noble of you, it's not a goal for you, son. That was a goal for me. Now, it's time to make one for yourself. A home will fill your mind with new ideas. It's a great experience. When I think about the day I bought this place, it always brings a smile to my face. It was the biggest purchase I'd ever made and it was the one thing which was entirely mine."

My eyes fall to the table and I look at my clean plate that had been filed with strawberry crepes. "Then I was thrust upon you, taking some of your home away. And what you really want is your home back and me to find my own. I understand now. I'll call the real estate lady and tell her the deal is still on. I didn't think about you wanting your old life back, the one you had before I came along."

The weight of his hand on my shoulder has me looking at him. "Son, that's not it at all. I know your mother and I call you our happy mishap but you were a true gift from above for me. I assume to your mother as well. I don't know as we hardly converse at all. She and I never were conversationalists."

"So, that's not it? Then why do you want me out so badly?" I ask as I don't understand and I usually understand almost everything.

"You need to make your own life. I've watched you following me and my life patterns and that's not fair to you. You're deeper than I ever was. Or your mother, for that matter. I feel as if you think there's only one way to live life but there are many ways to live it," he says, making me wonder if he's on to something.

"I think I do want to live the way you and Mother do, Papa. I see your faces are always happy. I want to be like you two. I want to live the life you two have," I say and watch a frown cover my father's face.

His hair has gone completely gray. But he's still what people call a handsome man.

He stills gets all the ladies he cares for!

"Son, I am getting older with each passing minute. And it's beginning to settle in with my retirement, that I have set myself up to live alone forever." He looks around at the empty room around us. "The servants move about like ghosts to make sure I'm never bothered, the way I used to ask them to do. But that was back when I was a busy man with the weight of the world on my shoulders."

"Are you saying, you're unhappy now, Papa?" I ask as he hasn't seemed unhappy to me in the least.

He nods. "I don't know how to talk to women. I flirt with women I know I can or talk business with women who are in my business world. But I have no idea how to talk to one like she's my friend. I don't want that for you. I want more for you."

"You've told me, on many occasions, when you have a relationship, it means arguments, unhappiness at times, and putting people before yourself and what you want. Are you changing your mind, now?"

"Not for me, no. I'm old and set in my ways. I couldn't put up with that now if I wanted to attempt to. But you've led a life that's been led by me and I think it's time for you to follow your own heart for a while. See what you really want in your life. That's why a home of your very own is the best place to start," he says then looks out the window to watch a sparrow fly past it to a nest in the tree next to it.

"And if I decide to make my own party room and live life the way I've come to know it, will you be disappointed in me?" I ask as I've never seen my father like this before.

With a shake of his head, he says, "I will never be disappointed in you. Not ever. Live however you want to. But do it because you want to. Not because you think anything is expected of you."

My mind is a mess. "You seemed proud of my male prowess."

"I am proud of you no matter what, Cyprian. I always have and always will be." He gets up and pats me on the back. "I'm going to take a nap. Do whatever it is you want to, son. Stay here, buy the house and move, whatever it is you want. I will always be proud of you."

WATCHING my father leave the room, I get up to head to the office. I've always done what I thought was expected of me. I never once realized that nothing was expected of me.

Making my way to the waiting Mercedes my father's driver is driving me to work in today, a dreaded Monday, I let the driver open the door for me and watch as he closes it, without a word said between us.

It's odd, how lost I suddenly feel. It's as if the rug has been pulled out from underneath my feet that I had been steadily treading upon for decades.

I can do whatever I want to?

I SHOULD FEEL GREAT. Nothing is expected of me and anything I want to do, I can. Papa will still be proud of me and so will Mother. So, why do I feel so alone?

The car pulls out of the large horseshoe drive and onto the road. I find myself pulling out my cell phone and tapping a message to the real estate lady. I'm going to take the estate. I'm going to live alone out there and see what it is I want to do with my personal life.

Businesswise, that's settled. I am to remain the CEO of Libertine Investments until I find another to groom to take over my place. Not a child of mine, obviously. Children are still off the table for me. I'd have no idea how to appropriately raise one of them.

With my own home, I could decide to keep women there overnight and into the next day, week, month, or year if I wanted to. And all this time, I thought my father would lose respect for me if I ever tried to keep a woman or women for more than one night.

I suppose I'm too literal of a person to understand everything. The little nuances that some people get, I just don't. Maybe with this advanced thought process, I was born with, I lost the ability to read between the lines. Or even realize I didn't have to follow my parents' exact footsteps.

I feel free but completely petrified for some reason. My first step at finding out who I really am and what I really want is upon me. I'm about to buy my own place to live and see how I want to live.

Who really knows what will happen to me...

6

CYPRIAN

Six months into living in my own place and I've yet to find the 'me' that I want to be. I love the 'me' I have been and think that's the real me.

It's Friday night and I have a young woman named, Cookie, sitting in my lap as my driver takes us back to my estate. I haven't made a party room at my place yet as Papa's is still fantastic so why give that one any competition?

Pulling up to the last convenience store at the edge of town before we leave it to go out into the country where I live, my driver goes inside to pick up the essentials I'll need for the night's activities.

"OH, is he getting us some things for tonight?" she asks me as she plays with my hair.

"Yep. You got anything you'd like?" I ask her as I push back her brown hair.

"Whipped cream," she says then runs her hand over the swell in the front of my pants. "I feel like a banana split if you get my drift."

"I do and I'll make sure you get some of that. I think some cherries would go well with that too," I say as I pick her up and take her off my lap. Rolling down the window, I lean out. "Ashton, can you add whipped cream and try to find some cherries too. And I want the ribbed condoms this time."

He nods and Cookie giggles as she climbs back onto my lap and plants a kiss on my lips. "Ribbed for her pleasure," she says when she pulls her lips off mine and erupts into giggles again.

I laugh and pull her face back to mine to enjoy a bit more of her twisting tongue. A knock on the window has us pulling our mouths away from each other and we look to find Ashton waiting at the window. I roll it back down. "Yes, Ashton?"

"They're out of ribbed. The cashier says there are none in the back and she said this Friday night you should try something new, like keeping it in your trousers, sir." He chuckles. "She's a spitfire, that girl. Anyway, do you have any other preferences or should I get what's on the shelf?"

I FIND MYSELF A BIT PISSED. "Who is this girl, cashier, who thinks she knows me?"

"Oh, just the same young lady who waits on me every Friday and Saturday night when I pick up your supplies. She's a hoot. I always leave with a laugh and a smile when she waits on me. She means nothing by it. She's a comical person. So, I'll just pick up another kind. I'll ask her if any of the ribbed will be in tomorrow," he says then turns to walk back inside.

"Oh, Ashton," Cookie calls out. "I'd love a fountain drink. Surprise me, will you?"

He nods and throws up a peace sign as he walks back through the glass doors. I find myself craning my neck to see if I can see this spitfire cashier he's talking about. The glass along the side of the store where the checkout counter is located is too dark to see through.

· · ·

"CYPRIAN, I really need to use the ladies room. How far is it to your place?" Cookie asks me as I'm still trying to catch a glimpse of the girl Ashton is talking to then he breaks into laughter.

I have every reason to believe it's at my expense and a heat fills me. I move Cookie off my lap. "Go inside and use the ladies room in there. I need to go now too."

As we get out of the car, I see Ashton cut his eyes at me and his smile vanishes. The man is around 50-years-old. When he calls someone young, it can mean they're a couple of years younger than he is. But I am dying to know who this woman is.

She's making fun of me, that's for certain!

ASHTON PUSHES THE DOOR OPEN. "I'm done. She managed to find a package of ribbed in a return bin behind the counter. Come on, now."

He seems nervous as hell for some reason. "She has to pee," I tell him as we keep going toward the doors.

"Home is but a few minutes away. I wouldn't recommend using these facilities, sir," he says then he holds up the large fountain drink. "Look, miss, I have your drink here. It's a Mr. Pibb."

"Oh, yes! I love that," Cookie gushes and turns back to accept the drink from him. "I can wait until we get to your place, Cyprian."

"Great, get back in the car. I'll only be a minute. I really have to go. I can't wait," I say then push the glass door open.

A little chirping bell rings, announcing my arrival. "Hello, welcome to Ty's Quick Stop," I hear a woman say but see no one.

"Hello," I say and make my way to the back of the store to where I see the bathroom sign. Only, I'm looking down each aisle to see if I can get a look at the cashier Ashton was talking about.

I find a short woman, putting bags of candy on the shelf. She has on a green smock and looks at me with a toothy grin. "Hi there. Can I help you find something?"

I raise my eyebrows at her and chuckle. "No, I think I'm good."

Making my way to the men's room, I find myself chuckling as I go. I don't know what got into me. I was so mad a moment ago about what the woman said but now that I see it's just a little, older woman, with most likely no real life outside of this little store, I'm anything but mad.

Going into the bathroom, I find it smells clean and almost sparkles. The door across the little hallway squeals open and I hear a soft voice say, "Women are filthier than men, Gina. Did you know that?"

The woman's voice is on the deeper side of the female octave. It's smooth and has the slightest French accent to it. It's not like anything I've ever heard before.

"CAMILLA, I know you've only been a cashier for six months but I've been one for fifteen years. Of course, I know women are nastier than men when it comes to public restrooms. The things I've seen and smelled," the women I recognize as the short older woman says.

The other one cuts her off as she says, "No, don't tell me. My stomach is still lurching a bit with what I just had to clean up." I hear her walk past my door and her footsteps keep going. "I wonder why moneybag's car is still parked outside. I found the pervert the kind of rubbers he wanted."

Pervert!

"I DON'T KNOW," the other lady says as she has no idea it's me, the moneybags pervert, in here.

"That man is a mess, I bet. Obviously, he's wealthier than any human needs to be and the way he buys condoms is a crime. Who actually screws that much each night but only on Friday and Saturday nights? It's ridiculous to need a new pack for each night. I bet he's old and bald and has to pay for his women. That's the only thing that makes any sense to me."

"Most likely," the other lady says. "He only started coming here just about the same time you started. His driver says he moved into an estate just outside of this side of town. I haven't seen him at the grocery stores or anything. I'm sure he has servants to do that kind of thing."

"An estate just outside of town. I bet he bought the old Franklin estate. I live right down the road from him then. In a little duplex, I rent, out that way. I might have to take a jog up the street one day and see if I can spot the fat bastard," the one I now know is called Camilla says.

I think I've heard enough. Pushing open the men's room door, I make my way to the soda machine. "Are your fountain drinks good?" I ask, without looking at either of the women.

"Our coffee is better. But I'd recommend a bottled water over either of those things," I hear that smooth voice say.

I listen as her footsteps move behind the counter and I walk over to the cooler to take a bottle of water the little shit has told me about. "Thank you. You're right, water is much better for the body. You a doctor or something?" I ask with a chuckle because no doctor would be working a crap job like this.

"A scientist, actually. I won't get my doctorate for another two years but I will be one then," she says.

I stop chuckling and open the door to the cooler and take a bottle of water and turn around slowly.

A scientist!

I can't wait to lay my eyes on the woman who will be the first person I have ever called out on talking shit about me.

As I turn around, I see no one behind the counter. Then the little woman pops up in front of me. "Will that be all, Sir? Are you ready to check out?"

I look around her to find the other woman. "Not yet. I'm a little hungry but there's nothing healthy jumping out at me. Perhaps the scientist has some suggestions for me."

"Nuts are on aisle three at the front of it. There's a package with a mixture of them that are about the healthiest thing you can get here," I hear her but don't see her.

So, I move on to aisle three and find the packages of nuts. There are six varieties. "Which ones do you recommend, doc?"

"The package on the row closest to the front. They have almonds and those are great for men. Women too, but especially for men," I hear her say but still don't see her.

"Are you going to school here?" I ask as I try to follow her voice.

"Clemson U, yes. I'm working here to make ends meet. And you, sir?" she asks.

I FIND her voice coming from the area of the counter and make my way to it. But when I get there, I still don't see her. "I dabble in this and that. Where are you?"

A head with a tight black bun, with curls that have escaped, comes out from under the counter. "Under here. I had to add money to the vault and you have to climb under this thing to do it. It's a real pain in the butt."

Watching her climb out from under the counter and smooth her green smock that fits her curvy body extremely well, I see her eyes when she lifts her head up. Gorgeous, blue eyes, framed by lush dark lashes, find mine. Her rosy red lips curve into a smile, showing brilliant white teeth that look amazing in contrast to her creamy caramel skin. "Will that be all, sir?"

"Huh?" I ask as her beauty has rendered me speechless.

She looks at the water and package of nuts in my hands. "I can ring those up for you if you're done shopping, sir."

I place the things on the counter top and stammer, "Sure, uh, yeah, that's going to do it."

Two little beeps have my purchases done and she looks at me with that pretty smile again. "Three fifteen, sir."

Handing her my credit card, I see her smile vanish. "Oh, sorry, sir." She points at a small sign on the counter that says they don't accept credit card payments for less than five dollars.

"Damn," I say. "I never carry cash. I'll put them back."

BEFORE I CAN TURN AWAY, her hand on my arm stops me. "I got this. You have a nice evening, sir. Drink all that water and eat all those nuts, and have a healthy evening, it's on me."

I look at her name tag and smile. "Thanks, Cami. I'll repay the favor."

"No need," she says as she looks at her name tag. "Did you call me, Cami?"

"I did," I say with a chuckle. "I'm afraid I have a habit of making up women's names on my own. Sorry. That's rude of me."

"Think nothing of it. I think that's kind of sweet. See you around then, sir. You come back and see us." She turns to walk away to get back underneath the counter.

"Cyprian, not Sir," I say then lean on the counter top. "You can call me, Cyprian."

She stops her retreat and smiles at me again. "Cyprian? What a beautiful name."

"Thanks," I say and open the bottle of water. "What're you doing when you get off work tonight, Cami?"

"Going home to study," she says and looks a little nervous, suddenly. She fidgets a bit and I find that cute.

"DO YOU HAVE TO? I mean, I'd like to get to know you a little bit," I say. The sound of the door opening and someone coming in, I barely notice as I look at her and can't seem to take my eyes off her. "I bet your hair looks amazing when you let it out of that bun."

A pink blush covers her cheeks then I hear a man's voice coming from behind me. "Mr. Girard, I just realized you were making purchases. I forgot to tell you about their payment policy here," my driver says and I watch Cami's face go from pink to red.

"You're him?" she asks as she steps back three full steps, as if I have leprosy or something terrible she might catch.

"Who?" I ask. I know damn well, who but I have to ask.

"The condom man?" she asks.

Now it's me who's blushing. My driver slaps a five-dollar bill on the counter. "There you, go, miss. We'll be going now."

THE SOUND of someone coming in fills my ears and when I hear Cookie's voice, I cringe, "Cyprian, are we going to get to your place and get the night going or what?"

Cookie is about as bimbo looking as they come. Nearly white hair with blue tips, she's skinny and pale. Not a beauty in the light but she looks good in the dark, where I picked her up at my father's party a little earlier.

Cami ducks her head and grins. Her amusement at my choice for the evening sends prickles through my skin. I take my water and nuts and leave the store in shame. "Come on, Cookie."

A short burst of laughter I hear come from Cami, I am positive, as she hears the woman's name.

I'm shaking with anger mixed with embarrassment, the addition of humiliation makes the emotional cocktail complete as I slam into the backseat of my car.

"That was brutal," I mumble as Cookie tries to climb back onto my lap.

"What was?" she asks then slurps her drink.

"Nothing, never mind," I say and close my eyes as I lay my head back on the seat.

What she must think of me...

7

CAMILLA

With a name and face to put to the perverted moneybags, as I had dubbed the man with what must be a nearly insatiable sex drive, I find I've thought all wrong about him.

"He wasn't fat and bald at all, was he?" I ask Gina as I help her clean the shelves where the can goods go.

"No, he was not," she agrees as she nods.

"He was actually very nice looking," I add as I wipe the top of a can of green beans.

"Yes, he was," she agrees again.

"Did you see how tall he was when he walked out the door? The tape on the door frame read six feet and three inches," I say as I think about how he filled that door frame nearly completely. "He was all muscles too."

"He had nice light brown hair, dark brown eyes too," Gina adds as she hands me a clean rag. "Use this one, honey. That one's merely pushing the dirt around."

What about those high cheekbones?" I ask. "And that Roman nose? It was the most perfect nose I recall ever seeing in my life. And his lips. Man, were they something. The top lip was a bit fuller than the lower one was."

"I suppose that's why he needs those condoms every weekend," Gina says, taking me out of the trance I was putting myself in as I thought about the man.

"Yeah, he's a male-whore. I know, I know," I say as I shake my head to clear it.

"He was flirting with you, Camilla. Do you suppose he was about to invite you to join him and that other woman?" she asks me with a grin. "And if he had?"

"Of course, not!" I shout and walk away as heat has suddenly invaded me. "You know I'm not that kind of woman. I know it's rare at my age of twenty-five to have only been with three men but I have to have feelings for any man I have intimate relations with. My parents and grandparents would kick my butt if I did it any other way."

"What about what you would do if you didn't have them to tell you what to do, Camilla?" she asks me, making me think about it.

"I'm a product of my raising. That belief runs through me, hardcore. I won't be a notch on any man's bedpost. No matter how gorgeous, sexy, and viral he is," I say as I make my way back to the counter.

"Are you describing moneybags, pervert, there, Camilla?" she asks with a laugh.

"He has a name now Gina. Cyprian Gerard. That last name is French," I say as I look out the window into the empty parking lot. It'd be nice to see that long black car pull back up into it and get to see that man one more time before I go to sleep.

"Like yours, Camilla Petit. But you still have a bit of an accent and he doesn't have one at all," she says as she joins me behind the counter.

"My father came here when he was a boy and my grandparents still speak it frequently. I wonder how my family would feel about him," I mumble to myself.

"Camilla, he's a rogue, a Romeo, a Lothario. You'll have to watch yourself so as not to let him charm you. He's much too handsome and I'm sure when he turns on the charm, he's almost irresistible," she says, reminding me he has to be kept at arms-length at all times.

"Do you suppose he'll keep coming in here, merely to hit on me?" I turn the outside lights off, so we can close the store.

"Most likely. He was looking at you with fire in his eyes. To tell you the truth, if I was a younger woman, I'd do it. He's rich, built like a one-ton tank, and the most handsome man I've ever laid eyes on. I'd give him a roll in the proverbial hay. But I was a bit of a whore myself, back in the day."

I have to laugh at the short, fifty-something woman. "Gina, you're a trip. Let's go home. Tomorrow night we'll see what happens. I doubt he had a second thought about me. I mean, why would he? And even if he did, it doesn't matter. I'm not a bimbo and he's obviously into them. If you took a good look at Cookie, you'd know that." We break into laughter as we lock up the store and walk to our cars.

"See you tomorrow night, Camilla. You have a nice night."

Getting into my little '67 mustang, I make my way down the road and notice the lights on at the old Franklin estate. It sits back off the road. A long driveway leads up to it and it's gated.

My mind wanders off to what the hot man is doing right now and then I find an animal crossing the road and have the jerk the wheel to miss hitting it.

"Shit!"

I have to get that man off my mind. He's definitely nothing but trouble!

BOOK 2: THE WOLF

A Bad Boy Billionaire Romance

By Michelle Love

8

CYPRIAN

The light show my father has had put on for tonight's party, has mock fireworks, sparkling over our heads in his ballroom. Two women have me in their clutches. For the first time ever, I'm trying to figure out how I can ditch them before I go home.

Someone has filled my mind all day and even into the night. The young woman from the convenience store has my thoughts muddled. I had a bouquet of red roses delivered to the store for her today. Ashton told me she works every weekend, so I'm pretty positive she got them when she got to work and I hope they brought a smile to her face.

I didn't put a thing on the card except, 'To Cami, From Moneybags-Pervert.' I hope it made her laugh.

MY SIGHTS ARE SET on her for tonight. I could use the sound of her slight French accent, cooing in my ear as we play around in my large bed a little later on tonight.

Ashton told me the store closes at two tonight and I plan on being her last customer. I've made a plan that's foolproof, as she will have to give me a ride home as I'm going to have Ashton drop me off there.

She seems the type of person who wouldn't leave another one of her fellow human beings in a bind. When I get her to my place, I'll offer her a drink. A little nightcap, I'll call it.

She'll accept, so as not to be rude. And after our little drink and some well-placed kisses from me, she'll come, willingly to my bed. It's all set out and I see no reason why it wouldn't work.

But I have to get rid of the women, who have their claws dug into me, holding me tightly, so as not to lose me to someone else for the night. I keep forgetting their names, and that's not like me.

"I need to check the time," I tell the one on my left. My watch is on that wrist.

"Why, are you ready to go?" she asks. "Because that's cool with me. We can leave now."

Wiggling my arm away from her, I check my watch to find it's almost one-thirty. "Not yet," I say. "I need to make a visit to the facilities. I'll be right back."

The women exchange worried looks, then the one on the right says, "We'll go with you. We can help you in your bathroom endeavors."

A sense of fear runs through me that I won't be able to ditch them and I blurt out, "I have to take a crap!"

BOTH OF THEIR expressions show me, my words were inappropriate. "Oh!" the one on the left says. "You go take care of that then. We'll wait for you right here."

I'm let go by both, with my bathroom talk and finally, set free. Off I go with a wave, neither aware I will not be returning to them. Not on this night, anyway.

Slinking out through a side door that's hidden behind the stage, I find Ashton waiting for me as I had directed him to. "Are you sure about this, Sir? She's not really your type." He opens the back door of the BMW that he brought me in tonight.

"I am sure and every woman is my type. What are you talking about?" I ask as I slide into the car's backseat.

"But you'll have to work for this one. You've never had to work for a woman in your entire life," he says as he shakes his head. "Best to stick with what you know."

"You are irritating me, Ashton. Just take me to the damn store, okay?" I pull the door closed as he seems intent on stalling me.

If I miss her because of him, he's going to hate the outcome!

As HE GETS into the driver's seat, he looks back at me. "Are you sure?"

"Yes! Drive, damn it!" He has me nearly shaking with worry that we'll miss her. "You seem a bit protective over this woman. What's the deal, Ashton? Do you want her for yourself? Perhaps she'll give you a little taste, I don't care. After I've had mine, though."

"See, that's what I'm talking about. She's not the kind of woman you're used to. And the answer is, no, I am not interested in her in a romantic way. She's a good kid. I think you're setting yourself up for disappointment. That's all," he says as he finally starts driving.

"Do you think I'm incapable of wooing her? I assure you, I do have the skills required to reel in a woman who is unsure she wants to give herself to me. It hasn't happened often, this is true. But a few have wavered at my bedside and I had to entice them into it. I can handle a bit of work when it comes to getting what I want." I lean back and look at the stars overhead, through the moonroof.

"I think she's a bit too spirited for you. And I doubt she'll fall into your bed easily. If you are depending on her to quench your sexual thirst tonight, I fear you will go to bed thirsty, Cyprian," he says as he looks at me through the rearview mirror.

"Do you really think so?" I ask as I turn my head to watch the city lights begin to dissipate as we near the edge of town. My heart starts to flutter with excitement as I know we're getting closer to her.

"I do, sir," he says and I find myself a bit worried that might happen as well.

"Perhaps it will take some time to get her where I want her. I only want her once. That's all I've ever done with any woman, one time and one time only. That way no one gets attached."

"I DON'T THINK she's that kind of person, sir. But you seem set on trying. This may be a goal you cannot reach," he says as he pulls into the parking lot of the store she works at. Parking at the side, instead of the front, like he usually does, he stops and turns to look at me. "Are you sure? You've never been turned down before. I don't know how you'll handle rejection."

His negative vibe is rubbing off on me as my insides go gooey. I have to get away from him. "I'll call you if she won't give me a ride."

He nods as I get out of the car on my own and wave at him to drive away. Checking my watch, I see that it's three minutes until they close and go around the side of the building to get to the entrance.

Just as I put my hand on the door, the outside lights go off. I push the door open, anyway and see her and the same woman she was working with last night, standing behind the counter. Cami is quick to say, "We're closed. Oh, it's you."

"HELLO TO YOU TOO," I say, feeling more than a bit put off.

"I've already shut down the registers. Looks like you're a minute too late to buy your Saturday night condom fix, sorry," she says as she reaches for something from under the counter.

"I have some leftover from yesterday, so we're all good. I have ten of them, to be exact. Do you think that'll be enough for tonight?" I ask as I lean on the counter.

She looks at me as if I'm daft, as she says, "How the hell should I know? How many tramps do you have in the car tonight?"

"None. And I have to ask you for a huge favor, Cami. My driver, Ashton's, wife became ill, suddenly. He had to drop me off here, so he could go get her and possibly take her to the hospital. I told him to do it. Time was of the essence for his poor wife, after all. I assured him, you would take me home. That is what neighbors do for one another, isn't it?" I have my fingers crossed behind my back, a thing I've never had to do before.

"Ugh," she groans and I find myself completely surprised. "I was going to go home and have some wine and watch some crappy television. I'm off tomorrow from school and work. It was going to be a chill night. But I suppose I can take an extra five or ten minutes to drop you off. It is on my home, anyway." She comes around the counter, unzipping her green smock and taking it off, tossing it on top of the counter and revealing a very nice set of tits.

Her tight white T-shirt is showing off a lacy blue bra and now that I can really see her ass in her tight black jeans, it's perfectly round and absolutely edible.

"You may not know this but I happen to have a whole cellar of fine wines from all over the world. I also have this dope home theater, I've yet to use. Want to come over for a while?" I ask her as she takes a set of keys out of her pocket.

"No thanks," she says like what I've just offered isn't cool at all.

Then I notice the flowers on the shelf behind the counter. "Aren't you going to take those with you?" I ask as I point to the large and expensive crystal vase full of red roses.

"Why would I take the manager's flowers?" she asks as she looks at me with a blank expression.

"THOSE ARE YOURS," I say as I make my way behind the counter to get them.

"And how do you know that?" she asks me as she crosses her arms in front of her.

I pull them down and take the card I wrote on at the florist's shop and hand it to her. "Because I sent them to you. Didn't anyone tell you?"

"Obviously not," she says as she rolls her eyes and takes the little card I'm holding out for her. Then she smiles and laughs and it makes it all worthwhile. "You're funny."

Step one, complete...

9

CAMILLA

Gina is giving me a thumb's up as Cyprian gets into the passenger seat of my car. I give her a thumb's down, making her shake her head. Then I get into the driver's seat and look at the hot man in my car.

He's wearing a tuxedo and looks too good to be true. "What kind of grand ball did you attend tonight?"

Running his hands over the lapels of the expensive garment, he smiles at me, revealing perfectly straight, white teeth. His lips are caramel colored with a hint of pink. They look delicious. "My father puts on formal parties on Saturday nights. All men are required to wear tux's."

"Fancy," I say and back out of the parking space. I put the car into first gear and see him looking at how close my hand is to his leg as I move the gear shift.

"You know, I've never driven a stick," he says. "Maybe you would be kind enough to teach me." He looks into my eyes and I have to avert them, quickly, as my stomach just went very tight with just that look.

"Maybe," I say. "So, tell me how you managed to escape the party with no woman, Cyprian."

"It wasn't easy, let me tell you. I had to make a daring escape to get away alone tonight," he says, making me wonder why he'd even want that.

"In all of my six months of working here, there hasn't been a single Friday or Saturday night that you haven't had your driver come in and buy condoms for you. What gives?" I ask as I pull out onto the main road out of town.

HIS HAND TOUCHES mine as it rests on the gear shift. "Can I move my hand with yours as you shift the gears, Cami?"

Heat is coursing through me and I have to shake my head to clear it. He frowns as I make the motion, not meant to answer his question. "Yeah, you can. That way you can get an idea of where the gears are."

His frown moves easily into a smile and his hand rests on top of mine. "Good. I'd really like to know how to drive a stick. This is a cool classic car. Most don't drive something like this around. Was it a gift or did you buy this, yourself?"

"Papa gave it to me when I graduated from high school, seven years ago," I tell him and try hard to ignore the pulsing that's going on in my nether regions.

IF I'M GETTING this horny over his hand merely touching mine, not even holding it, I have a serious problem!

"Papa, is that what you call your father?" he asks as he smiles like crazy for some reason.

"Yes, that's what I call him. My mother is called Mama. Papa is originally from France. His parents moved to New Orleans when he was seven-years-old. My grand-mere and grand-pere still live there, only a few houses down from where my parents live." I stop talking as I feel as if I'm rambling on, nervously.

"I call my father, papa too. My mother, I call, mother. She and I are not very close. She lives in Los Angeles. She sent me here to live with my father when I was five."

"Wow," I say, without thinking. "Sorry, my bad."

"Sorry? Why?" he asks, looking confused.

Even confusion on his face doesn't make him any less attractive at all!

"I WAS BEING judgmental about your mother. Sorry," I say as I see the huge black, wrought iron gated entry nearing. "This is it, right?"

"It is," he says. "And now you will know the code to the gate." A smile moves over his entire face and I see a little spark of evil in it.

"You can get out and push in the code. I don't need to know that," I tell him as I pull to a stop just far enough away from the control panel to allow him to get to it.

"Pull up, Cami. I'm not afraid for you to know the code to my gate," he says with a laugh.

With a shrug, I pull up and roll my window down. "Okay then." I position my finger over the keyboard, waiting for him to tell me the numbers.

"696969," he says as I look back at him, catching him smiling.

"Seriously? Damn!" I punch it in and the gates open. "I was right. I called it right from the get-go."

"About?" he asks as his hand moves back over mine to help me shift gears.

"About you being a pervert," I say with a laugh.

"I'm not happy with you thinking that way about me," he says and taps the top of my hand. "I'm not perverted. I am a sexual creature who enjoys having sex with many different women. But I am not perverted."

"Okay, think that if you want to," I say as I make my way up the long drive to his monster-sized home. "This place is huge."

THE ENTIRE FRONT of the house is lit up. The landscaping is magnificent. You can't see it from the road. "You like?" he asks as I pull to a stop in front of the front door.

"It's gorgeous. You've had a lot of work done on it. It looks great. Well, see you around, Cyprian," I say as he opens his door.

He stops and looks back at me. "Come inside. I'll give you the grand tour."

"I really should get home," I say, as I don't trust myself to be alone with the man. Especially in his home!

"WHO DO you have waiting for you, Cami?" he asks as he looks at me with no emotion on his handsome face.

"No one," I say as I look into his dark brown eyes.

"Then come inside. I'll pour you some wine. Take you on a tour of this gorgeous home and maybe then you will decide to watch a movie with me in the theater. Please," he ends his request.

"K," comes out of my mouth without me knowing it would.

What have I done...?

10

CYPRIAN

With a couple of glasses of red wine poured, I take them over to where Cami is standing, looking at one of my paintings that's hanging on the wall of the bar room. Her eyes are moving over every last inch of the painting I made of a stallion, prancing around in front of a stable of mares.

Placing her glass on the bar next to her, I lean over her shoulder a bit. "Do you like it?"

"I do, it's so lifelike." Her finger moves just over the canvas where I signed my name. "I can't read the writing. Who is the artist?"

"I am," I say then take a sip of the wine.

"No way!" She turns to look at me and takes a step back. "For real?"

"For real," I tell her then pick her glass up and hold it out for her, she takes it then I extend my arm for her to take. "Come with me and I'll show you the house."

SHE PLACES her hand in the crook of my arm and I lead her to the next room. "This is what I call my study."

"Strategically placed right next to the bar," she says with a smile. "Smart man."

"That I am. I was a child prodigy. Did you know that?" I ask her.

"Cyprian, I am not in the world of the wealthy. I don't know a single thing about you. Except you make large purchases of condoms on Friday and Saturday nights." She sips her wine as she looks around the room full of floor to ceiling bookshelves, filled with all types of books.

"I made my way through school very quickly. I was CEO of Libertine Investments at the age of twenty-five."

"Impressive," she says. "So, what other secret talents do you have, Cyprian?"

WITH A GROWL, I lean in close and whisper, "If you'll come to my bedroom, I can show you some more of my talents."

Her laughter peels through the air. "You are funny!"

I'm thrown off be her and straighten up, moving on to the next room. "I wasn't trying to be funny. But on we go." Pulling the door open, I take her into my meeting room. "I've yet to have a meeting in this room but if I ever need to have one at home, this is where it will take place."

"Like a board room, huh?" she asks as we walk through the large room with redwood siding covering the walls.

"Just like a board room, yes." I push the next door open and we're in the small kitchen. "If I ever do have a meeting, this is where my staff will make the food to serve at it."

"This kitchen is three times as big as the one in my duplex apartment. Pretty cool, I must say. State of the art appliances and everything." She stops and looks at the granite countertops. "You've spared no expense, haven't you?"

"Of course," I say. "You see, everything I did to upgrade and renovate this place is a tax write-off. Why spare expenses when it helps to offset the taxes I have to pay each year?"

"Pretty clever, Cyprian. Your mind works like a machine," she says, giving me another opportunity to throw in a sexy remark.

LEANING IN CLOSE, I whisper, "That's not the only thing that works like a machine, Cami."

Laughter again sends me into a state of confusion. "Oh, Cyprian! You are a card!"

A card?

A DOOR LEADS off this small kitchen to an outside patio and I decide to take her out there for a while. Maybe the cool night breeze and the sounds of the night will have her going to another place in her mind. A sexual place. Because she's sure not in one right now!

"Perhaps a brief pause on our tour to take in some of the night air," I say as I take her to the door and open it. I leave the light off on purpose, so she can mellow a bit with only the stars and moon to light the night.

"This is beautiful. Even in the dark," she says as I help her to sit on one of the small sofas on the deck.

I TAKE the seat next to her. The sofa is so small our legs touch and I rest my hand on her thigh. "It's peaceful out here. I spend at least fifteen minutes each night when I come home, outside on one patio or another. This place has six patios, three decks, this being one of them and five balconies. The master suite has a massive one. You'll love that one. I have a bed out there, covered with mosquito netting."

I can feel her pulse race and she turns her head to look at me. "Cyprian, can I ask you hold old you are?"

"Thirty-five. And you are?"

"Twenty-five. I'm ten years younger than you and I'm having a hard time figuring you out. Most men your age are married. They have families already and everything. Why don't you?" she asks me the way an innocent child would.

I run my fingers along her jawline as I answer her, "Camilla, I am not a man who wants those things. My life is full enough as it is."

"Do you think you will always be this strong and viral, Cyprian?" she asks me as her eyes search mine.

"Why do you ask that?" I trace her lips one time then rest my hand on her collar bone, stroking it with my thumb.

"I ask that because one day when you're old, you will want to have someone around. My parents and grandparents have been married for years and years. They tell me all the time how life wouldn't be worth living without the other. I know it's important to make a life with someone. Only one person, who you can grow old with."

"I don't think that way," I say as I move my hand to run over her shoulder.

"Perhaps you should think about the way you've been leading your life and how it will affect the end of it. Can you imagine, lying alone in your bed, unable to get up from the aches and pains that come along with old age. And have no one to help you up or go get something for you. That sounds terrible to me," she says.

"To be honest, I don't think about the future in that way. I think about business in the future but not me in the future. I suppose things will work out for me as they have for my parents. They're both still single and living their lives the same way they were when they were young."

"How boring," she says then takes a sip of her wine. "How very boring to do the same things over and over again. No growth. The same people at the same parties every weekend. The same thing, week in and week out."

"FUCK! YOU MAKE IT SOUND BAD," I say without laughing.

"Isn't it?" she asks as she looks at me again.

"And what is it that you do, Camilla? What is so fascinating about your life? Please, educate me," I ask her as I sit back, taking my hands off her.

"Well, I am a scientist which might not sound exciting but it really is. I put things together to create new things. I pull things apart to see how they work and then put them back together again. My job is vast. I never do the same exact thing twice. The only boring part of my life is working at that store." She finishes the glass of wine and places the empty glass on the table. "Now you tell me about what it is you do."

"I read the New York Times every weekday morning as I eat my breakfast," I tell her.

"Is it always the same thing?" she asks with a cocked eyebrow.

"No, well, yes and no," I say. "Mondays are pancakes, Tuesdays are scrambled eggs. But not the same thing every day."

"Hmm." She taps her finger to her chin. "Now I think I see why the never-ending, turn-style of women. You do the same thing, day in and day out, the only variable is them. I bet you've slept with only a handful of them more than once."

"Wrong!" I tell her and get up, holding my hand out for her. I've never slept with any of them for more than the one night. But I'm not about to tell her that.

"Is my visit over?" she asks as she takes my hand.

"No," I say then drain my glass of wine too. "Your drink is finished and we're in need of refills. The kitchen we just left has more wine in it. Come on. There's more house to see and I think you'll love the theater room."

I pull her along with me and kind of hate how she has the gears moving in my head. I've never thought of my life as boring. Nor that of my parents either. Who does she think she is?

"CYPRIAN, what are your plans for tomorrow?" she asks as we walk inside.

"We go to the horse races on Sundays," I tell her, making her laugh.

"So, Friday and Saturday are party nights. I never see you on the weeknights. You must work you ass off and get home late on those nights. And Sundays are spent at the track. Would you like to change it up some tomorrow?"

"What do you have in mind?" I ask her as I pour us more wine.

"How about you and I spend the day together, watching movies while we bar-b-que and just hang out. I saw a swimming pool. We could chill out together. A nice, peaceful day. What do you say?"

Looking at her and wondering what the fuck she's doing, my mouth opens on its own, "Yes. I say, yes to that."

Whoa! What just happened...?

11

CAMILLA

After an hour of touring his home, I wave goodbye to Cyprian, who's standing in the driveway as he walked me out to the car. He tried to give me a kiss but I turned my head and he only caught my cheek. It made me giggle and him smile.

"See you at noon, Cami," he calls out as I pull away.

"I'll be here," I call out to him.

"Bring your bikini," he shouts as I drive off.

I have no idea what the hell I'm doing with the man. I can't believe I made a date with him. And I can't believe he accepted it!

NEVER, have I wondered what the rich do. But finding out how he has lived all these years, doing the same thing day in and day out, is mind numbing to me. I went to the same club three weekends in a row, once when I was younger. That third night was so dull to me. The same faces, the same music, the same atmosphere. It was terrible!

I don't see how he's done the same things for so long. He told me how he'd watch his father's parties when he was a little kid. When he was only fifteen, his father asked him to join the parties. He was swept into that life so early.

It's sad, really. But he doesn't see it that way at all. I feel sorry for him. And I think he's in need for someone to shake his little world up. I'm not sure I should be the one to do that but the want to do it is coursing through my veins.

The man needs some substance in his life. Work, parties, and gambling on horse races are all fine and dandy unless that's all you do.

He does have his painting. He is a true artist. Perhaps that's what I see inside of him. He has depth. More so than I believe he's aware of. To help him find some of that, is a thing I feel I could do.

PULLING into my half of the driveway between the two apartments that make up the duplex, I turn the car off and get out. Getting my phone out of my pocket to use the light so I can unlock the door to my house, I see it's nearly four in the morning.

I spent more than an hour with the man I had no plans of spending any time with. Just as I push the door open, I remember the flowers he gave me in the back floorboard and turn back to go get them.

With the vase of flowers in hand, I go back to the front porch and find a little skunk standing on the step, looking at me. Terror flows through me as it lifts its tail, spraying the inside of my house before it runs off.

"No," I whine as I hold my breath and walk inside. "Ugh!"

Straight back to my bedroom, I go as the smell has already taken over the front of the house. I hope I don't smell like the damn stink the small rodent has plagued me with.

What will Cyprian think if I smell like a skunk tomorrow? Crap. I'm going to have to cancel.

But I don't have his number. Crap!

12

CYPRIAN

Making my way to my bedroom, I find myself not sleepy in the least. I don't know what it is about that woman but there's something different about her.

I also can't believe I accepted a date, of sorts, with her. I've never had any one-on-one time with a woman at my home. Other than the usual thing. But afterward, they are taken home by my driver and I am left to sleep.

I'll be spending the entire day with Cami. The whole day. What the hell will we do?

She didn't ever seem to get my, not so subtle, hints about what I want to do with her. Either that or she was just ignoring my advances on purpose. But how could she, is she made of stone?

Maybe Ashton was right. Maybe she's not the kind of woman to do anything with a man without some type of a commitment. Which I will never give her.

So, I may spend the whole day with her and still see no benefit from it. What will I do then? Make another date?

Surely, not!

. . .

No, I'll move on, letting Camilla Petit stay in the past as a woman who simply lost out. She's the one who'd be losing out, after all. Not me.

I can have pretty much any woman I want. She's the one who'll miss out on the experience I can give her. It's her who will be unhappy about missing out on having amazing sex with me. Not the other way around.

Climbing into my bed, I pull the blanket up to cover my naked body. I was an early fifteen the last Saturday night I went to bed without having tons of sex. It feels odd.

I'm kind of wound up but I don't exactly feel bad about it. Spending time with Cami, tonight was interesting. Not exactly fun but it was enjoyable, even though we really didn't do anything but walk around my house and talk.

Odd, but a good odd. I wonder what tomorrow will bring. She and I will be next to naked as we swim. That's when I'll be able to get to her. And if she'll allow it to happen once then I can see it lasting all day long. Then I can move on.

I should let the staff have the day off. She'll probably be much more susceptible to my charms if no one is around at all. I'll have to turn up the charm on her. That's for sure.

But why am I bothering at all with the woman when I can go to the track tomorrow with my father and some of the women from this weekend's party and get some action there?

Why, indeed...

13

CAMILLA

A dog's barking wakes me up from a deep sleep. I was dreaming about Cyprian and I, in his gorgeous home. I was helping him host a small get-together with some people he wanted to impress.

It was all so weird. And now that I'm awake, I can smell the damn skunk stench and I know I have to smell like that too. To the kitchen I go, climbing out of bed and holding my nose as the stench is much worse in the front part of the house where the little stinker let loose his horrible musk.

It's hard to believe that same musk oil is used in some perfumes. But it is and perhaps I can formulate something that will work with the odor rather than overpower it.

Some vanilla, cinnamon, brown sugar which I'll need to burn first. A few drops of lemon oil should help. I find a couple of cans of tomato sauce. Opening them, I take them to the bathroom with me and slather the stuff all over my body and saturate my hair with it as well.

. . .

CATCHING a glimpse of what I look like in the mirror has me laughing as I look like something out of a horror film. "Nice," I compliment myself.

After an hour of sitting with that stuff on me, I shower it off and go to make my concoction that I'll put into a spray bottle and douse myself with. Then I'll go see if Cyprian is even home. There's always the chance he's decided not to spend the day with me and go on about his typical Sunday routine of gambling, women, and sex.

Once I'm dressed in blue jean shorts, and a tank top that covers my black bikini, I head out to the car and take my aviator sunglasses from the visor and put them on.

Flip flops and clutches don't work well, so I slip mine off and drive barefooted up the road to the estate I left so late last night. I wonder if the light of day will have Cyprian thinking differently about hanging out with me.

Pulling up to his gate, I press the naughty numbers into the panel and the gate opens for me. I drive up and park in front of the house and am shocked to see him waiting for me at the front door.

"HEY, YOU," he says as he lets out a long whistle.

I slip my shoes back on and get out of the car as he comes to open my door. "Hi," I say, a little shyly.

"Look at that hair! I knew it'd look gorgeous when you let it down." To my horror, he takes a chunk of it and takes a big whiff of it. I prepare myself for humiliation as I squeeze my eyes shut. A thing he can't see as my glasses hide it. "Wow, your hair smells amazing. Like nothing I've ever smelled before. You have to tell me what shampoo you use. It's off the charts."

HOW DO I EXPLAIN THIS?

I laugh as he takes my hand and pulls me along with him. "I made it myself," I manage to come up with."

"You're kidding me," he says as he stops and sniffs my neck. "Your whole body must smell like that. And you made this yourself?"

With a nod, I say, "I did."

"You really are smart, aren't you?" he asks as he tugs me along.

"That's what they tell me," I say as I pull my shades off as we walk inside. I lay them on a table near the door, so I don't forget them when I leave.

"You should patent that and sell the formula or something. It's that good." He stops and closes the door then stays in front of me as I've become trapped between him and the door. "Did you miss me after you left me last night?"

Laying my palms against his chest, I smile at him. "Does that mean you missed me, Cyprian?"

"What if I told you I did?" he asks and runs his nose along my neck, taking in another whiff of me.

"I'd say that doesn't sound like a man who says the things you say. So, what are we doing first? I'm starving and making something on the pit was my idea of what to do first."

He presses his body against mine, pinning me to the wall as he looks down at me. "I kind of thought we'd get this sexual tension out of the way first."

"Think again," I say then slip down and get away from him. "Is your staff around? I'd love to talk to your cook."

"I gave them the day off," he says as he catches my hand and pulls me back to him. "We're all alone." He wraps me up in his strong arms and I laugh.

"I'm not here for your sexual enjoyment. So, let's get to the main kitchen and see what we have to cook. I'm dying for some jalapeno wraps. I hope you have some and some cream cheese. I'm sure you have bacon. Who doesn't have bacon, right?"

With a chuckle, he says, "You seem to be chattering away, nervously. Are you feeling nervous for some reason, Camilla?"

"Me?" I ask and hear my voice go up a little too high.

"Yes, you." He lets me out of the hold he had on me and leads me to the kitchen.

"I'm not nervous. Just hungry," I lie.

THE TRUTH IS he's making me hot and bothered and I have to find something to distract myself from that. I am not a woman who gives her body to a man without true feelings.

"The kitchen is well stocked, I'm sure. So, let's go put together what you want. Maybe, once you've eaten, you'll calm down. There's nothing at all to be nervous about. I can be very gentle or rough if you prefer," he says, ending with a growl and stopping to pull me into his arms again. "Which do you prefer, Cami?"

His obvious plan is to get me into his bed and mine is to stay far away from it. Placing my hands on his chest and pushing him back a bit, I say, "When I first make love with a man, I like it gentle. If you must know. Later on, I like it rough now and then. But today there will be none of that. As you are aware of, after our talk last night, I do not have casual sex. If you want me to leave, I will."

His eyes soften as he looks at me and a smile curves his lips. "I don't want you to leave. I'll ease up on you. Just remember, though, I do want you that way."

"Yes, I can tell," I say as I pull out of his arms and look at the swell in his shorts. "That's pretty obvious, Cyprian. Now, can we go to the kitchen?"

With a sigh, he takes my hand and off we go to the kitchen. I hope he doesn't act this way much more. I don't know how long I can actually take it!

14

CYPRIAN

"Yeah, well, I think some cloves of garlic would taste great wrapped up with all that other stuff," I argue as she's refusing to put them in the jalapeno wraps she's put everything but the kitchen sink into.

"I don't see it lending a flavor that will combine with the chicken, shrimp, cream cheese, bacon and the pepper," she says as she rolls a piece of bacon around one of the filled pepper halves.

"But I already peeled a whole thing of it," I say as I gesture to my work.

I SEE THAT," she says as she glances at it. "How about you chop up a yellow onion and chop up that garlic too, we can sauté them to put over the steaks we're going to grill."

"I can do that," I say and make my way to get an onion. "I've never cooked before. This is kind of fun."

"I would be surprised but since you come from money, I'm not one bit surprised. You wouldn't happen to have some beer in this place, would you?" she asks as she wraps another stuffed pepper. "I can make a beer run if you don't."

"You're not going anywhere. I have every beer they make. Name your poison," I say as I walk over to the third fridge and open it.

Her eyes move over the fridge full of all kinds of beer. "Wow, okay how about that one there? It has a skull and crossbones on it that looks cool."

"Okay, it might be too much for a little thing like yourself but I'll be sure to take good care of you if you get yourself drunk," I say as I open the bottle and take it to her.

SHE LAUGHS. "Little thing? Really? No one has ever called me little. I'm anything but that."

I slide my hand along her waist, which is fairly thick but not too much. "I think you're perfect and I do see you as a little thing. You are smaller than I am."

She smiles, shyly as she looks down. "Who isn't? You're built like He-man."

"So, you have noticed my fine physique? That's nice to know, Cami. I thought you weren't looking at all." I leave her to go get my own beer and turn back, quickly to find her watching me.

Her eyes move back to the pepper in her hand and her cheeks go pink. I turn back around and feel pretty good about how today will go. She thinks she's got the self-discipline to withstand my advances but I can already see cracks forming in the wall she has up.

Looks like today might be more fun than she anticipated...

15

CAMILLA

With a fantastic lunch behind us, we sit at the edge of the pool, dangling our feet in the water. "You are a very good cook. You rival the one I have on staff here. You wouldn't want a job, would you?" he asks me with a little smile on his handsome face.

"I have one and a career is soon to follow. Thanks, though. We could, however, make this a Sunday thing. Even if I have to work, it wouldn't be until seven in the evening. We could spend the afternoon with me teaching you how to cook and perhaps how to drive my car."

"We'll see. I don't make long-term plans. Never have. Want to get in the water?" he asks as he pulls his shirt off, revealing a very nice six pack and some great pecs. His monster biceps have me wet already and I can only nod my answer at him.

When he stands up, pulling me up with him, I'm surprised as he takes my shirt from the bottom and lifts it off, over my head. His fingers move quickly to unbutton my blue jean shorts and he shimmies them off me, leaving me standing in front of him in my black bikini.

A wolf-whistle follows then he has me in his arms. "Hold on tight, Cami. We're going in."

I wrap my arms around him and hold my breath. He runs and jumps and into the water we go. All the way under and when we come up I find my hair in my face and hear him laughing. He tilts me back and my hair is pulled back off my face with a slicked back look. "Thanks," I tell him for helping me out.

"Yes, that's a bunch of hair you have there. I couldn't let it smother you," he says as he walks along, still holding me.

There's never been a man who picked me up and carried me before. I'm not huge but I'm not small either. The way Cyprian can pick me up, like I don't weigh a thing, is pretty cool, in my book.

I wish he wasn't such a player.

Our bodies touching, skin to skin has me thinking things I shouldn't. I find him setting me down on some kind of a bench at the edge of the pool and he places his hands on it in front of me and lets his legs float out behind him. "Cyprian, where do you see yourself in say, five years?"

"Here, doing what I do. Working. Making people money. I suppose you'll be a big scientist by then." He moves his hands off the bench and onto my thighs.

I push away a lock of his light brown hair that's fallen into his face. "I hope so. Summer's nearly over and my classes will be starting up again. I'm only taking one summer class now and I'm not very busy but when the summer ends and my classes begin, I'll be swamped all the time."

"Then you should get in some fun while you still can," he says as he moves in close.

I pull back. "By fun, you must mean sex and that's not the kind of fun I can have with you."

"Oh, but you can," he says and attempts to kiss me again.

Moving my head, his lips land on my cheek, but not far from my lips. I have to fight myself not to turn and take the kiss he's offering. But I manage. "Cyprian, you're being silly." I laugh it off and find him pulling me into his arms.

Our bodies are flush and I can feel the thump against my stomach as he grows. Even though the water is cool, my body is hot as hell. "One kiss, Camilla. One sweet kiss then I will leave you alone, for a little while."

"No," I say, quickly.

Leaning over me, holding me tight, his mouth moves up my neck until his teeth take my earlobe and he nibbles it. My knees go weak and I'm glad we're in the water or he'd know the effect he's having on me. "Are you afraid it will leave you wanting more?"

I don't know what to say. The answer is, yes but I don't want him to know that. "Cyprian, please stop."

His arms go loose and he lets me go. Moving back, he swims backward. "Okay. Do you want to come jump off the big rock with me?"

I nod and swim after him as he makes his way to the large rock at the other end of the pool. My body is still tingling from his attention and I don't think coming to hang out with him was smart.

This is much harder than I expected it to be...

16

CYPRIAN

"**R**aiders of the Lost Ark? You want to watch that old movie. I can get things that are still in the theaters and that's what you want?" I ask Cami as she's curled up in one of the leather theater lounge chairs with a soft, light blue blanket wrapped around her.

Her hair is still damp and hanging around her face in spiral curls and all I want to do is scoop her up and take her to my bedroom. Then take her to Heaven with me. But she's very good at keeping herself out of men's bedrooms, it seems.

"I watched that movie only one time when I was a kid and I liked it and never got to see it again. If you don't want to watch it, I guess I'll understand," she says with a mopey voice.

"We can watch it," I say as I push the button to order the old as hell movie. "There's this new one out with a lot of car races and cool shit like that. But we can watch what you want to."

I GRAB us a couple of bottles of beer and a bag of popcorn and go sit in the chair next to hers. She leans her shoulder against mine as she takes the bottle I'm handing her. "You know, it's only four in the afternoon. We can watch the one you want to next if you want. It'd mean I'd have to hang out with you longer than expected but I will if you want."

"We could heat up some leftovers in between the movies," I say, feeling kind of excited for some stupid reason. "That sounds cool."

She grabs a handful of popcorn out of the bag that's resting between my legs and my cock stirs as the bag moves against it. I'll be leaving that right where it is!

TAKING THE REMOTE, I start the movie on the big screen and dim the lights. I'm happy to find her resting her head on my shoulder. "Thank you, Cyprian. You're a nice guy."

I'm so not a nice guy!

Her hand moves over my leg and she leaves it there. She seems more than comfortable with me and I am beginning to feel very comfortable with her as well. It's so strange.

"Don't do that!" she shouts, suddenly.

"What did I do?" I ask, as I have no clue.

"Not you, silly. Indy," she says with a giggle.

Going back to watching the movie, I feel her jump when a painted face of some tribesman pops up on the screen. She buries her face in my chest. "Tell me when this part is over."

CHUCKLING, I run my hand through her hair. "It's okay, Cami. I won't let the scary man hurt you. He's gone now."

She peeks at the screen and I run my arm around her, she rests her head on my chest and I can't recall a time I've ever felt this satisfied. It's crazy!

More tribal action comes on and she climbs over the armrest that's between us and climbs right onto my lap as she hides her face in my chest again. "God, I don't remember it being this damn scary. Tell me when it's over, please."

"I don't think it's scary at all. You're kind of a big chicken." I laugh at her and she smacks me in the chest. "Ow."

"I'm not a chicken. Is it over yet? I hear Indiana talking again."

"It is but you can stay where you are," I say as she looks up at me. "I like you cuddled up on my lap."

Gazing into her sapphire eyes, I find myself inching toward her. And she's not moving away from me, for once. Closer, I go and find my heart pounding.

"Cyprian?" she asks.

"Yes."

"You understand the kind of person I am, right?"

I nod. "You're a good person."

"I mean the kind of person I am about sexual relations," she says. "I can't be with you like that without knowing you better and having a commitment."

Commitment!

THAT STOPPED ME. "Cami, I'm not a commitment kind of man. I told you that before. Just because we've shared a little time doesn't mean I want more."

She scrambles off my lap and into the other chair. "I'm not some easy tramp. Sorry you wasted your time. I'll go. I'm sure you can call one of those whores you know."

Before I know it, she's slipped her shoes on and is hightailing it out of here. "Cami, wait!"

She's hauling ass and the bright light as she throws the door open blinds me. "Just leave me alone, Cyprian. I can't believe I entertained the thought you could be a decent human being."

I manage to catch up to her as she gets to the front door. As she opens it, I grab it and push it closed, trapping her between me and the door. "What do you mean by that?"

"You're shallow. A hollow man. You have no depth. You have no heart. You will die alone. And I won't be one of your casualties." Her eyes have gone hard. Judgment fills her expression.

"Who are you to say those things? You don't even know me," I shout at her.

"And who does?" she asks as she moves her hands to her hips. "Do you even know who Cyprian is?"

"Of course, I do."

"Explain him to me," she says as her expression changes. She looks softer and more open.

"WHY SHOULD I?" I ask her as I run my hand over her smooth cheek. "Your skin is as soft as rose petals. Did you like the flowers I sent you? You never said a word about them."

"I think they're beautiful. The crystal vase is something I'll keep forever. Thank you." She moves her face and her lips touch the palm of my hand.

A heat streaks through me and I feel the pulse begin in my cock. "Cami, please don't leave." I bite my lip as I wait for her to tell me what she's going to do.

"Cyprian, I'm afraid of you."

"You think I'll hurt you?" I ask, as I have no clue why she'd be afraid of me.

"I know you will." She caresses my cheek. "You see, I am in touch with myself and I know I cannot have a taste of you. I will want more and more and you won't give that to me."

"You think you'd like to have me around more often?" I ask as I push a lock of her hair off her face.

"Nothing would make me happier." She leans in and kisses my cheek.

I PUSH HER BACK, gently. "I'm not a liar. I am not a user of women. I am a man who is very busy all week long and on the weekends, I merely want to relax, unwind, and recharge for the next week. I don't want a relationship and doubt I ever will."

"Thank you for telling me the truth, Cyprian. It's a nice thing for a man like yourself to do. I appreciate your honesty. I have to be honest with you too. I am a woman who doesn't sleep with men she's not in love with and has a commitment with. We can be friends," she says.

I step back, ending our physical contact. I'm doing nothing, other than making myself frustrated by it. "I don't keep friends. I have people I work with and people I party with and that's it. There's no place or time in my life for friends. So, if we aren't going to fuck, I guess you can leave."

Her entire body goes rigid and her eyes glisten with what seems to be tears. "We are not going to fuck. And I am sorry for taking up your precious time, Cyprian. Good luck with your life. I fear it will be one of great loneliness."

I watch her walk out the door and find myself feeling lonely right away. I don't recall ever feeling lonely. Not ever. I'm fine being alone. I always have been.

Turning around to try to find something to fill my mind and stop thinking about her, I see her sunglasses on the table and sigh as I pick them up. Going back to the door, I open it and find her head is resting on the steering wheel and she has yet to leave.

"Hey, you forgot your sunglasses," I shout.

I make my way to her and when she looks up, I see tears streaming down her face.

What the hell have I started?

Camilla

"Shit!" I hiss as he's caught me crying over him and now I feel really stupid. I turn the car on and start to peel out but he gets to the passenger door and I might run him over if I do.

"Cami, don't cry," he says as he opens the door and gets into the car. "You're making me feel terrible."

"Thank you for bringing me my glasses. Bye." I take them out of his hand and shove them on the dashboard.

His hand moves over my cheek as he wipes the tears away. "I've never made anyone cry. Not ever. This is awful. Come back inside. Please. Let's try this again. I'm sorry."

"No, I can't go back inside. This is my problem, not yours. You see, I have this thing where my heart jumps ahead way too fast. It always has. It's part of the reason I'm single right now. I fall head over heels in love and when it doesn't work out, it leaves me shattered. I need to learn to reign in my emotions. I wear my heart on my sleeve and that's a dumb thing to do."

"Love?" he asks as he frowns. "Cami, that word shouldn't even be bantered about right now."

"You think I don't know that, Cyprian?" I shout at him. "I had a dream about us last night. I was with you, in this house, helping you with some kind of a get-together. It was like we were married or something."

"Married?" he says then laughs.

"I know, what a joke," I say and find the tears stinging my eyes again.

He stops laughing and wipes them away again. "Cami, please stop crying. It's kind of tearing me up inside."

"I would think you'd be used to seeing women cry over you." I sniffle and reach over to take some tissues out of the glovebox.

"No one has ever cried over me. I don't date. There has never been anyone who didn't know where they stood with me. No one has had any reason to cry over not being anything more to me than a sexual partner for the night. And the truth is, I have never had sex with any woman for more than one night or day."

I'm not surprised and he can see that on my face, I suppose as he looks down. He seems ashamed.

"If that's how you want things to be then why did you come for me?" I ask as I have no clue as to why the man sought me out last night.

"I can't explain it, Cami. You've filled my mind since the moment I met you. I thought we'd have a nice time and some fun in bed then you'd be out of my mind and I could think about important things again," he says, appalling me.

"Do you hear yourself?" I ask him as he seems to think what he's said is perfectly fine. "I'm glad you're being honest but, Cyprian, that's terrible. You want to have sex with me so you can forget about me. And you basically called me, unimportant."

"I didn't mean that. I'm sure you're important to lots of people. But I don't have time for people to be important to me. If you spent one day with me at work, you'd understand, completely."

"Is your job so encompassing that there's absolutely no room for a person to share your life with? Because if that's so, then you should change things around. There are plenty of rich people in this world who have time for families."

"Would you stop talking about things like families and sharing lives together?" he shouts. "You're sparking things inside me that have me wanting to run as fast as I can away from you."

I LEVEL my eyes on his. "Are you afraid of me, Cyprian?"

"I'm not afraid of anything. I merely don't want to talk about things that are never going to happen for me. Because I don't want them to. I don't want a wife or even a fucking girlfriend. I sure as hell don't want an entire family. God knows I have no time for all of that. And no want for it!"

"Then what are you doing, sitting in this car with me? You shouldn't even be talking to me. I strive for all the things you don't want any part of. So, why are you sitting here?"

"That's an excellent question." He gets out of my car, slamming the door behind him. I watch him walk all the way to his front door and he slams it behind him too.

I suppose that means this is over...

BOOK 3: THE SEDUCER

A Bad Boy Billionaire Romance

By Michelle Love

17

CYPRIAN

The lights of the last business in town, before we leave the Clemson city limits, catch my eye, the way they've done every night for the last week. It's Friday and I'm going home. I'm not in the mood to party at all.

The damn woman haunts me. Day and night, she's there, in the back of my mind. How she managed to squirm into my head is still a mystery. But she's there, going nowhere.

I've tried hard to forget her and go on but it seems impossible. Her words echo in my brain, 'you will die a lonely old man.'

Will I? Is that my fate? Does it have to be?

My driver, Ashton, slows down as we approach the store she works at. A car is turning in front of us, causing us to stop and just as we do, she walks out of the store, coming to the gas pumps with a rag and a bottle of cleaner.

Her eyes dance as she greets one of the customers who's pumping gas into their car. It's a man, she's talking to. The tall man is smiling like crazy at her and she's unaware of the fact he finds her attractive.

. . .

"PULL IN, ASHTON," I say as I watch her smiling and laughing as the guy regales her with his wit.

"Are you sure, sir?" he asks me as he looks into the rearview mirror with raised brows.

"I am." I run my hand over my Armani slacks then brush my hair back and sigh as we pull into the parking lot. I don't need anything, except to hear her voice.

Once he parks, I sit and wait, watching her as she cleans the gas pumps and talks to the man who hasn't left yet, even though he's done pumping his gas. She's oblivious to how he's watching her every move.

Three short steps he takes and he's standing behind her as she's kneeling, wiping the bottom of the pump. His hand moves over her shoulder and she turns to look up at him.

Her head is shaking and his is nodding. He's asking her out, I bet. My heart is pounding as I wait to see what she does.

"Do you want me to get out and get you something, sir?" Ashton asks me.

"No. I'm getting out when she goes back inside." I can't take my eyes off her. I haven't seen her at all since Sunday when I walked away from her.

I was angry at her for judging me and my life. But that anger turned to contemplation as I thought about how I've been living. She wasn't wrong about anything she said about me.

I am hollow.

BEING LESS than perfect is a thing I knew I was. But I never knew I was less than human and selling myself short with how I've lived and have always thought I'd live my life.

Camilla is moving away from the man now, looking over her shoulder and saying something to him as she goes and he watches her. I open the back door of the Mercedes, Ashton picked me up in, and step out of the car.

Her eyes move to look at me and she stops in the middle of the parking lot. Then she ducks her head and hurries to go inside. I meet her at the door and open it for her.

She says nothing to me as she moves past me. I follow her, closely, staying right behind her as I'm sure she means to hide from me, in the ladies' room perhaps.

I'm wrong about that, I see as she gets to the cooler and reaches out for the handle. "Stop," I say. Placing my hand on her shoulder, I hold it tight enough that she can't get away from me.

"Why?" she asks as she doesn't bother to turn back to look at me.

"Because I want to talk to you." I take her by the shoulders and turn her around.

Her eyes are bright with defiance. "There's nothing to talk about. You want something I won't give. End of subject. Moving on." A slight tremor moves over her red lips then she licks them.

SHE'S upset and I am to blame, once again. "I'm sorry."

"For what? Being who you are?" she asks as she shakes her head. "Don't be. It's me who's sorry. Sorry, I ever spent a minute with you. That was my fault, though. I could read you like a book. I knew your modus operandi. It was me who sold all those condoms to your driver for you to use on countless women. It was foolish of me to think you wanted me for any more than a one night stand."

"I can't stop thinking about you," I tell her and watch her eyes go hard.

Her body tenses even more as her face goes red. "What the fuck do you want me to do about that, Cyprian? Wait, I know. Fuck you, right? Do that, so your mind can be rid of me and you can think about more important things. You're out of luck. I'm not a woman who does that kind of thing. Seems you'll be stuck thinking about me."

"I deserve that," I say as I hold her hot gaze. "Come to my house after you get off work. We should talk."

Slowly, she shakes her head. "You are insane if you think I'm going to go to your house, so you can attempt to make me feel sorry for you and your thoughts about me and how they're messing up your life."

"Have you thought about me, at all?"

Her eyes cut to the side and her body sags a bit as she sighs. "It doesn't matter." She looks back at me. "So, let me help you find your Friday night condoms, Cyprian."

I shake my head. "I don't need any. I'm not going to my father's party tonight. And most likely, I still won't be feeling like going tomorrow."

She grins as she looks down and moves her tennis shoe over the white floor. "I see."

I CAN SEE she's happy I'm not going and it prompts me to ask about the man I saw her talking to outside. "Did that guy ask you out?"

"Huh?" she asks as she looks up at me. "How did you know that?"

"I was watching you. So, you told him what?" I bite the inside of my cheek to hold my tongue in case she tells me something I don't want to hear.

"I turned him down. He's not my type." She looks away as the door chime takes her attention. "I need to get back to work. Surely, you understand that."

Dropping my hands off her shoulders, I release her and nod. "I understand. If you change your mind about tonight, give me a call." I slip my card with my personal cell number on it, out of my pocket and put it into the pocket of her green smock. "I am sorry, Camilla."

With a nod, she leaves me, standing by the cooler as some woman takes a soft drink out of it and looks at us. The woman's eyes move to meet mine. "You two okay?"

I shake my head and turn to leave. My feet move, slowly. I don't want to leave her. I want to hear her say she'll come to me in a little while. I want her to forgive me and I want to tell her all the things I've been thinking about and ask her what she's thought about.

Instead, I'm walking past the checkout counter where she's

ringing up another customer. And older man who's looking at her as her eyes are drooping. "You look blue, sugar. What's got you so sad?"

Her brilliant blue eyes move to me and I flinch as it makes me feel terrible. She's right, I am a terrible person. I give her one last, pleading look and she looks back down. "I'm not sad for me, Bernie. I'm sad for someone else. Someone who doesn't understand what life's about."

With that, I leave the store and go get into my car. "Take me home, Ashton. This was a huge mistake."

He keeps his mouth shut as we leave the parking lot and head home. But his eyes look at me off and on, in the mirror and I know he wants to say something.

"You have something you'd like to tell me, Ashton?"

"It's just that I told you this would happen, sir. She's not like the women you've known. I'm afraid your father, hiring escorts to fill his parties, has left you with the idea all women are that free with who they give themselves to. That young woman isn't an escort. She's just a normal girl and wants normal things."

"That woman is far from normal, I expect. And you are right about me not knowing a thing about normal women and how to interact with them. So, I will read and educate myself on how to do that. Because I can't think of anything else, except how I can see that woman again. And have her stop being mad at me. I long to see her beautiful smile. I long to hear her laughter. I long to feel her skin pressed against mine."

"Maybe you can read up on things and figure it all out, sir. You are one smart man, after all," he says and then I find we're home and I get out of the car.

My heart is heavy and my mind is full. I have got to find a way to get her to forgive me.

I want a chance with her, a real chance...

18

CAMILLA

Locking up the store, I find my hand shaking as I hold his card in the other hand. He's all I could think about after he came to the store.

He's all I've thought about this whole week.

THE WAY he walked away from me on Sunday was jarring. He was cold in an instant and made the decision to walk away, so quickly. I believe he has that ingrained in him. Hasty retreats when things aren't going the exact way he wants them to.

Walking to my car, I glance at my co-worker as the teenage kid gets into his car. "Night, Kyle."

"You working tomorrow?" he asks me.

"No, I have this weekend off." I put the key into the lock on the car door and unlock it.

"You got any plans?" he asks.

Shaking my head, I say, "None at all. See you next week."

He nods and gets into his car. After he pulls out, I look at the card in my hand and slip into the driver's seat.

Cyprian didn't go to the party he's gone to every Friday and

Saturday night since he was a child. I know it's because of me and that has me wondering if Cyprian is capable of change.

What if he is and I am the one who can help him with that? What if he has this one opportunity to live a full life, with love and companionship? What if I ignore him and the feelings I have? What will happen to the man then? What will happen to me?

My heart hurts. It has since he walked away that day. And I have a feeling he can do much more harm to it than anyone else has ever been able to. But I find my fingers moving over my cell phone screen anyway.

It rings only once. "Cami?" his deep voice says and I feel a heat move through me.

"I know it's late," I say.

He quickly says, "Not too late for me to see you. I've been waiting up, hoping you'd call. Will you come over?"

"Will you promise not to make any attempt to get me into your bed?" I ask as I pound my head on the steering wheel, as I don't know what I'm doing.

"Can I touch you? I miss the way your skin feels."

"I guess some touching won't hurt," I say, though I think it might.

"I'll be waiting at the door for you, Cami."

I end the call and pull out of the parking lot. I'm probably going to regret doing this. But something inside of me is telling me that man needs me. And something else is telling me to hold tight to my heart that is so quick to fall in love. He's a gamble. And I'm not the gambling kind.

The gate pops up much faster than I thought it would. I push in the numbers and drive through it. I see him waiting outside, in his pajamas. No shoes, his T-shirt is light blue and his pajama bottoms are a dark blue. He looks like something I should run away from.

A heartache in PJ's, waiting to claim me.

. . .

HE COMES TO MY DOOR, once I stop, and opens it. I'm pulled up into his arms and he holds me, tightly. "Thank you, Cami. Thank you for coming."

He's holding onto me as if I'm some life preserver he's been tossed, in a stormy ocean. "You okay?"

"No," he says. "I have so much I want to talk to you about." He lets me go and takes my hand. "Come inside."

I go along with him and have to wonder if I'm taking on more than I can manage. He's not the same man I saw on Saturday and Sunday. He's kind of a mess.

He takes me inside and pulls me along until we're on a patio where he has a bottle of wine and a couple of glasses, waiting on a table for us. A platter of cheese, crackers, and cut up bits of fruit are in the middle of it. He takes me to a small sofa, covered in dark green upholstery. I sit as he goes to get the things off the table and places the tray next to me.

"This is for me?" I ask as I watch him fill the wine glasses.

"It is," he says. "I figured you'd be hungry after work." He places a glass of wine on the table beside me and goes to sit on the other side of the tray.

"That was very thoughtful of you." I pick up the glass and take a sip then pick up an apple slice.

"You stay on my mind, Cami." He looks at me as he takes a drink of his wine.

"You had things you wanted to talk to me about?" I ask as his gaze is making me feel kind of naked.

"You were right about me, Cami. I am a shell of a person. I am empty and had no idea I was. You see, the women I've been accustom to, have all been escorts my father brought in to entertain us. I don't know how to romantically handle a woman like yourself."

"FIRST OF ALL, using the word, handle, is offensive," I tell him then pick up a cracker and place a piece of creamy white cheese on it.

"Okay, noted. What word should I use in place of that?" he asks as he looks at me with a serious expression on his face.

"How about we call it, getting along with, instead of handling?" I ask as I move the tray to the low table in front of us. "If I keep that right beside me, I will eat it until there's nothing left on the plate."

With a smile, he scoots closer to me. "I'm glad to have it gone." His hand moves over my arm, up and down it goes, with a soft caress. His chest rises as he takes a deep breath. "To be able to touch you is a relief."

Sparks of electric current follow the path he's making over my arm and I put my hand on his leg and rest it there. "So, you really did miss me? That wasn't a line?"

"A line?" he asks. "Cami, I don't even know any lines. I've never had to use them."

"Tell me about these parties with escorts you've been attending since you were, how old did you say you were?" I ask as I gently squeeze his thigh, relishing in how well muscled it is.

"I was fifteen when I was formally introduced into my father's world." He takes a drink.

"You started having sex then too?"

He puts the glass down and looks away as he says, softly, "Yes, it was."

"With your father's consent?" I ask as my parents would never consent to such a thing.

He nods and keeps looking away from me. "Sex is sex in my family. It's what you do at the end of the week to help relieve the stress the work week has brought down on you."

"How mechanical," I say then take a long sip of wine. "And your mother and he, how do they get along?"

"MOTHER GETS along fine with my father. She doesn't come once a month like she did when I was young. She does make it for the holidays. She sleeps with other men when she's here. Never my father. Not even once that I'm aware of."

I reach out to touch his cheek as he keeps looking away from me. "Are you upset about that?"

"Upset isn't the right word. More like, confused. They are cordial to one another. There is and never has been any bad feelings between them. I was a mistake, their happy mishap, they call me."

I gasp and move my hand to my heart. "They call you that!"

"You make it sound horrible, Camilla," he says as he looks at me with wonder.

"It is. To be called a mistake is terrible. Were you treated like a mistake?" I ask, completely appalled.

"I don't think so. I was treated well. I lived my first years with Mother. She stayed at home with me, thanks to money my father sent her. I don't recall any bad treatment. Then she took me to my father's when I was five, so I could go to school. She wanted to get back to her career."

"Which is?" I ask then take a drink.

"Stripper," he says, as if it's no big deal.

I NEARLY CHOKE on my wine. He pats my back and takes the glass out of my hand, so I don't spill it as I gasp for air. Finally, I regain control. "She's a stripper?"

"Was," he corrects me. "Now she runs an adult nightclub my father bought for her."

"Okay, not a lot better but that's something," I say and he hands me back the glass of wine from which I take another sip. "So, she took you to your father to go back to stripping, okay. Had you known your father before she dropped you off with him?"

"No, I had never met him."

"How long did she stay with you, so you could get to know him before she left you?" I ask him and watch his face pale.

"She didn't. She brought me to him and kissed my cheek after she introduced us and then she left, telling me it would all be fine. And, eventually, it was." He takes his wine and downs it.

I am horrified and move in close to him and take him in my arms.

"Cyprian, that's awful. My God, what you must've thought. You must've been so afraid."

His hand moves through my hair as his lips graze the place just behind my ear. "I was."

Things are beginning to make more sense now...

19

CYPRIAN

Throughout the night, we talked and talked until we found ourselves unable to stay awake to talk anymore. And now, here we lie. I moved our little party into the house then laid out a blanket on the floor in front of one of the fireplaces. I gave her one of my T-shirts to put on, so she could get out of her work clothes and be comfortable. She looked cute as hell in it.

The atmosphere was just right to get Cami's guard down. She let me hold her as we talked about me, and my past. She told me a lot about hers too. She and I come from extremely different worlds. I don't think either of us would like the others.

She told me, she never wants to meet my parents, and for fear she'd blurt out how she feels about them and how they raised me. It's odd how I feel about her. It's as if she's becoming protective over me. No one has ever been protective over me before.

Her family would hate me. She didn't say that. I just know they would. The son of a former stripper and a man with no sexual morals. A thing I didn't know my father was until Cami schooled me on it.

And, apparently, I am that way too. A man with no sexual morals and no idea how to get some of those elusive morals she spoke about.

I cannot lie and say she's turned my mind around where casual sex is concerned. In my life sex, has served a purpose. To let off steam. To relax after a hardy bout of pleasurable activities and that's it.

CAMI TOLD me she supposed that's exactly what sex is and that's all I've ever had. Making love is different, she said. And I have to wonder if she's right.

She moves, slightly. I hold her tighter, not wanting her to wake up and make some excuse to leave me. She settles into my arms and begins to snore a bit. I kiss her cheek then lie back down.

Her ass hits me as she scoots back and it settles right at my juncture. The morning has me ready to go and I can't stop myself from grinding into her. I stop when she moans.

She reaches back and runs her hand along the arm I have wrapped around her. I'm stiff as a board as I wait to see if she's going to finally let me have sex with her.

Moving a little, I press myself against her ass and pump a bit, making her moan more and press her ass against me. Getting braver, I move her hair to one side and kiss her neck. She groans, "Cyprian."

At least she's aware it's me back here. I whisper in her ear, "Camilla." Then I take her earlobe and deliver a gentle bite.

Pushing her ass even harder against me, has my cock quivering in anticipation and now I'm aware I have no protection with me. The condoms are in my bedroom.

Now, how to move this upstairs and into my room without giving her a chance to think about things?

GIVING special attention to her neck, has her making some great sounds and letting me grind into her, so I pull her backward as I stand up and slip my arms around her to pick her up with me.

As she's jostled with the movement, her eyes open. At first they're dreamy and she makes a small smile. "Cyprian." She leans her head on my chest as her arms wrap around my neck.

"Shh," I shush her and start to carry her away.

Her fingertips roam over my chest. We still have on our clothes and that will have to be dealt with delicately as well. If I hurry, she'll surely come fully awake and if I take too long, she might also start thinking and I can't have that.

She seems to have fallen back to sleep as I make it to my bedroom. I open the door, which I'd left ajar, and quietly kick it closed. Just as I get to the edge of the bed, which is made, I lie her on one side and go to the other side to pull the blankets down.

As I walk back to her, finding she's snuggled down on the pillow, I pull my shirt off and drop my PJ bottoms. Taking a deep breath, I start to pull my T-shirt off her, gently taking it from the bottom and lifting it up until it's just underneath her tits.

Her eyes fly open. "Cyprian! What the hell are you doing?" She sits up and grabs my hands. "You're naked!"

"You were into it. Don't you remember?" I ask her as she looks at me with wide eyes.

"Would you cover yourself, for God's sake?" she shouts at me.

I pull my PJ bottoms back on, quickly and see her pull the shirt back down to cover herself. "You were into it, Cami."

"I was asleep!" she rolls off the bed and gets up. "I'm going home. I trusted you, Cyprian!"

"WAIT, please. I swear to God you were into it. Stop and think for a second." I grab her arm to stop her from leaving and she snaps her head to look at my hand.

"I was asleep!" She jerks her arm hard and I let it go, so I don't hurt her.

"Cami, I'm sorry," I say as I sit on the bed. "I am. I thought you were awake and wanting it as much as I was. I am sorry."

She spins around and looks at me with tired eyes. "Cyprian, if we ever do that, it needs to be a thing we discuss and are ready for. Not a thing that happens if we're together and have too much to drink. Or are hanging out, fall asleep in each other's arms, and barely awake. I, for one, would like to be fully present for our first time. If there ever is one."

"You're dead set on being in love and having a commitment, aren't you?" I ask as I realize this woman really is going to be a hell of a lot of work to get her where I want her.

Her face goes soft, the indignation gone. "Cyprian, of course, that's how I want it to be. I thought, after last night, you understood me better."

"I do." I look at her, standing in my bedroom with my T-shirt on, her hair a wild mess and I find her the most beautiful woman I've ever laid eyes on in the morning. And I have seen many.

"Then why would you do such a thing?" she asks as she puts one hand on her hip and pushes her hair back.

"I want you," I say, simply. "And if you will be truthful with yourself, you want me too. Or you wouldn't have pressed your ass against my cock, Cami. You wouldn't have moaned at how it felt and you wouldn't have let me kiss your neck the way I was kissing it. You have a hickey or two from my attention to your sweet neck."

HER HAND MOVES to her neck as her face goes pale. "No!" She rushes to look in the mirror over my dresser and pulls her hair back, revealing two, very nice sized purple spots on her long and elegant neck. "This looks terrible!"

Getting up, I move in behind her and wrap my arms around her and look at the marks I left on her. "I like the way they look." I turn her in my arms and look into her eyes. "Admit it. You want me as much as I want you, Cami."

"Okay, so I can admit that. But I am very self-disciplined. I can wait until what we have is real." She runs her arms around me and hugs me. "If it ever gets real."

Holding her and looking in the mirror as she hugs me, makes me think about what she's saying. So, I pull her with me to sit on the bed and hold her hand. "Cami, I don't think I know how to love. I haven't ever been very close to anyone. It could take a very long time or it might never happen. What then?"

"Then you and I are not meant to be. You see, I will not sell myself short. I want a man who loves me. Who will be there for me through thick and thin. Who will cherish me and put me above all others. And I will never settle for anything less. Because I will do that for him too. If you feel like this is a waste of your time, I will certainly understand." She looks at me as if trying to see if I am capable of understanding her.

"Go home," I say.

She nods and gets up. No arguing. No questions. She just gets up and starts walking away from me. "Okay."

"Uh, don't you want to know why I said that?" I ask as I get up and go to her. She shakes her head and I stop her retreat as I take her by the shoulders and turn her around. "I want you to go home and get cleaned up and put on something nice. I want to spend the day with you. I want to take you somewhere nice for breakfast. We'll do a bit of shopping then eat somewhere nice for lunch. Maybe take in a movie and go somewhere spectacular for dinner. I want to take you on a very long date. What do you say?"

"I'd like to say you will need to watch how you ask me out. I was sure you were done with me. Emotional whiplash is not a thing I like to have."

"Is that a yes?" I ask, as I'm still unsure about her.

She nods and hugs me. "You and I either have a long road ahead of us or a very short one, Cyprian."

"I hope it's a long one," I say. "Don't you?"

SHE LETS me go and shakes her head as she walks to the bedroom door. "I hope it's a long road that doesn't end in a dead end." With that, she's gone, leaving me with myself and wondering if this is worth it.

The woman's mind is set. It's love then sex. And if I never find the love for her, she demands, then I will never get a taste of her, and I will most likely never stop thinking about her.

I wonder if one can make themselves fall in love...

20

CAMILLA

"Did you ever watch a love story movie, Cyprian?" I ask him as he holds my hand and we stroll along the sidewalk that goes through a picturesque park in the middle of town.

He's been acting like a boyfriend. It has me thinking, he's trying to project the image of what I want. But I want more than a mere projection from him.

"No, why do you ask that?" he asks me as he pulls our clasped hands up and kisses mine then lets my hand go and runs his arm around me, kissing the side of my head.

"You've been acting different today. At breakfast, you cut up my ham when I had trouble doing it. At lunch, you kept feeding me your french-fries. And here we are, taking a walk in the park on our way to see a play put on by the local theater club. It's very romantic, and you are anything but a romantic."

"I thought this is what you wanted," he says as he stops and looks at me. "I'm doing what you wanted. Are you saying that, even if I become the man you expect, you will still find fault with me?"

"No!" I shake my head and find myself confused. "Cyprian, I want you to be you. I'm not trying to change you."

"But you are." He pulls me along again to continue on our way to the small, open-air theater on the other side of the park. "You're lying to yourself if you really think that. You don't want me as I am. You want me the way you want me. A perfect gentleman who is in complete love with his girl."

Suddenly, I see him for who he must really be. A man who does what's expected of him. And that breaks my heart. "Cyprian, please be who it is you want to be. I will either like you or I won't but don't be a fake person with me. Please."

"I'm not being fake. I've never done the things we're doing. I feel light-hearted and free. I feel healthy and to be honest, I feel I have you to owe that to and it makes me think you are a very special person and I enjoy just being with you, doing anything at all or even nothing. So, sue me if you think I'm faking it. I'm not."

"You do seem light-hearted. And you do seem happy." I look at him from the corner of my eye and see the smile that's been on his face most all day long.

As we arrive at the theater, I see by the sign, it's Romeo and Juliet. "Have you ever seen this one?" he asks me.

"I've never been to a play at all. I have read the book and seen the old movie. Have you seen it before?"

He shakes his head as he heads close to the front and finds us a nice hill to sit on. He tosses the blanket he brought for us on the ground and sits down then pulls me to sit in front of him, between his legs. "Lie back on me, so you'll be comfortable. And, no, I also have never seen a play. We had a home theater like I have at my place. That's where I saw any movies I wanted to. Which weren't many, as I spent the majority of my time studying, once I got home from school. Weekends were full. Once I went to work, free time only came on the weekends and you know how I've spent them."

"So, this is new to us both. That's nice," I say as I lean back on him.

More and more couples come and spread blankets and get ready to watch the play. It's a very couple's kind of thing to do and I find it fascinating Cyprian could think this up on such short notice. Being he's never been a romantic kind of man.

His fingertips stroke my neck as he leans his head on my opposite shoulder. "You look so pretty today, Cami. I love the blue ribbon you have holding your hair back. And your soft, pink sundress is pretty too."

I smile as he seems to be trying so hard to say all the right things. "Thank you. You look handsome in your black slacks and pale green button up, yourself."

His lips press against my neck, where I used makeup to cover the marks he left there this morning. "You have yet to allow me to kiss your sweet lips, Cami." He nudges my head to look at some of the other couples who are exchanging kisses.

"What the hell," I say and twist a bit, so we can look at each other. I run my arm around his neck. "You've been a very good boyfriend today. I think you deserve a kiss."

His eyes sparkle as I push back a lock of his light brown hair. His lips part then he licks them and looks at mine. "It's because we're in public and it can go no farther than a kiss, isn't it?"

I NOD AND HE SMILES. "Of course, Cyprian."

"I'm going to make you wish we were alone, Camilla." His hand cradles my head as he holds me still for him. His face moves so slowly I have to fight myself not to move mine to meet him.

His lips, barely touch mine as he hovers. His breath is warm on my lips that are aching for him to press his to them. One tiny peck, he gives me, then three more in slow succession.

My heart is racing and my body is aching as he toys with me. Small pecks leave me wanting more and then his mouth is full on mine. His tongue moves past my lips and into my mouth, stroking my tongue in a way I've never felt before.

His fingers grip the back of my head as he tastes me, but only for a moment. Then his mouth is gone and I am left, panting. He says not a word, as he gazes into my eyes. "Did you feel that, Camilla?"

I blink and nod. "I felt something I've never felt before."

THE ACTORS COME on stage and everyone begins clapping. Cyprian turns me around and leans me back against him, wrapping me in his strong arms, leaving me nearly breathless with that one kiss and my mind moving in fast circles about what that was.

I've told myself, time and time again, not to fall for him as quickly as I've done with the others who've come before him. I have to guard myself against this man. He may seem to be acting like he's all about me but he isn't really this guy. He is a man who's never learned how to develop real feelings for others. And he is dangerous because of that.

But how am I to hold back now that I know what his kiss is like...

21

CYPRIAN

Dancing with Camilla in the cool night air, on an outdoor dance floor, I hold her in my arms, enjoying how her scent mixes with the breeze, sending me to a place I've never been. She is so easy to be with.

I've never argued with a person, other than at work. Honestly, I thought if a woman ever wanted to argue with me, I'd simply walk away from her. But I can't seem to walk away from this one. And I don't see myself ever wanting to.

She's made me feel things I've never felt before. And when we kissed, it was unlike anything I've ever felt. Fireworks went off inside my head. My body tingled all over. It was mind blowing!

We came to this place for dinner and dancing, a thing I always thought sounded lame as hell. But it's anything but lame. With her, anyway. She and I went shopping and I found myself buying us matching outfit after matching outfit.

She asked me if I'd watched a movie about love and I didn't lie when I told her, no. The truth is, I got a couple of books, okay ten of them, and read them between the time I saw her at the store and she came to my house last night.

Ashton had reminded me about how smart I am and I downloaded e-book after e-book to help me understand what love is and what people in love do. So, I did use that help but I don't see that as a bad thing.

She might, though. So, I'll keep that tidbit of information to myself. That was a thing one of the authors said to do. Women and men think differently, hence all the arguing that comes along with any healthy relationship.

I FOUND out that in any relationship where no arguing occurs, it's a shallow thing that's not healthy. My parents and I have shallow relationships. It's hard to tell myself that, as their child, who should be able to have at least deep relationships with his parents.

The part I didn't like about some of the information was that a person forms their core personality and beliefs in the first six years of their life. If that's true, then I'm in for a tough time of it, as from what I can recall, it was a time with relatively no emotions. And that might make it hard when it comes to finding love with Cami.

And I want to, so very badly. Now that I've read about how fulfilling love can be, I want to feel that too. But it did say you can't find it with just anyone. You need to have chemistry, connection, and common beliefs.

She and I have the first two but not the last one. But I am a work in progress. I may never look at sex the same way she does but I don't have to. I also don't have to talk to her anymore about that. I can simply agree with her and keep things easy between us in that department. That seems to be the one she's most concerned about.

The song ends and she pulls her head off my shoulder and looks at me. "That was nice, Cyprian. Thank you for the dance."

I take her hand, leading her back to our table and pull the chair out for her. The night is nearly over, as it's closing time, I see as the lights come up.

She smiles at me. "Time to go, Cyprian. I had a very nice time with you today."

· · ·

I TAKE HER HAND, helping her back up, then lead her to the car. I drove us today, so we could be alone and she'd feel more normal than being chauffeured around.

"I'm glad you had a nice time. I did too. I really did. It was surprising." I open the door and help her into the car and find her smiling.

She's smiled a lot today and so have I. Just being around her makes me feel happy.

I want to take her home more than I've ever wanted anything but I think that might make things take longer than I want them to. As I slide in behind the steering wheel of my BMW, I look at her. "What would you like to do tomorrow?"

"Another date?" she asks, looking surprised. "Do you think you can top this one?"

"I can try," I say as I start the car and head out.

"How about I let you decide? You did a pretty great job today. I'll do anything you want to."

"I'LL THINK ABOUT IT THEN." I drive toward the outskirts of town and take hold of her hand, holding it between us.

It's so hard not to ask her to come home with me. It's so foreign to me to go without sex for this long. I feel pent up and more than a bit frustrated.

I haven't told anyone a thing about her. My driver is the only one who knows about me and her, and no one else does. I'm a private person, anyway. And we are not a for sure thing either.

The gate to my place comes up and I keep going. She looks at me with a smile. "Not even going to make an attempt at it, Cyprian?"

"No, ma'am. I am determined to treat you like a proper young lady. I want you to know I hear what you say. I respect what you say. And I am striving to treat you the way you want to be treated."

She smiles as I pull into her small driveway. "I'm glad to have you understanding me."

Parking the car, I jump out and open her door and walk her to her front door. I'm not going to ask if I can come in, as that's improper.

According to one of the books I read. "What time can I pick you up tomorrow?"

"I suppose it depends on what you want to do." She bats her eyelashes at me.

"I want to spend the whole day with you again. Is that okay?" I ask her as I move her between me and the door.

"Okay, if you want to. How about eleven? We can go to brunch. I love brunch." She runs her hand through my hair.

"I'll make plans for that then. And now, may I have a goodnight kiss?"

SHE NODS as her arms go around my neck. I move in, slowly, watching her eyes dart back and forth and her lips begin to tremble. Her heart is going crazy as my lips touch hers.

Holding me tight, her mouth succumbs to mine. I dominate her as I take her with a hard kiss, demanding she kiss me back. Our bodies are flush as I press her against the door. Her body heats with the kiss and I can tell she's on fire for me.

My body is on fire for her too and I can barely control myself. But I find the strength to end the kiss. I have to leave her wanting more or she'll never give into me.

Her hands move down my chest. "Cyprian, I hope you're not disappointed."

"How could I be?" I ask her then lift her chin. "I don't think you could ever disappoint me, Cami." I leave a soft kiss on her plump lips. "Goodnight. I'll be here at eleven tomorrow."

"Goodnight, thank you for the wonderful day." Then she unlocks the door and slips inside.

As I make my way to the car, I feel tortured. I want her so bad, I can taste it. I lick my lips and taste her there. I want to taste every last inch of her and this waiting is the hardest thing I've ever had to do.

Driving back to my place, I feel the swell in my pants and it's uncomfortable as hell. I suppose a cool shower will ease this discomfort from being celibate longer than I have in twenty years. Plus, wanting that woman more than I've ever wanted anyone.

My cock is chastising my brain for picking a woman with such strong morals.

It wants to feel a woman and it wants it now!

I PULL through the gate and pull up to the house to find a long black car in the drive. Once, I park and get out, I see the back door of the car open and two women get out of it. Both are giggling and one has a bottle of champagne in one hand. The one with dark hair holds her arms open. "Your father sent us to you, Cyprian. I am Lola and this is Becca. We belong to you for the rest of the night."

Becca has long blonde hair and six-inch heels and a tight, red, short dress that barely hides her ample breasts. Lola is wearing a skirt so short it's almost not there and my cock is twitching to get to them.

"I can't!" I shout as I take steps back.

"What?" Lola asks as they come toward me, anyway. "Come on. Your father told us you've been without female company for over a week. What's wrong with you?"

"I'm seeing someone. I can't do this with you guys. Thanks, but tell my father, I don't need his help in finding women." I have to move to the other side of the car as they're still coming at me.

Becca takes over the pursuit. "Cyprian, we've been told about you by some of the other women at your father's party. Please allow us to experience you. We've already been paid, after all. And I have a few tricks you may have never seen before."

"What kind of tricks?" I ask without meaning to.

She wiggles her finger in a come-hither fashion. "I can make miracles happen with just this little finger."

"Like what?" I ask and I swear it's my cock talking because my brain is telling me I can't find that out, anyway.

Before I realize it, they're on either side of me and moving me toward the front door of my home. Cherry red lips are on mine as the door opens and we three spill inside.

My cock is throbbing to be set free as Lola puts her hand on it and undoes my pants with the other. She sets it free as Becca kisses me. We move backward until my back hits the wall and I feel the cool air as Lola pulls my pants and underwear down to my ankles then her wet mouth is on my throbbing cock and I am lost to them.

The animal in me takes over as the women fondle my entire body. Becca takes my hand and helps me to pull her tit out of the top of her dress. I squeeze it as Lola sucks me off.

My entire body is shaking with the release that's already beginning. It's been too long. I have no control over it. And just like that, I spurt into Lola's mouth and she moans as she drinks it all down.

You'd think I'd be spent, but I am anything but that. I move us to the next room. "All fours, Becca," I command as Lola rids me of my shirt. She looks over and sees the remote for the gas-lit fireplace and turns it on to light up the room a bit.

"I want to see this," she purrs as I push Becca's short red dress up and rip her lacy panties off. I'm in such a frenzy, I almost forget a very important thing.

"Fuck! Do either of you have any condoms?"

Lola pulls one out of her black bra and slides it on for me. My body is trembling as she does and I look at Becca's ass, riding up in the air, waiting for me.

With the condom on, I pull Lola up and kiss her hard. "Go upstairs, the first door to the left is my bedroom. In the drawer, next to my bed is a box of condoms bring them down. You're next!"

She giggles and runs off to fetch the things that will make this frustration leave my body. I turn back to the waiting Becca and run my hands over her pristine ass. Then plunge my cock into her and relish how it feels to be inside of a woman again.

Over and over I thrust until I feel the ache inside of me turn into ecstasy and find myself shouting and growling with the release. Panting, I lean over her body and let myself complete the act.

. . .

LOLA COMES BACK with the condoms just as I pull out of Becca and find myself a bit weak with the amount of fluid that's left my body. "I'm going to grab a bottle of water and be right back. Do either of you want anything?"

Both of their heads shake as they begin to undress one another and I head off to the bar in the next room. My body feels only a little bit less tense and I know it will take the rest of the night to rid me of all the tension the last week has given me.

Taking the cold bottle of water from the mini-fridge, I gulp it down in three large gulps. The girls' giggling stops and I find myself wondering why.

"Who the hell are you two?" I hear a deep female voice ask and I know it's Camilla.

My mind freezes as I have no idea what I should do. Then my brain goes into overdrive, sending my ass flying through room after room to get up to mine and put some clothes on.

Why did I let this happen?

What will she do?

I MAKE it to my bedroom and haul ass to the bathroom to clean myself then run to the dresser and put on underwear and shorts and a shirt. Then I pace back and forth as I scratch my head and wonder what the fuck I'm supposed to say or act like.

She and I have not said we're exclusive, that's a fact. I didn't ask her to come over here, another fact. She could've taken care of my needs but she refused to, yet another fact!

With such facts on my side, why is my entire body shaking? Why am I acting like the men I've made fun of countless times who are married and dabbling at the parties?

I am not married and not even in a relationship!

So why do I feel this way...

22

CAMILLA

"Cyprian!" I shout as I hold his used condom between two fingers. It has been tied up and is nearly full of his semen.

The women are quickly pulling on what little clothes they had on. "His father sent us. It's not his fault," the blonde says.

"Oh yeah?" I ask as she seems very nervous. "I think it may have been his fault that he fucked one of you. Is that all he's done so far?"

The blonde jerks her head toward the dark-haired woman. "She gave him a blowjob."

"Shut the fuck up, Becca," the one she called Lola, hisses at her. "This must be the woman he said he was seeing."

"So, he told you he was seeing someone and you fucked him anyway?" I ask then shake my head. "No, don't even bother to answer that. He should've never done it. It's not your fault. You're paid to do this, I suppose."

"Yes, yes we were. His father pays a lot of us to come to his parties for the weekend and we're expected to come on really strong to the men. It's our job," Becca says.

.   .   .

"I SEE THAT. Please, leave him to me," I say as I escort them to the door. A long black car is waiting outside and I guess it's for them.

Lola looks over her shoulder and asks, "For future reference, is he going to be a free man again? I mean, just in case his father tries to send us out to him again. We don't like to get into any kind of altercations with pissed off girlfriends or wives."

"He will be a free man." I shut the door and go to find Cyprian. "Come out, come out, wherever you are."

He's obviously in hiding and afraid to face me. I stop at the restroom just outside the entry room and drop the used condom in the wastebasket and give my hands a good washing.

I have no idea what got into me when I saw it. I just reached down and picked it up. It was right next to a torn pair of red panties I suppose belonged to the girl in the red dress.

As I continue my journey to find Cyprian, I see the tray of chocolate chip cookies I made for him, on the floor where I dropped them, and shudder at what I found when I got here.

Two naked women, kissing and touching each other. Cyprian's clothes spread from the entry room to the next room. The fireplace lit up, making romantic glows and, finally, the used condom and panties on the floor, amongst his shirt and the women's clothes and shoes.

I figure he's hiding in his bedroom, so I make my way to it and find the door is locked. "Afraid of me, Cyprian?"

I HEAR the door unlock and he pulls me into his arms. "Thank God, you're here. I wanted to call you but my cell phone was in my pants and they managed to get those off me. I finally got away from them and ran up here to lock myself away from them. My father sent them. I had no idea. I swear it!"

Pushing his chest, I make him let me go. "So, you were raped?"

"Raped? No," he says as he steps back. "Molested is a better word."

"Those little women molested you, Cyprian?" I ask. "Perhaps we should report the incident?"

"No, my father sent them." He looks at me with a sheepish expression.

"But you allowed them to do to you what they did and you fucked one of them. They told me everything," I say as I cross my arms in front of me. "And, just so you know, one of them asked me if you would still be in a relationship, the way you told them you were, any longer. I told her, no."

"We aren't in one. I just said that to try to get them to leave me alone. They seduced me, Cami! They both took a hold of me and pulled me into the house and had me undressed before I knew what was happening. One kissed me while the other took me into her mouth. I was blindsided by all the sexual stimulation. I couldn't help myself. You have to understand!"

"I have to understand that two women that small could make you do all that? I have to understand you lost yourself in the sexual desire for them?" I stop and shake my head. "Today was one of the best days I've ever had. It was, hands down, the best date I've ever been on. You were wonderful. Affectionate, funny, cute, sweet, lovable, and it was all a lie."

"It wasn't a lie, Cami! It was real. It was the most real thing I've ever done in my life. Being with you, I feel more of a person than I ever have. I've felt like a robot, going through the motions, most of the time. Sex is exactly what you said it was, mechanical. An act. Much like any other act that requires a bodily function where you expel bodily fluids. That's how I think about it."

"Oh, so what you did down there was just like when you take a shit. You find a toilet, any one will do, and you release yourself into it. Then you flush it all away and no one should even worry about what you just did. It was a bodily function, everyone has to do, in order to live. Is that pretty much how you think about what you just did?"

HE SITS on the bed and looks up at the ceiling. "Pretty much."

"You will never be the man for me. You will never be what I need in my life. And I think it's better I figured that out before I fell head over heels in love with you, Cyprian. Because I could fall so easily for you. Thank you for fucking those girls, minutes after our date ended. Thank you very much for bringing to light that you are not a man I want in my life."

I turn to walk away but he stops me as he asks, "Why were you over here in the first place?"

I turn back to him with eyes full of tears. "I was bringing you a plate of cookies. I wanted us to share a couple of them and a glass of milk then I was going to leave you with another goodnight kiss." I turn away again.

His hand on my shoulder stops me. He turns me to him but I can't look at his handsome face. It's just too hard. "Cami, I need sex. I need it. You don't seem to understand me. If I give you the commitment you need, will you give me the sex I need? Then we can make this work. I do care about you and I do love spending time with you. You are my most favorite person and if I lost you..."

"You already have," I tell him before he can say anything else. "I will not be holding you to me with a sexual rope. I will not be held to you with a commitment that doesn't involve love. I cannot trust you, Cyprian."

"I go all week without sex. On the weekends, I've had an abundance of it for twenty years, Cami! You cannot expect me to go cold turkey, with no idea when I will get to feel the inside of a woman again. When I'll get to feel, soft breasts, pressed against my chest. When I'll get to feel sweet lips on me. You can't begin to understand my needs. I have them too, Camilla."

"I cannot change my entire way of thinking, just so you can get off. I don't have sex, I make love. You don't have real feelings about anything or anyone. Any woman will do for you to relieve yourself in. I can't handle that. Sorry, Cyprian. You're asking for more than I can give you."

I pull away from him and leave him in his bedroom. I'm not trying to punish him or manipulate him in any way. I am merely trying to keep myself from getting hurt any more by him.

Making my way down the stairs, I let myself out of the house and get into my car and drive all the way to the gate before the waterfall of tears overtakes me.

Why does he have to be so damn corrupted...?

To be continued...

BOOK 4: LADY KILLER

A Bad Boy Billionaire Romance

By Michelle Love

23

CYPRIAN

The horses thunder down the track in front of us. The afternoon is warm and I find myself pulling my jacket off and rolling up the sleeves on my white button-down. "Have a mint julip, Cyprian," my father says as he passes a tall, slender glass down to me.

I am sandwiched between two brunettes. Simone has green eyes and Joanie has dark eyes, nearly black. They latched onto me as soon as I came to my father's private booth. He's now the new owner of Charlemagne's Choice, a feisty thoroughbred he's had his eye on for some time.

Joanie places the cold drink in my hand. "Here you go, drink up. I have plans for you soon."

Simone looks around me, at the other woman. "Back off, Joanie. I want him all to myself."

"Ladies, there is no need to fight over me. I won't be needing any special attention from either of you. I'm not feeling it, today. Sorry," I tell them and earn a frown from them both, and my father.

"Come with me, son," he says as he gets up and goes to the back of the small but elaborately decorated room. He rests his hand on my shoulder as I meet him. "What's been going on with you? You haven't been coming around to the parties. Did the girls I sent you last night treat you well?"

"Papa, I've messed up. I met someone. A good woman. A great woman, actually. The girls you sent me, ruined that for me. She wants nothing more to do with me. She caught us. And I am devastated." I take a long drink of the minty liquid to numb the pain that's overwhelmed me since she left me.

"So, you think you found a woman? Like a girlfriend?" he asks as he goes behind the bar and mixes himself up something to drink.

"I did," I tell him as I take a seat on one of the tall barstools. "But I blew it. I should've sent the girls away but I let them toy with me."

"If you had a special lady friend, why did you feel the need to mess with the girls I sent you? Is your special lady not sexually satisfying you?"

I cock my eyebrow as I say, "She wants love before sex. And she doesn't want sex, she wants to make love."

His laugh is low and deep as ice cubes splash into the amber liquid in his short glass. "Love? What do any of us know about love?"

"I HAD to read some books on it. The life we've led had nothing to do with love. But I want to experience it. I want to experience it with her. Camilla Petit is her name. She comes from New Orleans, originally. And she is gorgeous, sweet, funny, and amazing. And I blew it, all for a piece of ass. I am morally corrupt, just like she said I was."

"She called you names?" he asks then takes a sip of the concoction he made himself. Making a face, he looks around the bar and comes up with a single cube of sugar and drops it into the glass.

I watch it melting as I say, "Not exactly. She's not mean. She's honest. I don't know why I did it. I really don't. I think it might be because I have been conditioned to accepting sex." I look at my father. "At times I feel like a machine, work, work, work then play, play, play. It matters to me where I make my money from but when it comes to me, personally, well, it hasn't mattered where I got sex from. But Cami wants a commitment, which I offered her. She refused it.

She wasn't willing to accept the condition of sex being part of the commitment. And I was left alone. Papa, I've never felt more alone in my life."

"You are feeling sad and hopeless, aren't you?" he asks me as he stirs his drink with a red swizzle stick.

I lean on the bar. "I am."

"Do you see what love and relationships do to a person? This is exactly why I've stayed the hell away from them. You see, I had myself a girlfriend in high school. At first, it was great. Then she and I started bickering over nothing at all. She wanted a hot dog and I had bought her a hamburger. I was thoughtless, she told me." He stops and takes a drink as if the memory stirs things in him, he'd rather be left alone.

"So, was she your only girlfriend?" I ask as I sit up and listen to him.

"No, I had another one in college. She was smart and classy. The kind of woman you can take home to mom and dad, you know?"

"I do know. Cami is that kind of a woman. Very respectable."

He nods. "Well, then you can expect her to want you to be just as respectable as she is. That's how mine was. She hated my drinking. Said it wasn't a thing she wanted me to do, except on occasion. So, I modified my nightly Scotch to every other weekend when we went to social functions."

"There's nothing wrong with that," I say. "It's a healthy way to live."

"It is. And if it would've been my decision, it might not have started to bother me. But that wasn't enough. You see, I found my love for the racetrack while I was in college. And she found gambling to be deplorable. So, she told me she didn't want me to do that anymore." Another long drink has his glass empty and he stares at the bottom of it.

"She was controlling," I say as I nod.

"As are all women of that nature. The ones you can bring home to meet the parents are all the same. The want you to straighten up and fly right by their side. They will dress you, make you eat what they deem, appropriate. They will make you bend to their rules of how things must go if you are to stay in a peaceful existence with them. Which, by the way, is quite impossible, even if you bend until you break."

"I read where things are not supposed to go peacefully in healthy relationships. Arguments occur because men and women see things differently. The key to a happy relationship is learning compromise. But even once that's learned, arguments will still occur. There is no getting around them," I tell him as he shakes his head.

"Why would you want that?" he asks as he looks deep into my eyes. "Why would anyone?"

"I guess to procreate. It's bred into us." I look back at the ten women my father brought along to the races today. "You want women around, Papa. The women you want around are paid, though. They will act however you want them too. If you want docile, they will be that. If you want aggressive, they will be that. It's an act. The whole thing, including the sex, is an act. It's not real."

"But it is peaceful. There are no arguments. They may be paid and it all may be an act but what isn't, son? Isn't life just a series of acts you must do each day? We must get up every weekday and attend to our work, whatever kind you have. It's an act. No one really wants to be doing it but it has to be done."

"I LIKED to go to school and I like to go to work. I find it stimulates my brain. I need that stimulation. I crave it."

He shakes his head. "I did not. I did what I had to, in order to make the kind of money that would support the lifestyle I imagined for myself. And I made that happen. You came along and I saw my chance to groom you to take over and give me the rest of my vision. The freedom to never work again. To completely relax."

"And I'm glad I can give you that. I am different, though. I need the problems and I love to solve them." My wheels start moving as I think about what I've just said.

I love to solve problems!

. . .

COULD I have made the decision to be with those women last night, in order to create a problem where there wasn't one? Could I have done that, so I would have to use my brain to fix the problem between me and Camilla? Am I really that person who does that kind of thing to themselves?

"You are different, Cyprian. So, this woman you're upset about, how come she broke things off with you? Had you given her a commitment already?" he asks as he looks behind the bar and comes up with a platter of meats and cheeses.

"We did not have a commitment, no," I say as I pick up a slice of salami.

"Then why would she end things? You were a free man. Did you not explain that to her?" he asks as he piles meats and cheeses on a cracker.

"I did but it did no good. She was right to do it. We had barely finished an amazing date. Literally, five minutes after I dropped her off, I was with two other women. It hurt her, I saw it in her eyes. She was devastated. And now, so am I."

"I can give you some advice. It's a mental game, one sometimes must play when trying to get a woman. I've never used it, as I lost any want to mess with relationships after those two nightmares." He comes around the bar and takes a seat next to me.

"I'm not into games, Papa."

"If you want a relationship then you should know, you will have to play some. Now, jealousy is a great catalyst. You want this woman to know you will not sit around and wait for her to come to her senses. She needs to know that."

"I think she already does. She's not dumb, Papa. She's a scientist. She's extremely smart. She'll be on to me, quickly," I tell him, as I'm skeptical about making her jealous. She simply ended things with me with the first bit of that.

"If you don't want to play that card just yet, then keep the pressure on her. Send her flowers and candies. See her as often as you can. Is there somewhere she goes you could show up at?" he asks as he watches another set of horse's race.

"She works at a little store at the edge of town. That's where I met her."

"She's a supposed scientist who works at a store?" he asks as he shakes his head. "She's a liar, son."

"No, Papa, she's not. She's still in college, at Clemson University," I say then laugh at my father's skepticism.

"IF YOU HAVE a place where you can go see her that's what you need. Be nice to her even if she's short with you. Remind her of any good times you had together. And end every short visit with an invitation for her to come to you. If after a while that doesn't work, you can get aggressive with her. Treat her like you own her."

"That woman will never accept that kind of treatment. Not ever. That would be a fatal mistake. But you may be right about the seeing her every chance I get. I will put that plan into action and see what happens."

"I'm telling you, son. Show up with a pretty girl on your arm and watch her move mountains to get you back into hers," he says, making me think he might be right. But I'd like to give a shot at the other way.

I've already hurt her enough as it is...

24

CAMILLA

"Men have needs, dear," Gina tells me as we clean out the coffee machines in the back of the store.

"I have the need to know I'm loved first and that I love the person I'm about to give myself to. What about my needs?" I ask as I slosh bleach water around in one of the glass coffee pots.

She stops scrubbing a pot someone left on the burner too long and coffee burnt to the bottom of it. "It sounds to me, that date he took you on and how he acted toward you, showed promise. He cares for you, at the very least. And I can see you care for him."

"He's a man with no morals," I say as I rinse the pot and place it on a rack to dry.

"Teach him what you expect. In turn, he'll teach you what he expects. And that means he expects his girlfriend to give him the sex he needs to function. You don't understand how some men's minds work. I've been married three times. I've studied the beasts. They are simple creatures. Feed them, coddle them when they need it, and keep them happy in the bedroom, or where ever they feel like getting frisky. Don't be such a prude, Camilla."

Prude!

. . .

"I AM NOT A PRUDE, GINA!"

"I think you are a bit of one. How do expect you and this man to know if you are compatible? Let's say you don't have any sex and you fall madly in love with one another, if that can happen without having any sex? Then you get married and the wedding night comes and boom, he sucks! What then? You got yourself into a marriage with a crappy lover."

"I didn't mean we had to wait until we got married," I say with a huff. "I'm not that bad. I just meant until we were sure we didn't want to see other people. That's all I meant,"

"But, didn't you tell me he did offer you that? Just before you left him?" she asks.

"Well, yes," I say as I toss the dishrag I wiped my hands on, into the dirty rag bucket. "But he had one condition. Sex being the condition. I'm not into that."

"You aren't into having sex being a part of a real commitment?" she asks as she shakes her head. "You're being unrealistic. Why have a commitment at all if not for that reason?"

"Life is about more than sex, Gina," I say as I walk away with the chirp of the door that means we have a customer. "I'll take care of this one. You have your hands full."

"Not to a man, it's not!" she calls out to me as I leave the backroom.

"Welcome to Ty's..." I stop as I see Cyprian, waiting at the counter.

"HI," he says.

I shake off the panic my body is suddenly filled with and walk forward. "Let me guess, you need more condoms?"

"No," he says as he places his hands on the counter top. "I need you. That's all I need."

"Aww," comes from behind me as Gina is eavesdropping.

I turn and glare at her. "Those coffee pots won't clean themselves, Gina."

"Hi, Gina," Cyprian calls out to her. "How's it going tonight?"

"Well, and you, sir?" she asks.

"It would be better if a certain someone would forgive the imbecile I have been and see fit to give this old dog another chance," he says.

"Aww, Camilla, don't be a stubborn fool. Why, I'd jump through hoops for a man like him," Gina says and I wave my hands to shoo her away.

I TURN BACK as she disappears to the back again and I make my way to the man who has torn a hole in my heart with his immoral ways. "Cyprian, look, at this point, there are no hard feelings on my part. You are the man you are. I merely cannot deal with that."

"I was a fool who was in a state of sexual frustration. I am not blaming you for that, I am merely stating a fact. And all that can change but that's up to you, Cami. I want you. I want all of you. I want to see you every single day. I've never wanted to see anyone that much." He smiles as if that's going to make anything better.

"Lucky me," I say, sarcastically. "And let's pretend for a minute that it is possible for me to give you sex whenever you need or demand it. Because there will be certain situations which will arise when I will not be able to have sex. Physical reasons, you know?"

"I am not an addict, Cami. I do have the ability to deal with the fact you are unavailable for that at certain times of the month and when you're sick. It's not like I need it all the time. But I do want it on the table. I need it on the table. I'm willing to give you the commitment. It will be only you, I see. I will stay away from my father's parties and the track but I will expect you to fill that empty space."

"Cyprian, I hate the way you make things sound. It sounds like a business deal you're making with me. In return for your faithfulness to me, I am to let you fuck me whenever you please," I say then huff and cross my arms in front of me.

· · ·

"ISN'T THAT, essentially what a relationship is, Cami? And there's no reason to use vulgar terminology when describing sex. Also, it won't be anytime I please. It's not like you're my sex slave. It will be a relationship. We promise to be faithful to one another while also seeing to each other's needs. I'm sorry if you feel I'm being too straight forward. I don't know any other way to be. I know business and that's the way I think is best to handle this thing with you," he says and thumps the counter top with his fist. "Come to my place when you get off and we can hammer out any details you want."

I laugh and shake my head. "Cyprian, I am not about to sit down and write out a contract for us. Bye."

I walk away, leaving him staring after me. He turns away and leaves and I feel a weight on me.

Did I have to be that hard on him...?

25

CYPRIAN

"Give me her address," my father says as I sulk on the sofa in his den. "I'll go talk to her. I'll explain things to her about you."

"Papa, she'd rip you apart. She doesn't like how you raised me," I let him know before he makes a huge mistake.

"Rip me apart?" he asks as his hand flies to his chest. "I highly doubt that."

"I don't. She's pretty snappy with her words. And she is sure to have some choice ones for you. I've been at her store every night this last week. She's brutal," I say and take another long drink of the Scotch my father gave me to settle me after another brutal night of trying to unruffle Cami's very ruffled feathers.

"I'll take my chances. Her address, Cyprian? Please don't make me find it for myself." He picks up his cell phone, getting ready to make a call that will get him the information he wants.

"Papa, you need to let me fight my own battles with her. I did this to myself. I should've sent those women away. I do deserve this." I take another drink and watch him tap away at his phone. "What are you doing?"

"Your mother is in town. I'm sending her to go talk some sense into the tenacious woman."

"PAPA, no! She isn't Mother's fan either. Please, let me handle things!" I get up and pace around the room. "Why must you bother yourself with my personal affairs?"

"I've never butted in before," he says. "I just can't stand to see you so unhappy. I have to do something about it."

"You have butted in before. Many, many times. The day you asked me to come to that first party that was you butting into my personal life. You taught me that was the only way to socialize. You cheered me on when that woman, that grown woman, led me up the stairs to my bedroom. The whole room did. No wonder I am immoral and incapable of having a normal woman. Cami's right, I am asking too much of her and I'm just now realizing that." I move toward the door. "I have to get out of here."

"Cyprian!" my father calls out. "You are not at fault here. You did nothing wrong. You and she had no prior commitment. Stop apologizing. Be a man!"

I HURRY AWAY, ignoring him. He's wrong and I know he is and now I know I've been wrong too. Ashton is waiting in the car for me as it's Friday and I told him I wanted to talk to my father, briefly but I wanted to be gone before any of his guests arrive.

He's out and opening the back door of the Cadillac he drove me to work in today and I get in. "Take me to Cami's."

"Sir, that's such a bad…"

I interrupt him, "Just do it!"

He closes the door as he shakes his head and goes around the car to get in. He's quiet as a church mouse all the way to her house. I see her car in the drive and get out.

She opens the door just before I get to it. Her green smock is in her hand. "I don't have time for this, Cyprian."

She tries to go past me but I grab her arm. "I only want to tell you one thing, Camilla. I want to tell you I am sorry and I'm taking my offer off the table."

She stands perfectly still and looks into my eyes. "You are?"

With a nod, I turn and leave her alone. I'm not trying to hurt her or manipulate her. I am merely giving her the information that I will no longer be asking her for anything. I've tried to rush things just so I can get her into my bed and I am done doing that to her.

Tonight starts a new way of living for me. And I don't need Cami in my bed to make changes. I need to be the best man I can be and stop thinking about my damn sex life or lack thereof.

She's right, there is more to life than just sex. There's so much more and I'm about to discover just what else there might be in this big old world that I've left undiscovered.

If love is meant for me, it will come my way. But I can't take Camilla, just to give me the experience. It's wrong in so many ways.

As I get back into the backseat of my car, I see Cami getting into hers and I have to wonder what she's thinking about what I said.

I hope she wasn't hurt by it...

26

CAMILLA

An entire week has passed without me seeing hide nor hair of Cyprian. I watch each night for one of his many cars to pass by on his way home after work but have yet to spot one.

He told me he was taking his offer off the table but I didn't think that meant he was really done. There's an empty spot inside of me with him gone. I didn't realize it was there until he left me completely alone.

I find myself looking at my cell phone many times a day and thinking about giving him a call. Which I know I shouldn't do. I'm sure he's staying at his father's and getting all the ass he can since he missed out on so much of it as he wasted his time on me.

It's Saturday night and I'm closing the store, looking around for any sign that Cyprian is around, maybe looking out for me. I see no sign and know I went too long and too far. He's over me.

I DESERVE IT, I know I do. I gave him no slack at all. As time has passed, I made some realizations about the man. His past is a thing I didn't take into consideration when I was so hard on him for being with those escorts, as they call themselves.

He is a man who has had terrible examples in his life. I should've been nicer to him about it. I could've said things nicer to him. I didn't have to give in and take him up on his offer but I didn't have to be so mean with how I told him things.

As I look back at all the different things I said, as he came in each night, I have to admit I was harsh. And I'd like to apologize for being so judgmental. It's really not like me at all.

Driving down the road, I see his gate and look up the drive and see the house is all lit up. I wouldn't dare pop in on him.

Never again will I subject myself to that!

BUT I MIGHT GIVE him a call to tell him I'm sorry about how I talked to him. He has the capacity to be a good man. I saw it that day on our day-long date. It's there, just beneath the surface.

A surface that's been hardened by a life of repetition with no influences to show him how a loving relationship works. And I talked to him as if he was to blame for that.

He was a child, for God's sake!

Pulling into my drive, I find myself feeling extremely remorseful and I go inside and plop down on my sofa. The pale green fabric is threadbare as the furniture came with the place.

Still looking at my phone, I know it's late. It's two-thirty in the morning. Instead of calling and waking him up or hearing tons of women in the background, I find it safer to send him a text.

-I'd like to apologize to you for the words I've said. I understand if you don't want to talk to me. I'd love to apologize to you in person or at least over the phone.-

WHEN NOTHING COMES BACK, I place the phone on the coffee table and go to bed. I had an idea he'd want nothing to do with me. And he's right to be that way.

I berated the man who had nearly no control over what he did. That had been ingrained in him, since he was five-years-old. Only ten years later, sex was thrust upon him. And I tore into him like he had complete control over himself.

It's like screaming at a person who can't see, for stepping on your toes. Cyprian did do things wrong. But it was obvious by how he acted that he knew it was wrong. He never knew that before.

Everyone he was around, accepted him having sex with whoever he wanted to. I go on one date with the man and think we're a couple and treat him like I was his wife.

Was it shameful for him to screw two women after dropping me off minutes earlier?

For certain!

THE THING IS, I never gave him a chance to talk it out with me. I just judged him, harshly and walked away. Every bit as coldly as he did to me, in the beginning.

I don't deserve a second chance. I know that. But I do want him to know I am sorry for how roughly I've treated him. It was wrong and I merely want the opportunity to tell him that. But it seems he doesn't want to give me that and I have to accept the fact, I will not get what I want. And I'll have to learn to be okay with that.

But, damn, this feels terrible...

27

CYPRIAN

After a two-week retreat to cleanse myself from the poisons that have been fed to me since birth, I have found a guru to help me find the inner me who's been shoved down my entire life.

Tabitha is a fifty-year-old woman who looks much younger, thanks to learning how to live life in a positive manner. She's had just as many hardships as any of us who attended her retreat have had and she has managed to not only overcome them but learn from them and use them as stepping stones to help her get out of the hole she was in. She taught us a lot of techniques to use to help us achieve the same goals.

Our phones were the first things to go, so we could immerse ourselves in getting to know our true selves. The instructions told us to leave them at home, which I did.

During the retreat, I found I want more from this life than I ever imagined. I never took the time to stop and think about what it was I wanted.

Kids have always been a thing I thought I was incapable of raising but I found a deep desire to see myself in another human being. So, now kids are part of what I want to experience in my life.

Tabitha says we only get one life and we should live it to the fullest, which means something different for each person. She's a wise woman. Her little sayings run through my head often.

I'm about to walk into my home, for the first time in two weeks, and pick my phone back up and begin my normal life again but with a whole new attitude.

Work is to be eight to ten hours a weekday and no more than that. I thought I couldn't take any time off. Somehow the company made it just fine without me for two weeks, so I think they can manage to have me a few less hours each day.

Each weekend, I am to schedule something I've never done before. This upcoming weekend I will go skydiving. Tabitha says it was an amazing experience and everyone should do it at least once in their lifetime.

Sunday's should be days for reflection and one should take it easy. Rest as much as you want to and find something uplifting to read or watch. I got a book from the Oprah book club site and will be reading that on Sunday.

My body and mind feel so much better than I ever recall feeling before. I do believe finding Tabitha's website and going to her retreat was a great thing for me.

TODAY IS Sunday and work begins tomorrow. Back to the normal world I go then and have to see if I can really incorporate some of what I've learned into my real life.

Ashton pulls to a stop at the front door. "Here you are, sir. Did you miss the place?" He stars to get out of the car to help me out.

"No, Ashton, let me get my things. I appreciate your help but I can do for myself," I say as I open my own door.

He pops the trunk, so I can get my bags, and I find him getting out, anyway. "Cyprian, I am paid to do this for you. Allow me to do my job, please."

"I've been spoiled for too long." I pick up one bag and find him picking up the other.

"Spoiled is not what you've been, sir. You pay me to do this for you." He begins to carry the bag to the door and I follow behind with the one I picked up.

"Ashton, you don't need to call me, sir. Call me by my name. You're older than I am. You shouldn't talk to me as if I am your superior. Tabitha says we are all equals and should act that way." I wait while he disarms the security system he had put in while I was away.

I asked him to get that done for me just before I got out of the car at the airport the day I left for the retreat. I also had him change the code to the gate. I want no more surprises from anyone.

Once he's opened the door, he hands me a card. "This has the codes for each panel, Cyprian. And as far as calling you, sir, that's a thing I've grown accustomed to, so it may pop out now and again. Take no offense by it. I'm old and set in my ways."

"Speaking of old, just how old are you, Ashton?" I ask him as I thought he was around fifty.

"I am fifty-three," he says as he takes my bag inside.

"Well, I'm not trying to be rude at all but Tabitha is fifty and she looks much younger. She says taking supplements along with a diet rich in raw veggies and organic spices is the key to that. You should let me give you her diet plan. It could take years off you. And it might help your wife too," I tell him as we go inside.

"That's very nice of you," he says. "Shall I take these up to your bedroom?"

"No, I'll do that. I just want to settle in and meditate for a little while."

"I'll leave you to that then." He turns to leave and I take the bags and make my way to my room. "Good to have you back, Cyprian."

"I hope it's good to be back, Ashton. See you in the morning. We will see how this all goes."

GETTING INTO MY BEDROOM, I put my things down and see my cell phone, sitting on the bedside table where I left it. It seems the maid has plugged it into the charger and it's ready for me to see what I've missed in the last two weeks.

I told my parents what I was doing and both were very supportive. My father conceded that he had no idea how to parent, he wished me luck on finding the 'me' I want to become. Mother was a bit put off by where I was going. She thought it sounded cultish but told me she approved of me trying to better myself.

It did feel kind of like a family with Tabitha. She made us all feel at home on the small farm we stayed on. Small cabins dotted an area in the back of her quaint farm home. There were six of us. She says she keeps the groups that small, so we can all get her special attention.

She'll be coming into town on Wednesday. She's going to do a workshop with my staff at work. I think they all could use a dose of her mental medicine. I can't wait to see what they all think after hearing her talk.

Sitting on my bed, I pick up my phone and find myself afraid for some reason. I've hidden from my reality for only two weeks but it's felt like an eternity.

I'm not wanting to come back to it.

BUT I MUST, so I start looking through my phone and when I open my text messages, one pops up at me. "Cami."

I've put her in a place in myself for safekeeping, leaving the obsession out of it. She's apologizing for how she spoke to me. And my heart is thumping hard in my chest.

Tabitha said it would be a bad idea to get involved with anyone right now. She described my soul like a wound that has been opened and scraped and needs to heal before bringing anyone else into it. The desperation I felt before is gone. But the want for Cami is still present.

So, I decide to leave that alone for now. I'm not strong enough to handle her right now. I have to give myself time to heal and acclimate to my surroundings once again. This time, doing things my way.

But I do text her back to let her know I got the text and am not ignoring her.

-CAMI, thanks for the apology. It's appreciated. I've been working on myself. When I feel ready, I will come and see you. Then we can apologize to each other in person and put the past where it belongs.-

THAT SHOULD EASE her thoughts about me if she was worried or something. I didn't mean to worry her with my leaving. I just had to work on myself.

I wonder if she was worried about me...

28

CAMILLA

It's been a week since I texted Cyprian and he's just now texting me back, telling me he was working on himself and when he's ready, he'll come talk to me. I'd like to see him right now but it sounds as if he's ready to put me in his past. A thing I'm finding hard to swallow.

I have the day off and it's barely noon. To sit just down the road from him and not go over there will be hard to do. But I suppose I have to.

-Cyprian, thanks for answering my text, I was worried about you. Glad to know you are okay. I look forward to the day you feel like talking to me again.-

GETTING OFF THE SOFA, I grab my running shoes and decide it would be best to run off some of this anxiety I'm beginning to feel. I didn't realize he'd crept so deep inside of me that the idea of him leaving me behind is affecting me so much.

It's not as if I had any grand ideas he and I'd end up together. I didn't think that at all. I assumed he was at his father's place, fornicating like a rabbit with random women. To find out he was some-where, working on himself, is so very different from what I was thinking.

I take off out of the house and start running in the direction which will have me passing by his estate. It's a long shot I'll even catch a glimpse of him or him of me but it's a gamble I'm willing to take.

I just want to see him, even if only for a moment!

JOGGING DOWN THE COUNTRY ROAD, my mind refuses to stop thinking about the man. I wonder where he went to work on himself. I wonder if he did that for himself or me. I wonder if what he learned about himself made him think he and I are too different and would never work out.

I know I've had those thoughts. Taking him home to meet my family would go over very badly. I feel the same way about him taking me to meet his parents, who I think should've never been allowed to have a kid in the first place.

Maybe he and I aren't meant to be together.

MAYBE THERE'S someone else in the world meant for him. A woman with tons of patience and empathy. A woman who can help him work on his demons. A woman who will be everything to him, the way I wouldn't allow.

What's wrong with me?

I HAD a chance to be with a gorgeous, muscle-bound, nearly perfect specimen of male anatomy and I stood on my high morals, refusing to give him the one thing he needed from me. Everyone at work thinks I'm an idiot. Not just a little one either, a huge idiot who has blown her chance with a man who could buy and sell this entire town.

With Cyprian missing, I Googled him and found out he's beyond wealthy. He's uber-rich. A multi-billionaire, who's highly respected in the business world.

I saw picture after picture of him with his colleges. Some of whom are women and he didn't look like a man-whore at all. He looked like he treated them with respect. It was a thing I didn't see in him.

It was my misfortune to have judged him before I really knew him. I saw him as a womanizer and nothing more than that. I saw him as a man I needed to guard myself against.

And now it's most likely too late to let him know I was wrong. I was wrong for withholding my affection. I was wrong for trying to make him be someone he wasn't. I was wrong on so many levels, it's not even funny.

Suddenly, my train of thought is broken as his gate comes up. I jog in place as I look at it and can see the house that looms far back off the road.

Fuck it!

I jog up to the security box and tap in the code, 696969. Only to find it buzzing at me. The code's been changed!

Hurrying away, I have no want for him to see me on his camera, I see now is at the gate, pointing in my direction.

What an idiot I feel like!

HE'S CHANGED THE CODE, no doubt to keep me out. He has moved on, that's obvious. I have to do something to get him out of my mind.

Something huge!

MAYBE I WILL ACCEPT the next date that's offered to me. I have to do something to get him out my head. He's made a place there and even in my heart. I have to do something to move him out. He's moved me out of where ever I was in his head.

Could he have a girlfriend? Could he have found a woman more compatible with him and left me behind? Did I let that happen to me? To us?

Have I been a fool...?

29

CYPRIAN

The week has been long as I've had to drive by the store Cami works at each night, knowing she's there as I see her Mustang parked at the side of the store. But Tabitha and I have talked every day about how I need to guard myself against everyone right now. I've followed her advice and only texted my parents that I still need time away from them to get my head on straight.

It's Wednesday and Tabitha is doing a workshop with my staff. It was my idea and no one was really on board with it. I had to insist, though. I need people around me who understand how I need things to be.

I'm waiting for the workshop to end as I invited Tabitha to stay at my place for the night instead of putting her up in a hotel room. She was kind enough to open her home to me and others like me, I can repay the favor.

The door to the meeting room opens and my employees come out. It's nine at night and most of them seem to be impatient to get out of here. They all give me smiles and nods as they file past me but no one says anything.

Finally, Tabitha comes out, looking happy and radiating positive energy the way she always does. Her blonde bobbed hair is bouncing as she nods at me. "It went fantastic! Thank you for setting this up. I do believe your staff has been brought to the light, Cyprian!"

My secretary, Mrs. Peterson, looks over her shoulder at me and then at Tabitha then looks away. I didn't see new beginnings in her brown eyes. I saw concern.

Why would she be concerned?

TABITHA LINKS her arm with mine and allows me to escort her out of the office. "I'm sure some of them get it and some don't. That's how things go. Like you say, we are all on different levels."

"That we are, Cyprian. And I think I can help you tonight with your situation with the Camilla woman. Do you think she'll be at work? I think it's essential for your recuperation if I meet her. I'd like to gauge her true persona. I fear you might have only been taking her at face value and thinking her beauty means she's a good person. Which hardly ever means that. Most beautiful women are hard-hearted."

"Surely, you don't really believe that Tabitha," I say as we get to the car. Ashton opens the back door of the town-car, and I let her get in first.

When I get in, I find her frowning at me. "I know it to be true. You see, Cyprian, many men are easy targets for women of beauty."

"You're beautiful, yourself, Tabitha. Are you saying you have used that to hurt men?" I ask her as I watch her light blue eyes dance.

"I have." She looks me in the eyes. "As old as I am, do you really think I'm beautiful?"

With a nod, I say, "I do. You are beautiful. A glow radiates within you. You're a beautiful woman, inside and out. I am privileged to know you."

She laughs a bit. "And I, you. You handsome devil."

. . .

HER HAND RUNS over the top of mine and she takes my hand and holds it. "Do you need some of my positive energy?" I ask her as she told us at the retreat about the different ways we can share our energy and receive it. Holding hands, hugs, and things of that nature are perfect ways to receive positive energy and give some away as well.

"I am in need of some," she says. "You see, I am going to need all I can get, so I can stay positive when I meet this woman who has motivated you to make changes in yourself. I'm afraid she will see my work with you as a threat."

"I don't see why she would," I say. "We aren't a couple. That was her doing. Well, my messing around had everything to do with that but still, she never saw fit to accept my apology and give me another chance. I don't think she wants me. I believe the damage I did is irreversible. It's a thing I am working on accepting. Something I did caused such a reaction it must've dissolved any feelings she was growing for me."

She looks away then back at me. "I hope you're right."

I'm a bit stunned by her words. I hope I'm wrong!

"PLEASE JUST DO me a favor and hold tight to my hand or maybe even put your arm around me, to lend me your positive energy, so I can handle my reaction to her. After what you've told me about her, I'm finding it hard to like her. I want to like her."

"I don't hold what she's said to me against her. Neither should you," I say as I don't understand her right now.

"I've come to care about you, Cyprian. You are a rare gem of a person. Your father and mother, I can understand why they did, what they did with you. They were unaware of what they were doing, after all. I feel, Camilla is very aware of what she was doing to you. Withholding sex to make you do what she wanted you to. It's a manipulation some women use on men."

"Well, I don't think she was trying to manipulate me by doing that. She has good morals. She wanted to be in love first. I can see her point. It's pretty respectable."

"And outdated. And out of the question once she knew about your circumstances of having so much sex since you were only fifteen-years-old. She should've been more supportive of what your needs were instead of making you feel immoral for them. And she is a scientist as well. An educated person, who should know going cold turkey on anything, rarely works. So, please do hold her accountable for what she's said and done. You have to, for your own self-preservation."

I don't say it out loud but I don't think I can hold her accountable for doing what she did. She was trying to preserve her own morals, after all. But I have no want to argue with Tabitha. "I'll try my best."

She pulls our clasped hands up to her heart. "That's all you can do, Cyprian." Then she kisses my hand and lays our clasped hands back on the seat between us.

As we near the convenience store, my body starts to sweat and my heart starts to pound. Seeing Cami, after almost three weeks is going to be hard. Because I think I'll want to throw my arms around her and ask her for more than she can give me right now.

And more than I can give her as well...

30

CAMILLA

The store is dead at nearly ten on a Wednesday night and I am bored out of my mind as I've gotten everything on the to-do list, done. I let Mary, the older woman I was working with tonight, go home early. Her back hurt and there's no reason to keep two people here with no customers and all the work done.

Leaning on the counter, I look out the window and think about closing early and wondering if that would get me fired. Most likely it would.

A black car pulls up right in front and my heart skips a beat. "Cyprian!" I wait to see if it is him, which I'm pretty sure it is.

The door opens and he gets out and I find myself wanting to run to him and grab him up in a hug. Walking around the counter, I freeze and walk backward to get back behind it. He has a woman with him and they're holding hands.

Tears burn the back of my eyes, making me blink them like crazy to get rid of the shininess that has to be going on in them. The chirp of the door opening has me taking a deep breath to steady my nerves which are overloaded. "Hello, Cyprian," I say with a shaky voice.

"Cami, how are you?" he asks as he lets the woman's hand go and puts his arm around her. "This is Tabitha. She's helping me to make some much-needed changes in myself. She's been a Godsend."

"Good," I say but I find myself not meaning it. "So, you are feeling better about yourself then. That's fantastic. Nice to meet you, Tabitha."

SHE EXTENDS her hand and I shake it, feeling her hand tight on mine. "Camilla, I wanted to meet you. Cyprian has told me every last detail about your little fling."

Fling!

"IS THAT WHAT HE CALLED IT?" I ask, instantly pissed.

"No," he says. "I didn't call it that. What we had was much more than a fling. It was ill-timed, though. I wasn't the man you needed."

"Nor were you the woman he needed," she says.

I want to scream at her but I don't. "I suppose I wasn't. I was wanting to speak with Cyprian, in private, to talk to him about the harsh things I've said to him and apologize for them. His past was a thing I didn't take into consideration when I spouted the hateful things I did. I was hurt and I struck out at him. I've felt terrible about that."

"For how long?" Tabitha asks me.

"What?" I ask as she's confusing me.

"He told me he came to see you every night after he got off work for a week. He apologized over and over to you and you sent him away each and every night, making him feel like a deplorable human being," she says as she looks at me as if she's an attorney wanting her client to get a much better apology than what I gave him.

"Look, lady, I really don't have to explain myself to you. Cyprian and I can talk later, in private."

She holds her hand up, stopping me. "No, you won't. I'm staying with him tonight and I've counseled him about you. He's much too raw for you two to talk alone at the moment. You have a tendency to be abrasive with him and I simply cannot allow it."

My eyes leave her and go to Cyprian, who is looking more than a bit sheepish. "Is that how you want it, Cyprian?"

He nods then looks down. "Tabitha is a smart woman."

"I can see that. I can see she's got you by the reins." I cross my arms over my chest because I can see right through the woman.

SHE LOOKS young at a glance but when I look hard at her, I can see the lines at the corners of her eyes. I'm sure she's in her late forties or so and she has a gleam in her eye for Cyprian.

Of that I am sure!

HE LOOKS AT TABITHA, who he still has his arm around. "Since you're right here, do you think she and I could talk alone for a moment? Perhaps in the back?" he asks her.

Her head shakes as she looks at him and runs her hand over his cheek. "Cyprian, you are much too fragile."

"Ha!" I laugh. "He's not fragile. He is a strong man. I've never seen him like this and quite frankly, I don't like it." I walk around the counter and find her moving in front of him.

"No, you cannot be alone with him right now. I was afraid of this." She looks back at Cyprian. "We need to leave now."

He nods and backs out the door as if I'm a terrorist, trying to get to him. "Cyprian, call me later. Please."

HIS EYES BORE into mine as she backs him up. "He will not be calling you. I can see it in your eyes. You are not the woman he thinks you are. You are a selfish and manipulative woman. Out to get his money, most likely. Hence the reason you withheld sex until you forced him to find some love for you in his heart, thus trapping him, eventually into a marriage."

I look at Cyprian. "She's nuts and you know that. Call me, Cyprian. I care about you. I miss you. And I'm worried about you. Call me."

He's pushed out the door, still looking at me. It's obvious she's using her expertise as a con artist to get to him. My heart is pounding and I find myself following them outside. She has him in the back before I can get to him and it has me madder than I ever recall being. Even when I caught him with those escorts!

She will not get away with this...

31

CYPRIAN

My head is spinning as we walk into my house. "I would like to talk to her, Tabitha."

She takes my hand and pulls me along with her. "Show me your home, Cyprian. We can have some wine. You need to forget about that woman. She is bad for you. I fear she is the reason for your mental breakdown."

"I wouldn't call it a mental breakdown. I simply wanted to be a better person, Tabitha." I stop and she has to stop with me.

"Show me to my room first, please." Her eyes sparkle at me.

Ashton walks in with her suitcase. "I'll take this up there too."

She shakes her head. "It's fine. Leave it by the door. I'll take it up later, Ashton. Be a dear and leave us alone. I need to help Cyprian through what looks as if it might turn into a crisis if I don't intervene with some drastic actions."

I look at Ashton who gives me a frown. "You sure about this, sir?"

"What?" Tabitha asks as she shoos him out the door. "This man is safer with me than anyone who is currently in his life. Goodbye. See you tomorrow. If I leave then. He may need my help for a while."

He looks at me again. "Sir, are you absolutely sure about this?"

Tabitha looks back at me and puts her hand on her hip. "Cyprian, will you tell him you're sure?"

I nod my answer and he turns and leaves me but I can tell he doesn't want to. My hand is snatched up again and then she runs my arm around her waist. "Okay, I'll show you where your room is, Tabitha. I suppose you'd like to freshen up."

We go upstairs and she notices the many doors up here. "Which room is yours?"

I gesture to my door and she smiles. Then I walk all the way to the end of the hallway and catch her frowning. "Why so far away from yours, Cyprian?"

"For your privacy," I say. "I want you to feel like you have some." I open the door and stay at it while gesturing for her to go inside. "Here you go. I'll be downstairs in the main living area at the bottom of the stairs when you get done."

She takes both of my hands and pulls me into the room with her. "Cyprian, we need to talk. I can see you need more help from me. You'll fall back down that rabbit hole that is Camilla Petit, if I don't do something drastic."

"You keep saying that." I look at her and wonder what the fuck, drastic, means.

"IT MEANS, you are in need of some physical help. I need to help your energy field with some skin on skin touching. I am not effectively filling you with positive energy with hand holding or even by putting your arms around me. You are searching for the negative, which is Camilla Petit, to fill you again. I need to fill you with some of my positive energy."

"Skin to skin," I ask as that sounds kind of like she wants to be naked with me.

She takes a step back and begins to unbutton her sheer tan shirt that covers a brown camisole top. "Take off your clothes, Cyprian. I need to hold you, skin to skin, to deliver a good dose of my positive vibes to you. You're in desperate need of them."

"I can't do that, Tabitha." I shake my head as she continues to undress in front of me.

"You can, Cyprian. It's merely one human being helping another. I've done this on occasion with some of my other patients. It works wonders. Like I said, I will stay with you until I see an improvement on your handle on how you want to live your new life." By the time she's done talking, she's standing, stark naked, in front of me, holding her arms open. "If you're unsure of how much it will help you, hug me with your clothes on and mine off and see how good it feels. See how much better you feel."

I'm frozen and unsure about any of this. But she steps forward and takes my hands, placing them on her ass as she hugs me tight. "Tabitha."

"Shh. No talking. Close your eyes and feel the energy I'm sending to you. My entire body is sending you positive energy."

I do as she says since I'm not naked and try to feel the energy she's sending me. She was right on the other occasions. Holding hands with others and hugging them did help me feel more positive energy.

AFTER A FEW MINUTES of her holding me, she lets me go and looks at me then unbuttons my shirt. I take her hand, stopping her. "Tabitha, I don't think that's a good idea."

"Nonsense," she says. "I can still feel the negative coming from you." She quickly takes my shirt off and puts her body back in my arms and places my hands on her ass again. "Give my cheeks a good squeeze. Think of them like the stress balls I gave you all at the retreat. Use them to ease your tension."

Her breasts are smashed against my naked chest as I do as she's said and my mind is being dragged into a very bad place. I try hard to think of this as therapy but my cock is thinking other thoughts. "Tabitha, we have to stop this. I'm having inappropriate thoughts."

"It's not inappropriate to want to feel more. We can do that. We can exchange our energy. I will take your negative while you take my positive. I can rebuild my energy much more quickly than you can, after all. Let me help to heal you, Cyprian."

Her hands find the button on my slacks and she has my pants down, quickly followed by my underwear. "Tabitha, I can't. You said I'm not to be doing anything like this, remember?"

"With anyone you currently know as they are all out to hurt you, Cyprian. I am here to heal you. Now come with me to the bed and bury yourself in my positive chamber, so I can take away your pain and fill you with light."

She lets me out of her arms and looks down at my shoes and socks, the only thing left on me. "Kick those off and ditch the socks too. We need skin to skin with nothing in between us, for this to work."

"I'll need a condom. I have some in my bedroom," I say, trying to escape this situation I feel has gotten out of hand.

"No need for one. I am clean and healthy and on the pill. So, you can relax. Come on, Cyprian. I can help you more than you know."

As I let her lead me to the bed, I find myself fighting this with every step.

Am I really about to do this...

BOOK 5: THE RAKE

A Bad Boy Billionaire Romance

By Michelle Love

32

CAMILLA

Cyprian's car pulls back up to the front of the store and I ready myself for another battle with the broad who seems to think Cyprian needs to be defended against me, of all people. Instead, it's his driver who flies into the store. "Can you come with me, Camilla? Cyprian needs you!"

Making a drastic and quick decision, I grab my keys from under the counter to lock the store up, turning off the lights as I go. "What's wrong?"

"That woman," he says as he hurries me out. "She's going to take advantage of him. I can tell it. Come with me."

I get into the passenger seat as he jumps in the driver's seat and peels out of the parking lot. "Ashton, what if he wants to be with her?"

"He doesn't. He seems clueless about the woman and her motives. I can read her like a book. She wanted to be shown to her room right away and wouldn't allow me to accompany them to take up her suitcase. She actually told me to leave them alone, so she could do something to him to avoid a meltdown or some shit like that."

"A meltdown?" I ask. "Has he had one before?"

"No," he tells me. "That woman's pulling something over on him.

I'm not sure if she just wants in his pants or if she wants much more than that but she is one determined woman and that has me worried about Cyprian."

"What if I go in and catch them going at it, Ashton?" I shake my head. "I can't see that again. I can't! It hurt too much last time."

"He needs you, Camilla," he tells me as he pulls up to the gate and punches in the code.

"But what if they're having sex?" I ask him. "Is that a real possibility?"

HE'S NOT SAYING a word as I watch his expression change from worried to sick. "I hope not. I didn't see that want in Cyprian's eyes but I sure as hell saw it in hers. He's not one to turn down sex, just so you know. But with her, I feel she's using a trust he's put in her to manipulate him into it. A thing I can't stand. I'll be with you, Camilla. I just know he'll be more responsive to you."

We stop in front of the door and my heart stops beating. "Please, don't let him be with her that way!" I get out of the car, my body shaking like a leaf.

Ashton punches in a code at a new box on the outside of the front door. The light turns green and we go inside. A suitcase is right next to the door and I hear nothing.

"Let's go upstairs," Ashton whispers.

I follow him, nearly sick as we go up the stairs and I still hear nothing. Just as we get to the top of the stairs I hear Cyprian's voice, saying, "Really, I can't. I didn't expect this from you, Tabitha. I'm going to my room. I'll see you in the morning."

Ashton and I drop back to hide on the staircase. It seems Cyprian can take care of himself. But as I peek around Ashton, I see Cyprian is carrying his clothes and is naked. Anger fills me and then that damn woman is in the hallway, naked too. "Cyprian, come here. Don't be like that. I'm merely wanting to transmit my positive energy to you, via penetrating contact. You don't even have to make any strokes if you don't want to. Although that does help to get more out of it."

He stops his retreat and spins around. "That's called sex, Tabitha! Do you think I am some naïve boy?"

My entire body is shaking with pure hatred for the woman. "Cyprian, as your therapist, I must insist on this. You are close to a breakdown. Closer than you realize."

BEFORE HE CAN SAY A WORD, I barrel around Ashton and run right at the woman, screaming like a banshee, "You fucking bitch!"

Her eyes go huge and she quickly steps back into the room and locks the door. I pound on the door but she's not about to unlock it.

"Cami?" Cyprian asks as he comes up behind me.

I turn around and see he's pulled his pants on. "What the hell were you doing naked, Cyprian? Do you have any sense at all?"

"Yes!" he shouts at me. "And thank you for coming!"

My body's shaking and I pull him into my arms and start bawling like a baby. "Cyprian, what have you gotten yourself into?"

"Shh, don't cry," he whispers as he strokes my hair. "It's alright."

I pull away from him and shake my head. "Why were you naked?"

He pulls me with him down the hallway and then he sees Ashton. "You brought her here?"

He nods. "I saw what that woman had planned for you, even though you didn't. I had to get her to come help me. I knew she'd have the right amount of anger to handle that old bitch."

Cyprian smiles at the man who's driven him around for the last few years. "Thanks. I was pretty sure she'd hound me all night."

"And she would've too," Ashton tells him. "I'm going to take her to a hotel for the night and make sure she gets her ass on a plane in the morning. Please tell me you'll have nothing else to do with that woman."

CYPRIAN NODS and looks like he's a bit smarter now. "You can count on that. I never saw it in her. I had no idea she'd do something like this. I'll report this on her website so future clients will know how she is. She told me she'd done this sort of positivity sharing with some of the others she's helped."

I shudder with how awful the woman is. Preying on people who come to her for help. "Positivity sharing? I'd like to share my fist with her face, the nasty whore."

The creaking of the bedroom door behind us has us all turning back to find Tabitha dressed and looking mad, of all things. "Nasty whore?" she asks as she comes toward us.

Now it's me and Ashton who get in front of Cyprian to keep her away from him. "Yes, you are one devious, malicious bitch of a whore. What you've done is a crime. This man came to you for mental help and guidance and you used his trust to manipulate him into having sex with you. You are one of the lowest people I've ever had the misfortune to run into," I tell her as I glare at her. "I'd like nothing more than to rip your fucking head off and play soccer with it."

"Would you, now?" she asks with a condescending tone. "Cyprian was well aware of how we use physical energy to help heal others. He did spend two weeks with me. Voluntarily, might I add."

"And I suppose you're trying to tell me, you and he have a special connection or some shit like that?" I ask her. Cyprian takes my hand and holds it tight, behind me.

"Not like that, Cami," he whispers.

THE WOMAN SQUARES her narrow shoulders and looks past me to Cyprian. "I've never hurt you and never would. I am only here to heal you. You are breaking down right before my eyes with these people to aid you in the most negative of ways. Anger is flowing through them and they're all over you, sending you into a negative state of being. If you tell them to leave, I can take that negativity away."

"By having him fuck you?" I ask then shake my head. "No fucking way. Cyprian's driver will take you to a hotel now and you will get your ass on a fucking plane that will take you back to wherever you came from. If you so much as send a fucking text to Cyprian, I will blow you up on social media and ruin your farce of a career."

"Who would believe you?" she says with a laugh.

Ashton steps forward and takes her by the wrist. "Oh, there's more than a few people who can corroborate her accusations. Time to go." He pulls her along as she tries to get Cyprian to look at her.

"Cyprian, please. You know I won't hurt you," she says as she's pulled away.

"You already have," he says as he looks at me.

"Get her the hell out of here, Ashton," I say as I run my hand over Cyprian's cheek. "Would you care to drive me back to the store, so I can close it, the right way?"

He runs his hand over my cheek. "I would. Thank you, Cami."

"What are friends for?" I ask as I take his hand and start walking down the hallway. "You might want to put on a shirt and some shoes."

We stop just before his bedroom door for him to get the clothes he left on the floor. Instead of picking them up, he picks me up in his arms and hugs me tight. "I've missed you more than I realized, Cami."

"I've missed you too. But I knew I was missing you," I say then find his mouth on mine and I melt into him like a chocolate candy bar on a hot July afternoon.

Could we be on our way to making things work...?

33

CYPRIAN

Her body feels right in my arms as I kiss her the way I've only dreamt about being able to do for what seems like a very long time. The way she's wrapping herself around me has me thinking she's finally forgiven me for my stupid weak moment.

Easing the kiss, with soft pecks, I find tears in her eyes and not ones of anger this time. "Cyprian, I'm sorry I let you leave with that woman. I shouldn't have."

"Don't blame yourself, Cami." I let her out of my arms and pick up my shirt and put it on. "I've being grasping at straws to reinvent myself. I shouldn't have gone to a retreat put on by a person with no real credentials, in the first place."

"Why are you trying so hard to make big changes, to yourself?" she asks as I pull on my last shoe and take her hand to head out.

"I need to make some changes. I'm not what I can be. I've made some discoveries about myself, while I was at the retreat. It wasn't at all bad. Tabitha wasn't like that when I was there with a group of people. She only started that crap once she and I were alone. I don't know what got into her."

"You are hot as hell, Cyprian. That's what got into her." We go out to the garage and I watch Cami's eyes light up as I turn on the overhead lights. "Shit! You have a lot of cars, Cyprian!"

"Pick the one you want to take," I say as I wait by the peg board with all the car keys on it.

SHE POINTS at the red Lamborghini. "How about that one?"

I look at her with uncertainty. "Cami, I haven't driven that one yet. It was delivered while I was gone. Do you think you can handle it?"

"Me?" she squeaks as she shakes her head. "I'm not going to drive it. Plus, I have to pick my car up. You pick which one you want to drive."

"Or you could leave your car there overnight and come back here with me. We could take a little cruise in the Lambo. What do you say?" I ask her and find myself crossing my fingers behind my back.

After a long moment, admiring the car, she nods. "I say, yes." She looks at me then winks. "I think you could use some company, after what you've been through."

With a laugh, I pick her up and carry her to the car. "Good! Tomorrow, I'll drive this little beauty around to get used to her."

"I'm so excited! Come on, Cyprian. Let's see what she can do!"

I help her get into the driver's seat and watch her eyes roam all over the car. "You like it?"

"Love is the only word one can use for something this special," she says.

"I agree," I say and close her door. And I'm not talking about the car, either.

After I get in and strap myself down, I put my hand over hers as she places it on the console between us. "You ready for this?"

She nods. "Are you?"

With a nod, I say, "More than ready. Let's take off, baby."

"I'm more than a bit uneasy about this," she says as she looks at the intimidating dashboard.

"There's nothing to be uneasy about. It's just different. Take it easy, though. This thing has a lot of horses," I caution her.

. . .

I HIT the remote to open the garage door and she pulls out, slowly. "Oh my God, I can feel the raw power already!"

Now, I'm feeling nervous about her driving and have to look out the window and bite my lip, so I don't say the wrong thing and fuck things all up again.

Down the long driveway we go and she's doing well. "How's it feel? Think you can handle it on the open road?"

She laughs and it kind of scares me. "Hold on and let's see!" The gate opens and she eases out of it then turns onto the desolate road that goes into town. "Here we go!"

I grab my seat and hold on tight as she peels out. "Shit!" I scream as she flies down the straight stretch of road.

My heart is in my throat as we haul ass down the dark road. "Wow!" she shouts as she goes.

LOOKING AT HER, and watching her smile with excitement, I find myself smiling too. Even though I'm scared shitless. I am scared in more ways than just this one.

This might be the real deal. She just might be the girl for me. And I am so far from being the man she needs and deserves. I'm not sure how to do this.

My first try at improving myself has failed, miserably. I can't rely on myself to make the right decisions about how to go about changing the man I am. And I have to change for her. I know I do.

But do I have it in me to become the man who is perfect for her...?

34

CAMILLA

Vanilla ice cream drips down my arm as I hurry to the kitchen to wash it off. My drumstick ice cream cone, Cyprian bought for us just before I closed the register down, has sprung a leak as I've taken too long to eat it.

He's sitting on the counter top, smiling at me as I make a run for it before I get ice cream drops on my clean floor. "You better hurry, speed demon!"

I laugh as he's come up with a clever nickname for me. He claims I was driving his car excessively fast. I think I was driving it appropriately, as it is a monster of a machine.

Making it to the sink in time to stop the drip from making it to the floor, I pop the rest of the cone into my mouth and wash my sticky hand and arm off. Suddenly, I feel arms go around me and I'm turned to face Cyprian. My mouth is full of the cone and he smiles at me and kisses the tip of my nose.

Waiting for me to swallow, he kisses me with soft kisses until I am putty in the man's hands. "Cami, I want you to know something."

After a few more small kisses, I ask, "What would you like me to know?"

More kisses come then he says, "I'm not going to ask you to make love with me tonight."

RUNNING my hands up and down his bulging arms, I find myself a bit disappointed. "Cyprian, I can be what you need me to be for you." I bite my lip and wait to see what he says about that.

A smile moves over his face, taking over his sultry expression. "Cami, we can take this slow."

I nod but think we have been taking it slow. It's been over a month since we met and have hung out together a few times now. Both of us realize we missed one another. And now that I'm putting sex on the table, he's taking it off?

What the hell?

But I stay quiet about it as he takes my mouth with a deep kiss that sends a wave of need all the way through me. I don't usually make out this hard with someone if I'm not intending on going all the way with it. I think Cyprian is in store for a shock if he thinks he can stop at just making out.

WITH MY ARMS wrapped around his neck, he pulls my legs up and I wrap them around him. He moves with me then sets me on the stainless-steel prep table and grinds himself against me. Suddenly, I think about what time it is and how the store's alarm is about to set itself. "Cyprian, we have to get out of here!"

He growls and pulls me off the table and takes my hand. "Yes, we do!"

Grabbing my keys off the counter, I follow him out the door and lock it. We don't even get to the car before I hear the three beeps that mean the store's security system has been activated by the main office. "We barely stopped messing around in time. We'd have been locked in until six in the morning if we had stayed any longer."

He opens the passenger door with a smile on his handsome face. "That would've sucked. Mind if I drive, speedy?"

I get in, laughing. "Nope, not at all. I'm dying to see if you can control yourself with this beast."

"Control is my new middle name, baby." He closes the door and goes around the car and gets inside.

"Control?" I ask him as he puts on his seatbelt.

"Yes, I will be exercising my control with you." He takes my hand and kisses it as he looks at me. "I will become the respectable man you need."

"I've told you not to change for me." I frown at him.

Starting the car, he takes off, spinning the wheels and burning out of the parking lot. "Whoa! This is a powerful thing, isn't it?"

He seems to be onto other things and our conversation about him needing to change for me is put in the past, quite quickly as he turns up the radio to just below a deafening level and heads toward town.

It's a little past midnight, making me think his plan is to drive for a while before we go back to his place. And what will happen when we get back there, I wonder.

He's said he's going to be exercising his control with me. I'm a little worried he thinks we can make out like crazy and do nothing more than that. He must think that's how I want it. Which is far from true.

I've had to fight myself to stay strong where he's concerned. His touch turns me inside out. His kiss fills me with desire. I can't make out with him and that's it!

He takes a sharp left and we get onto the highway. With the flip of a switch, I see a radar screen light up and he looks at me with light in his eyes. "Hang on, baby! The highway is clear!"

"Shit!" I scream as I hang on and he accelerates.

LIGHTS FLASH by so fast they're like strobe lights. I find I'm still shrieking as he goes down the road. I close my mouth and my eyes but can still feel the car's energy as it hauls butt down the empty highway.

Finally, he slows down and we're both panting as he turns the radio down. "What a rush, huh?"

I can only nod as my stomach is in my throat. He takes the next exit and we head back toward home, going a moderate ninety miles an hour. Finally, I manage to swallow enough times, my tummy goes back to where it belongs. "That was amazing!"

"You look like you were about to pass out," he says with a chuckle "Did I scare you?"

"Hell, yes you did! But I found trust in you, eventually." I laugh as exhilaration runs through me.

"I'm glad you found trust in me, Cami." He touches my hand with his fingertips. "I'm going to show you all night, just how much you can trust me.

I blink at him as I have a fear I know what he's going to do to me. And I have no idea if I can take that kind of pressure. "What are you going to do, Cyprian?" I ask to make sure I'm right.

"You'll see. I am going to learn more about self-control. You are an expert at it. You can help me." He gives me a smile.

I feel a bit sick as I know he thinks I'm some kind of expert at keeping myself somewhat chaste. But I had made a decision to give him what he needed if he ever gave me another chance.

Now, he's sitting here, telling me he wants me to show him how to keep things from going too far. "How far do you want to go?" I ask him as I have no clue.

"You tell me," he says as he pulls up to his gate. "You are the expert at knowing the point not to go past, after all."

I am not!

I HAVE no idea how far we can go before I need it all. And I have an idea he wants to test his limits tonight. That means mine will be tested as well. I'm not sure I can handle it!

As he pulls back into the garage, I have to ask, "Cyprian, do you feel ready to make the commitment of seeing only each other, yet?"

He looks at me for what I deem, too long, before he says, "Cami, I want to be the man you deserve before I go that far. I want to be sure I can be the best man I can be before I ask you not to see anyone else."

"Does that mean, you and I can go out with other people, if we want to?" I ask as I'm unsure what the man wants.

He sighs and gets out of the car and comes around to help me out. His arm goes around me as he helps me up and his forehead rests on mine. "If you feel you want to go out with someone else, you are still free to do that. But I can tell you right now, I will try to monopolize your time."

"And what about you?" I ask him as he's making me feel uneasy about things.

"I have no want for anyone else right now. But that door is open to me as well. I don't want either of us to have to go through a break-up if we don't think we can be what the other needs. Do you agree with that?"

"I suppose that's how everyone who dates, without a commitment, does things. So, I agree to those terms." I'm not sure how I feel about things but at least we're going forward, somewhat.

"Good," he says as he puts his arm around my waist and takes me inside. "Tonight, we get to know one another on a different level. We know all about each other's pasts and families. Now, we can get to know what kinds of things we like to do. And you can teach me how to control myself where sex is concerned."

With a sigh, I go with him to explore unknown territory and find I'm more nervous than if he was taking me straight to his bed.

How am I going to handle this...?

35

CYPRIAN

The ambiance is perfect as we sit on a leather sofa in front of a picture window that overlooks the back of the estate. A full moon fills the upper left corner of the huge window and stars dot the sky.

Cami and I sit right next to one another, our legs touching as I have my arm around her shoulders. "I have no idea how to be gentlemanly about this, Cami. You have to teach me what's expected."

She shifts a bit to look at me. "With the other women, the escorts, how did that work? Did you pick them or did they pick you?"

"They most often picked me. There were very few times when I found one I had to have. But there were a few times." I play with one of her curls that she's let down out of the bun she had them trapped in.

I gave her a T-shirt and a pair of my pajama bottoms, instead of having her too close to naked with only the T-shirt on. I changed into a pair, too. We both have the same amount of clothing on and have had no alcohol to lessen our inhibitions. I'll need my wits about me to learn how to do this only to a certain point.

"Did you have to entice those women to come to your bed?" she asks.

I smile at her naivety. "That's not how escorts work. I merely pointed and wiggled my finger and that was all I ever had to do."

"I see. And just how did that all go? Did you have foreplay?" She searches my eyes and I find myself wondering if she really should know this. "I need to know how your experiences were, so I can gauge where your weaknesses are."

"Well then, you should know there would be one, two, or three women each time. Foreplay was going on even while we were still in the ballroom at the party. Once we took it up to my bedroom, we pretty much got down to business."

I watch her expression go scientific as she nods. "How many orgasms would you typically have in one session?"

"It varied. Anywhere from five to ten. And most of the time, we'd sleep until morning and have another session, where I climaxed another three to five times." I tell her and she seems to be taking it all very clinically, which is better than I expected. But then again, I never expected her to ask me for such details.

"And you did this on Friday and Saturday nights?" she asks as she seems to be tallying things up in her head.

"Yes. In total, there would be up to ten times on Friday night. Add five more for Saturday morning. Add ten more for Saturday night. Another ten for Sundays."

"Ten on Sundays too?" she asks, looking puzzled.

"Yes, around five in the morning. Then we'd go to the track and those times were usually one by one as the women would hit me up, one at a time and we'd have quickies in the bathrooms. Or other secluded areas." I say and see her frown a little.

"So, you like to have sex in semi-secluded places," she says as she's weighing the information I gave her.

"I didn't say I liked it or preferred it. It's just how I was introduced to it all. I want to find my own way to enjoy it now. I want to do things with you and find our own way." I run my hand over her shoulder and trace her red lips as I look into her sapphire eyes. "I want to be a different man for you, Camilla."

She nods. "I can see, no matter how many times I tell you not to change for me, you will never listen, will you?"

"I WANT to change for myself too. And I don't have to have that many climaxes every weekend. That was mostly because there were so many different women who were around. Plus, I never had sex on weeknights or Sunday nights. If you and I do decide to become exclusive, then I could have sex on those nights too. It's not that I have to have that much sex. I just have had that much. Do you understand?"

She nods and looks at me in a different way. "Will it offend you if I treat this somewhat like a science experiment? I'll still have real feelings, don't get me wrong. But I'd like to see if a man who's lived this way, doing the same thing, sexually for twenty years, can really make this big of an adjustment."

"It doesn't hurt my feelings at all. Go right ahead. I'm more than interested, myself," I tell her as I run my hand through her satin-like dark curls.

"You will need to be completely truthful with me," she says as she plays with my bicep. "You will need to let me know if you begin to feel it necessary to climax while we're still in the phase of teaching you self-control. And if we move on to a committed relationship, you will need to let me know if you are happy and comfortable with the amount of sex and type you're getting. It's vital I know that and you be truthful. Don't worry about hurting my feelings."

"Okay," I say and move my lips over her cheek until they come to her ear. "Can we begin?"

"We can," she says as her hands move over my back and I move around in front of her and hold the back of her neck as I move my mouth back to hers.

OUR LIPS PRESS TOGETHER, using no tongue, I kiss her with little pecks, alternated with long kisses. Her lips part after a while and I venture in. Our tongues intertwine and we explore one another's mouth, learning how it feels to be aware of the kiss.

It's not as hard as I thought it'd be to keep my cock from running off with me. I'm not allowing my mind go into the dark, I'm staying focused on the kiss and that's it. When our mouths part, she asks, "Are you okay?"

I nod and move my hand to her breast. "Second base?"

She nods and pulls me back to kiss her again while I massage her breast. It becomes a little harder to control myself but I think about Cami and how much I respect her and how I need to treat her respectably too.

Her body is soft and supple as I run my hand under the T-shirt and cup her naked breast in my hand. I'm doing fine with this, so I push it further. Pushing her to lie back on the sofa, I kiss my way to her breast and take it in my mouth while I play with the other one.

Her hands run through my hair and she moans a little. Her moan has me smiling as I can see she is into it and even that still has me controlling myself with her.

It would be at this point that my dick would already be rock hard and aching for relief. But so far I'm comfortable. It occurs to me that Cami may not have had sex in a long time and this may be more difficult for her.

Pulling my mouth off her delicious tit, I look at her and find her biting her lip. "Cami, how long has it been since your last orgasm?"

She looks up at the ceiling. "It's been a long time."

"I'm doing fine with this. And I'd like to really test myself with you. Could I give you an orgasm, no penetration, of course?"

She eyeballs me for a moment then sighs. "That wouldn't be fair to you."

THEN I GET a bright idea as I recall a kid back in high school who was so proud to tell everyone who'd listen how he and this one girl dry humped until they came.

"Have you ever dry humped?" I ask her as I gauge her reaction. "I never have. I think it might be a way we could release tension while not exactly having sex. What do say to that?"

She looks a little nervous. "Won't your pj's get kind of nasty?"

"I can change them. But we don't have to go that far if you think it's an inappropriate thing to do. Is it too physical for you? Is it too invasive? Too much too soon?"

"It's not really having sex. So, I think it'll be okay." She pulls me back but I stop her.

"Wait, that's not helping me to learn how to make-out without having my own release. Can I use my mouth to give you an orgasm?" I ask her as I think about the other way defeating my purpose. "Also, I want tonight to be about you."

She looks at me for a long time. Her body is tense as she makes her decision. "It's not fair to you."

"I need to learn about self-control. Please."

WITH A SIGH, she nods and I move my body over hers. "Okay, but a little dry humping to start out with. I want to see if that does anything for me. This may sound insane but I'd like to have a hard-on when I taste you for the first time."

She moans and pulls me to her. "Damn it, Cyprian, you are a Rake, aren't you? You are irresistible." Her mouth is hot as I've gone too far for her to retain self-control.

I'm not sure if that matters or not. It's me she's counting on to keep my cock out of her.

Am I up to that yet...?

36

CAMILLA

His tight and taut body is all over mine, grinding against me, making the soft cotton material move back and forth over my clit, igniting a hunger in me.

I can't believe he wants to do this without going all the way!

I'M close to going over the edge when he stops kissing me and pumping away on me and moves down my body, pulling the pajama bottoms down only far enough so he can get to the goods.

I arch up to him as he blows on me. My fingers curve into the soft leather of the sofa. He blows and blows until I'm about to go crazy, I want his mouth on me so damn bad.

Just before I beg him, his lips touch me and I moan, long and hard, as his tongue moves in ways I didn't know were possible. "Cyprian. Yes."

He hums his response, sending a vibration deep into me. I can't stop moaning and twisting as he makes magical things happen inside of me. On and on he goes, giving me his intimate kiss which rivals what he can do with his mouth.

One thought keeps coursing through my head. I don't ever want to let him go. I want him more than I did before. I can't think of anyone else doing this to me.

I want to scream out that I'm his and his, alone. I want to shout it out loud for everyone to hear. No one can make me feel this way. No one!

My body starts to tremble as it grows closer to reaching a place it hasn't in over a year. My moan goes a pitch higher and then one more as the wave climbs to new heights. I shriek with my release and find him holding my ass in his strong hands as he pushes his tongue into me and sends me even deeper into the sweet ecstasy he's found in me.

When my body eases, he looks at me with my juices wet on his face. His dark eyes are ravenous, like that of a wild wolf's. He swallows hard, making his Adam's apple bob in his throat.

I FEEL as if he's working against himself right now. His chest is heaving as he tries to steady himself. I pull my shirt off and wiggle my finger at him. "Would you make love to me now, Cyprian? Because I'm pretty damn positive that I do love you. Do you think you might love me too?"

He nods and pulls his shirt off too. Then he goes savage and yanks my pajama bottoms all the way off then drops his and picks me up. I wrap my legs around him as he holds me higher than he is and looks at me as he lowers me to him.

"I have beaten you," he growls. "I have made you into what I was afraid of."

I shake my head. "No! No, I know I love you. I do. You haven't beaten me. This is right. It's good. We care for one another. This means something."

"I want it to," he says as he grits his teeth. "Are you on birth control?"

"Yes, you can be free with me, Cyprian. You're safe with me. I'm clean and you must be too with all the condoms you've bought from me." I giggle a little, earning a snarl from him.

"I've never done this without a condom, sheathing me." His eyes grow bright and hunger fills his face. Then his eyes roam over the room and he stops them on something.

GRABBING MY HAND, he pulls me along with him as he makes quick strides toward a small round table with a few chairs around it. He spins me into his arms to face him. "Cyprian, can you tell me you love me?"

He nods as he caresses my cheek. "I love you, Camilla. I think I've loved you before I even met you. Now, don't be afraid by this, but animal lust is burning inside me. I'm about to get very aggressive with you but after that, I will make love to you. It's been too long and I have to get this part out of the way."

My heart is racing as excitement runs through me. "Do what you need to do."

His mouth crashes onto mine so hard, I taste a bit of blood as one of us has cut the other. I can't feel any pain as adrenaline runs through me. I'm shaking with anticipation of what he's about to do to me.

He ends the hard kiss then turns me around, quickly and pushes the top half of me down on the table, holding me down with one hand and running his other one over my ass.

Two hard slaps have me quivering with need then he slams into me and goes brutal on me. Slam after slam is made as he slaps my ass hard every so often, sending heat pouring through me.

I've never been treated this way and I'm on fire with how animal it is. His breathing is hard and even that has a lusty tone to it.

"Do you like it?" he asks between clenched teeth as he smacks my ass again.

"Yes," I say and it comes out quivery.

"This is fucking, Camilla. This is all I've ever done. This is all I know. You will teach me how to make love in a little while but first I will show you what I know how to do."

"I'm not complaining, Cyprian," I manage to say as I've never been this stimulated before.

I find I'm pretty pissed at myself for holding the man off at all. He's amazing!

MY BODY STARTS to shake and my knees go weak as he takes me harder and more furiously. I shriek with the hardest orgasm I've ever had and he groans as he comes along with me. Then his teeth are on my back as he leans over me, biting me with his release.

I know it should hurt but it doesn't, instead it sends me even deeper into the zone he's putting me into. A level of Heaven I have lived my life unaware existed.

Before we're all the way through with the orgasms, he pulls me up and I find him lying me on the floor where he moves over me. His eyes are glistening as he looks at me. "That was fifty times better than anything I've ever done before." He kisses me, softly and sweetly. "Now it's your turn to show me how you like it."

Wrapping my arms around him, I pull him to me and hug him. "No, you know exactly what you're doing. I don't need to teach you a damn thing. I think I've only been with men who were doing it all wrong. Show me your ways, Cyprian. Take me into your world. Mine's a bore."

He laughs and gets up, picking me up with him. "To my bedroom then. The staff gets here at seven and I'd rather them not find us in here."

"Do you really think we'll still be at it by then?" I ask as he carries me up to his bedroom.

"Far past that, baby. Far past that. I've never had such a feeling. You may tire of me and the appetite I've found for you," he says then growls again.

"I don't know. I've found one for you as well." I lean my head against his wide chest as he goes up the stairs.

"I'm sorry I've managed to change you instead of the other way around. I was trying so hard to be the one to change."

"I know you were." I trace a pattern on his chest as I think about how I've never been that fulfilled and he's not even done with me yet. "I promise you. The way I've been doing it would leave you wanting more. Now I've seen what it can be like, you'll play hell getting rid of me."

HE STOPS on the top step and gives me a serious look. "I can't imagine wanting to get rid of you."

I sigh as he kicks his bedroom door open and takes me inside. "I hope you don't get tired of me."

"I hope you don't get tired of me," he says then tosses me onto the bed. "So, you want the real deal, huh?"

I nod as I look at him and turn to lie on my side, watching him stand at the side of the large bed. "I do."

"How many times have you ever climaxed in a single night?" he asks me as he opens a drawer next to the bed.

"Um, the most I can recall is two. And a few hours apart."

He shakes his head as his hand comes out of the drawer with a large dildo he turns on and it begins to glow pink. "Then you need to be conditioned to what will become your new normal." He drops the thing which is vibrating and pulsating on the bed, making it vibrate too then he reaches back into the drawer and comes back out with a pink lace piece of cloth. "I'll tie this over your eyes, so you can't let anything else interfere with your experience."

He picks up a remote and loud music fills the room. It's got a hard beat and makes my insides shiver with the deep base of the music. I sit up and he puts the blindfold over my eyes. I can still see shapes but nothing else.

He hoists me up the bed until my back is against the headboard. Propping pillows behind my head, the next thing I feel is cold metal on my wrist then he pulls my left arm up and cuffs me to the bed. I find myself biting my lip as he does the same thing to the other.

Moving my legs up until my knees are bent, I feel him moving in between them and then the vibration begins on my clit as he touches the machine to me.

I can see his shadow as he moves his body up mine, taking the thing off me. His lips touch my ear. "Do you trust me, Cami?"

"Yes," I say as I feel my insides squirming in anticipation. I have never done anything like this!

"If it gets too much for you, I want you to say the word lemon. You will shout for me to stop but I won't. If you really need me to stop, say lemon."

"Why would I tell you to stop?" I ask as I can't see that happening.

"Sometimes the pleasure can become so great, you want away from it. Hence, cuffing you to the bed. But I want to go on as much as possible, so I can get you on my level. Okay?"

"Yes," I say and feel fear, suddenly. "No one's ever died of an orgasm overdose, have they?"

"Not under me, they haven't. But then again, I've only dealt with professionals. So, you be sure to let me know if you can't take it anymore."

My heart is racing as he leaves one hard kiss on my mouth then I find the vibrator placed on my lips. "What?" I ask but it's too late. He's put it into my mouth.

Back and forth he goes with it. I suppose he's teaching me how he likes his blowjobs which I'm not experienced at, so I may as well learn on this thing.

His cock is moving over my stomach as he moves the thing in my mouth. It's growing harder and harder. Then the thing's pulled out of my mouth and he slides it into me. I have never used one of these things and the sensation is totally different from anything I've felt before.

It's stimulating everything and then something is placed against my rectum and I tighten up.

"Push, Cami."

"Huh?" I ask. "Push what?"

"Like you're taking a shit," he says.

"What is that you have there?" I ask as it feels kind of small.

"My little finger. Now push and stop asking questions. Just feel it. Experience it."

I shut my mouth and do as he's said and feel his little finger enter me. I moan as he pumps and everything is going at me at once. I feel an orgasm tapping at the door and explode when he turns the vibrator up even higher.

I'm screaming with the way it feels. It's not stopping, it's climbing higher somehow and he makes the vibrator go even faster and it warms up. His little finger is moved and a larger one goes in and I shout as the orgasm won't ebb. It's hard and making me want to squirm but I can't. My hands are immobile with the cuffs and he has my legs held down by his, somehow. I can't move and the pleasure is too much.

"Cyprian, stop!"

HE PULLS the vibrator out and then I'm filled with him. "Yes, you're primed for me. Your pussy is wetter than I bet it's ever been. It's pulsating all over my cock. I've never got to feel how wet a woman can get. It's amazing. Keep it going, baby. Keep it up. You're better than anyone I've ever had."

With his praises, I manage to stop feeling so overwhelmed and get into a rhythm with him. The hard orgasm is finally subsiding into a dull throb as he moves, expertly.

"I love you, Cyprian," I whisper, raggedly.

"I love fucking you, Cami. I'm completely addicted to you now." He bites my neck and I shudder.

Addicted? I was looking for something else there. And he loves fucking me, not me?

Have I just made the worst decision I ever could've made ...?

37

CYPRIAN

Yellow rays peek through the curtains as Cami is nestled in my arms. She did better than I ever expected her to. And my need for her is still raging. I thought I'd have her once and be over it but that was far from true.

Nibbling her neck, I whisper. "I have to go to work but you can stay here."

She grumbles and moans. "I can't. You need to drop me off at the store to pick up my car. I have a test later this afternoon at the college. It's a final, I can't miss it."

"Then get your lazy ass up, girl," I joke with her as I give her a light smack on her ass.

"Ow!" she groans as she rolls over. "I'm sore all over."

"I bet you are," I say then kiss her swollen lips. "I think tonight I'll add some spice to it."

Her sleepy eyes open and she squints at me. "Um, you need more spice?"

I nod and smile at her then get up, pulling the blanket with me to uncover her naked body which wears my marks all over it. "I did eat you up, didn't I?"

. . .

HER HANDS MOVE over her body and I love the way they look as they do. "You did." She smiles at the memory.

Throwing her clothes on the bed, I make my way to take a quick shower. "Do you prefer blondes or brunettes, Cami?"

"Um, I guess blondes. I consider you in that category. I never had a type before." I glance at her over my shoulder and wonder how she'll take what I want to watch her experience tonight.

As the warm water pours over me I think how lucky I am to have found a woman who is normal with an abnormal sex drive much like mine. It was destiny that brought us together, I can see that now.

When I get out of the shower, I find her dressed and pulling her wild hair into a ponytail. She smiles at me when I come into the room. "So, how's this going to go, Romeo?"

"I'd like you to stay over as much as you can," I say then go to find a suit in my suit closet.

"Okay. I have to work tonight. Only until eleven, though. Is that too late for you?"

"No, that'll work for me. I can't wait for tonight." I pull my clothes on then go and take her up in my arms and deliver a kiss to her sweet lips. "You're a rare find, Camilla Petit. I suppose it's the French in you that has you so daring."

SHE GIGGLES and a pink blush fills her cheeks. "I suppose so. I am sore, though. I'm not sure how much I can take tonight."

"No worries, a softer touch will be used on you tonight. You do trust me, don't you?" I ask her to make sure.

She nods as I take her hand and lead her out of the house to the waiting car. Ashton meets us at the door and opens it for us. "Well, good morning you two. What a surprise this is."

"Good morning, Ashton," Cami says as she ducks into the back seat.

"Get used to this. She'll be here a lot," I tell him. "Did you get the crazy lady on a plane yet?"

"I did," he says with a nod. "At six this morning. She's no longer an issue."

"Cool," I say as I get into the back seat with Cami.

She rests her head on my shoulder as we ride to where she works. I nuzzle her cheek and whisper, "I can't wait to get at you tonight, baby."

She sighs and looks at me. "I love you, Cyprian."

Looking into her blue eyes I see it there. It wasn't before and now it is. To be in love with someone with the same kind of adventurous sex drive is a thing I never even wished for.

"I'm going to show you things you never even thought about before, Camilla."

She shivers and I find that a good sign. "You are?"

"I am. You will never be bored with me. Not in bed anyway." I kiss her waiting lips and relish how they feel on mine.

All too soon, we pull up at the store where her car is and I have to let her go. Walking her to her car, I hold my hand out for the keys and unlock it for her. "Until tonight," she says then gets into her car.

I wave and go to get back into mine. I cannot wait to see how she takes my surprise!

I know it's a thing she's never done before...

38

CAMILLA

My body has been on edge all day with the thoughts about what Cyprian has in store for me. I'm just about to start shaking with nervous anticipation as I pull up to his front door.

He meets me at it with a tall glass in his hand. "Drink this down fast. It will steady your nerves and ease the soreness from last night."

I gulp it down without bothering to ask what it is. It tastes like a lemon-lime soda. "Thank you," I tell him as I hand him the empty glass back.

He takes my hand and leads me straight up to his bedroom. "I bought you something pretty to wear. It's open in the crotch area." He stops at the edge of his bed and I see a dark blue lacey negligee on top of the blanket. "Go put it on and get your hair out of that bun. Make yourself look sexy for me, baby."

I smile as he sits on his bed, wearing only a pair of dark blue, satin pajama bottoms. As I change into the little thing, I look at myself in the full-length mirror. I've never worn anything like this. I look kind of sizzling hot!

. . .

WITH MY HAIR, free, I look positively savage and smile at my reflection. "Ready to get dirty?"

Leaving the bathroom, I find the lights have been dimmed, the music is on but not loud, and Cyprian is waiting for me with a blue satin blindfold and two sets of the same color blue, fluffy hand cuffs are lying on the bed. He points at something across the room and I follow his finger and see a video camera. The light's red, it's not on yet. "You still trust me?" he asks with a wink.

"Oh, Lord. You want to record this?" I ask, feeling shy about it.

"I do. It's the first time you'll be experiencing this and I'd like for you to be able to see it later." His smile is broad as he seems so excited about this new thing he's going to do to me. "With your permission, of course."

"What are you going to be doing?" I ask. "Because if it's going to look odd or parts of me will be too much on display then I'm not cool with that."

"No, nothing gross. Nothing to make you look ugly or anything like that. I merely want it, so you can see for yourself how you enjoyed it all."

"Well, okay then. I do trust you. Cyprian, do you really love me or love doing this with me?" I ask as it's stuck in my mind what he said last night.

He moves his hands up and down my arms. "Both."

I sigh and nod. "I suppose I can handle that."

"I love having sex and when it's with you, it's beyond compare. Thank you for that, Cami." His lips touch mine for a moment. Then he's stepping back and holding up the handcuffs. "Ready to get into position?"

"Is the safe-word still, lemon?" I ask as I get onto the bed.

"It is. Tonight, I want you to really think before you say it. I'd rather you not say it at all. Just like last night. You made great strides in getting your body up to where mine is. I think you can handle just about anything I can," he says as he closes the cuff around the bedpost.

"I'm not too worried about it. You're teaching me a lot about just what the human body is capable of. I find it both interesting and enjoyable." I sneak a kiss on his cheek as he leans over me to cuff the other arm to the bedpost.

"Good. Tonight, will be an eye opener into the world I come from, Cami. You see, I'd like to get to a place where you feel comfortable going to my father's for a party every now and then."

I GULP as that is something I'm unsure I can handle. "I don't know about that, Cyprian," I say as he takes the blindfold and puts it over my eyes.

"It's your ignorance of why we do what we do at those parties that has you thinking that way. I'm going to show you why we do what we do at them. Didn't you feel more relaxed than you've ever been, today?"

"Well, yes, I did. But my mind is cool with it because of how much I care for you."

"And I care for you and I care about making you happy in every way possible. Do you feel that way about me?" he asks as a feather is ran over my chest.

"I do," I say and find him leaning over me.

His lips touch my ear as he whispers, "Prepare to go to a place you never dreamt could be so satisfying." The music goes loud and he moves away from me.

I CAN'T SEE a thing through this blindfold. My body is tense with what he's about to do to it. He pushes my legs apart then I feel cool air being blown on me. His hands squeeze my tits and I feel the drink kicking in as I relax.

I'm in his hands and he knows how to make things work inside of me. So, I give myself up to him and let him work his magic on me. His tongue runs up and down my folds. It's wet and cold. An ice cube is rubbed all over my sore area. It makes it less sore as the soft tongue moves over it.

Soft kisses are peppered over it. So soft, I can't believe it. His hands leave my breasts and the feather is ran all over them, in their place. His mouth leaves me for a moment as he asks me, "Do you like the way that feels, Cami?"

"Yes," I moan.

"Do you want more of that?" he asks and runs the feather over me where he's been kissing.

"I do. Please give me more, Cyprian."

"As you wish."

SOFT LIPS TOUCH me again and kiss me, so deep and intimately, I can't quite get over it. I could just let him kiss me like this forever. It feels so good. I'm not sure how he's managed to learn to lighten up his kiss like this. It's amazing.

His hands move over the lace fabric of the negligee, covering my stomach. His touch is light as well. I suppose that's what he meant about things would be much softer tonight.

His intimate kiss is starting to work and I arch up as I orgasm. "Good, Cami. Let it out."

I arch up and moan as the kiss goes on then I hear the sound of a vibrator. His lips are near my ear as his body hovers over mine. I can feel the tip of the vibrator on the edge of my vagina. "Let it all go, Cami."

It sides into me and moves back out. He's holding himself all the way up off me and somehow he's managing to move it as if he's wearing the thing.

"Do you have that strapped onto you, Cyprian?" I ask as it feels that way to me.

His lips are touching my ear again. "Shh, do you like it?"

The warmth of it is nice and the vibration is too. "I do."

"You want it harder and faster?" he asks me.

"Yes," I say as I moan and he moves it that way.

Over and over he goes until I'm groaning with another orgasm. Then soft lips are on mine and I taste myself as a small tongue goes into my mouth as the vibrator keeps going in and out as my body erupts with the hard climax.

THE LIPS ARE SOFT, small, and the way the tongue is moving in my mouth is different. The body that's now laying on top of mine is light and small.

My God! It's a woman!

What the hell has he done...?

To be continued...

BOOK 6: THE LOTHARIO

A Bad Boy Billionaire Romance

By Michelle Love

39

CAMILLA

"Lemon! Lemon! Lemon!" I screech, once I manage to twist my head enough the woman has to stop her kiss.

"Lemon?" Cyprian asks as if he's completely surprised. "You're not in any pain, are you?"

"You mother fucker!" I shout. "Get her off me and get me out of these fucking cuffs!"

The woman scrambles off me. "She's mad, Cyprian. This was a bad idea."

"Mad doesn't begin to describe what the hell I am," I say with a low tone to try to get some kind of control over the emotions that are rushing through me like a tidal wave.

"Baby," Cyprian says with a soothing tone to his deep voice.

"Shut up!" I shriek. "Get me out of these things!"

Finally, I feel him unlocking the handcuffs. With one hand, free, I pull the blindfold off and see the other woman, a small blonde, standing in a corner. She has on the same thing I do and I see Cyprian is still in those blue pajama bottoms.

He's leaning over me to release the other handcuff and as soon as he does, I slap the shit out of him. "Fuck you, you pervert!" I roll off the bed as he looks at me with a stunned expression and a red hand print, whelping up on his face. A face that did look handsome to me but now sends anger through me so intense I've never experienced the likes of before.

"Cami?" he asks as I run toward the bathroom. "Cami, you liked it."

"Shut up!" I scream at him and slam into the bathroom and turn on the shower to nearly scalding hot.

Ripping the little negligee off, I throw it at the wastebasket and get into the steaming hot shower and grab the shampoo, filling my hand with it and rubbing it all over my hair, face, and body. All the while I'm screaming and can't manage to stop doing that.

The bathroom door opens, somehow. I did lock it, I'm sure I did.

"Cami, baby," he says with a little cooing sound. "You liked..."

"I'm going to kill you! Get out!" I scream so loud I'm sure people can hear me from a mile away.

He laughs. The mother fucker is fucking laughing at me and I come completely unglued and jump out of the shower and tackle his ass. I scratch, bite, and punch him everywhere I can.

I can still hear him laughing and it infuriates me even further. "Camilla Petit, calm the hell down." More chuckles follow his words and I can't believe him.

Worn out, I get off him as I've managed to knock him to the floor and have straddled him, buck naked as I am, and find myself weak and full of sadness. Tears start flowing like rivers and I get off him and get back in the shower to rinse the soap off me.

I can't look at him. I can't talk to him. He's sick.

"Cami," he says, soothingly as he gets in the shower with me, as he's taken off his PJ bottoms. His arms go around me and I bat them away.

"Don't, Cyprian," I cry out at him. "You need to get away from me. We're done."

"No, we're not, Cami. I just went further, faster than you were ready for, that's all. I'm sorry, baby. I didn't know you'd react so badly to that. You were liking it."

Then my stomach churns and turns and I am puking my guts up. Holding myself up with the tiled wall, I vomit until there's nothing left inside me. Cyprian holds my hair back and rubs my shoulders.

I look up at him through tear-filled eyes and can't believe he'd do such a thing to me. "I trusted you," I croak. "And you did that to me. I can never trust you again. Not ever. We're done. I don't even want to be your friend anymore. You're sick."

HE ROLLS his eyes and smiles at me. "I am not sick. Tons of people do things like that. And once you watch the video, you'll see how much you enjoyed it. And I did too. Watching you getting off like that..."

I dry heave again as he talks about what just happened as if it was a beautiful thing. When I manage to stop, I look at him again. "I'm leaving. I'm not watching that."

"Are you a homophobe, Cami?" he asks with a deep chuckle.

Shaking my head, I slip out of his grasp, thanks to the water on my skin, and get out to grab a towel and wrap it around me. "I am not anything like that. What people do is their business. You did that to me without asking me about it. That's unforgivable."

He turns off the water and gets out of the shower and wraps a towel around his waist then reaches out and pulls me into his arms. "I can't let you go. You're mad right now and there's no way I can let you leave. We'll have a few drinks and..."

I scream and he stops talking. "I am leaving and you are to leave me the hell alone. I've never been so upset in my life. If I had a gun, you'd be dead already."

He looks shocked I've said that and lets me go. "You know what? Fucking leave then! You fucking liked that and you fucking know it! Your little act of being Miss Goody-Two-Shoes isn't a thing I'm buying. You liked what I did to you and you liked what I had done to you. So, fucking leave if you want to!"

I'm left in his bathroom, stunned and amazed, as he storms out.

My clothes are in here, so I put them back on and run my hands through my wet hair then try to gather my strength to walk out the door and most likely find him fucking that other woman.

CLOSING MY EYES, I leave the bathroom and walk into his room. I find him lying in his bed and don't see the other woman in the room. "Where is she?"

He doesn't even look at me as he says, "I sent her home. She was worried you'd try to beat her up."

"I'm not even upset with the poor woman. She was only doing what you paid her to do. I'm upset, no scratch that, upset is too small of a word, I'm furious at you, Cyprian. And you don't seem to care at all." I stand still and watch him as he closes his eyes.

"Camilla, I will say this only one more time. You said you trusted me to make you feel good and I did. End of argument." He opens his eyes and looks at me then picks up the remote from the nightstand and presses a button. I see the large television screen that's hung on the opposite wall, light up.

On the large screen, it's me on the bed and my stomach lurches. "Cyprian," I say as I turn to walk away.

"Come here, Camilla," he orders me.

I turn back and look at him with my heart full of sadness. He was a man I put my trust in and he has hurt me more than he can understand.

The sound is turned up and I hear myself on the television panting and moaning as the other woman kisses my intimate areas. "I can't believe you expect me to be okay with what you did. It speaks volumes about the real man you are. You are a sexual deviant wrapped in a very pretty package. You can think I am one too and just trying to hide it. I wanted to be with you. Not anyone else. I was giving myself to you. Not another person, woman or man. I let my inhibitions go with you, and I only ever meant to do that with just you. And you went and took the trust I placed in you and misused it. Goodbye,

Cyprian. I'm not a woman who will be ordered around or used. We are done."

I walk away and as my hand touches the doorknob, I hear him say, "Please, don't go."

I STAND THERE for a long moment as I think about the man and all he's been through and how he's so different than I am. I think how he must've meant something else by what he did. But when it comes down to it, I cannot allow myself to trust the man. I cannot allow my morals to be corrupted by him and if I stay with him, he will surely corrupt every part of me.

Twisting the doorknob, I leave him, saying nothing else because there are no words that can make it right. The trust is gone and without that, you have nothing.

If this is the right thing to do, why the hell does it hurt so damn bad...?

40

CYPRIAN

Watching her walk away from me, again, is so much harder than it was before. I know she can be what I want but her damn morals are in her way.

I turn my attention back to the television and watch her being very pleased with what was happening to her and have no idea why she freaked out. It wasn't until the other woman kissed her on the mouth that she wanted things to stop.

Some women don't like that and perhaps I should've gotten to know Cami and her hidden sexual wants better before I brought the other woman into play. I wasn't going to have sex with the other woman, I merely wanted Cami to get to feel the soft touch of another woman. Almost every woman I've been with, liked that.

I watch the television and can see her body go tense as soon as their lips meet. She wrenches her head, making their kiss end and then she's screaming the safe word and my expression is one of confusion.

When I was taking her cuffs off, I wasn't able to see her face. Now that I can, I see she was disgusted and somewhat hurt. Then her hand flies back and she slaps me.

I run my hand over my cheek and still feel the heat from the hard slap. Pulling the blanket back, I find small scratches where she clawed at me. There's a bite mark on my arm and I find myself thinking a little differently.

She was like a wild animal!

COULD she really have felt so upset with me for doing that? Or is she just mad because I pushed her further than what she was ready for?

I turn the television off as the scene has become anything except what I intended it to be. I bought all the clothes to match so we'd have our own little video of us. It was meant to be romantic and a keepsake.

Pulling the blanket back up, I lie down and think about going to sleep. I need to. Work will come early in the morning and today the only thing that kept me going was my plans for tonight. With the way things turned out, on my mind, I doubt I'll be any good at all tomorrow.

The darkness encompasses me as I close my eyes and try to think of nothing at all. But her face keeps coming to my mind. She was clearly upset. I'm lying to myself about her being anything less than disgusted with me.

Is she going to stick to being done with me? Can she really end it, just like that? Will she end it?

I CAN'T TAKE her words at the moment, as she was angry and most words spoken in anger are taken back, eventually. Maybe tomorrow will have her seeing things differently.

If the shoe were on the other foot and she had me tied up and blindfolded and brought in another man, secretly, and had him do the exact same things to me, how would I take it?

I lie here and imagine that and feel my stomach wrap in on itself. Yes, that would be uncool in my book. But women are different. I've watched countless women get off on each other's touch. Cami will come around. She has to.

But what if she doesn't?

What will I have to do to win her back again...?

41

CAMILLA

The smell of bleach fills my nostrils as I empty out the mop bucket. "Gina, you don't understand. I can't tell you why I broke it off with him. It's too ugly."

She looks at me with a frown. "How ugly could it be? The man looks like a Roman God. He'd have to do something very wrong for me to end things with the likes of him. Add in all that money, and you have a gold mine right there, honey. And, for some reason, you just keep on walking out on him. Are you sure you're not legally insane?" She laughs and I'm finally sick of hearing her go on and on about how great Cyprian is and how dumb I am.

Placing the empty mop bucket in the corner, where it goes, I walk around the corner and scan the store to make sure no one is in it. Looking back at her, I say, "So, you want to hear the terrible thing he did to me?"

She nods and tosses the rag she was drying dishes with, in the sink and comes to me with wide eyes and open ears. "Tell me about it."

"He had me handcuffed to his bed and blindfolded," I say.

She laughs and shakes her head. "Honey, that's fun!"

Shaking my head, I say, "No, that's not the part I had a problem with. You see, the night before, he showed me some things about the way he likes to be intimate and I liked them too. I liked them a lot and maybe he got the wrong idea about me. Maybe he got the idea that I was a slut and he could do anything he wanted to me. I don't know. All I know is the man went too far."

"LIKE WHAT?" she asks as her eyes go even wider. "Did he beat you with whips or chains? My first husband was into that and I liked it at first then it got old."

"No, he didn't do that. I kind of half-ass expected that and was prepared for something along those lines. No, what he did was worse. He violated my trust," I say as I can't seem to get the words to come out of my mouth.

"How'd he do that, Camilla?" she asks. "Did he hurt you, physically?"

"No," I say then walk away to find my cup of coffee.

She follows me to the checkout counter and seems to be confused. "He simply violated your trust, you say. But tell me how he did that."

I find my stomach knotting up as I recall it all and have to run to the bathroom. "I'm going to be sick."

Gina waits and says, "My God! What did he do to you?"

I barely make it to the bathroom before it all comes up. Everything I've eaten all day, which wasn't much as my appetite has been non-existent. Splashing water on my face, I look at my reflection and want to cry.

I see the same woman I was yesterday at this time but I know I'm different now. I'm a woman who has been with another woman. When people ask, I will have to say that I've dabbled in that department and that makes me furious at Cyprian. That should've been my call, not his!

. . .

I'M NOT GOING to lie and say it didn't feel good, what she did to me. But I thought it was him the whole time and that's where my head is all fucked up. My heart is pounding and I lean against the wall to stop myself from hyperventilating as I'm breathing hard and fast. "Stop. Calm down."

Finally, I manage to catch my breath and go back out into the store. Several customers have come in and I see Gina waiting on one of them. A nice-looking man comes up to me and asks, "Excuse me, do you keep the condoms behind the counter or something? I can't find any out on the shelves.

Anger boils up inside of me and I shout, "Pervert!" Then I spin around and go to the walk-in cooler and try to stop shaking with the anger that's consuming me.

Tears well up and I can't stop them. I run out of the cooler, going to the counter and grab my things and leave the store without saying a word because I can't talk right now.

Everyone is watching me as I haul ass to my car and then I stop, dead in my tracks as Cyprian is standing next to it. I look around and don't see any of his cars. He's gotten dropped off, so I have to take him home. "No!" I turn around and start running.

I have no idea where I'm going but I'm running like the wind to get away from him. He's not going to pull me back down to where he's at. I'm not going!

SUDDENLY, a pair of strong arms wrap around me, stopping me. "Hey there. What's wrong?"

I blink to try to get some of the tears out of my eyes and when I can see, I see it's the guy who asked me out once. "Sorry, I have to go." I look over my shoulder and see Cyprian coming my way.

"Hold her for me, will you?" he calls out to the man holding my arms.

"Oh my God," I say under my breath. "Please let me go. Don't let him get me."

"Did he do something to you, Camilla?" the guy asks me and I nod.

This guy is nowhere nearly as built as Cyprian and I get afraid for him, immediately when he says, "Hold up there, buddy. He says you did something to her."

I cower into the man's chest and pray he decides to let me go, so I can run away from Cyprian. A few more people circle around us as the guy has brought more attention to us all.

Cyprian gets close enough to whisper, "Are you happy now, Cami? You've caused a scene with your theatrics." He puts his hand on my shoulder. "Come on."

I look up at the man with terror in my eyes. "Don't let him take me. Please."

He looks at Cyprian. "Tell you what. Why don't you leave her alone for a while? It seems you two have had a fight or something and she needs to calm down."

"Cami, come on," Cyprian says again. "You know I've never hurt you and I never will. Now come on. Stop being so dramatic. We need to talk."

Gina comes outside and shouts, "Should I call the cops, Camilla?"

"Should she?" Cyprian asks me. "Or should you stop being crazy?"

Now he's made me mad and I find my backbone straightening as my courage builds. "You know what, you're right." I look around at everyone that's gathered around us. "Come on, Cyprian, I'm taking you home."

"That's better," he says as the guy lets me go and Cyprian and I walk, side by side, to my car.

Gina's looking at me with confusion. "You going home, Camilla?"

"I am. Clock me out, please. I have some business to take care of."

SHE GIVES me a nod and I walk away with the man who doesn't realize he's about to get his ass handed to him. His arm runs around my shoulders as he leans in close. "You had me worried, baby."

"You should be," I say as I unlock the passenger door and open it for him then walk around to get into the driver's seat. He looks at me with an odd expression then gets into the car.

I suppose he thinks he can handle me but he's far from being right. I slip into the seat and start the car up and leave the parking lot, nice and slow. The group of people is still lingering around, to make sure things are okay, I'm sure.

"Cami, I couldn't think about anything today except for the fact you're mad at me," he says and puts his hand over mine.

I move it after I change to fourth gear and shake my head. "I don't care."

"You must," he says as he reaches up and pulls the rubber band, that's holding my hair in a ponytail, out. My hair cascades over my shoulders and he takes a lock of it and pulls it to his nose, taking a sniff. "I missed this scent this morning when I woke up, alone."

I don't bother to speak as I'm mentally preparing myself for what I'm going to say to get him to understand, we are through. The gate comes up and I punch in the code and in we go.

When I stop in front of his door, he looks at me for a second then grabs the keys, turning off my car and yanking them out of the ignition then getting out of the car.

My first instinct is to scream at him as panic floods my system. Then I realize he'll be handing them back in no time and telling me to get the hell out of here.

So, I get out and walk behind him as I take off my green smock and toss it in the open passenger window as I pass by it. I crack my neck and knuckles and find him looking back to see what's making the noise. "You thinking about hitting me?"

I shake my head. "You thinking about trying to get me to change my mind about you?"

He nods and punches in the security code on his door then opens it and we go inside. He takes my hand and leads me all the way through the house and out to the garage. Placing my keys on the pegboard, he takes the Lambo keys off it and hands them to me. "I'm giving you the Lambo, Cami." He reaches into his inside jacket pocket and pulls out a paper. "I put the title in your name today. It's yours now."

I take the keys and step to one side then look at him and smile. "No, thank you." I place them back on the pegboard and take mine back. "And you can wipe your ass with that fucking title, you prick."

Turning to go back inside and leave, I feel his hand on my shoulder. "Cami, just stop being this way. It doesn't suit you at all."

Spinning back, I throw my hand back to slap the shit out of him but he grabs my wrist just before I can connect. "Damn you!"

"I'm not going to let you hit me, Cami." He pulls me along with him and we end up in the kitchen. "You look pale and I'm sure you haven't eaten much today." He doesn't let me go as he gets something out of a bag on the countertop. "I picked this up for you on the way home. It's a cheese burger and you're going to eat all of it."

"Sure," I say as I take a seat on a tall stool at the island in the middle of the huge kitchen. "Suddenly, I am very hungry." I take the burger and begin to eat it. He lets my wrist go and looks at me with a wary expression.

"What can I get you to drink?" he asks as he makes his way to the fridge.

"A beer. Better make that three of them. I don't care what kind. Something strong, none of that light shit," I say and take another bite. I'm preparing myself for battle and I'll be damned if I go into it with an empty stomach and no stones to tell him what I think of him.

He places one beer on the countertop. "Let's start with one, shall we?"

Looking right into his dark eyes, I pick up the beer and down it. Placing the empty bottle back down, I say, "Another please."

He frowns and takes the empty bottle, tossing it into the recycling bin. I watch him get another one out of the fridge as I take another bite. The burger is delicious and I want to ask him where he got it but that would be too conversational and I don't want to have a conversation with the man. I want to piss him off. And I want to do it, thoroughly!

. . .

SLIDING THE BEER TO ME, he takes the seat next to me. "About last night."

I hold up my hand. "I don't want to talk about that. I'm eating and that subject matter makes me sick."

He nods and looks away. "I thought about that. I thought about if you'd done that to me. Not another woman, as that would be fine but another man. I did find it to be a thing I wouldn't want."

"Great. Too late for me, though," I say as I take another bite, followed by a drink of the beer. "You say if I brought a woman in and had her suck your cock and screw you that you'd like that, huh?"

"Yes," he says as looks at me. "I have done that many, many times, after all."

"And you should get back to that, Cyprian. You really should. You need to leave me the hell alone and get back to the life you know and love. Don't let me stop you or get in your way," I say as I slam back the rest of the beer. "How about another?"

"You're going to get drunk?" he says but gets up to get me another beer.

"I am. I am going to get drunk tonight and wash this shit out of my mind. I am going to get back to the woman I was before I met you." I take the last bite of the burger and watch him as he looks back at me with defiance dancing in his dark eyes.

"I see." He brings me another beer but keeps it in his hand as he takes my hand and pulls me up, wrapping his arms around me. "I love you, Camilla Petit." He brings his lips toward mine.

"If your lips touch mine, they will be met with a bite," I say and find him stopping.

"You told me you loved me, only yesterday. How could you stop so quickly? Unless you were only telling me what you thought I wanted to hear?"

"I thought I loved you. But that was before I knew you for the real man you are. A pervert who destroys women's trust."

"If you call me a pervert one more time, I may find it necessary to punish you, Camilla." His eyes dart back and forth as if he's being serious.

"If you lay a hand on me, you will bring back a stub, Cyprian. I am not the woman to think you can do that to." I level my eyes on his and find him letting me out of the hold he had on me.

"You have too much anger going through you still. I thought, by now, you'd have come to your senses about last night. It wasn't ugly or perverted. You looked beautiful. I watched the recording many times and you're face and body told me you did enjoy it." He walks away from me, slowly.

"You would watch it over and over again. Tell me how you liked the part where I slapped the shit out of you," I say then grab the beer he's placed on the counter.

My body is about to start shaking as he reminds me about last night. I take a drink and blink back the burning of the tears that are threatening me, yet again. "I've thrown up more today than I ever have, and I had the flu once. I've cried more too. Are you still sure I enjoyed that?"

"You did, until your misplaced morals got in your way. It's merely sex, Cami. Nothing more than that. It's people making others experience pleasure. You're making it into something society has changed it into." He slips his jacket off and then unbuttons his white shirt and takes it off. "My body can bring your body much pleasure and vice versa. So why are you fighting everything so hard?"

"You should never have done that, Cyprian. And the fact you won't apologize and keep shoving it down my throat, tells me who you really are and I don't like that man. You know many women who will do what you want. Go to them." I take another drink as he eyes me like a wolf does its prey.

"Camilla Petit, I have set my sights on you. It is you I want and need. I crave you. I was willing to change for you. When I found, you liked the same things I do, well, I had to venture out and see if you could really be a part of the me I was. If you think you can't then I can change."

I shake my head. "I have never asked you to change for me. Not once. I have repeatedly told you not to. While I liked what you and I did, alone, I don't see myself ever wanting more than you in my bed. But for a moment, let me stick this picture in your head. Me in bed with you and another man. Let that little picture sink in, Cyprian."

"THAT'S NOT a thing I've ever done. I like to be the dominate one in the bedroom. I like to rule over the women I bring to it. I like to orchestrate the scene to satisfy us all. And I'd like you at my side while I do that."

"I don't want your dick in any other female, or male, for that matter. I don't want your lips on anyone else's either. I don't want their mouth on you, anywhere. I want you all to myself. It may sound selfish but here, in normal society, it's widely accepted." I place the beer on the counter and bait him some more. "So, I'm going to ask you something and see if you see fit to give me what I want."

"Shoot," he says. "The world is at your fingertips, baby."

"This Friday night, take me to your father's party and let me have sex with another man while you watch. If you like seeing me being aroused by another person, that is." I watch his face go into a blank expression and his Adam's apple lurches in his throat as he swallows hard.

"I thought you had to have feelings for a man before you allowed him to have sex with you? God knows you made me wait," he says as he looks into my eyes. I think he's trying to see if I'm serious.

I'm not sure if I am or not. But I say, "Since you brought a person into me who I had no feelings for, I figure why not do it with a random man too. Fuck, I've already been desecrated, what's one more? And this time a man."

Pacing in front of me, he seems to be thinking. I see a vein start to thump in his forehead. I've never seen that happened before. Finally, he stops and looks at me. "I can't do that. I can't see another man's hands on you, much less him taking you."

"But you let that woman take me," I say and watch him shake his head.

"It's not the same. I suppose it's because she can't get you pregnant and a man can. I don't know, exactly. I just know I can't stand to even think about another man on you, in you. The thought, alone, makes me crazy. And why would you even want that, if you love me?" he glares at me as I shrug.

"I'M JUST SAYING if you think watching another woman give me pleasure is what gets you off then why not let another man do it too?"

"Look, I can live my life never seeing that again. I can do whatever it is you want. You want a plain, old, boring sex life? I can deal with that. God knows I've had enough wild sex already." He moves around the counter to come to me.

I get up and move away from him. "Boring sex life? Is that what you think I want? Is that how you felt when it was only you and me?"

"No, I didn't mean it like that. You're putting words into my mouth." He comes toward me and grabs my arm before I can get away.

PULLING ME INTO HIS ARMS, he puts his hand under my T-shirt. His hand closes over one of my breasts and I take in a sharp breath. "Cyprian, no."

"I take responsibility for hurting you, Cami. I promise to never do that again. Now, can we get back to where we were? I want you. I'll do anything for you." His lips touch my ear then he bites my earlobe. "I'm addicted to you. You're sweeter than any drug ever made."

I press my hands against his chest as he's driving my body crazy. "Cyprian, please don't do this to me. I can't," I say but his mouth is on mine, stopping me from saying another word.

My mind is telling me to push him away and leave but my body is craving the man. He takes one of my hands and wraps it around his neck then he picks me up and carries me with him.

I want to stop kissing him, I want to stop liking it. I want to have more will power. But it's fading fast. The anger is fading.

. . .

HE LAYS me on a sofa and touches something on the table and fire springs to life in a fireplace. "I love you, Cami. Forgive me."

I stare into his eyes and see more in them than I did before. Maybe he does love me. But do I love him, anymore?

SITTING UP, I stand up and shake my head. "I can't right now. I don't trust you. I don't know if you can earn it again. Plus, the fact you still think you'd like to have sex with other women is a huge red flag."

He grabs my hand as I try to leave. "So, my honesty has cost me. Is that what you're saying? Because I don't want to be in a relationship if it means I have to hide things about myself or lie."

"You still don't get it, Cyprian. I thought you told me you were a child prodigy? When did you stop listening? I want you to be whoever the hell you want to be. I will accept who you are or I won't. At this point, who you are right now, well, I can't be with you. I have to be able to trust you and I can't right now."

"How can I make it up to you?" he asks as he pulls me back into his arms. His lips graze my forehead then he kisses me again. "Cami, don't leave me this way. This is killing me."

"I have to be true to myself. I am sorry you don't understand. Just give me space, please. I need space and time. Maybe I'll get over this feeling and maybe I won't. But you pushing at me, so soon afterward, is just pushing me away." I push his chest and he lets me go.

"Take the car I gave you," he says then reaches into his pocket and pulls out a wad of cash. "And this." He holds it out to me.

"No, Cyprian. You cannot buy me." I turn to leave and he stands still.

My heart is aching but I know I have to do this for myself. I must put myself first. I can't lose myself in the man.

"CAMI, LOOK AT ME, PLEASE," he says.

I stop and turn around. "Yes?"

"I love you," he says then blows me a kiss. "I will be here, waiting for you. You come or call or send me a message and I will be there. I am sorry for hurting you and making you lose trust in me. And I hope you can forgive me in time. Can I hear you tell me that you love me one more time? You see, no one but you has ever told me those words before. No one. And you are the only person I have said those words to."

What he said shouldn't shock me but it does. He's a 35-year-old gorgeous man with tons of money and no one has ever seen fit to ever tell him that he's loved. Not even his parents.

"I love you, Cyprian. I suppose I always will. But I love myself too and I have to uphold myself to the standards I have and will always live my life by. I hope you can understand."

He nods. "Thank you, Cami."

I nod and leave him. Again, I am walking away. Each time I've thought it was the last time, I'd be leaving him. Yet, I've managed to come back. But this time he's really gone too far and I know who he really is and I can't be with someone like him.

I wonder how long it will take for the pain to leave my heart...?

42

CYPRIAN

The moon still glows as it fills the sky and the stars still shine up in the dark sky. Life moves on, even though mine feels as if it's over. She's left me again and this time I don't think she's coming back.

With no idea of who to talk to as making friends was never a real concern of mine, I've asked Ashton to come over and talk to me. The emptiness I'm feeling is overwhelming. And my father's advice isn't a thing I think is right for this situation. He and I are too much alike for him to actually help me.

"So, you brought a woman into your love life, without Camilla's consent?" he asks me then takes a long drag off a cigar.

I told him everything. And he's been quiet for about five minutes. "I did. Now, what can I do to get her to forgive me and understand I'm an idiot?"

Ashton shakes his head as he looks up into the night sky. We're out on a patio, the light has been bothering me all day and into the night. I have a migraine that could kill a horse.

"Cyprian, there's not a thing you can do. That was terrible. She's probably feeling violated. Much like a rape victim," he says then looks at me. Not in a judgmental way but like a man who's trying to get me to see right from wrong.

THAT LINE IS SO THIN, in my mind, it's nearly invisible. "Rape is too strong of a word, Ashton. And she was enjoying it, up until she realized it wasn't me."

"That's because she was trusting that it was you. You know damn good and well, you knew what you were doing. You knew she had no idea it wasn't you. What's worse, is she's aware of how much thought you put into the whole thing. It was premeditated. I'm telling you, that wound will leave a scar so deep, it may never go away." He looks away from me and shakes his head again. "Best to move on and leave that woman alone. Entirely, Cyprian."

His words are sinking in deep. I never meant for her to feel that way about what I did. I only wanted her to feel amazing things. That's all!

"ASHTON, I have to fix things. I have to! I didn't think the way you are, about it. I guess she feels exactly what you're talking about. My God! I have to fix it. I have to!"

"It's too late, boy." He gets up and walks over to the large potted plant at the edge of the patio and stubs out his cigar. "Leave her alone. Your face will only remind her of what happened to her one crazy night when she was in love with a man who made her do things that were never in her mind to do."

I double over as my stomach cramps. "My God! What have I done? I am a monster, aren't I?"

"You were created, Cyprian. Stay with the world you grew up in. You weren't meant to be with a normal woman. You were made to be a man with a love for money and many, many women. Camilla is a special woman and she deserves to get to live a normal life. You will only ever hurt her. You're not meant for that kind of life."

The pain inside my body is excruciating. "Ashton, something's wrong."

He walks over to me and touches my head. "You're not hot. You have no fever. Why are you doubled over?"

"Ashton, something's wrong. I can't straighten up. I think I need to go to the hospital," I look up at him and see him shaking his head.

"It's guilt, son. It hurts, huh?" he asks as he runs his hand over my head. "I'll get you something stout to drink. It'll knock the edge off."

He walks away and I find myself gritting my teeth with the pain in my abdomen. I have to admit this is my first bout with guilt but fuck it hurts like hell.

I pick up my phone and call Cami. It rings and rings but she doesn't answer. I don't know why I thought she would. She left me only an hour ago. The anger is still white hot inside of her.

Why did I do that to her? What the hell is wrong with me? Is there any way I can change what I've done?

Ashton returns with a dark glass of something and hands it to me. "Sip on this and take a hot bath. This is what it feels like to fully understand your role in her pain. Yours is manifesting itself, physically. Hers is invisible. Her mind is where it resides and I'm sure she can feel it in her heart. I told you to leave her alone. You shouldn't have pushed yourself on her. She was a good girl, Cyprian. She has to feel tainted by what you've done to her."

Getting up, I stagger into the house and make it to the first bathroom. Starting the water, I take my clothes off to get into the hot tub to try to relieve this pain in my gut. It's so bad, I can hardly think.

And what thoughts are filtering in are about her and that seems to make it worse.

What have I done...?

43

CAMILLA

"**D**id you hear about the rich guy, last night, Camilla?" Kyle asks me as I come in for my evening shift at the store.

I pull my green smock on and shake my head. "Are you talking about that guy I used to see?"

"Yeah, Cyprian Girard. It was on the news. I was driving down the road when the ambulance left his house last night. There was a long black car following it and a BMW came out after that one."

I stand perfectly still and look at him. "What happened to him? I just saw him last night." And I had ignored five calls from him after I left him!

HE HAD APPENDICITIS. He was sent to surgery and he's yet to come out of the anesthesia. The reporter said it happens sometimes. He seems to be in a coma."

My knees buckle and I have to hold the counter to stay up. "What hospital? Did they say?" I find myself taking my phone out and calling him. I cross my fingers that, by some miracle, he answers it and tells me he's okay. But I don't get that.

"I don't know if they did say the hospital or not. It was the channel six news. Maybe you could check their website," he says and I go to that next.

I find out which one he's in and look at Kyle. "I need to leave."

He shakes his head. "I don't know how to close the store. You have to stay, Camilla."

I'm stuck! I'm fucking stuck!

HURRYING TO THE OFFICE, I start trying to find someone to come in to take my shift, who can close the store. The first call goes unanswered. "Of course, Gina isn't answering. She has some high school reunion tonight. Damn!"

There's only three of us who know how to close this damn store. Then I make a decision. I'll leave and be back in time to close. I get up and walk out to tell Kyle what I'm going to do when three men in suits walk in.

I stare at them as Kyle greets them. "We're from corporate. We have a pop-inspection and audit to do. Are you the night manager?" one of them asks me.

I nod and another one gestures to the office. We should start up as soon as we possibly can. This could go until late."

"The store locks at one-fifteen tonight. It can't go longer than that," I say as I go with them to the office.

"We can override that. It could take up until four or five. Depends on how well you all have kept the records and things in order," the other guy says and I feel the blood running out of my head.

"All night?" I ask. "I really need to leave for at least a little while, please. I just found out my boyfriend is in a coma in the hospital."

One of the men sighs, "Honey, we've heard every excuse in the book. You aren't going anywhere, unless you're ready to quit this job."

ONE OF THE men holds up his hand. "And that's not an option right now. You see, if you leave and things are found to be out of order and money or inventory is off, it's you who'll be prosecuted to the fullest extent of the law. So, take a seat and let's get this going.

My heart is pounding and I look out the office door at Kyle. He looks a bit panicked too. With a shrug, he turns around and I find myself feeling more unstable than I ever recall feeling.

God, I hope he wakes up...

44

CAMILLA

The rising sun has me blinking and pulling on sunglasses at six in the morning. The manager is coming in as the three men and I are leaving after the all-night audit we managed to pass.

She gives me a look as she comes to the door we're leaving. "What's going on?"

One of the men hands her a paper. "Here's a copy of our findings. You passed. You have yourself a very competent night manager. Keep up the good work."

"I want the night off," I tell her as I go to my car.

"You got it!" she shouts after me. "Take the next three nights off. And thanks!"

I'm a zombie as I go to my car and drive out to my house. I'm going to shower and change then call that hospital and find out if Cyprian woke up. If he did, I'll talk to him over the phone then sleep. If he didn't wake up, I'll go up to the hospital.

I keep thinking this is my fault, somehow. Maybe the stress of our breakup caused it. I'm a scientist, I know that's not very plausible but stress can do some weird shit to the body.

An experiment with lab rats where there was a very dominate

female had all the other females becoming infertile as she was so aggressive to them anytime a male was introduced into their enclosure. It was weird but true.

Going into my house, I find my body trying to give up on me. My eyes go to my bed and my body migrates to it. "No! Cyprian's in a bad spot. Come on!"

I shake my head to ward off the exhaustion and go to the shower. It helps me refresh and wake up some. I hurry to bathe then get out and throw on jeans and a T-shirt then slip on some sandals. My hair has to be tamed a bit, so I put it into a clip to hold my wild curls down. Then I leave the bathroom and find my phone.

The damn battery is dead so I plug it into the charger and make myself some coffee as it charges up, so I can turn it on. The pot is shaking in my hand as I fill it with water.

Suddenly, I'm overwhelmed by sorrow and slowly, go to the floor, leaving the coffee pot in the sink as I start crying. "Why didn't I answer his calls?"

Have I missed any chance of ever hearing his voice again? Have I missed any chance of ever having him in my life? What have I done?

My phone makes a beep as it comes back on. I pull myself up and turn the water off and go back to my phone and find the number to the hospital. "AnMed, how can I direct your call?" a woman answers the phone.

"I need to ask about a patient."

The phone makes some clicking noises then another woman answers, "Patient care."

"Hello, I'm wanting to know if Cyprian Girard has woken up yet," I blurt out.

"And you are who to him?" she asks with a professional tone.

"His girlfriend." I cross my fingers.

"Oh. Um, well. I can't tell you anything more than what room he's in. His family has asked that of us."

"Give me his room number." I pick up a pen and write 228, on my hand, when she gives it to me. "Thanks."

Dropping the pen, I grab my purse and keys and head out to the hospital. It's about forty minutes away.

A long as hell forty minutes...

45

CYPRIAN

Bright light filters through beige curtains, a steady beep is near my head, filling my ears as antiseptic stings my nose. "I made it," I croak out.

The pain was unbearable. I asked Aston to take me to the hospital but he thought it would be better if an ambulance came to get me. He called my father and he got to me before the ambulance did.

I called Cami more times than I can remember. She never answered any of my calls. I guess she's done with me. And I cannot blame her.

"Hey there," a soft voice calls out to me.

I turn my head to find a nurse, in pink scrubs coming into my room. "Hi," I say and find my throat is so dry.

SHE SMILES and picks up a cup of water with a straw in it and gives me a drink. "The IV is keeping you hydrated but it can't help the mouth stay that way. How's the pain level, Mr. Girard?"

I recall the paramedics asking me that and telling them to register it between one and ten. It was a ten when they had me. "A five." I point to my side. "Here is where it hurts."

She nods. "That's where they made the incision to take out that pesky appendix that ruptured on you a couple of nights ago. That will no longer bother you."

"What did I do to make it give up on me?" I ask as I don't recall ever finding that out in the past. "What makes them rupture?"

"There's nothing you could've done to prevent it from happening. It just happens to some people, not all. There's no way to tell. You can be sure it won't happen again, though. It's outta there!" She laughs and checks my machines. "You gave your family quite a scare with how long you took to wake up. They'll be glad to see those pretty brown eyes, open."

"Did anyone else come to see me?" I ask her. "A beautiful young woman with curly black hair and dark blue eyes, perhaps?"

Her green eyes droop at the corners as her lips form a straight line. "No. Would you like me to help you call that beautiful young woman?"

"No," I say then think twice about it. "Maybe."

She picks up the phone next to the bed. "Give me her number and I'll call her for you."

"Is my cell phone here by any chance?" I ask. "I don't have her number memorized."

She shakes her head. "There's no cell phone in here. Sorry. Perhaps she'll see the news when they report you woke up and come see you."

"I'm on the news?"

She nods. "Yes, your story was. Clemson is waiting to hear you've woken up. Everyone will be so relieved. You had many worrying about you."

"Not many know me," I say as I doubt her words.

WITH A GESTURE to one side of me, she says, "Then where did all these get-well cards and flowers come from?"

Turning my head, I see a ton of cards and flowers as well as balloons. "Wow!"

"Yes, wow. So, I'm going to run out to the nurses' station and deliver the good news and send your doctor in to see you. Should I call your father and mother? We have their numbers."

I nod and she leaves me. My heart thuds in my chest as I now know my story was on the news and Cami has not even checked on me.

Somewhere, deep inside of me, I thought she would give a shit. I suppose what I did was so bad, she never wants to see me again. And it's pretty obvious she doesn't care if I'm alive or dead.

It's both good and bad to wake up alive. On the one hand, I have life. On the other, what good is it if you have to live it all alone?

A man in dark blue scrubs comes into the room, looking pretty happy. "Hi, man am I glad to see those eyes open. Mr. Girard, I was the man who administered your anesthesia. When you didn't wake up, you had my nerves frazzled."

"Sorry to do that to you," I tell him then look out the window. "What time is it?"

"A bit after seven in the morning. So, do you feel groggy at all?"

"No, I'm sore and stiff but my mind is growing sharper with each passing moment." And becoming more and more aware of how Cami really feels about me.

SHE'S DONE WITH ME. I should leave this town. If I run into her, it'll just continue to fuck my head up.

"Do you have anyone to help you at home, Mr. Girard?" he asks me as another man walks in with tan slacks and a gray button-down, a clipboard is in his hands.

"I have my staff."

"Great," the other man says. "I am Doctor Wilkins. I performed the surgery. You didn't get to meet me. This guy had you out by the time I got to you. The procedure was complete and you will need to give yourself a full month to completely recover."

The nurse comes back in and takes over where the surgeon left off, "No heavy lifting. Nothing over 5 pounds. No tub baths. Showers only."

My father walks in and says, "How about sex, doc?"

The nurse looks at him then at me. "A month, I'm afraid."

The surgeon taps my leg to get my attention. "Seriously. None until you see your personal physician for your one-month post-op appointment. And that doctor will be the one who will release you or won't. If you don't take good care of the incision and do what the orders say, you will end up needing more time to recuperate."

I look back at the nurse as she pushes my hospital gown up so the doctor can inspect his handiwork. "By the look of those abs and the rest of you, it'd bet you make vigorous exercise part of your daily routine," she says.

"I do. An hour every day." I smile at my commitment to keeping myself fit.

"Yeah," the surgeon says. "No more of that. Not until your doctor releases you. You can take small walks, no more than a half-mile. Then you can ease up to a mile."

The nurse takes over again. "No more than that."

"I know, I know. Until my personal physician releases me. Got it. Now, when can I get the heck out of here and go home?" I ask them all.

"Are you sure you have adequate care at home?" the nurse asks. "Because we have many nurses who could take shifts, taking care of you at your home. Your father has told us you have a large estate and you could have constant care. If you have no one else to do that for you. You will need tons of help, Mr. Girard. I cannot express that enough."

"I'll set it up, son. You'll have nurses there to help you. Don't worry," my father says to me then my mother walks into the room too.

"CYPRIAN, YOU'RE AWAKE!" She sounds so happy. She's all over me, kissing my whole face.

"Mother!" I say as I laugh. "You've never been so affectionate to me before."

She takes my hand and holds it to her cheek. "My baby wouldn't wake up. I was a mess. A complete mess, Cyprian. Did I hear them talking about you needing nurses?"

"You did. I think the staff will be enough. I don't need any nurses. I'll be fine."

"Nonsense," Papa says as he steps up to the foot of my bed.

I laugh a bit and find it hurts, so I stop.

But the idea of having women all around me, living in my home has me worried.

What will Cami think...?

46

CAMILLA

T he smell of the sterile environment has me rubbing under my nose as it threatens to make me sneeze. Not many people are moving around yet as it's still pretty early.

I get onto the elevator, finding two more people getting on with me. I push in the 2 button and they each push in other floors. We get to mine first and I step off and look up and down the long hallway.

Easing down the hallway, I try to settle my nerves by twisting my hands in front of me. It's not helping.

I know Cyprian will be glad to see me if he's awake. If he's not, I don't know how I'll cope with it. If I never hear his voice again, I don't know what I'll do.

The numbers tick off as I walk down the hallway. I pass a room with someone crying with low and long moans. It's heartbreaking. The door is slightly open and I can't help but peek in and see an old man sitting by an old woman, who seems to be sleeping in the hospital bed. "Bertha, please come back to me," he whispers.

The sight and sound hurts my heart and it makes me wonder what I am willing to offer Cyprian if and when he wakes up. I see the numbers 228 on the next door, just across the hallway and my heart stops.

Walking across, I listen at the closed door. "Don't worry, son. You'll be well taken care of. I'll only hire the prettiest nurses to care for you."

I lean my ear on the door and listen harder. "Papa, you spoil me."

It's Cyprian!

He's awake!

And asking for nurses?

"ONLY THE BEST FOR OUR BOY," a woman says. I assume it's his mother. "Only the prettiest."

I hear him laughing and shake my head as I was so damn worried. And for what?

"I'll get you a list of available nurses, Mr. Girard," another woman says.

"Pictures with their files, please," the man I think is his father, says.

Cyprian laughs again and I walk away. He doesn't need me.

Any woman will do...

TO BE CONTINUED...

BOOK 7: THE SENSUALIST

A Bad Boy Billionaire Romance

By Michelle Love

47

CYPRIAN

P ink and odd shades of green fill the sky outside the window of my hospital room. My father sits in one of the chairs, staring out the window, as do I.

"A hurricane," my father says. "You're being so stubborn, Cyprian. A hurricane is coming and you're being released in a couple of hours and instead of coming home with me, you're choosing to go to your place and not even taking a nurse with you. Are you trying to kill yourself?"

"No," I tell him as I get off the bed and show him how well I'm getting around. "Look at me. It's been two days and I barely feel a thing. I'm fine. And I'd rather ride out the storm at my place. I've called the staff and they have the necessary things in the house. Even if power is lost, I have a generator for the kitchen."

He turns his attention to me, instead of the foreboding evening sky. "It's the idea of you being all alone, Cyprian. At least let me come over. I get it. You don't want to be around women when you're unable to perform because of your injury."

"It's not that. It's about my needing time alone. I've been going about things so very wrong. I'd like to get into my bed and read until I know how to make the changes I need to."

"This sudden urge to become someone different is annoying." My father gets up and gets his cup of coffee. "I don't understand it. The woman you were doing it for has lost interest in you. Can't you see that? You've been in this hospital for five days and she's not even made an inquiring call about you. She has to know you're here. It was on the news."

I WATCH him take a sip of the coffee which is now cold. He makes a face and puts if back down. "Papa, you should leave. Go home. Relax and get ready for the storm to hit. They said it would be around ten or eleven tonight. Ashton is driving me home, anyway. He's waiting outside for me. As soon as the doc comes to check on me, one last time, I'll be set free."

He nods and picks up his jacket. "I'm not making any headway with you anyway. You give me a call when you get home and settled. And if anything happens, you let me know. If you need anything..."

"I know," I interrupt him. "I'll call you. Now go home. Mother went back to Los Angeles yesterday. It'll make me feel better to know you're at home, having a hurricane party rather than sitting with me at my place, bored and lonely."

With a pat on my back, he leaves me without saying another word. In his defense, he's been trying to talk me into going home with him the entire day.

Going to the bathroom, I run my hand through my hair and look at my reflection. "Who are you trying to change yourself for?"

Shaking my head, I go back into the hospital room and sit in the chair my father left vacant. I don't know how to explain to anyone why I feel the need to make changes in myself. Everything looks rosy, on the surface. Inside, I'm a mess.

Twice I've done sexual shit that's gotten me on Cami's bad side. I can't seem to learn the difference between right and wrong. To have been taught that, early on, would've been helpful.

A lesser man would stand on the fact he was taught deviant

sexual practices and that would be that. Women would comply or he'd simply not deal with them.

So, why am I so hung up on Camilla Petit?

SHE CLEARLY DOESN'T CARE for me. Leaving me like this, proves that much. But I still care for her. As a matter of fact, I need to try to call her to make sure she's got somewhere safe to be, during the hurricane. If she'll answer my call that is.

My cell phone is still at home. Once I get there, I will attempt to contact her and make sure she's okay. I don't care if she hates me or not, I will not let her anger stop her from being someplace safe for the storm. Her little duplex apartment is nowhere nearly good enough for her to ride the storm out.

The door opens and in sweeps the doctor. "Hey there, Mr. Girard. Are you ready to leave us?"

I get up and shake his hand. "I am." Lifting up my shirt, I show him the stitches which look excellent. "See, it looks great, don't you think?"

He nods and writes on a paper on his clipboard. "It does. If you can sign all these papers for me, I'll get you a wheelchair and a nurse and you will be on your way. You're doing so well. I think all that worry over having full time nurses around you was a bit too much. You'll be fine. Did your staff at home manage to get you set up for this hurricane we're about to have?"

"They did," I tell him as I sign page after page of release papers. "I'll be fine. The place is huge."

"Oh, I know. I saw it just a couple of days ago. An ex-student of mine lives out that way. She and I met again when she was here in the hospital. It had been a few years since I had seen her and something just sparked inside of me when I saw her again. No longer my student and she was available, had me asking her out to dinner and she accepted. We had a nice night out. I'm hoping to see her again soon but she told me she's just coming off a bad semi-relationship, she didn't want to talk about."

My hackles start rising as he goes on about this woman he's looking forward to dating. I sign the last page and hand him back his clipboard. "So, she's a neighbor of mine?" I ask him and feel my stomach going tight.

"Yes, she pointed out your estate. She said she heard about your hospital stay from the news and asked if I knew anything about how you were doing."

When he says nothing else, I ask, "And you told her?"

He shakes his head. "I told her I wasn't allowed to talk about my patients."

With a nod, I find myself asking him, "And her name is?"

"Camilla."

Mother fucker!

"I THINK she's one of the cashiers at that convenience store at the edge of town. I think I've seen her before. Long, dark, curly hair, right?"

He nods and smiles. "Her hair is gorgeous. Her eyes are like jewels, don't you think?"

"I really haven't looked at her that hard. She's a bit on the thick side," I say, trying to get him to stop liking her.

"Her curves are incredible," he says as he shakes his head. "And man, don't get me started on her plump, completely kissable lips. Man!"

Suddenly, I feel terrible. "Guess I just didn't look at her the right way. You think you two might hit it off?"

"I hope so. She's a great girl. And a hell of a scientist. She will do amazing things one day, mark my words." He walks toward the door to leave. "You have to wait for your ride out. But you're free to go as soon as they come for you."

He leaves and I sit on the bed and look out the window at the clouds that are starting to roll in quite heavily. All I can think about is she went out with someone else. She has to be done with me. And now a doctor is after her.

A normal man with money and a career. A great catch for a

normal girl, like herself. And she should have a great guy. She really should. Who am I to stand in her way?

A male nurse comes in, pushing an old wheelchair. "Your chariot, sir." He gives me a grin.

I take a seat and say nothing. My mood is grim, to say the least. He wheels me away as I think about Cami and my doctor and them having an evening out. Dinner, dancing, drinks, normal shit like that!

Jealousy is coursing through me, sending terrible thoughts into my head. Thoughts that shouldn't be there. Things like going to get her and dragging her to my place where I'll keep her until she teaches me how to be the man she needs.

IF SHE'D WRITE me a manual, then I could follow it and she'd never have to look for another man again. I'd be her everything. I'd be all she would ever need or want in a man.

The glass doors slide open and I point to the BMW, Ashton is picking me up in. "There he is."

Ashton sees us and gets out of the car to open the back door. "Classy," the nurse says as Ashton tips his hat at us.

"Thank you, sir," Ashton says as I get up and get into the car.

Just as the door closes, I recall my doctor saying he met her in the hospital. That means she did come to see me. But what the hell happened? Did she meet him again and just blow me off?

That seems unlikely. But what did send her away without seeing me...?

48

CAMILLA

"Do you have any more toilet paper in the back?" a woman asks me, excitedly.

"No, sorry. We're all out," I tell her as I scan the three cases of water she's buying. "Are you completely out at home?"

"No, I've got about twenty rolls but you never know what might happen with a hurricane. It might be days and days before the stores open back up," she says as she scans the store for anything else she might want to horde.

"I'm sure we'll all be back up and running in no time, ma'am. Will this be all, today?" I ask her as I try to ignore the tons of other customers who are literally taking everything off the shelves they can.

THE WOMAN LOOKS over my shoulder at the six cans of soup I bought myself before they were all gone. "Can I have those?"

"I bought them, already. So, will there be anything else?"

She pulls out a hundred-dollar bill and places it on the counter. "I'll trade you this for that soup. All six cans." Her dark brown eyes hold mine as she is dead serious.

Politely, I push the money back to her. "No, ma'am. Your total is sixteen, fifty."

"I only have enough food at home for nine days. I may need that soup. Please," she stomps her foot as she says the word, totally negating it.

"Nine days, you say! Wow!" I shake my head and pick up the cans of soup and put them in a bag and hide them under the counter so no one else sees them and tries to take the only food I'll have.

Slamming a twenty down, she glares at me as if I've committed a horrible crime. I make her change and watch her leave, carrying all the heavy bottled water.

The next person in line steps up. "And I'll be needing three hundred dollars worth of gas on pump 1. That's me in the truck in that spot," a small red-haired man tells me.

"I can't set the pump for that amount. How about ninety dollars, that's more than enough to get you through this hurricane." I wait to see what he says as he seems to be getting upset.

"I have tons of old milk jugs in the back of the truck. I can handle the load," he says. "Make the sales in increments. That'll work."

"No, it won't. You see, I can't allow you to get gasoline in a container that's not approved for it. You can't fill up old milk jugs with it. Sorry. I can let you fill up your truck but nothing else, unless you have an approved gasoline container." I watch as he turns a shade of red I haven't see on a human before.

"Look, I need that gas. So just take my money and turn the damn pump on for me. Don't look at where I'm putting the gas. I won't tell anyone about it."

WITH A SIGH, I shake my head and look out at the store that's gone crazy. The cooler is bare, the shelves are too and the sudden onset of beeping tells me this man is really going to be upset. "That beeping sound means the underground tanks are empty. We have no more gasoline, sir," I tell him and watch him explode.

His fit is huge and I'm reminded of Yosemite Sam in those old cartoons as he blows his top. Gina manages to get the loud beeping to go away but the effect it had on our customers is still going.

It seems to have sent them into a frenzy, even worse than they were before. A sudden crack of lightning has everyone going quiet. Then someone shouts, "Shit! It's here!"

With no more time to waste, the man stops his fit and hauls ass out the door, presumably to get to another gas station before all is lost. I go into automated mode and scan things like a robot, taking money and making change like a champ.

Gina and I work, side by side, to clear up the customers and get them out the door. With a few more swipes of the last of the merchandise our store had, we are done.

I hurry to lock the doors and turn off the outside lights. Gina closes her register as I look at the empty store. "Man, the first day back is going to be a nightmare too."

"It is," she agrees. "But that'll be day shift's problem, not ours, thank God. Hurry up and close down your register. We need to get the hell out of here."

Moving back to my register, I quickly take the money out to drop it in the safe and punch in the code to shut it down. The machine has worked more than it's ever had to before, with all the sells it had to make on this crazy day.

Just as we get it all finished, the wind picks up. The howling of it makes me shiver and I find the rain is falling in sheets. "We're going to get wet," Gina says as we look out the glass door.

THE WINDOWS HAVE BEEN BOARDED up and we were instructed to place a piece of plywood on the door before we left. It's leaning against the wall next to it and I don't see us being able to accomplish the act, now the wind has picked up.

Gina picks up the hammer and six nails that were left for us to do the job. "I'll hold it up and you hammer," I say as I pick up the heavy thing.

Then into the rain we go. Me with the heavy board and Gina with the things to put it up with. I can hardly see as the rain pelts me in the face. The wind has it coming at us, sideways.

Gina locks the door then I do my best to get the large piece of wood to the door and hold it while she hammers in the nails until all six are used. She tosses the hammer in the empty ice container and locks it up.

Finished, we can go home. So, we go to get into our cars, soaking wet and cold. "Good luck," I call out to her.

"You too, Camilla. Hope to see you soon!"

Getting into my car, I'm a shaking, shivering mess. I start the car and ease out of the parking lot, barely able to see as the rain is coming down so hard.

We should've closed an hour ago but with the onslaught of people we didn't make it out before the storm hit us, even though we were told to close the store early, we're barely making it out at midnight.

I can go about fifteen miles an hour and even that seems too fast. The road is covered with water. The windshield wipers are doing nothing to help me see. I'm most likely going to end up in a damn ditch.

Am I doomed to spend this hurricane in a ditch with nothing between me and the storm but my car...?

49

CYPRIAN

The rain is pouring and the thunder is rumbling so loudly, I can hear it before I open the garage door. I'm going out to get Cami. She hasn't answered her cell phone for me at all. But I saw the hordes of people at her store and her car there, so I know she was merely swamped and not ignoring my calls. It's midnight and I'd assume she's made it home but I can't let her stay there.

Taking the four-wheel-drive truck, I make my way out of the garage and am met with a torrential downpour. I knew it was bad out here but not this bad!

I have to go slowly down the driveway that has water flowing down it as if it's a stream instead of a paved road. I have to roll my window down to punch in the code to open the gate and get soaked doing it.

As I pull out of the gate, I see a set of headlights to the left and turn toward them to see if that's her. The car is barely moving as I go toward it. The rain's so hard, I can't tell if it's her until I get right on it.

Rolling my window down as I see it is her, I wave at her to follow me and turn around and drive around to get in front of her. My large truck will shield some of the rain and make it easier for her to drive, I hope.

Going at a snail's pace, I pick up my cell and call her. "Cyprian," she answers the call.

"Follow me to my place," I say in as a commanding tone as I dare to with the tenacious woman.

"I'm not about to argue with you. I'm freaking out right now. I was thinking I'd have to spend the storm in a ditch or worse. Your place sounds like Heaven to me. I also left the soup I got myself to eat, while I ride out the storm, at the store. So, I was going to be starving too. Thank you."

RELIEVED TO HEAR she's grateful and won't be a pain in the ass about my help, I say, "Good, and I have tons of food, just follow me, Cami." I end the call as I want her full attention on driving and find myself smiling like an idiot as I look at her headlights in my rearview mirror.

I'm going to have her home with me and she cannot leave anytime soon as the hurricane will keep her ass trapped with me. I realize that sounds a little creepy but I'll take her any way I can get her.

Finally, we get to the gate again and I'm soaked once more as I roll the window down to put the code in. The gate opens and in we go, all the way to the garage. I open two of the doors, so she can pull into a place I made for her, just in case I did manage to get her here.

Once I have the garage doors shut behind us, I feel so much better. Getting out of the truck, I realize just how wet I am and when I see her, I find she's completely drenched. "My Lord, look at you!"

She gives me a frown. "I'm freezing, Cyprian. Do you think I could borrow some of your cozy pajamas?"

I nod and take her hand, leading her inside the warm house. "Of course. A nice hot shower is what you should take first. I'll warm us up something to eat while you do that. You can sleep in the bedroom across the hall from mine."

I catch her smiling. "That's very nice of you. Thank you. Were you looking for me, or on your way out?"

"Looking for you. I tried to call you several times but I saw you were busy at work. I was going to ask you to come here, anyway. That little apartment of yours isn't sturdy enough, in my opinion." I lead her up the stairs and to the room across the hall from mine.

When I open the door, she looks around and whistles. "Man, this is a hell of a lot nicer than where I was going to spend this hurricane. I had planned on making the tub my bed for the duration of the storm. You know, in case parts of my house blew away."

I SHUDDER at the thought then say, "The bathroom is fully stocked and I've already taken the privilege of putting some things for you to wear in the closet and the drawers. I had bought you some things if you'll recall." I gesture for her to go inside. "I'll be in the kitchen when you're done. I'll be waiting to eat with you."

She turns to look at me with a quizzical expression. "You were planning on me staying, huh?"

"I wasn't going to take no for an answer. Your safety is more important to me than almost anything. I was prepared to throw you over my shoulder and bring you, kicking and screaming, if I had to." Then I close the door and leave her alone.

I'm trying so hard to keep my hopes at a moderate level that she will see fit to forgive me. I know there can be nothing physical right now, anyway. That does take the pressure, to get her into my bed, off.

After changing into dry clothes, a dark brown set of pajamas, I go to the kitchen and open a bottle of expensive red wine and take a tray of lobster rolls, my chef left for me, out and pop them into the oven I already had heating up. I see a casserole dish of homemade mac and cheese and pop that into the oven as well. A salad is in another bowl and I take it out and place it into a nice crystal bowl and decide to set the table in the small dining area that has large windows, so we can watch the storm while we eat by the fire's light of the fireplace that's in that room.

I find long white candles in the cutlery cabinet in the room and find the set of dishes I want to use too. I smile all the while as I place a deep red table cloth over the small, round table.

White dishes accent it perfectly and I find the scene gorgeous and more romantic than any meal we've consumed together thus far. And I pray many more will come.

The sound of the oven timer beeping has me going back to the kitchen and finding the food is nearly ready. Our salads and wine, I take back to place on the table and then go back to get the dishes out of the oven.

When I walk back in, I see her, standing at the island in the middle of the large kitchen. Her feet are bare and she has on the deep blue, silk pajama set I bought for her on our day long date.

HER HAIR IS wet and hanging in loose spiral curls around her freshly washed face. "You look gorgeous."

She smiles and looks down. "I look like a drowned rat but thank you."

Picking up the hot dishes with some pot holders, I nod in the direction of the drawer with the trivets in it. "Can you grab two of the trivets and bring them?"

She grabs a couple and follows me to the dining area. I hear her gasp as she sees how I've set it all up. "Cyprian, this is beautiful!"

"Thank you. Can you place those on the table, so I can put these down?"

She hurries to do that and I set the things down and pull her chair out. She looks up at me as she sits. "Thank you. This is really nice. I was going to eat cold soup out of a can if the electricity went off. This is so much better."

I take a seat and pour us each a glass of wine. "Being that we're trapped here, together, all alone, I'd like to initiate a truce. No talking about anything we might argue over. I don't want either of us to feel upset at all during this storm. Agreed?"

She nods as she sips her wine. "Agreed. We're just a couple of people who are forced by nature to be together right now. We can talk about all kinds of things. Just not anything about us, as a couple, or anything that's in our past, as a couple. Deal, Cyprian. So, tell me about your appendix bursting. Was it the worst pain you've ever felt before?"

No, losing her was.

IN THE VEIN of staying away from fights, I don't utter the thought. "I have never been in more physical pain in my life. I thought I was dying."

Her hand touches mine as her blue eyes find mine. "Cyprian, I did come to see you in the hospital. When I heard about you, the next night, I tried to leave work and get to you. But things went crazy for me. An all-night audit nearly did me in and I wanted you to know I was worried about you."

"You were?" I ask as her hand moves back and forth over mine. "So, why didn't you come and see me, Cami?"

"This may sound stupid but I got to your door and heard everyone talking and laughing. Nurses were mentioned. Pretty nurses. Pretty nurses who'd be taking care of you. It sent a bad taste to my mouth and I left." She looks sheepish about her actions.

I want to bring up her date with my doctor but that will certainly be an argument, so I leave it out that I know that tidbit of information. "As you can see, I didn't follow my parents' advice. All on my own, might I add. I had to put up a fight about it but I won."

She blinks at me a few times then points at one of the dishes. "Would you pass me that? It looks delicious."

It seems she's stifling something she wanted to say but I let it go and take her plate instead. "I'll put it on the plate for you. It's hot. Lobster rolls, mac and cheese, and salad is what I pulled out of the fridge my chef stocked for us, for the hurricane."

"For us?" she asks as she looks at me with a surprised expression. "Just how long have you been making the plan for me to be here for this hurricane?"

"Since I saw the weather report that said it was coming our way. I had the staff working overtime to get everything taken care of so we'd be safe. I care about you, Cami." I place the food on her plate and set it down in front of her, seeing a frown on her face. I don't ask her why she has it, I think I know why.

THERE'RE MOST likely things running through her head, she'd like to say to me but is thinking better of it. I pretend not to notice anything as I go about making my own plate. From the corner of my eye, I see her take a drink of the wine then she shakes her head as if shaking off her bad thoughts.

I hear her sigh then she says, "Well, I am glad you came to find me and I am glad to have your hospitality during this rough time. I am grateful for you and I want you to know, I care for you too, Cyprian. If things were different..."

I stop her. "No, no. No talking about anything like that. So, tell me how crazy people were acting at your store. I saw, on the news, some footage at various stores and it looked like a mob scene. Was yours that bad?"

She nods as she swallows a bite of food. "It was a nightmare. Gina was the only one with me. And just as we got the store closed, we had to nail a piece of plywood on the front door. That's when we got drenched. People were acting insanely."

"At least you made it out, unscathed, Cami. That's what really matters. I saw one report where a cashier was pushed down when she was unable to make a gasoline sale to a small man who wanted to fill up milk jugs with gas. That was on the ten o'clock news."

"A little man, with red hair?" she asks in surprise.

"I believe so," I say as I watch her eyes go big.

"He was in my store. And boy did he have a fit when I told him I couldn't sell him the gas. I guess I'm lucky he couldn't get behind the counter to get to me." She laughs then and smiles. "How funny, huh?"

"I suppose that's one way to look at it. I'd have been one pissed off man if I'd seen him push you around." I take a drink of the wine to calm my sudden onslaught of protectiveness.

I find her smiling as she takes a bite of the lobster roll. I smile too as I think how great it's going so far. And wonder if we can both manage to keep our words and tempers under control for the entire hurricane. If we can manage that then maybe she'll see fit to give me one more chance to prove I can be the man she deserves.

But what will I do if she doesn't...?

50

CAMILLA

As we walk up the stairs to go to bed, I notice Cyprian's face go tight and his hand goes to just above his right hip. "Does it hurt?" I ask him as I put my hand on the small of his back.

"Up and down the stairs is the worst," he tells me. "Other than that, it's not really bothersome."

I keep my hand on his back to steady him as much as I can until we get to the top of the stairs. The thought about telling him I went out on a date with his doctor, is banging at my brain. My conscience is telling me to speak up before he finds that out some other way.

We made the truce, though and that would be a fight for sure. So, I keep my mouth shut about that. Instead, I say, "Will you let me see to the wound, Cyprian?"

He nods as we get to his bedroom. "I have the stuff in here to take care of it."

I FOLLOW him into his bedroom. The room where good times and bad times were had. His television on the wall is on and it reminds me of what I saw on it the last time I saw it on. My stomach goes tight and I have to shake off the bad feelings.

"Get into bed and I'll take care of you," I tell him as I help him into the bed.

After he lies down, I push his shirt up and see the small area where they made the incision to remove his appendix. Six stitches were used to close it up and it looks pretty good. "How's it look to you, doc?" he asks with a grin.

"Excellent workmanship, but with Dr. Jenkins as your surgeon that's to be expected." I take an alcohol wipe out of the packet and find him frowning. "This burns, I know. It's important to keep the area very sterile."

"No, it's not that. It's nothing," he says but I feel he does have something to say. "Go ahead."

Just before I place the alcohol wipe on him, I find myself asking, "If you have something you want to say, you can say it, Cyprian. I promise not to get mad at you."

"How'd you know my surgeon's name?" he asks then grits his teeth as I press the wipe to his stitches.

Suddenly, I realize what I've said and panic. "Um, uh, I told you I went to the hospital. I saw him. I saw him come out of your room."

"He doesn't wear a nametag," he says as he looks at me.

"No, I know he doesn't. You see, he was one of my professors when I was a freshman in college. That's how I know him," I feel the guilt of withholding information to be too much as I put some of the antibiotic ointment on the area then place a bandage over it. "You should keep this covered. That way the stitches won't catch on any material and it'll stay much cleaner and actually heal faster."

"Good to know," he says then pulls his shirt down to cover himself. "Do you mind going into the bathroom and getting my antibiotic pills. I'm supposed to take one within this hour."

I nod and go to get the medicine and find I'm mad at myself for feeling so torn about telling him about the date I had. The man has done much worse and we were not together, so there's nothing to feel bad about.

So why do I then?

HE'S SITTING up in the bed when I come back in with the pill and a small cup of water. "Here you go," I say as I hand him the things.

He takes them and swallows the pill with the water then places the empty cup on the nightstand. "Thank you, nurse." He smiles and pats the place on the other side of him. "I don't suppose you'd like to cuddle tonight. The storm is raging and we could lose power."

As if he's magic, a loud clap of thunder has us both looking surprised and the lights go out.

"Shit!" I say and have to put my hands on the bed to make my way to the other side of it. "We can keep our clothes on. There's nothing wrong with that."

Climbing into the bed, I find his left arm wrapping around me. He pulls me close to him. "I could use the company too. That wind sounds a bit scary, doesn't it?"

"It does. The lightning and thunder, the hard rain, and the winds combine to make chilling sounds." I snuggle into his side, relishing how great it feels. "Cyprian, why can't it always be just like this?" Then I realize I've spoken about something our truce has banned. "Sorry, don't answer that."

His lips touch the side of my head. "The answer is that it can be. It can be just like this or any way you want it to be."

My heart hurts with how badly it wants to believe him. "Let's talk about something else. There's been something weighing heavily on me and I want to get it out in the open. Mostly because it was a one-time thing that won't be happening again."

"What's weighing on you?" he asks as he strokes my hair and I catch him taking in a whiff of it then sighing.

"I went out on a date with your doctor." I thought the weight would vanish but it's still there, so I go on. "We went to eat and then he took me back home and we kissed at my front door."

"Oh," he says but I can feel his heart rate increase. "You said it was a one-time thing. So, I suppose the kiss wasn't great."

"It was okay but when I kissed you, it was much better. Do you suppose you've ruined me for anyone else?" I ask with a laugh.

"God, I hope so," he says then kisses the top of my head. "Thank you for telling me that. I have something I'd like to get off my chest too."

Now, I'm scared!

WITH CYPRIAN, the things he wants to get off his chest just might make me crazy with jealousy or sick. "Okay," I say with much hesitation.

"I knew you went out with him. He told me just before he released me today. He had no idea I knew you, though."

Leaning up to look at him as much as the lightning outside will allow me to see him, I ask, "So, you knew that?"

He nods and kisses the tip of my nose. "I was jealous if you want to know how I felt when he told me the name of the woman he was interested in. And you have yet to let him know you won't be going out anymore."

Lying back on his chest, I say, "I know. I told him I was coming out of a relationship. But I suppose he's going to keep calling if I don't tell him I won't be seeing him anymore. He's a nice man. A great catch. But I can't be with someone who doesn't stimulate me. I mean, he does stimulate my mind. We have tons in common in that area."

"You mean, sexually, don't you?" he asks me with a low voice. A silky, sexy voice.

"That's what I mean," I say then sigh as I move my fingertip over the soft pajama top he has on. "I see no reason to lead the man on when that kiss left me wanting no more of them from him."

"You're not just saying that for my benefit, are you?" he asks me as his hand caresses my shoulder.

"I'm not. I wish I was. If you want me to be honest, I think another man is exactly what I need, to get over you."

"I don't want you to get over me. I want you to tell me what it is you want in a man. I want to be whatever it is you want."

I lie still and fight myself not to make this into an argument. We are just two people talking about what we like in a person who we see a future with. That's all!

"You tell me what you want in a woman, first."

"I never had any want for a woman, for more than one thing, until I met you. So, let me educate you on the perfect woman for me, Cami. She has to be my intellectual equal. She has to be caring, sweet, and supportive. She has to be beautiful, inside and out. Her hair has to feel like silk when I touch it and smell amazing when she's lying next to me. Her voice has to be on the deep side, smooth as a Tennessee whiskey, and soft as cashmere. But that's not all. She has to have these deep blue eyes that I could look into forever, without ever getting tired of it. Her juicy red lips must look pretty with a smile and a pout. She must stir places inside me nothing and no one ever has before. Tell me, Camilla Petit, do you know anyone like the woman I've just described to you?"

His words have my heart pounding and my eyes are tearing but I don't want to cry. I have to swallow back the lump in my throat to answer him, "You are very good with words, Cyprian."

"Those are my exact thoughts about you, Cami. They came straight from my heart. I meant every single word I just said. So, now it's your turn to tell me the kind of man you're looking for."

"What if I told you that I have no idea what kind of man I want to spend the rest of my life with?" I ask him as I really don't know.

"Is that why you're always telling me to be who I am and you'll like me or you won't? Because you don't even know what it is you want? That makes a lot more sense to me."

"Good, so you be who you want and I can stop saying that to you. This was a great talk, I think."

"For you, maybe. Not so much for me," he says as he holds me tight as the wind picks up more speed. "Crap, it's getting bad out there."

"Why was the talk not so great for you, Cyprian?" I ask as I rest my hand on his chest, feeling his heart beating.

"I'm a person who has used books and knowledge to fill my brain and make me the person I am. I've never gone on instinct, alone. I take things very literally. I make decisions based on evidence and facts, never do I make them with my gut feelings. Until you came along. You hit me right in my gut and instinct told me I had to get to know you. I fought it, at first. I called it animal magnetism and lust. I lied to myself that was all there was."

"So, I brought out this thing in you that you've never exercised. Instinct. Huh, that's pretty cool. You see, as a scientist, I too rely on facts and data to make my decisions. In that way, we are alike. But I've also relied on instinct from time to time, especially in my personal life." I lift my head to look at him and find him staring back at me.

Lightning flashes, making his eyes light up and I find my lips pressing to his without even thinking about it. Perhaps I've over-thought everything.

Our mouths move together, not in heated passion but in a hello kind of way. A way that says, I've missed you. A way that says, I love you.

When our lips part, I find him looking at me with softness in his expression. "Camilla Petit, I love you. I love you more than I knew I could."

I gulp then say, "I love you too, Cyprian. But I don't know if love is enough. I don't know if you are capable of turning away from your old life and that style. I'm deeply afraid of you becoming bored with me. So afraid, it makes it hard to trust a relationship with you."

"I cannot see myself ever getting bored of you, Cami. I don't know what the future holds but I know what I want right now and I want you and only you. I know I've made huge mistakes, the likes of which you've never had to deal with. But I can make amends for them. I wish I could go back and change them but we both know I can't. So, tell me what you expect. It may sound insane to you but I need to know."

"Okay," I say as I'm seeing more inside him than I realized was there. "I expect you to be faithful to me. I expect you to never bring into the bedroom anything we haven't discussed beforehand. For a while, this trust me thing, you want, will have to end. Before you bring in any kind of thing into our love making, I want a heads up."

"Got it," he says with a sigh of relief. "I can do that. I can do anything. With you, Cami, everything feels so amazing, anyway. Just lying here with you and talking, is better than any night I've had at any party. I swear that to you."

I graze his cheek with my hand and kiss him again. I know he can't do anything sexual and am keeping the kiss chaste enough not to provoke that. Moving my lips off his, I lie back down, using his large bicep as my pillow and look up at the ceiling that sparks with the light show outside. "Cyprian, this will be the last chance for us. I can't keep coming back."

"I know that. But you have to know there will be disagreements. But I promise not to make huge mistakes, anymore. Okay?"

"Okay, I know fights will happen but leave the ladies out of things and I can handle almost anything else. So, we are agreeing to give this thing one more shot," I say then find myself snuggling into his body and feeling more relief than I have felt in forever.

"Are you ready to try to sleep, baby?" he asks me with a kiss on my cheek.

"I am," I say and feel better about everything.

How did we manage to find each other in the middle of a raging storm and come to such an agreement? How will this all work out?

Can I really believe Cyprian can be happy with just me...?

51

CYPRIAN

Though a storm rages outside, I slept like a baby with Cami in my arms. Her soft snores leave warmth on my neck where she's nuzzled her face. I slide my hand up and down her silk pajama covered back.

Content is how I feel. Happy, satisfied even more so than I knew was possible without any sex occurring between us at all. She has to be the one for me. I didn't even know this type of feeling existed!

THE PROPER AMOUNT of time to wait before proposing is foremost on my mind. The perfect engagement ring, the perfect venue to be married in are also right there. I wonder how long she thinks an engagement should last. I hope not a long time!

"CYPRIAN," she groans as she stirs. Her hand moves over my chest and her lips touch my neck. "Are you awake, baby?"

"I am," I say then kiss the top of her head, her curls a chaos of spirals and fuzzy ends.

She picks her head up and looks at me. "Have we survived the hurricane?"

"I'm not sure. I do feel like I'm in Heaven, waking up with you like this." I kiss her red cheek where she was lying on it.

She smiles and puts her head down on my chest. I couldn't sleep in the pajamas as I'm used to sleeping naked, so I got up and pulled them off sometime during the night. She begins to realize that fact as she runs her hand over my chest. She inches down until she finds out I'm totally naked. "Bad boy," she murmurs.

With a low growl, I say, "Only with you." I take her hand and kiss it and wish I could do more than that but I can't.

"I'm going to go down and make us some breakfast. I'm going to bring it up to you. You can take a shower while I do that." She goes to get up and I hold her still.

"You are forgetting, we have no electricity. The kitchen should still be running. If the backup generator came on. But we have a water well, that means if there's no electricity, there's no water. So, no showers for us until we get some juice back in this place.

"It's still raining, isn't it?" she asks as she pulls her head off my chest and sits up, looking toward one of the windows.

"Yep," I say as I look out the window too. "But I bet those crews are already getting to work on restoring power. We'll just have to make do with what we have."

She runs her hand over her massive amount of hair. "No water! My hair!"

Stifling a chuckle, I get out of bed and hear her make a little groan as I walk, naked, to the bathroom. I wrap a towel around my ass to help myself not get too heated up and find the package of rubber bands I bought for her a while back. When I come back with them, I see a smile curve her lips. "I have saved the day."

She takes them from me as she agrees, "You have." She climbs out of the bed and hurries off to the bathroom. "I'll get my hair tamed and go down to get our breakfast."

"I can go down, you don't need to bring it up to me," I tell her as I pull my pajamas back on.

She stops and spins around, shaking her finger at me. "You will not. You told me the stairs were hard on you and I won't let you go up and down them for at least another day. I will be waiting on you today, Cyprian."

Though that sounds amazing, I have to protest some, just to make her spark a bit. "I can do it, Cami. You don't have to spoil me."

I SIT on the edge of the bed and watch her as she walks back to me. Her hands move over my shoulders as she looks at me with serious eyes that speak to me. "I don't consider it spoiling you. I want to take care of you. Please let me." She ends her plea with a kiss on my lips that sends shards of pure happiness through me.

"Well, if you're going to say, please, then I have to allow you to take care of me. No one, since my nanny, has taken care of me. It might be nice." I lie back as she pushes at me, gently.

"Good, it's settled. Now, since we're on our own here, I'll go into the library and get us some things to read. Any preferences?" She walks away to tend to herself and I think about what I'd like to read.

When she comes back out, I tell her what I want, "Would you bring that large book on the middle shelf of the first bookcase next to the door of the library? It's full of Shakespeare's plays. I want us to read Romeo and Juliet, together. That sounds fun to me."

With a smile and a laugh, she walks out the bedroom door. "As long as you realize, we cannot act out the love scene, my Romeo."

"I'm aware of my limitations, my Juliet."

She leaves me alone but I've never felt less alone in my life. She's here with me and I never want to spend another night without her. And I want her to quit that job which will keep her at work until late most nights.

It's bad enough school is about to start up again. But those are day classes and I work days, anyway. Nights must be for us. And now I must figure out how to get her to do that.

. . .

BEFORE I KNOW IT, she's back in the bedroom with a tray of food and the book. "I have pineapple, orange juice, scrambled eggs, bacon, and milk to make sure you have some calcium. Whole wheat toast rounds out our breakfast." She places the tray over my lap, as I sit up straight, then she kisses my cheek. "Will there be anything else, my lord?"

With a smile at her willingness to see after me, I say, "Only for you to climb up in this bed with me. I must feed my lady, so she too gains great strength. In only a month, I will bring you to my bed chamber with a goal in mind."

She laughs as she climbs up on the bed, next to me. "A goal, you say? What kind of goal does my lord have for me?"

I bite my lower lip as I put a piece of bacon to her lips and she takes it into her sweet mouth. "The goal is to fill your belly with my seed, my lady."

The whites of her eyes grow as her eyes grow large. She nearly chokes on the food and I find myself feeling bad about saying that as I gave her a bite. I hand her a glass of juice and she drinks some then says, "Cyprian, you're joking, right?"

Shaking my head, I take her hand in mine. "I am not joking, Cami. I want to do this all the right way and I may have been kidding a bit about only a month from now. But I want it all with you. The whole enchilada. The marriage, the family, the whole thing, baby. It's all I've thought about since we made up last night."

She looks stunned and I find it hard to believe. Her lips open then close then do that several more times before she says, "I have a career I'm only just about to begin. I have one more year of college then I'm on to working in the field I've spent so much time learning about. Kids are far from now. Say, five years or maybe more."

"We can wait on that then. Although, I'd really like you to consider doing that sooner than five years. But that's negotiable. Everything is." I give her a bite of eggs. "How long of an engagement would you like to have?"

Shaking her head, she swallows then says, "Cyprian, we're just dating. That's all we're doing right now. We're seeing if we can become people who know they can depend on one another in this life."

"Haven't we just proven that? I sought you out to be sure you were safe in a terrible storm and you want to take care of me when I'm down. What else is there to prove about how much we care for each other?" I ask her and offer her a sip of milk.

She holds up her hand, "Lactose intolerant. You drink that."

I take a drink and watch her wheels spinning about what I've just said. So, I toss it all out there, since she's incorporating it into her mind. "I want you to quit your job. I want you to move in with me, let that little place go. I want you to drive the car I gave you. Go to school and do no more than that. I will pay for everything. And I'll give you your own account that I'll make regular deposits to."

"I don't want to be a kept woman." She shakes her head to emphasize just how much she doesn't want that.

"IT WON'T BE like that. I merely want to help you through, what will be the hardest school year. Once you begin your career, if you want no money from me, then I'll stop the deposits and you can do with the account whatever you want. And if you do want me to keep putting money into it, I will do that. Whatever you want, Cami. Anything you want, I will give it to you, freely and willingly." I take her hands in mine and smile at her as she looks shocked.

I can feel her hands shaking and see her body doing that too. "Cyprian, I'm afraid I'll lose myself if I allow that."

"How?" I ask her as she's making too much out of it. "Your car will remain in the garage. You will have money and time to do what you need to in order to become the rock star scientist I know you're on your way to being. I merely want to help make it easier for you to reach the stars you're grasping at. Let me, Cami. Let me help you. It would be the only thing I've ever done for another human being. Please, let me!"

"I'll have to think about it. My independence is a thing I cherish," she tells me as she searches my eyes for understanding.

"I have been somewhat independent my entire life. I've had financial security but the security of people, I've lacked. I want to provide you the thing which has been provided to me. And from you, I want the security of knowing I have a partner in this life. I didn't realize I even wanted one until I met you."

"Cyprian, I feel as if you are making me your everything," she says as tears glisten in her eyes.

"I am. And once our children come then they too will be part of our everything." I kiss her cheek and find it warm. "Don't be afraid of this. Don't let fear of me finding you boring, do that to us. Have no fear of that, I don't."

"Just because you say not to have it, doesn't make it stop. And now I fear you will suck me into a vortex that will turn me into a spoiled rich woman. Not a thing I ever saw myself being." She looks at me with fear and I find it funny.

WITH A CHUCKLE, I say, "I have money. When you get me, you get that too. We will share our lives. When I get you, I get love and companionship. No need to worry, we'll share everything."

She takes the juice off the tray and downs it like it's a shot then looks off into space as she says, "I'm going to be driving a Lambo to school. I'm going to have access to more money than I ever have. I'm going to be Mrs. Cyprian Girard, one day."

"One day soon, I hope. If you'll have me," I say then pop a piece of toast into her mouth that's hanging ajar.

She chews it then looks at me. "I have nothing to offer you."

Taking her by the chin, I give her a wink. "What you have to offer is more valuable than anything in the entire world. You see, love is what I've been poor in. All I need is your love and understanding as I grow into the man I will become with you by my side. You are the missing element in my world. Do you think that of me?"

She blinks rapidly as she thinks. "My life was missing something. I didn't know it was. It wasn't obvious. You see, I have always been one who falls in love much too easily. And men fall in love with me too easily as well. Cyprian, all my relationships, which have been but a few, have ended with the men leaving me. I haven't broken up with anyone, except you."

"And I have left you once too. That happened in the past. It's over and we are something completely different. You were young back then. You don't have to worry about me leaving you. I love you. I adore you. I cherish you. And I'm never letting you go. I will dance through hell to make you happy. I will climb mountains to get you the stars you want." I stop talking as she looks even sadder.

"Cyprian, I hate your parents. This will never work," she says as tears start to flow.

I LAUGH AND HUG HER. "Don't most wives hate their in-laws? Not a big deal. Hell, we won't even spend holidays with them. They celebrate in ways we wouldn't want us or our kids to be involved in."

"My parents will love you, I think. I mean, you are very good to me. And the fact you saved me during this hurricane will show them more about your character than I could ever tell them. But a wedding would mean all of our families have to come together and that's worrisome."

"Then we will elope. There is nothing you can come up with that I will not have an answer to," I tell her then move the tray of half-eaten food away and push her down and kiss her to let her know everything will be fine.

As long as we're together, it will be fine, won't it...

BOOK 8: THE LIBERTINE

A Bad Boy Billionaire Romance

By Michelle Love

52

CAMILLA

The lush foliage of New Orleans looms under us as Cyprian's private jet flies over my hometown. He looks out the window, leaning over me as he's given me the window seat. "It looks positively uninhabited down there. Where do all the people live?"

"Underneath the canopy of trees. Have you ever taken an airboat ride?" I ask him as he seems to be intrigued with the way the terrain looks wild and free.

"I have not. Do you think that's something we could do? Does your family own one?" He looks excited.

I GIGGLE. "No, but there are tons of swamp tours. It's been awhile since I've been on one. Since my entire family is home for my last visit of the summer, I think one is in order. I hope you don't find alligators frightening. The men who drive those things delight in trying to scare anyone they see the least bit afraid of the creatures."

"I've never been around any before." He wraps his arm around me and holds me tight. "Can I count on you to protect me, Cami?"

"Sure, Cyprian. I'll do my best," I say as we see the small, private airport near my family's home break out of the trees. "Here it is. It won't be long now. And there's Papa's car, waiting for us."

"I am beginning to get nervous," he tells me as he slips his arm off my shoulders and takes my hand. "Have you told them everything?"

With a nod, I say, "I have. I told them we've been seeing each other for a couple of months and moved in together two weeks ago. I told them about me quitting my job and how you're going to pay my way through the rest of college and all that jazz. My father was a bit apprehensive but told me he trusted my judgment."

"Okay, so there's nothing I need to know other than that, right?" he asks as I shake my head. "What about my parents? What did you tell them about them?"

"Oh, well, about them." I scratch my head as I kind of sugar coated them to my parents. "You see, here's the thing, I kind of embellished them a bit."

"Embellished? You mean lied, Cami?" He looks at me with fear in his dark eyes.

"Lied is too strong of a word. I told them your father is retired and lives alone in Clemson in a mansion. And that's true. I told them your mother is the owner of a nightclub in L.A. and that's true too." I look at him to see what he thinks about that.

"It's an adult nightclub," he says. "And she is an ex-stripper."

"Who cares about what she did in the past? Not me!"

He shakes his head. "And I am to leave that out, I suppose."

"Please," I say as we start to land. "They don't need to know everything. If we play our cards right, we'll be three kids into a marriage before our families ever have to meet."

He smiles with my words and kisses me, gently. "When you put it that way, how can I argue?"

"You can't," I say and take a deep breath as the small plane starts to descend. "I hate this part."

. . .

He holds my hand a bit tighter as we land and gives me that smile that makes my heart go pitter patter. The last couple of weeks have been so nice and quiet and completely amazing. I still worked, as I gave them my two weeks' notice and had to give them time to hire another person. But now I'm officially free from that job and feel excited about being able to start school in the fall with nothing else to do but learn.

Once the jet lands, we get out and my father and younger brother get out of Papa's Lincoln Continental to greet us. The warm, sultry air hits us as we go down the stairs someone from the airport has pushed up against the plane. I find myself waving like I'm in a parade as my father and brother watch us. "Hi!"

Papa meets us at the bottom of the stairs and picks me up as he hugs me tightly. "Mon canard, I've missed you," Papa says with his thick French accent."

"I've missed you too, Papa," I say as he lets me go. Then I gesture to the gorgeous man to my right. "This is Cyprian Girard. Cyprian, my father, Thomas Petit."

Cyprian extends his hand and my father takes it in a firm handshake as Cyprian says, "It's an honor to meet the man who raised such a wonderful woman."

Papa smiles at me then looks back at Cyprian as he lets go of his hand. "Call me Tommy, Cyprian." He gestures to my brother, "This is Camilla's younger brother, Carlyle."

My brother shakes his hand. "Nice to meet you, Cyprian."

"You too, Carlyle. Your sister tells me you're going to LSU in Baton Rouge. She says you're majoring in business."

We follow them to the car as Carlyle says, over his shoulder. "I am."

Cyprian looks at me, giving me a wink. "You should let me know when you're ready for an internship. I can offer you one next summer at Libertine Investments if you'd like. It comes with a car and a one bedroom apartment while you're working."

I watch my brother's blue eyes light up. "Oh, yeah?"

"Yeah," Cyprian says with a smile. "So, you just let me know before March of this coming year and I'll get that approved by the board."

Papa looks at us as he gets to the car. "Don't wait, son. Tell the man, yes, right now."

Carlyle smiles and nods. "The answer is yes, Cyprian. Thank you so much."

Cyprian opens the back door, letting me get in first. He whispers, "I think this is going well, so far. Don't you?"

"I do," I tell him then kiss his cheek.

I see my father's eyes glance at us and a smile moves over his face. "You two look sweet together. My daughter has never looked as beautiful as she does under your arm, Cyprian."

I blush and lean my head on his shoulder. "Thanks, Papa."

CYPRIAN SIGHS WITH RELIEF, I suppose. Things are going well. It looks as if we'll have no problems with my family. But he's yet to meet my big sister. She's always been protective over me. It was she who bawled out two of my past boyfriends when they dumped me. Both with no real explanation as to why they found it better to leave me than to try to work things out with me.

She thinks I'm perfect, I know I'm not. I know I can be hard to deal with at times. I know how I was with those other guys. Sometimes I was cold and distant. At times, I was bitchy. With Cyprian, I'm trying to watch out for those things. I'm really trying with him, more so than I've ever tried before with anyone else.

"Your sister arrived a couple of days ago, Camilla. Her husband had to stay in Cape Town to work," my father tells me. "Do not bring up his absence as she gets teary-eyed when anyone does. I fear their marriage has hit a rocky patch."

My heart freezes. If she's having a rough time, she tends to make others have one as well. "Is she keeping it together for the kids, though? Not wearing her heart on her sleeve, is she?" I ask, hopefully.

My brother looks back at me. "She is doing well for who she is." He looks at Cyprian. "Our oldest sister is a bit much at times. Her passionate personality can be somewhat hard to take. She is much more French than any of us, including our Papa. And your last name is French as well, Cyprian. Tell us how your family is. Is your father a passionate man? Is he married to a French woman?"

"My father isn't married," Cyprian says as he ignores my hand tapping on his leg to let him know to guard his words. "My mother is American and my papa is of French descent but he's never been abroad. He was born in the states to a family who was third generation immigrants. He has no real connection to that country any longer."

"So, your parents are divorced?" my father asks. "Mon conard, has been tight-lipped about your family."

I LEAN over and whisper to Cyprian, "That's his little nickname for me. It means, my little duck."

He leans over and kisses my cheek. "I know. I think it's cute."

I blush as I seem to have forgotten, Cyprian is a very smart man. I seem to forget so much about him and who he is. Perhaps I have a problem getting to really know people. Maybe that's what had my other relationships going south. I should pay more attention to what he says, I think.

"So, they are divorced?" Papa asks, again.

Before Cyprian can answer, I do, "No, they were never married. Can this inquisition end now? I don't want Cyprian put on the spot about his family. His family is small. He, his father, and his mother makes up the little family who are very busy living their own lives."

Cyprian gives my knee a squeeze. "I don't mind answering your father's questions."

"I mind them asking too many things," I say and peck his cheek. "Let me guard you a bit. Once we get home, you will be met with more than you will care for."

"She's right," Carlyle tells him as he looks back at him. "Catarina is one hell of a big sister."

Cyprian chuckles. "Is she now? A passionate creature who looks after her younger siblings. What's not to like about that?"

"You'll see," I say as we pull into the driveway of my parents' modest home on the outskirts of New Orleans. "For here we are."

Why did I decide to bring him home to meet my family...?

53

CYPRIAN

Teal eyes land on me as we enter the Petit home. Straight black hair frames her plump face, which is beautiful. Her bronze lips part as she looks me up and down. "You must be Cyprian Girard. Just so you know, I have already researched you. You were news, recently. How are you feeling after having your appendix removed?"

"This is my sister, Catarina," Cami tells me as she gestures to the bold woman who continues to look me over.

I reach out for her hand and she places it in mine. I kiss the top of it as she narrows her eyes at me. "It's a pleasure to meet you, Catarina. Your sister has told me much about you."

"So you will understand when I dig deep into you, Cyprian," she says, making a chill run through me.

CAMILLA HAS MADE IT CLEAR, I am not to go divulging too much about my past with women. She thinks her family would never allow her to be with me if they knew it all.

Cami shakes her head. "No, Rina. He is not to be bothered with your incessant curiosity. He's been through surgery only a couple of weeks ago and I am fiercely protective over him. So, don't push me."

Catarina looks at her younger sister with a smirk on her face. "You will have to leave his side sometime, dear sister."

Cami looks at me and winks. "Stay close, Cyprian. Lions await you."

I nod and find another woman coming into the room. "And this is the new man in my baby girl's life. It's nice to meet you, Cyprian. I am Anashe, but you can call me, Ana." Cami's mother has a British accent, as do the majority of people who come from Cape Town, South Africa, I suppose.

I take her extended hand, delivering a kiss to the top of it as I bow a bit. "It's a pleasure to meet you, Ana. I can see where your daughters get their great beauty from."

Out of the corner of my eye, I see Cami smile. The corner of my other eye catches, Catarina frowning as she says, "Spoken like a true, libertine."

Cutting my eyes at her, I respond, "I see you know the moniker of the investment company my father started before my time. You see, he meant it not as the one definition that means a man who behaves sexually immoral. He meant it as the definition that means, free thinker. But you probably know that, if you read up on me and the company I am CEO of."

She nods and smiles an eerie smile at me. "Of course, you would say that, Cyprian. You and I have much to discuss when we have a chance to. Perhaps wine on the back porch later will find us chatting about you and your past that's shaded a bit more than some."

I find Cami, pulling at me to go with her somewhere. "Don't mind her, Cyprian. Come with me, let's put our things in my old bedroom." We wheel our luggage down a short hallway. She opens the third door on the left and I find a pink bedroom.

"Your mother hasn't changed a thing since you left, has she?" I ask as I go inside with her.

With a shake of her head, she closes the door behind us. "No, she's left all of our bedrooms the exact same way we left them. Did my sister intimidate you, Cyprian? I'm sorry about her."

"She loves you. I find it sweet. I can handle her, Cami. Don't worry." Taking her in my arms, I hold her tight and kiss her long and sweetly. Gazing into her eyes once I've set her lips free, I find her to look even sweeter. "Your family is gorgeous. Our children will have great genetics. We're sure to have us a houseful of pretty kids."

She smiles and bats at my arm. "A houseful is a bit too many. Especially with the size of your home."

"I have room for at least nine kids. You can give me nine, can't you, baby?" I tease her.

"Rogue," she says as she wraps her arms around my neck and kisses me more deeply than she's done since my surgery.

HER TONGUE MOVES over mine as her hands move up into my hair and my hands travel to her rounded bottom. I pull her into me and find my cock springing to life. That can't happen yet, so I pull my mouth from hers. "Naughty vixen."

She smiles and lays her forehead against my chest. "With you, I am."

I look at her small bed and see we'll be sleeping nearly on top of one another. "This next couple of days will have me exercising my self-control, I see. You will lay nearly on top of me."

She pulls out of my arms and giggles. "I can make a pallet on the floor if you doubt your ability to control your urges, Cyprian."

Pulling her back into my arms, I kiss her again. "No way. I will sleep with you for the rest of my life. Nothing like my self-control will ever get in our way."

She runs her hand over my cheek and I see my world in her deep blue eyes. Taking her hand, I hold it to my lips as I gaze at her and think about how lucky I am to have found her in this huge world we live in.

Is it possible to love someone so completely...?

54

CAMILLA

The smell of chicken and dumplings fills my nostrils as Cyprian and I go into my mother's kitchen. We find her, stirring a pot as my sister tosses flour coated balls of dough into a huge pot.

My three-year-old niece, Sadie, and one-year-old nephew, Sax, make their way to me but stop just short as they seem a bit shy about Cyprian. I let his hand go and pick them both up, holding one on each hip.

"My, my, those kids look good on you, baby," Cyprian says with a chuckle.

"First things first, Cyprian," my sister says.

"Shush," my mother reprimands her. "Your sister is twenty-five, plenty old enough to be thinking about children. I'd like a few more grandkids."

"I meant they need to be married before any talk of that happens. That's all I meant by that comment." My sister looks past me at Cyprian. "Is that in the cards for you?"

He laughs and sits at the small round table in the kitchen. "I'll let that be a mystery for a while, Catarina. You are quite the big sister, aren't you?"

"I am," she says as she eyes him. "And you are an enigma, Cyprian."

"You don't trust me to do right by your little sister?" he asks.

I FIND their banter annoying and butt in, "It doesn't matter what she thinks. Mama, can you please tell your eldest to mind her business and her manners?"

My mother nods as she stirs the pot of boiling deliciousness. "Camilla is right, Catarina. Leave her man be."

I put the kids down and sit next to Cyprian who leans over and whispers, "I love being called your man," He leaves a quick kiss just behind my ear, sending heat through me.

This celibacy thing while he heals is as close to torture as I've ever been. Sleeping with him each night has left me waking to him gloriously naked, while I keep my body wrapping in night clothes, afraid of what would happen if we were both naked.

He has been a rock of self-control, which I find amazing. The man seems to be transforming right before my eyes. His normal demeanor of raw sexual prowess has nearly disappeared.

I see him gazing at my niece and nephew who've gone back to playing at the little table my mother has made for them in the kitchen. "You remember me telling you the kids' names, right?" I ask him.

He nods. "Sadie and Sax, right?"

"Yes," my sister says. "My husband had to stay in Cape Town. My mother's from there. Did Camilla tell you that?"

"She did. She and I have talked about so much these last two weeks. We now know one another inside and out." He drapes his arm across my shoulders. "I'm sure your husband, Peter, misses you and his kids very much. He's the manager of a hotel there, right?"

"He is. If he misses us, I have no idea. I've yet to speak to him since we got here a couple of days ago. He's not answered my calls," she says as she looks at the pot instead of us.

"Are you sure he's okay," I ask her as I'd never be okay with anyone not taking my calls after such a long trip.

"He's fine. I called the hotel and his assistant told me as much. He just doesn't want to talk to me is all." She throws one last dumpling into the pot and walks over to the sink to wash her hands.

I get up and go to help them by picking up the bowl of flour, tossing out the unused portion and washing the bowl while my mother chastises Catarina. "Not in front of the c-h-i-l-d-r-e-n."

"Why did you spell, children, Grandmama?" Sadie asks.

CYPRIAN FIGHTS himself not to laugh I see, as he holds his mouth shut. Then he gets up and goes to the little table where the kids are playing with a coloring book and colors. "My, my, how smart you are. Can you read, Sadie?" he asks her, diverting her attention.

My sister looks at me as I smile with his efforts. Her shoulder touches mine as she whispers, "I can see you think he's hung the moon, little sister. Believe me, men are incapable of keeping up their act of being good. Because it's just an act. Once they have you trapped, or so they think, in a marriage with children you share, then they go right back to who they were before you came along. So, beware, Camilla."

I don't say a word in response. She's obviously unhappy with her marriage right now, that's all. She's always been happy with her husband. I have no idea what's happened but I have no doubts she'll be bending my ear with the details before the night's over. She's not one to keep her problems to herself, totally opposite of me.

I can't help but watch Cyprian color with the kids as he perches on a tiny chair. Sadie, who was shy, is getting bolder with him as she reads to him from one of her children's books. He seems impressed and she seems proud of herself.

Sax is looking at Cyprian from under his thick dark lashes. I can see his curiosity is getting the better of him as Cyprian is talking to his big sister. Before Cyprian realizes what's happened, Sax has moved off his chair and is leaning on Cyprian's leg, listening to his sister read and helping Cyprian color his picture.

Cyprian looks over his shoulder at me and gives me a grin that tells me he's quite happy. "Looks like you've made a couple of new friends," I say as I wipe my hands on a dish towel and make my way to him.

He nods and I see pink stain his cheeks. Then I recall how he's told me he never made any real friends. Thanks to his father promoting school was for learning, not building friendships. Then work started and he told him the same thing. My poor Cyprian was held back from so many things.

I run my hands over his broad shoulders and stand behind him. Then find my sister looking at us and sighing just before she leaves the kitchen. My mother shakes her head as she turns the stove off and moves the pot to let the contents thicken. "She needs your help, Camilla. She's not herself and she's not telling us everything. Could you go see if you can get anything out of her? I'll entertain your young man if you'd do that for me."

I kiss the top of Cyprian's head and give her a nod then go to find my sister who's not quite herself. Into the living room I go and find her walking out on the front porch, so I go out there too and see her lighting a cigarette., "What the hell are you doing, Catarina?" I ask as I close the door behind me. "Mama and Papa will kill you if they see you doing that. You know that."

"I have to do something to ease my stress. You have no idea." She takes a long drag then I take the thing away from her, toss it on the ground, and stomp on it until it's out.

"Killing yourself, slowly, isn't the answer." I pull her with me to sit on the rockers on the porch. "Talk to me."

Her hands are knotting as she holds them in her lap. "Peter has taken on a mistress and expects me to accept that."

"Whoa!" I say then let out a whistle. "Man, I have to tell you, it's not completely unexpected, with his religion and all. Mama and Papa warned you, it could happen. But you said mistress, not wife. Is there a chance he won't marry her too?"

"I suppose he's testing the waters with her. I hate it. I hate all of it," she says then I see the tears starting.

"Look," I say as I run my hand over her leg to try to comfort her. "Maybe we could talk to him. Maybe we could get him to see reason."

SHAKING HER HEAD, SHE CRIES," He won't even answer my calls. I begged him to come with me and he told me this would be the perfect opportunity for him to get to be alone with this other woman, who he's refused to allow me to even meet yet. So, here I am in New Orleans, knowing my husband is having sex with another woman in our bed."

My gut turns on itself as I think about how she must feel. "Leave him, Rina. Don't stay in that kind of a marriage."

She shakes her head. "It's not that easy. He'll be able to keep the kids away from me if I do that. They are citizens of South Africa, after all."

"You've dug yourself a real whole. You will have to come to terms with things. You married a man who can take more than one wife at a time. You knew this could happen. So, take that for what it's worth. You took a risk and lost. Life goes on. It's just sex, right?" I say, quoting Cyprian.

"If that's all it is then why does it hurt so damn much?" she asks me as she tries to suck it up.

"I wish I knew."

We both turn to see who's coming outside as the screen squeals on them, we see it's Cyprian. "Catarina, your son has a diaper that's in need of your attention. Your mother sent me to tell you that. I'm sorry to be the bearer of bad news." She gets up and rushes past him wiping her eyes. He takes her by the arm, stopping her. "You're crying."

She nods and tries to pull away. "It's nothing."

He lets her go and she hurries inside then he comes and sits in her empty chair. "Care to tell me about it?"

"I most likely shouldn't but this might be an area you can actually be of help with. You see, her husband practices a religion that allows him to have more than one wife and he's looking into taking another, as we speak."

"Oh," he says as he looks down then he looks back at me. "She had to know this might happen."

"I told her that too but it's hitting her hard."

"When that's practiced as a religion, it's more about making more children than anything else, from what I've read. So, it's just sex, really." He looks at me as if I can understand the concept.

"She and I come from a family who believes there is not a thing, as just having sex. I have no idea why she married a man who could legally do such a thing as add another wife to his plate. She did, though. Everyone cautioned her but she did it anyway. Peter promised her he'd never do such a thing. Seems he lied."

Cyprian nods. "Men lie to get what they want."

I stifle a gasp as he speaks so openly with me. "You are also a man."

"That I am," he says then places his hand on my arm. "But I am a man who has spent over half his life having meaningless sex with more women than most. And I have found the one woman who brings out more in me than I knew was inside of this mind and body. I have no want for any other."

"But someday I might not be enough. You have to admit that." I watch his brow furrow.

"Please don't think like that. I can't predict the future. For all I know, it will be you who tires of me. You could be the one who cheats or lies. No one knows what will happen. All I can promise you is right now."

I don't say a word as I recall how much Peter was in love with my sister. He treated her like a princess. He gave her tons of jewelry and took her to Cape Town and bought them a huge, lovely home. And now he wants to add a woman into his life. And the same could happen to me, I suppose. Cyprian has been honest with me about being fine with two or more women.

"Cyprian, if I told you it would be okay, would you want to add another woman into our lives or our bedroom life?"

"Don't, Cami. Don't do that. This is a thing between your sister and her husband. A man she knew could take more wives if he wanted to. You and I don't have that. We will have a traditional marriage. Leave us out of them, okay?"

"This is just a, what if, thing," I say. "What if you were a man who was part of a religion that allowed you to have more than one wife? Would you want one?"

He moves off the chair and gets on his knees in front of me, taking my hands. "Camilla Petit, you are the only woman I have ever seen a future with. Don't take paths that might be or could've been. We are on one path. That's to marry and become a family of our very own. Don't think any other way."

As I look at him, I know he's right not to let my mind stray into places that might be dangerous to our relationship. I see he has faith in us and that gives me some faith too.

So what, if my sister was foolish enough to marry a man she took his word he'd never take another wife, even though he would be able to if he wanted. I'm not her and Cyprian and I can't be compared to what she entered into with the man she married.

She was warned. She shouldn't have married him. She should've never trusted the man.

I look at Cyprian with his good looks, money, and charm. I should be wary of them. A woman can easily fall victim to all of that. A man like Cyprian could make a woman believe anything he told her to.

A man like him could break me into more pieces than anyone else ever has. He could take my heart and pull it apart.

But would he do that to me...?

55

CYPRIAN

Though Cami has stopped trying to bait me with what if questions that pertain to her sister, I find her still being a bit on the standoffish side. Which is making it harder for me to do what I had planned to do on our visit to her parents' home.

The dinner went smoothly enough. Her father seems to like me as does her mother. When Cami told them about me coming for her the night of the hurricane, they both looked at me with adoring eyes.

Her sister, on the other hand, looked at me with accusing eyes. She seems to be looking through the man I am becoming and seeing the man I am trying to leave behind.

The backyard is large and Cami and I are sitting outside, enjoying the night air as we sip on some white wine. The screen on the back door squeaks open then slams shut. It has us looking to see who's joining us, rather than star gazing.

When her sister pulls up a chair, with a bottle of beer in her hand, I feel a definite chill. "Catarina," Cami says. "Did you get the kids to sleep already?"

"I did. I want to get some advice from your man, Camilla." She takes a long drink of her beer, while she waits to see if Cami will approve her request.

Without looking at me to see what I have to say about it, she gives her older sister a nod of approval and I feel prickles of heat run down my spine. What has she gotten me into?

CATARINA LOOKS at me as she lowers the tall brown bottle off her full lips. "Am I pretty to you, Cyprian?"

Oh, shit!

"THAT'S NOT a loaded question at all, is it?" I ask with a chuckle.

Cami nudges me. "It's okay to answer truthfully."

I weigh my answer, carefully before I speak, "You are very pretty, as is your mother and your sister. In fact, the whole family looks like something out of a movie."

Cami smiles and leans in close to me as we sit on a large swing that's hanging from an ancient oak tree. "Good way to say it, babe."

Her sister eyes me. "You are good with your words. I knew a man like that once."

Cami cautions her, "He isn't Peter, Rina. Don't go hostile on him."

"If you had me, would you want anyone else?" Catarina asks me.

"Another loaded question," I say. "I don't know you. If you're asking me, by your looks alone, would I ever want anyone other than you, I have to say I have been with many beautiful women and did want more. It wasn't until I met this little beauty beside me that I found myself only wanting her."

Cami looks at me with a frown on her face. "That's not exactly true."

"Okay, at first, it wasn't. But then it became true. You know that," I say then kiss the side of her head.

"Have you hurt my sister?" Catarina asks me then takes another drink.

"I have," I admit. "I have hurt her deeply and I have to tell you that I am ashamed of the pain I've caused her and have made a vow to her and myself never to do that again."

"Huh," she says as she puts the bottle on the ground next to her chair. "How have you hurt her, Cyprian?"

"Never mind about that," Cami tells her as she takes my hand. "That's our business and that's behind us. It's taken a lot of work to get that behind us and I won't be bringing it back out to banter about with anyone. Okay?"

THE CONVICTION in Cami's voice makes my heart swell. It's the first time I've heard her say anything like that. I kind of feared what I did would haunt us forever. But it sounds like she really means it's behind us.

I give her hand a squeeze. "I love you, Cami."

She smiles and bats her long lashes at me. "I love you too."

Her sister, clearing her throat, has us turning our attention back to her. "I assume my little sister has let you in on my predicament."

I nod. "She has."

"Any advice on how to handle sharing my husband with another woman?" Her eyes glisten in the moonlight as she holds back her tears.

"You knew who he was and what he was capable of doing when you married him. Cami told me you two dated for two years, were engaged for one year then married and immediately started your family. Tell me, has he spoken to you about the number of children he wants?"

"As many as he can have," she says then picks up her beer and drinks the rest of it.

"And you were okay with that?" I ask her as she doesn't look to be fine with it.

The way her head shakes tells me she jumped into something without thinking it through. "No, I wasn't. You see, I have committed what he called a crime against our marriage. While visiting my parents, when Sax was two months old, I went to a doctor here and got a birth control shot that lasts three months. I've visited them every three months to keep the shots up. I did this without telling him about doing it."

"Oh, shit!" Cami says. "Why did you do that?"

"Obviously, I wanted a break between babies. I did the same thing after I had Sadie. Only now that I haven't gotten pregnant again, Peter's found me out," Catarina says as she looks up at the sky. "I just wanted a small break between having babies, that's all."

"His religion doesn't allow that," I tell her. "I know you're aware of that. I know me saying it doesn't help a damn thing. But you made a commitment, knowing these things. Is the woman he's thinking about adding as a wife in the same religion he is?"

She nods and Cami mumbles, "You're fucked."

I give her a look that tells her to have a bit more compassion. "Look, Catarina, there's not much you can do but to accept this. Unless you want to give up any life with your kids in it."

"I'll never do that," she says as I see her tears glistening in the moonlight.

"THEN ACCEPT YOUR FATE. You went into that marriage with your head on straight. You looked at the odds and thought you could handle them. But I would offer you this bit of advice. Consider getting off that birth control and giving your husband what you promised him you would. Before making such a drastic commitment, though. I'd ask him if he'd consider not taking another wife if you'd do that for him and your marriage."

"I don't want to do that. I want to stay on birth control and when my children are grown, I'll leave him then." She looks at me as if to ask me if that's even possible.

"He can divorce you and keep the kids anyway if you go with that plan. You must realize that," I tell her and watch her melt into a puddle of tears.

Cami gets up and goes to hug her sister, shushing her and telling her things will be okay. It doesn't sound as if they'll be okay but who am I to point that out at this moment?

Cami looks at me and her eyes go bright as she does. "Catarina, let me talk to Cyprian in private. If he agrees then I'll tell you my plan in the morning."

Her sister nods and sniffles as she tries to pull herself together and I give Cami a look that says, I have nothing I can do about the man or their marriage.

Cami comes and takes me by the hand, leading me back into the house and all the way into her old bedroom. "Cami, there's not a thing I can do."

"What if I told you there is something you can do?" she asks as she begins to change into her night clothes.

I start ditching my clothes and make it into the bed first. She eyes me as I do. "I'm not going to even attempt to sleep in pajamas, baby. It's humid as hell here."

SHE NODS in agreement and finds a thin nightgown out of a dresser where she has left some of her clothes. I sigh as she pulls it over her head. How I wish the one month mark was here already.

I pull the blanket back and she slips into the little bed with me and leans up on her elbow, looking down at me. "Okay, hear me out before you say a thing, please."

I nod but know there's no plan that could possibly work out for her sister. I wish there was but there just isn't a thing anyone can do. Her sister made her bed, now she has to lie in it.

And maybe with another woman too...?

56

CAMILLA

"So, you see it might work. Peter's not a bad man. I think what my sister pulled, left him thinking he had no other choice but to take another wife. If he was around us more, I think he'd find it in his heart to allow her a few years between children. I think it's being in his home country that has him wanting to save face."

Cyprian looks away then back at me. "He'll only be allowed a work visa. That means he'll have to leave the country at least once a year."

"And that's when you'll have him take a month in France to give that manager a vacation. He can take Catarina and the kids with him for that month. It will work, I know it will!" I am over the top excited that I came up with such a great plan.

"You do realize this requires me buying two hotels. Plus, hiring another manager for the France hotel. And I'm not even in that business. I'm in investments," he says as he looks doubtful.

"So, you buy two hotels and hire managers to do the rest. You are rich and you did tell me whatever I wanted, you'd give me. Well, I want two hotels to help my sister keep her family." I look him square in the eyes and ask him for the first thing ever and wait to see if he will give it to me.

"Might I have a meeting with this man first, before I go getting into the hotel business, baby?" he asks me then pulls me to him and kisses the top of my head. "I will do it for you. I just want to see if I have to hire a real manager to oversee him or if he knows what he's doing."

I clap and giggle and kiss his face all over. "Thank you, thank you!"

He laughs as I kiss him then holds me back. "I suppose you want the American hotel to be in Clemson, so they spend more time with us, correct?"

I nod and he smiles at me. "I'm beginning to be able to read you like a book."

"You are," I say and cuddle into his side. "Man, this bed is little." I have to readjust and end up lying on his left side or I'll fall off the bed.

"I'm happy to have your attitude being more positive. It makes my heart go all bumpy." He pulls me up even more on top of him and I hug him tight.

So, I've asked him for something huge and he's agreed to it. Maybe this thing between us really is going places.

But should I really be incorporating my family into it, so soon...?

57

CYPRIAN

"That's a grand gesture," Cami's father says after we've told everyone our plan for keeping Catarina's family together. "Peter is a smart man. I can assure you he'll work hard for you, Cyprian."

I find the whole family is all smiles and then I go and do a bit more. "I'm not a man who knows a thing about the running of hotels. I can make the investment but that's about all I can do." I turn to Carlyle. "Can I count on you to assist Peter with this endeavor? That can be your internship and if you like that kind of work, I can make you a permanent part of the business structure."

He nods and I see his father looking at him with a ton of pride in his expression. "I sure would love that opportunity. Thank you!"

Catarina looks a little worried as she says, "But he'll ask about where we'll live."

"In the hotel," Cami says. "We'll have the top floor, renovated to accommodate your whole family."

Catarina nods then looks at me. "Are you some kind of an angel, Cyprian?"

I laugh. "Far from it."

Cami looks at me as she laughs too and I know she knows I'm no angel. "Well, we're off to go on a swamp tour. Does anyone care to join us?"

No one comes forward, so she and I leave her family behind to go see some alligators. We hold hands as we go out to borrow her father's car and I open the passenger door for her. "My lady."

She kisses my cheek then gets inside the car. When I get into the driver's side, I find her gazing at me. "I love you more than you can imagine."

"Baby, you've given me more in my life than anyone ever has. I feel like a part of a real family, for the first time ever. And it feels awesome." I take her hand and kiss it then run the back of it over my cheek. "Thank you."

"Thank you, Cyprian. Thank you for everything. The hard times and the good times. I'm the luckiest woman in the world."

Watching her smile like she is, has my heart doing flips. "This really is the best feeling. Do you think we can really get your family around us in Clemson?"

Then her head falls and she looks down. "My mother and father will never leave my grandparents, alone. And they'll never leave."

"I'm sorry," I say as I lift her hand back up to my lips. "But we can always visit a lot. I love them, Cami. They're great. Next to visit is your grandparents. We can go see them after our swamp tour."

She gets happy again as the smile returns to her pretty face. "Maybe things will go this well when I meet your parents."

I nod and drive away but I have a feeling things won't go as well as they've gone with her family. My parents are nothing like hers. She has a real family and I have a couple of people who never fully developed as grown-ups. That's painfully obvious to me now that I've been around a real family.

"Can you be brutally honest with me, Cami?"

She nods. "Sure."

"Do you think I'll make a good father?"

She looks at me with a smile and sighs. "I do. I really do,"

"Can I ask you another question then?"

"Sure."

"When do you think you can let me become one?"

She laughs and I find it a lighthearted sound. One that tells me she's not that far off from the idea. "We'll just have to see about that, Romeo."

I shut my mouth and bide my time. She's coming along much faster than I anticipated. Becoming a father might not be years and years away like she said it would be. Especially if we have aunts and uncles around to help care for our brood.

I look over at her and picture her with a swollen stomach, full of my baby and my cock stirs. I look away as that's still a no, no. Damn this recuperation is taking forever!

Can I really wait that long...?

58

CAMILLA

Our stay has extended to two more days, so Peter can fly in and meet with Cyprian. He's having him flown over by private jet and Peter sounded impressed when I overheard him talking to Catharina on her cell.

Cyprian, Catarina, and I are using Papa's car to pick up Peter from the small airport we flew into a few days ago. My family has taken to Cyprian better than I imagined they would.

"Is it odd that I'm so excited to see my husband?" Catharina asks us. "I mean, I know he's had sex with another woman while I've been gone."

"Let it go, Rina," I tell her. "Trust me, you can get over it." I look at Cyprian who goes pink with embarrassment.

My sister leans up from the back seat and pats him on the shoulder. "I could tell you were a bad boy. But you seem to have grown out of it."

"Great," he says as he seems at a loss for words.

We laugh a little as he pulls up to the airport and we see the black jet pulling in too. "Just in time," I say as we stop.

.   .   .

WE ALL GET out and in moments my sister is hugging her husband as Cyprian and I watch them. "What a married couple can get through, huh, baby," Cyprian says as he pulls me close.

"All I know is, you better never put my ass through that." I pinch his butt a little and he smacks mine, lightly.

"Nor you."

"Agreed," I say as my sister and brother-in-law stop hugging and kissing and come toward us.

Cyprian lets me go as he steps forward, extending his hand. "Hello, Peter. I'm Cyprian Girard, CEO of Libertine Investments. It's nice to meet you."

"Likewise," Peter says then stops shaking his hand to give me a hug. "How's my gorgeous sister-in-law?"

"I'm fine." I pat him on the back as we end our hug.

"Shall we?" Cyprian asks as he gestures to the car. "I've made lunch reservations at someplace called, The Grill Room that Cami has assured me is excellent food and a great place to discuss our business."

Peter gives him a nod as he opens the door for my sister who gets inside, all the while gazing at her attractive husband. It's no wonder she doesn't want to share him. He's an exotic beauty, that man!

I SCOOT across the seat to sit right next to Cyprian as my sister and her husband begin to make-out in the back seat. "Sorry about this," I whisper to Cyprian as I turn up the music, so we don't have to hear the heavy breathing coming from them both.

He leans over and whispers. "Get out your cell and make them reservations somewhere crazily expensive in the French Quarter for the next two nights. I think they need to rekindle their romance."

I do as he says and find myself smiling all the while. Cyprian is surprising me more and more with each passing day. He's insightful and helpful, and just plain wonderful!

"I love you," I tell him after I've received confirmation of the reservations at Ritz-Carlton.

He reaches into his pocket and pulls out a wad of cash. "Slip this to your sister when you get a chance. I don't want to leave them downtown without any money."

When I count the money, I shake my head. "Baby, this is too much."

He shakes his head right back at me. "No, it's not. Just give it to her."

I place the cash in my purse and think he's nuts but he has more money than I have an imagination of just how much it really is. If he wants to splurge on my sister and her husband, who am I to stop him?

As we pull to a stop in front of the restaurant to let the valet take the car, my sister has to pull herself off her husband and we get out and go inside. I find them both glowing and think I was dead on right with my idea of bringing him to her.

Once we're seated, Cyprian begins to let Peter know what he has planned. We don't want Peter to think this is just something to get him to do what my sister wants him to do. Cyprian tells him the plan and asks for his help.

Peter thinks he's negotiating but he has no idea Cyprian will give him more than what he's asking for. Just as Peter looks as if he's trying to make a decision about what to do, I open my mouth, "He left out the most important part, Peter. You will be getting a share of the profits each quarter and that will go all the way down to your children when they turn eighteen. Fifty percent of the profits, to be exact."

His dark brown eyes narrow as he looks at me. "You are kidding, aren't you?"

CYPRIAN CHIMES IN, "She isn't. I wanted her to tell you. You see, I'm an investor, not a person who knows how to run a hotel. That's why I'm willing to give you not only a salary but a percentage as well. Plus, I like your kids and want to give them something they can reap from what you sow."

"This is much too nice of you. I can't let you do this," Peter says, making us all stop and look at him.

Cyprian nudges me. "Take your sister to freshen up, will you?"

I nod and tilt my head toward the ladies' room. "Come on, sis. The men need to talk business." As soon as we get out of earshot, I let her in on Cyprian's gift. "My man has set you up good, Rina. You and your husband will be staying two nights at the Ritz."

"What?" she says as her eyes grow in size.

We slip into the ladies' room and I open my purse. "Here, put this in your purse. Cyprian gave it to me to give to you. He said you'll need some money to have fun while you have a little vacation. I'll help Mama with your children. Don't worry. Reconnect with Peter and see if you can get him on board with this venture."

"What if he doesn't want to do it, Camilla?" she asks as she seems worried he might not.

"Do your best to talk him into it. It means a lot to the kids too. This will set you all up for your whole lives. If you do smart things with it, that is. But I'm sure Cyprian will help out with great ideas about how to make the business work. He keeps saying he knows nothing about the hotel business but the man can read things and instantly become an expert. He's the smartest man I've ever met and I know brilliant doctors and scientists!"

"I hope he can talk Peter into taking this offer. I don't know what I'll do if he won't take it."

I don't know what she'll do, either...

59

CYPRIAN

"**M**an to man, no judgment," I say to Peter. "Why would you not accept this offer?"

"I have my reasons for wanting to stay in South Africa. It's my home country. I want my children to be raised there. I want them to know my religion and heritage," he says, making valid points.

"Clemson has a community where they can get that as well. You see, your children are half-American too. Shouldn't they get to experience and learn about this culture as well?" I ask him.

His eyes keep darting to the side and I think he has other reasons to want to stay right where he's at. "My family is back in Cape Town as well."

"You'd have lots of vacation time. Anytime you needed or wanted to go for a visit, not only would you be able to take that time off, you'd have access to the company's private jet to make the trip." I pile it on thick as I can see this man has that other woman on his mind.

He looks at me for a moment then says, "I suppose my wife has informed you all about me taking a mistress."

I nod. "That has nothing to do with this offer. You see, I am planning on marrying Camilla. I've never had a family and I'd like to help ensure your family has everything they need. Think of me as a brother, Peter."

HE NODS. "I have many, many brothers, Cyprian."

"I am sure you do. That's wonderful for you. Such a large and loving family," I say but find him shaking his head.

"Loving, no. Just large. But that's all I know. Can I be honest with you?" he asks me as he looks over my shoulder for his wife, no doubt.

"I wish you would."

"I am facing a lot of flak from my extensive family about my wife and her slowness to fill our family with more children. They've set me up with another woman. She's more than willing to make sure I have as many children as possible. So, leaving my home now would cause a rift in our families. This woman is a cousin of one of my brother's wives. A close family we've traded with for many generations."

"While I see your dilemma, may I ask you if you love your wife?"

He looks at me for a long moment. "Where I come from a wife is an asset. Love shouldn't enter into that agreement. She married me, agreeing to bear my children. As many as we were given. When she took birth control, she voided our agreement. I haven't divulged that information to anyone. Nor will I. You want to know why that is, Cyprian?"

"Let me guess, because you, my friend, love your wife."

He nods but says nothing as he takes a drink of his wine. After a long time, he says, "But I have never told her those words."

"You should. You should live your life for you and no one else except that woman and your children. I was also brought up in a family who thought love had no place in our existences. They were wrong. I had been living life almost the same way as you've described. I used women for sex and gave them nothing in return. Until I met, Camilla Petit. She opened my eyes and my heart to a different, more fulfilling way to live. You should forget about what you're leaving behind."

"Can I even do that?" he asks. "I'm not sure I can."

"When you have sex with your wife, have you found it more enjoyable than when you had sex with this new mistress?" I ask him as I hold his eyes to make sure he tells me the truth.

"I didn't feel a damn thing when I bedded the mistress. Except shame. That's the truth."

"Here's the deal, Peter. I love Cami and I love her family now too. Your family will leave you the hell alone about this. Would you like to know why that is?"

With a nod, he says, "I'd love to know why you think that."

I wink at him. "Because you will be sending so much money home to them, they wouldn't dare say a bad word to you. You know, afraid you'd stop sending them anything."

"Just how much money do you think I can make off that hotel, anyway?" he asks me.

"Well, there will be two of them, actually. There will be another in Paris. You will only work there one month out of each year. But you and your children will get fifty percent of the profits off that one too. So, how much money you make is all up to you, my friend."

"This is too good to be true," he says and I nod. "See, I told you it was."

"I do have a private condition for this," I tell him.

"And that is?" he asks as he leans forward.

THIS IS the whole reason I sent the women away. I'm not sure Cami nor would her sister approve of my doing this. But I feel protective over her and her family, so I will do what I think I need to, for their protection.

"You and I will have a side agreement, signed and kept in my attorney's possession. Only you, me, and my attorney will know a thing about it. It will state that, at any time, you take on another mistress or wife, you will lose everything to your current wife, Catarina. You will be deported, without a cent and without your wife or children. That's my one condition. As long as you live by that agreement, you and your entire family will benefit from it. If you don't, then you will go back to South Africa, penniless, without your family."

"You're a man who has more dark than light," he says as he looks me over.

"I have a darkness, you don't' begin to have. You see, I have lived a life even worse than your own. I could've had love and companionship the whole time but it was kept from me. Now that I have it, I will do anything to make it stay in my life. Cami is my life and her family means the world to her and that means it does to me now too. So, I will protect them all, the same way I will protect her."

"If I walk away, accepting nothing, then what?" he asks me.

"I wish you wouldn't do that, Peter. Like I said, I will do anything to protect them."

"Does that include having me killed?" he asks.

SHAKING MY HEAD, I say, "Surely, you wouldn't let it come to such a drastic thing. I am offering you wealth beyond your wildest imagination. A beautiful wife, who is willing to give you children. She's merely asking for a small break in between them. A very fair thing to give, in my opinion. You will be beyond happy, Peter. Do the right thing, man."

He drums his fingers on the table then looks up at me. "I have no choice, Cyprian. I will take your offer."

I hold up my glass of wine and he holds his up as we tap them together. "Here's to many years of being brothers-in-law, Peter, as well as business partners."

He doesn't say anything as he knows I have him by the balls. When my family is threatened, I'm finding I can turn into a ruthless man. But then again, isn't Peter the same way.

So, who is to say what I'm doing is wrong...?

BOOK 9: THE INTIMIDATOR

A Bad Boy Billionaire Romance

By Michelle Love

60

CAMILLA

ulling up to the college in the red Lamborghini, I feel more than a bit ostentatious. Everyone looks at me as I get out of the attention attracting door that lifts up.

"Whoa," a young dark haired guy says as he stops and looks at the car. "What do we have here?"

Closing the door, I hit the button on the key fob to lock it and take a step back to appreciate the car with the guy. "We have a pretty nice car my boyfriend gave me."

He cuts his eyes away from the gorgeous car for only a moment to say, "You should marry that man." Then he's right back to looking at the car.

WALKING AWAY, I think about what he's said and wonder why it is Cyprian has yet to ask me that all-important question. We've been living together for a bit over a month and he talks all the time like we're definitely going to get married and he mentions having kids a lot too. But the actual proposal and an engagement ring have yet to be heard or seen.

Not that I want to rush anything but I am beginning to wonder if

I'll get a real proposal or if one day, out of the blue, he tells me to pack a bag and whisks me away to Las Vegas. I don't know how I'd feel about not having a real proposal.

MAYBE I SHOULD LET Cyprian know that. No, that's much too forward. I'd better just wait to see what he has up his sleeve.

Making my way into the lab for my first class of the new year, my last year, I find the smell of formaldehyde, stinging my nostrils and get ready to get back into the mindset of learning all I can, while I still can.

Checking my phone, before I shut it off for class, I see my sister has sent me a text, asking me to meet her for lunch. She, her husband, and kids are staying in a house, Cyprian rented for them while they scout out a great place to make the new hotel.

Catarina is over the moon about it and must have something she wants to show me or talk to me about. I text back that I'll meet her for lunch and turn the phone off to get down to business.

This year is going to be so different with no job to go to every night. And I have Cyprian to thank for that. He's such a good guy, now that his past seems to be behind him.

61

CYPRIAN

"Thank you for meeting me, Peter," I tell Catarina's husband who's stepping off the elevator at my office building. "Follow, me. My lawyer is waiting for us in the small meeting room."

"So, you really had the contract drawn up?" he asks me as if it was ever a question.

I stop and turn to him and look him over. The man is tall, dark, and mysterious looking. I can see why Cami's sister fell for him. He's a charismatic man and seems to be used to getting his way. He's not a bit happy about the contract that's the main part of our deal.

"Peter, would you do right by her, if there was no contract?" I ask him as he looks at me with a blank expression. It tells me he wouldn't.

"Catarina and I made our vows and she's well aware of what they were and what she can and can't do and what I can and can't do. I do not feel this contract is a thing I need, to do right by my wife and family." He shoves his hands into the pockets of his expensive Armani suit I had delivered to him, along with top of the line clothing for his wife and kids.

I gave him and his wife cars to drive, I've already started his salary for managing the hotel that's not even purchased yet. I've set them up in a nice home. I've done all that and he still thinks I should merely trust him to do what his wife feels is the right thing to do.

PETER IS OBVIOUS TO ME. I can see right through him. If I don't make him sign this contract, he will go back to South Africa and add that other woman into his life, as well as Catarina's. I know it would break that woman.

Taking him to my office, instead of the meeting room, I decide to give him two offers. "Let's stop off at my office for a minute. I have something else I'd like to offer you."

He follows me into the office and I close the door behind us. "Good, I'm glad you're seeing things my way," he says.

With a chuckle, I say, "Far from it, Peter. You see, I've found a part of me I didn't know I had. Seeing Cami as my future, has me seeing her family as my future too. Protection for them has begun to course through my veins and that has me thinking you should be given a chance to change your mind."

"About?" he asks as I gesture for him to take a seat in the chair on the opposite side of my desk while I go take a seat in mine.

"How would you like to start fresh?" I ask him and see a puzzled expression could his face.

His dark brows furrow over his dark as night eyes as he asks, "I would like to know what you mean by that."

Lacing my fingers and leaning my chin on them as I place my elbows on the desk, I tell him what I mean, "Divorce your wife. Leave her and your children here and I will see they never do without a thing. You can go back to your country and live life the way you want to. I'll pay you to do that."

"Leave my wife and children?" he asks as he shakes his head. "Do you think I could even do that? They belong to me!"

"Then what's the big deal about what I'm asking from you? All I'm asking you to do is accept my gravy job offer and take care of your family. You're making it out like I'm asking you to do something you don't want to do."

"I should be able to take another wife if I want to. It is in my religion, after all," he says, and I find myself getting pissed at him.

"And you can, but divorce Catarina first. Let her go. It's not her religion to do such things," I tell him as he looks at me with a stubbornness in his eyes.

"She is mine. The children are mine. I'm not about to let them go," he says through gritted teeth.

"Then you're saying you will, willingly, sign the contract that states if you marry another, you will be sent back to South Africa, alone, leaving your wife and children here."

"Fuck! I guess I can sign the damn contract but I would not call it, willingly. I would call it, you forcing me to." He glares at me and I find a smile creeping across my lips.

"Peter, you're a very lucky man. You have a beautiful family and now you're going to be a very wealthy man. It's more than most dream of," I tell him as he looks grim. "So, let's go get that thing signed and then I'll take you to look at a building I think might be perfect for the new hotel. I've come up with a name too, Catarina's Quarters. It is because of her that you have anything, after all."

HE SLAMS his fist on top of the desk and growls. "I cannot do this! I will not allow this! She is my wife and those are my children and I am going to take them home. I am not a man who can be pushed around. Fuck you, Girard!"

I let him get up and walk to the door, then I say, "Have it your way, Peter."

He stops and turns back to me, slowly. "You don't mean to let me leave this building without signing that contract, do you?"

"If you walk out the door of the main lobby, without having signed that contract, I'm afraid a terrible accident will happen to you. But that's your choice to make. It doesn't matter at all to me." I lock eyes with him to let him know I'm the one who's calling the shots, not him.

Getting up, I make my way to the door and open it, walking out, I find him following me. I assume he's made his decision. It's too bad he had to be made to do the most basic thing in a marriage, be faithful.

As I open the door to the meeting room and see my lawyer sitting at the table, waiting for us, I notice a smile is on Peter's face. Maybe he's decided to be happy about things. He should be. He's getting more than he's ever dreamt of, after all.

I hope I'm doing the right thing...

62

CAMILLA

"I'm meeting Catarina for lunch, you should join us, Cyprian," I tell him as I've called him to see how his day is going. "I don't have another class until two, so I have a couple of hours to kill."

"We'll meet you two then. I have Peter with me. I took him to see a building I think might be good for the hotel. Meeting with you girls will give me the opportunity to let you in on the name I've chosen."

"Great, see you soon then." I end the call and pull up in front of my sister's house and honk the horn.

She hurries out, leaving the kids with a nanny she found soon after moving to Clemson. She looks happier than I've ever seen her as she gets into the car. "God, this car is so badass!"

"It turns heads, let me tell you," I say as I pull away. "Our men are meeting us at the restaurant. Text yours, tell him where we're going."

She pulls her cell out of her purse and taps in the information then puts the phone in her lap and sighs. "I'm so happy, Camilla. Happier than I've ever been."

"Good," I say and give her a smile. "It makes me happy to see you this way, Catarina. It's been a week since I've seen you. How's it all going?"

"Great." She nods as she looks out the window and sees people pointing at the car. She waves at them like they can see her, which they can't through the darkly tinted windows. "Peter has been a bit cloudy-headed with all the changes but he'll come around. He's never been given such an opportunity before. I think he's kind of blown away by it all."

"Cyprian has been very generous, I admit." I look over at her as I'm stopped at a red light. "But I have to tell you, it makes me love the man, even more, knowing he'd do anything for me and my family. He's a keeper, that's for sure."

Taking off from the light, I find a car full of young guys pulling up next to us and gesturing for Catarina to roll her window down. She giggles as she sees them too and rolls it down. "Hey, boys!"

They laugh and hoot and holler. She laughs and rolls the window back up. "You have a fan club, Camilla."

"I know. So, has Peter said anything about Cyprian? You know, does he like him?" I ask as Cyprian's not said much.

"I suppose he likes him. Peter's never been the type of man who lets me in on things. He's reserved and I have to say, I like it that way. The man remains a mystery to me and that keeps my interested in him. But, I'm sure he likes all the things Cyprian's doing for him." She pulls her lipstick out of her purse and pulls down the visor to look in the mirror.

"Cyprian's good at talking and telling me things. But he's not said much about Peter, even though they've spent some time together, looking for places to make the hotel. Cyprian doesn't know how to make friends. It wasn't a thing his father thought was good for him. He was groomed to take over his father's role as CEO of his company. Making friends would've gotten in the way of that."

She puts her lipstick away and looks at me. "Camilla, have you met his family yet?"

"No," I say and don't want to say any more about it. I've kept Cyprian's family and past, hush, hush.

. . .

THE RESTAURANT COMES UP and I pull into the valet lane and find Cyprian's BMW pulling up behind us with Ashton at the wheel. Two men open our doors and I look the one, who will be driving my baby, right in his eyes. He nods before I say a word. "Got it, ma'am. Be extra careful with this little beauty. No need to worry. I'll treat her like she was my own."

Placing a twenty in his hand, I say, "Please do."

Catarina laughs at me as we step up to the entrance and watch our men get out of the car behind mine. "You're moving into the role of a wealthy wife quite easily."

"It's weird, I know. But being with Cyprian is rubbing off on me. Is that a bad thing?" I ask her.

Shaking her head, she says, "I don't think so. He's a great guy. I hope he rubs off on Peter, to tell the truth."

Our men meet us with kisses to our cheeks and we all go inside. Cyprian's arm runs around my waist as we're led to a table by the hostess. His lips touch my ear as he whispers, "Did you miss me, baby?"

A chill runs through me and I smile. "I did. And you?"

"I did and I have great news. I had my follow-up appointment this morning and have been set free. Prepare to be devoured tonight, all night long." He leaves a bite on my earlobe and I go all wet in an instant.

Holding the chair out for me, I sit down and find him sitting next to me and moving his chair so close to mine, our legs touch. His hand runs over my thigh, resting on my knee and making me crazy for him.

The month has been long and I'm more than ready to spend a sleepless night with him, even though I have classes tomorrow. I move my hand over his leg too and take in his musky aroma and find myself breathing harder than one should while sitting at a table with her sister and brother-in-law.

When I look away from Cyprian, I find Peter watching us. "We found a place today," he says. "Cyprian has named the hotel. He's named it after your sister. What do you think about that, Camilla?"

I turn to Cyprian to find him smiling. "What's the name?"

"Catarina's Quarters," he tells me, making me and my sister smile but Peter's face remains emotionless.

"How sweet, Cyprian!" Catarina gushes as she runs her arm around Peter's. "I love it."

"I thought you might," he says and leans his shoulder against mine. "Do you like the name, Cami?"

"I do. I think you have to be the nicest man I've ever known." I kiss his cheek and he looks at me with gleaming eyes.

"To make you happy makes me happy," he says then kisses the tip of my nose.

"He is the absolute sweetest," Catarina says and I catch Peter making a quick frown.

"That, he is," I agree and give Cyprian's knee a little squeeze.

"Baby, I have something to ask you and you can say, no, but I really want you and I to make an appearance," Cyprian says. "It's my father's birthday. He's having a party, which I don't want to stay at but maybe an hour or so. We should go for a short while."

"A PARTY? AT YOUR FATHERS?" I ask, hesitantly.

"Camilla, what's wrong with you?" My sister asks me then looks at Cyprian. "Of course, she'll be happy to go with you."

He looks at me, though, waiting to hear it come out of my mouth. "Baby? What do you say?"

What can I say?

"OKAY, I guess it's time to meet your family."

He pulls me in for a hug and kisses the top of my head. "I can't wait. He's been wanting to meet you."

"Is your mother going to be there too?" I ask as meeting the two people who screwed him up isn't a thing I want to do.

"She will," he says. "So, you can get meeting them both out of the way. I can't wait!"

His enthusiasm doesn't help me at all. I don't know if I can control my mouth with them. The fact they didn't want him to have friends is huge, when you add in the fact they taught him to be a sexual deviant, well, there's no getting over the damage they did to him.

Can I actually hold my tongue with them...?

63

CYPRIAN

Despite the signing of the contract, Peter seems to be handling it well enough. The main thing is Cami's sister looks happy about things. As lunch wraps up, we all go back to get in our cars and get back to work.

"Can Catarina catch a ride with you guys?" Cami asks. "We hung out a bit too long and I have to make my next class."

"Sure," I tell her then give her a kiss goodbye as Ashton pulls up. "See you at home around five. We'll be expected at Papa's at eight."

The frown on her face was expected. I didn't think she'd be down to going but I need her to. I need her to show my parents that she loves me. They've both been on my ass about how much I'm doing for her family. They think I'm jumping the gun.

I DON'T, though. Nothing has ever felt this right. It's like I've finally stepped into the man I could've always been. A family man who handles things with ease. The man everyone looks to, to make sure everything is okay.

I let Peter and Catarina get into the car first then slide in, sandwiching her between us. Peter whispers to her, "Did you get what I asked you to?"

"I did," she says and seems like she doesn't want to talk about whatever it is. In front of me, anyway.

"Good," he says then places his hand on her leg.

She cuts her eyes at me and I see something in them that tells me she'd like to say something. "So, how are you liking Clemson?"

"I like it. I really do. It's great. What you're doing for us is great. I'm so glad you came into my sister's life. She's needed a man like you. She's had nothing but shit heads." She stops and looks at Peter who's frowning at her. "Sorry. A bunch jerks who broke up with her without seeing fit to give her any reason why."

"I honestly can't see why any man would ever break up with her. She's amazing." I look away as I can't imagine what she could've possibly done to make three men just dump her. It makes no sense.

"In her past, she's acted very differently with men than she does with you. In my opinion, it was her way of not giving all of herself to them that ended them all. She was reserved most of the time. I'm glad you think she's amazing," Catarina says then pats me on the leg. "She's as lucky to have you and you are to have her."

Peter clears his throat and I see him looking at her hand as she taps it on top of my leg. She quickly moves it and seems a little nervous. "On another note, what do you think about getting online to look for a place to buy in Paris to make a hotel there too, Catarina? I want it to be small, quaint, like the place I found here. No more than fifty rooms. Both will be exclusive places to stay. We'll cater to the rich. So, look for something along those lines, will you?"

"That sounds fun," she says as she pulls her phone out to start searching, no doubt.

I smile as she looks so excited then Peter says, "I will do that when we get home."

"Of course, you'll have the last say, Peter. But I'd enjoy looking too," she says as she continues to tap in what she wants to search for.

"When we get home, I'm going to send the nanny home and you will need to see to the children," he says.

. . .

HE SOUNDS irritated with her for some reason. And I find that not making me happy at all. "Let the nanny stay for a while. What will that hurt, Peter?" I ask as I look past her, at him.

He shuts up and looks out his window. No one speaks while we make the rest of the ride. When we pull to a stop in front of their house, he gets out and she quickly follows. "Thank you, Cyprian. I'll send you links to what I find," she says as she looks back into the car.

"Come!" Peter says and she hurries to walk a step behind him.

As I watch them go into their house, I have to wonder if he's always treated her that way or if it's something new. She doesn't seem the type of woman to put up with that. I know her sister isn't.

As we DRIVE AWAY, I find Ashton looking at me through the rearview mirror with that expression on his face that tells me he has something he'd like to say to me. "You have something you want to say, Ashton?"

"It's none of my business," he starts to say.

I finish his sentence for him, "But you're going to say this anyway."

"I am," he gives me a nod. "You should stay out of their affairs, Cyprian. I can see you not liking how that man treats his wife. It's written all over your face. But she married that man, so she knows who he is and what comes along with him. You need to butt out."

"She is going to be my sister-in-law, it's my responsibility to make sure she's happy."

He laughs and shakes his head. "Cyprian, that's not your responsibility. She's a grown woman who has made her own decisions. This will not end well if you get between them. I don't suppose you saw how dominant he is over her. You will only make things harder for her if you don't stop butting in."

"I have Peter where I need him. If he's mean to her, I'll find out and deal with him," I tell him as my insides begin to quiver with anger at how obvious it is he's dominating her.

"What does that mean?" Ashton asks with concern etched into his voice.

"It means, I have the man handled."

He goes quiet and says no more as he drives me back to the office. I know he must have an idea about how I have handled Peter. But he's not asking anything else about it. I wouldn't tell him, anyway.

I won't be telling anyone about that...

64

CAMILLA

fter a nice long, hot bath, I feel a bit more relaxed about meeting Cyprian's parents. The half bottle of wine didn't hurt, either!

PULLING ON A DEEP BLUE DRESS, I find some heels to match it and turn to find Cyprian has finally come home. "I thought you'd be here hours ago."

He smiles and comes to wrap me up in his arms. "I went and picked up some naughty things for later." The bag he was holding drops to the floor behind me and I turn to look at the things he brought home.

But he catches my chin, stopping me from seeing into his bag of goodies. "I have to approve of everything," I tell him as I eye him to let him know I mean I will be looking over everything to determine if it's a thing I want or not.

"I promise you, I'll never do anything to hurt you again. I swear it," he pulls me close and kisses me not so soft or sweet but hot and demanding.

· · ·

HIS TONGUE MOVES into my mouth as he maneuvers my hands until he has them behind my back and holds them with one of his. I can see we're headed for a night of restrictive touching, on my part. When his mouth leaves mine, we're both breathing heavy and my heart's racing.

He moves me backward, still holding my hands behind my back until we get to the bed. He sets me down and goes back for the bag. The first thing he takes out is a pink silk bra and panty set. He doesn't say a word as he holds the panties up and pulls the crotch and I see it split open as Velcro sides split down the middle. He tosses them to me with a grin on his handsome face.

"You want me to put these on now?"

He nods and shows me how the bra opens in the front and tosses that to me too. "And that. And one more thing." He reaches back into the bag and pulls out a silver ball. "We'll start with one for tonight. I want you to put this inside you, to keep you stimulated."

"You certainly are setting things up, aren't you?" I ask as I walk toward the bathroom.

His hand on my shoulder stops me. "Let me help you."

"That's kind of nasty, Cyprian." I look at him with more than a bit of apprehension.

He shakes his head. "Not nasty. Just dirty." He chuckles as he pushes the sleeves of my dress down and undoes my bra. He looks at my bare breasts then runs his hands over them. "I can hardly wait to feel these in my mouth."

"Cyprian!" I say as he stares at my tits like they're made of gold or something.

He ignores me as he puts the new bra on then pushes the dress all the way off and takes my panties down with it. I step out of them and hold up one foot so he can put the quick release panties on me, only to find him shaking his head.

Picking me up, he lays me down on the bed, pushing my legs up until my knees are bent. His eyes stay on mine as he takes the ball and inserts it. I gasp a little with the cold and the odd weight of it. Then he puts the panties on and picks me up.

He holds me close, our lips but a breath apart. Then he moves me back to where my dress is on the floor and has me step into the middle of the pool of fabric. Moving his hands down both sides of my body, he goes all the way down and grabs my dress, slowly moving it back up to cover my naughty underwear.

My body is hot and I would like nothing more than to forgo the evening with his parents and climb right into the man's arms and stay there for the duration of the night. "Cyprian." His fingers touch my lips, stopping me.

"Shh. I'd like for you to remain perfectly silent. I want to hear only one word from you tonight. When you're asked anything, I'd like you to answer with one word. Do you want to tell me what word it is I need to hear come from those juicy red lips?"

"You want to hear the word, yes," I answer him and watch his light brown eyes light up.

He nods and pulls me close, hugging me and making me wonder what all this is about. But it seems he really wants me to keep it quiet until he asks me something. Which seems kind of steamy and intriguing, so I'll play his naughty game.

Anything will work tonight, anyway. I don't even need a game to know I'm going to melt in the man's arms, no matter what he wants to do. I've been hungering for him since he came to find me the night of the hurricane. Keeping my mind in the right place, so he could heal, was an exercise in self-control.

Leaving me alone, he goes to shower and change and I decide to take a peek to see what else he has in his bag. I find a set of handcuffs with soft, velvety pink fabric, covering the steel. I gasp a bit as I see a small whip and pick it up. The leather is soft and glides over my palm, leaving a heat behind the strands of leather.

I look over my shoulder to make sure he's not back in the room. Seeing that he's still busy in the bathroom, I pull my arm up and slap the whip against my leg. I giggle as I see it doesn't hurt at all. It's just too soft.

It's the idea of it, is all it really is and that's cute to me. He's going to play like it's me giving into his wants and needs. In reality, I have just as many wants and needs as he does. But he has a like for the games and fantasy. Who am I to tell him, no?

I PUT the things back in the brown paper bag and sit on the bed, turning on the television to watch it while he gets ready. My phone rings and I see it's my sister, so I answer, "Hello."

"Hey, you are going to Cyprian's father's party, right?" she asks me.

"Yes, nosey." I roll my eyes as if she could see me.

"I just wanted to be sure. I feel in debt to the man for all he's done for us. I just wanted to exercise my big sister hold on you to make sure you give the man what he wants."

"You know he's doing what he's doing for you and the kids, right? I could tell by the way he acted at lunch that Peter isn't his most favorite person," I tell her as I look at my red painted nails and try to recall if I have ever gone for a manicure before Cyprian started taking me to get my nails done each week.

"Well, Peter doesn't try very hard to be likable, in Cyprian's defense. As a matter of fact, here lately, he doesn't seem to care if I or the kids like him, either. I think all of what Cyprian is doing is making him feel somewhat less of a man."

"Why do you say that?" I ask her as I watch Cyprian emerge from the bathroom and go to his closet to get dressed. Seeing him with only a towel wrapped around his waist sends a torrent of heat straight through me and I have to close my eyes to focus on what my sister is saying.

"Oh. He's got this dominating man thing going on. He must need to know he's still the one who wears the pants in the family," she says, pulling my mind away from the naked man in the closet.

"Dominating? Like how?" I ask her as I turn away from the closet and stop trying to catch another glimpse of him.

"Like, he's bought me a chastity belt I have to wear all the time and once the kids go to bed, he has me wear a slave collar. That kind of thing. Bathe him, wash his hair, and file his nails. You know that kind of stuff."

"Huh? Are you shitting me?" I ask as that sounds nothing like my sister. "Do you like that?"

"Like it?" she asks as if she doesn't know if she does or not. "It's never been my cup of tea. But, on occasion, he's needed me to be submissive to him. He's always come around, once he knows I know my place in his life."

RED FLAGS ARE FILLING my head as I think about Peter, lording over my sister. "You don't have to do those things if you don't want to. You do know that, right?" I ask her as Cyprian comes out of the closet, dressed in a tux and looking like a million bucks.

"He needs me to, right now. I can do it for him. Don't tell Cyprian, please. He already looks at Peter like he wants to tell him off more often than I'd like. I can't have Cyprian starting a battle with my husband over how he treats me. I'm used to it."

"Because he's beat you down to accept it," I say as my hackles have risen.

"Shit! Don't tell me you're going to be a problem too! I only wanted to talk to you about it. I don't want anyone to say a thing to Peter. Please."

"You ready?" Cyprian asks me.

I smile as I recall him telling me he only wants to hear the word, yes, come from me tonight. "Yes." I turn my attention back to the phone call. "Got to go, sis."

"Okay, bye, you guys have fun."

I put the phone in a gold clutch he's handing me and take the arm he's offering me. As we leave the bedroom, I'm filled with worry for myself and my sister.

Are we both fools over men...?

65

CYPRIAN

I've never been more nervous in my entire life!

My palms are sweating as I grip the small box in my inside jacket pocket. My father is looming ahead and Cami is looking a little frantic as she takes in the blue lights that are reflecting off the disco ball that still hangs above the dance floor of my father's ballroom.

HE'S SMILING as we approach him and I find my mother swooping in from the right. "Oh, you can speak freely, Cami."

She looks at me and winks. "Do you really think I didn't know that?"

I laugh, nervously as I watch her eyes grow bright. "Damn, I love the shit out of you."

Her mouth quirks into a half smile. "And later you will show me."

"You have no idea how much I'll show you." I make a growling sound as she runs her hand over my ass.

My father meets us with his hand extended. "Corbin Girard, Camilla. Nice to meet you."

She shakes his hand and nods but can't say anything as my

mother is next to him in a second with her hand extended as well. "Coco Mason."

"It's nice to meet you both," she says as she shakes my mother's hand.

"My son tells me you're going to be a scientist someday," my father says.

I pick up a couple of drinks off a passing tray and hand one to Cami. She looks at me with thankfulness in her pretty eyes then looks back at my father. "I am going to be doing something in that field, yes sir."

"Such a beautiful woman, she is Cyprian," Mother tells me. "I can see why you like her."

"I more than like her, Mother." I look at Cami and push a few of her curls away from her face. "I love her."

Cami's hand on my cheek sends tingles all through me as she caresses it. "And I love him."

"How strange, huh, Corbin?" Mother asks as she looks at us.

"He does look happy."

Cami smiles as she turns to look at them. "Does he?"

They nod and it makes her laugh. I take her in my arms and spin her away as a song comes on that I like and take her out to dance with me. "You make me happy, baby."

She giggles as I touch her bottom and moves my hand up to her waist. "You make me happy too, naughty boy."

Nuzzling her ear, I hiss, "You have no idea. Now, back to no talking, wench."

She giggles then goes quiet as she looks into my eyes as I spin her around the half-empty dance floor. Silently, we gaze at each other as I think about what I'm about to do.

The music slows as the DJ changes the song. I pull her in close, she leans her head on my shoulder and I see a throng of women cascading into the ballroom. The escorts have arrived and I wanted to be long gone before they got here.

It's been a good while since I've been at one of Papa's parties. No one ever discusses people who aren't present, so I know none of them has been told that I'm off limits. My presence in the middle of the dancefloor has several of them targeting me.

"Shit!" I hiss as I try to dance away with Cami before any of them can get to me. I hurry, moving Cami backward until I get to the stage, then I stop dancing and take her by the hand and go up on the stage with her looking at me with complete confusion.

"Cyprian, what the hell are you doing?" she asks me as I wave at the D.J.

I grin at her. "No talking except when I ask you something, remember?"

She nods and looks around at all the people who've shown up, suddenly. The DJ comes to me and I whisper, "Can you end the music for a moment? I need to make an announcement."

He gives me a thumbs up and the music stops, immediately as he explains, "Cyprian has something he'd like to say."

Looking at Cami, I can see she's nervous as hell. Her eyes are the size of saucers. I give her hand a gentle squeeze to try to calm her down a bit.

She jumps as cheers come at me from the women who have crammed themselves near the stage. Shouts come from them, asking me to pick them. One flashes her tits and I decided it's time to quiet them all down. "Ladies, and gentlemen, I have something I'd like to tell you all."

"You're hosting an orgy in your bedroom and all are invited!" one of the women shouts.

Cami looks at me like she thinks this is insane, which I know now, it is. "It's okay, baby."

"It's not," she whispers.

As I hold her hand, I look out at the crowd of people and say, "The lady next to me has done an amazing thing."

"I can do amazing things too, Cyprian. Let me show you," another woman calls out.

"No!" I shout. "No, don't show me anything. Let me finish. You see the amazing thing this woman, Miss Camilla Petit, has done without even trying to, is show me a man who was hidden inside of me."

"I knew he had to have more men inside of him," another lady shouts. "There was just no way only one man could bring that much pleasure to so many!" Laughter follows her words and I find Cami tugging at my hand.

"Just be patient, baby," I say as I hold her tight, not about to let her flee. "Okay, ladies, and I use that term loosely, how about you let me finish my tale?"

"Shush, everyone," my father calls out from the back of the crowd.

A HUSH FALLS over them all and I go on, "This woman has brought out things in me I never knew I was capable of. She's brought out love in me. True love, the likes I didn't know existed until I found her."

"Aww," the crowd moans.

I reach into my pocket and pull out the little box and get on one knee, looking up at Cami. Her hands fly to cover her mouth and I see the tale-tale signs of tears pooling in her eyes.

Reaching up for her left hand, she gives it to me and I find it shaking. "Camilla Petit, you are a gift from above. Your kind heart, gentle spirit, and take-no-shit attitude have won my heart. It will forever be yours. So, I'd like to make this thing we have official. Camilla Petit, will you marry me?"

Her whole body is shaking and the room is so quiet you can hear a cricket chirping somewhere far away. Cami shocks me as she gets on her knees in front of me and nods as she says, "Yes."

Slipping the ring on her finger, I say, "You have made me even happier than I was before. You are indeed an amazing woman and I am blessed that you've chosen me to spend your life with."

Kissing her has everyone clapping and I lift her up as we kiss. When our mouths part, she looks out at the crowd with a huge smile.

"Ladies, this man is mine! So, keep your hands to yourself, or you'll have me to deal with. I do not share!"

Laughter fills the room and I gesture to the D.J. to get back to playing music. As we exit the stage I find my mother and father have made it to the front and are waiting for us.

"I never thought I'd see the day when my Cyprian would settle down," Papa says as he pulls Cami into his arms for a hug. "Be good to him, please."

"Not to worry," Cami tells him. "I love him and will always be good to him."

MOTHER GRABS her up next as my father lets her go and shakes my hand. "Being married carries many responsibilities, Cyprian. That's why I stayed the hell away from it. But, I suppose you've thought that all out. I suppose that's why you've invested so much into her sister's family. I hope that all works out for you."

"Thanks, Papa." I see my mother letting Cami go and tears are in her eyes for the first time ever.

She takes me in her arms and whispers, "Congratulations, my son. I hope you don't plan on making me a grandmother anytime soon. That would spoil my reputation." She laughs to show me she's joking but I bet there's a lot of truth behind her words.

"I am going to do my best to make you a grandmother as soon as I can talk that little spit fire into it." Cami hears me and shakes her head. I nod and take her hand. "And now she and I must go. See you guys later in the week."

They watch us as we leave and so do most of the guests in the room. Just as I think we've made it, one of the women from my past steps in front of us "Hey."

"Trish, right?" I ask as if I don't know

"Come on, Cyprian. Introduce me to the woman who has stolen you away from us all."

"This is Cami," I say then step to one side.

Trish takes Cami by her shoulder, making Cami stop and look back at her. "Can I help you?"

"I just want to know one thing, Cami. How'd you do it? How'd you get him to want you and only you?"

Cami looks at me then back at Trish. "I didn't. It just happened."

"That's not true," I say. "She stole my heart and she keeps it under lock and key."

TRISH CUTS her eyes at me and frowns. "I'm sad to see you go, Cyprian."

Cami looks down and I pull her close, wrapping my arm around her. "Everyone should grow up, sometime, Trish. Goodbye."

Taking Cami, we walk away from the ballroom I watched parties going on in since I was a child. A thing no kid should've ever been able to watch. And I am happy to be walking away from that life. Happier than I've ever been.

How long can elation really last, I wonder...?

66

CAMILLA

The ring on my finger weighs a ton. The diamond is huge and the platinum band is wide and full of smaller diamonds. "I suppose my finger will build muscle to be able to hold this monster up."

Cyprian smiles and kisses the ring he's placed on my finger. "I suppose it will have to because it's never coming off you."

As Ashton pulls away from Cyprian's father's mansion, I look at all the cars that have come in after we did. The place was filled to the brim and that was a weekend normalcy for the man who's sitting next to me.

It's not lost on me what all he has given up for me. Not one ugly woman was in that ballroom. All willing to give their bodies to Cyprian for the night or longer. And he only wants me. That's hard to believe.

"Can you really walk away from that life, Cyprian? Can you really only ever want me?"

His fingers touch my lips. "Let's go back to the no talking thing. Only say yes when I ask you something. I don't want to talk about that place or that life. I want to talk about our future but, for tonight, I don't want to talk about anything. I want to experience you and you, me. It's been an eternity since I've let myself really feel you. So, what do you say to that?"

"Yes," I say with a smile and find his mouth on mine.

Ashton drove us in the limousine, so we have complete privacy as he takes us home. The ride is about a half hour and from the way Cyprian is maneuvering me around, I think he has plans on starting this in the car.

Hoisting my dress up, he moves me to straddle him as I sit on his lap. His mouth leaves mine only long enough for him to say, "Set me free, baby." His hands move mine to undo his pants then his move to my panties and he pulls them open. The Velcro snapping, loudly as he does. "Push."

I do as he says and feel the ball he placed inside me, slip out. The weight of it had me staying acutely aware of my sex and now that the object is gone, I ache to be filled with something much larger that can move.

Lifting me up, he puts me back down on his exposed erection and we both moan. He keeps me perfectly still as my body stretches to fit him and I find myself shaking with raw sexuality. My stomach is tight as he lifts me, slightly.

"CYPRIAN, YES," I moan as I feel his silky cock move inside me and nearly fall apart with how damn good it feels. "Oh, how I've missed this."

His lips press against my neck for the longest time as he holds me still then moves me again. "I have to go slow. My body has never been celibate this long and it's threatening to erupt much too quickly."

"The hell with it, baby. Get this one over with and out of the way. I know you can build up, quickly." I move faster and push his shoulders back, so he can watch me ride him.

He pushes my dress off my shoulders, it pools at my midsection. He pulls the bra apart in the middle as the Velcro comes apart, unleashing my tits and his hands move over them as he groans, "My God, I've missed these."

His large cock rubs parts of me that have been left alone far too long. It has me going over the edge before he does, but the spasms my body is making has him coming along for the ride. Simultaneously, we moan out, "Yes!"

Pulling me to him, he kisses me long and softly. Making little pecks, he says, "I love you. I love you so damn much."

"I love you, Cyprian. More than you will ever know." I feel his cock stirring back to life inside of me and move my body to encourage the growth.

More kisses we pepper each other's lips with and before I know it, the easy kisses have turned passionate. He moves and I'm on my back on the floor. His movements are hard and pounding as he takes me.

I am his for the taking. This man can have me any way he wants me. For the first time, I have completely given myself away. Mind, body, and soul, yet I've never felt more free in my entire life.

With one chance meeting, I found the man who was the missing part of me. And he has me to fill the place in him that had lain empty all this time.

His movements are harsh and so is our breathing. The last of the street lights leave us in the dark and he hurries to meet his end, taking me to mine. With a grunt and a groan, he's spilled himself inside me once again. "We're about to be home."

Getting up, he pulls me up with him and we secure our clothing. My hair's a bit of a mess, so I know our little escapade will not go unnoticed by Ashton when he opens the door for us. As we pull up to the gate, I see we've both managed to put all our body parts back where they belong, beneath our clothes. "We did it!"

Cyprian laughs. "Did you think we wouldn't?"

With a nod, I slide onto the seat and lean my head on his wide shoulder. "I had my doubts. You've made me feel so much better."

"And it's not over yet," he kisses my cheek as we come to a stop in front of the house. Cyprian pushes a button that rolls the middle between us and the driver down. "I got it from here, Ashton. Thanks, see you in the morning."

"Yes, sir," Ashton says and I find myself feeling elated, I don't have to face him with my hair wild and him well-aware of what we've been up to while he was driving us home.

As soon as he has me out of the car, Cyprian picks me up like I'm already his bride and carries me to the door. "Punch in the code, baby."

I punch it in on the keypad that's attached to the doorframe and in he takes me. All the way up the stairs and straight to our bedroom. Placing my feet on the floor, he steps back and spins his finger in a circle, a gesture for me to turn around.

As I turn around, I feel him move close behind me, pushing my hair to the side and kissing my neck. "I've missed you."

His tongue travels up the length of my neck until he reaches my ear then he nibbles on the lobe. My body sparks and I'm ready for him again. How, I don't know, but I am.

Unzipping my dress in the back, he lets it fall to the floor. Then peels away my clothing until I am naked and he's still dressed. Taking a step back, he looks me up and down and makes a growl as he points to the bed.

I walk away from him and get on the bed, lying back and waiting to see what he's going to have me do. He makes his way to me, picking up the bag he brought home earlier and dumping the contents on the bed. I watch him as he picks up the small whip. "Do you trust me?"

"Yes," I tell him as I've already tested the little thing. It's not that I don't trust him. Wait, that is exactly why I tried it out! But he doesn't need to know that.

"Get on your hands and knees and bring your ass to the edge of the bed, wench." He smiles to show me he's not really being a prick.

I smile too and do as he says. Without a word, I wait for him to do whatever he's going to do to me. One hand he runs over my ass, I quiver with desire and fight the urge to beg him to hurry things along. How he has me aching for him, I have no clue but he does!

I hear the sound of his zipper as his hand still roams over the hills of my bottom. The rustle of clothing lets me know he's finally joining me in being naked and soon my eyes will fill with his fine form.

Pressing his cock against my ass, has me shivering with need for him. "Cyprian," I moan as he toys with me.

A smack with the whip is what I get as he says, "No talking, wench."

"Yes," I say but it comes out sensual and he moans and smacks my ass with the whip again. "Yes, yes!"

"You like that, wench? You like it when I punish you?" He hits me with the soft leather again and I find myself soaking wet with how excited it makes me.

"Yes."

"Do you belong to me?" he asks me and hits me again.

"Yes."

With a growl, he runs a finger into me. "Are you all wet for me, baby?"

"Yes," I moan out as I press my ass back to him, so his finger goes in deeper.

"Would you like me to fuck you now?" he asks as he wiggles his finger.

"Yes! Yes!"

Pushing me down, he flips me onto my back and yanks my legs until my ass is at the edge and I am facing him. My eyes roam over his perfect body. His washboard abs are taut as are his pecs. His hands move to each side of my ass, his biceps bulge with the effort and he goes into me with one deft thrust of his hips. "Better?" he asks me.

My body relishes the way he feels inside me. So perfect, so right, so damn fulfilling. "Yes," I moan as my hands move over my breasts and

I look at him as he moves his body to make mine feel more pleasure than should be legal.

"Do you agree this pussy is mine and mine alone, forever?" he asks me as he thrusts hard, making my breath shoot out of my lungs with every one of them.

"Yes!"

"Good, girl." He pivots my body up a bit, making him hit a new place inside of me as he lifts me only a little.

"Uh!" I grunt as he seems to be hitting some amazing place inside of me and my body starts quivering as it nears the edge of a fantastic orgasm.

Harder he thrusts as he pulls me to meet him each time. It feels like he's bottoming out in me and I can't wait any longer. I fall apart as he goes so deep inside it seems impossible.

I scream as I let it all go and he goes that much harder and faster. My legs are shaking and I'm writhing with the intensity of the climax. It's not stopping and he's going at me furiously until his body goes into an orgasm that has him groaning so loud, I can feel the vibration coming through him and into me.

I watch him as his eyes close and his face flushes, making him glow. He's beautiful, amazing, and he is going to be my husband!

How did I get so damn lucky...?

CYPRIAN

"Cami, don't you dare be fucking with me!" I say as I lie in bed and look down at her after a night of fantastic sex and love-making, as well.

"I'll stop taking the pill, immediately. I want to have your baby, Cyprian. I want to give you the one thing you can't give yourself." She bites her kiss swollen bottom lip as a tear slips down one of her pink cheeks.

"Baby!" I pull her into my arms and hug her like there's no tomorrow. Peppering kisses all over her until I find her lips, yielding to mine and sending me into a passionate kiss.

She's going to have my baby!

CAMILLA

The drive to class has me calling my sister to tell her my big news. "Morning, Camilla."

"And a very good morning it is, Catarina. Cyprian asked me to marry him last night and I accepted, of course. And guess what else?"

"You're going to Vegas this weekend to do it?" she asks.

"No," I say. "Well, I don't know that for sure but who knows with Cyprian. Anyway, I've made the decision to start a family with him, right away."

"That's fantastic. My kids will finally have some cousins!"

"Is my breakfast ready?" I hear Peter ask, gruffly, in the background.

"He's a bear in the mornings, huh?" I ask.

"Here lately, yes. I need to go."

She hangs up without another word and I find myself feeling upset about it. Just as I tap the phone to call my parents and tell them the good news, I see a small black car zoom up next to me.

I ease off the gas as the car has some more daring individuals, wanting to race the Lambo. My phone rings and I see it's not a number I know but I answer it anyway as it might be a professor telling me something about a class. "Camilla Petit."

"Camilla Petit, I need you to pull to the side of the road. I have important business with you. It concerns your sister and her children. I'm in the black BMW behind you. Pull into the next parking lot," a man's voice tells me.

"Um, no," I say as I speed up a bit. "You can tell me anything you need to, over the phone."

"I cannot. The phone may be bugged. Your sister and her children are in danger. I need you to make your new fiancé stop his interference in my brother's life. Or it will cost your family much."

"What does Cyprian have to do with this?" I ask as I speed up a bit more.

"He made my brother sign a contract yesterday. If he takes another wife, he will be sent out of America and have to leave his wife and children behind. This is a thing my family cannot and will not allow. So, you see how important it is to get your fiancé to see reason. And I have one other thing you need to know."

"You don't have to tell me anything else. I will handle my fiancé." I'm so pissed I can barely speak. How could he do such a thing!

"You need to know this, Camilla. My brother is already married to the other woman he told Catarina about. He married her three months ago and she is pregnant. So, you see why this cannot be tolerated. He has to come back to take care of his responsibilities. And we will never allow his children to be taken from him. Your sister may not be happy with things the way they are but she entered into a marriage with him and had children with him and she and those children belong to him now. Make your man see reason or you and your family will never lay eyes on your sister and your nieces and nephews again."

"Surely, something can be done. My sister was beyond upset that he was even contemplating taking another wife, this news will devastate her."

"Catarina knew what she was doing. She was never forced or even coerced into becoming my brother's wife. Let your fiancé know this. If he doesn't tear up the contract and stop trying to intimidate my brother into doing what he wants, the same thing he's threatening my brother with will happen to you, Camilla."

Then the call is ended and I watch the black car in my rearview mirror slow down and turn off onto a side street. Changing my plans for school, I head to Cyprian's office to find out just what it is he's done to make a war between my brother-in-law's family and us.

And just what could he have threatened Peter with that could happen to me...

BOOK 10: THE HERO

A Bad Boy Billionaire Romance

By Michelle Love

69

CYPRIAN

My secretary buzzes me on the intercom at the same time the door to office flies open. Cami's face is beet red and she's panting like a lunatic. "How could you?"

"How could I what?" I ask as I get up and go to her, pulling her into the office and closing the door, so my gawking office staff can be left in the dark about whatever her problem is.

Her body is shaking as I attempt to pull her into my arms. She's having none of that, though, I find out as she shakes me off and steps away from me. "Don't! Cyprian, what the hell were you thinking?"

"Baby, you're going to have to calm down to speak to me. You're not making any sense."

"Peter!"

What does she know about my dealings with Peter?

I DON'T JUMP the gun and divulge more than she may know. "What about Peter?"

"You tell me and tell me right now. I'm going to give you only one opportunity to be truthful with me." I watch as she takes the engagement ring, I barely put on her finger last night, off.

"What are you saying?" I ask as I feel more than a bit shell-shocked by her tirade.

"I'm saying that you have one chance to tell me what it is you've done if you want things to stay the way they are. Because, in order to marry you, I have to trust you in all ways."

"How about you tell me what's happened to upset you?," I say and watch in disbelief as she walks over to my desk and places the ring on it.

"I see," she says and tries to walk out of my office.

Taking her by the arm as she walks past me I look into her eyes and see pure anger there and know she's been told about the contract. I have no choice. "I made Peter sign a contract that said if he ever takes another wife then I'll have him deported without your sister and the kids."

"Well, I can't be deported and I was threatened with, one of Peter's brothers, said was the same thing you threatened Peter with." She eyes me and I know the jig is up if I want to keep her. And I want to keep her.

"Damn it!" Holding her arm, tightly, I take her back to the desk, pick up the ring and hold it out. She shakes her head and continues to look into my eyes. "Fuck! Okay, so I threatened him with death."

"Cyprian! Why would you ever do such a terrible thing? He's the father of my sister's children. Her husband. He's to be your brother-in-law one day! Why would you do such a thing?"

"I've told you the whole truth. Can I put this ring back on your finger? It's making me nervous not to see it on you," I say as I hold it out to her.

"First, tell me why you did that."

"Because I see him as a bad man. A man who needed someone to make sure he was held accountable to your sister. She will be my sister-in-law soon and I feel a certain amount of responsibility to make sure she and all of your family is happy and treated well."

Her eyes soften and she holds out her hand. I slip the ring back on before she changes her mind then sit in the chair next to the desk and pull her onto my lap. Her forehead touches mine as she mumbles, "What am I going to do with you?"

"Love me," I whisper then kiss her cheek. "I did it for you, Cami."

"You have to tear up the contract. You have to allow him to leave. And you have to know my sister will be going with him. She has to or he'll take her and the children and we'll never see them again and apparently, I will be killed." She pulls back to look at me. "Do you see what you've done? You should've talked to me about what your idea was and I could've explained to you why that would be a horrible idea."

"So, you don't really care if your sister has to accept all that shit?" I ask because it was her who asked me to give him a job that would keep them here.

"I'm afraid my sister has to face the fact she married a man who could take more than one wife. She is the one who purposely took birth control in order to not give him child after child, the way he expected her to. And it's too late to change anything, anyway. His brother told me Peter married that woman already, months ago. They are expecting a child. My sister has to accept that now. No matter what. And Peter has to go back to South Africa to take care of that other wife."

"SHE'S GOING to be blown out of the water with that news, isn't she?" I ask as I play with a dark curl that's sprung loose from her bun.

"She is." She runs her hand through my hair. "Can you promise me that you'll never do anything like this again?"

"I can. I'm sorry. I was only trying to help."

"Make a mental note of what I'm about to tell you," she says as she takes my chin in her hand. "Threatening anyone with murder is a huge no, no."

"Noted," I say and feel my cheeks heating with embarrassment. "I guess I lack something in my brain that makes me understand things like that. I felt protective and with Peter being so dominating, it had me thinking I needed to dominate him, so your sister could be happy."

"My sister will have to make her peace with the life she's chosen." She eases her lips to mine and the kiss she gives me sends the butterflies that had swarmed my stomach into submission.

Everything will be fine. She's not going to leave me over this.

When will I ever learn...?

70

CAMILLA

With the contract in my hand, I leave Cyprian's office and make my way to give it back to Peter and try my best to smooth things out. Cyprian wanted to come with me but I explained how things would probably not go well if he was around.

All I want is for things to go back to normal. My sister and the kids come to visit a few times a year and most likely we'll never see Peter again, which is fine too. Now that I know he has another family.

I rehearse what I'll say all the way across town then find I'm on their street and see the black BMW that was following me, parked in the driveway behind my sister's car. I stop and wait and think about what I should do.

With no idea about what's going on, I give Catarina a call. "Camilla!" she answers the phone.

"Catarina, is everything okay?"

"No, did Cyprian tell you what he did to Peter?" she asks me then I hear shouting in the background.

"He did. Who's yelling?"

"Everyone. Did he call it all off?"

. . .

"He did. I was with him in his office when he made the call to leave Peter alone. I have the contract that's not worth the paper it's written on as it's totally illegal. It was a scare tactic but I wanted to give it to Peter, so he would feel some relief with it in his possession. I thought he might like to tear it up, himself."

"While that's really nice of you. I think it's best if you stay away from here. Three of his brothers arrived late last night. They're not in great moods with their brother's life being threatened."

I feel terrible my poor little niece and nephew are having to hear all this and it was Cyprian who caused it all. "Please let me try to smooth things out."

"Catarina, who the hell are you on the phone with?"

"Peter, just leave me alone. It's my sister," she says with a defeated voice.

"You tell her to come here. I want to have words with her."

Ending the call, I can't wait any longer for my sister to tell me I can go inside of their very chaotic home. Grabbing the paper, I get out of the car, keys in hand, locking the door behind me with my purse in the car.

As I get close to the back door, I plan on sneaking in, I find so much shouting going on and can't believe my sister hasn't put a stop to it. Instead of sneaking in, I throw the back door open and shout, "There's no need for all this! I have the contract and Peter is in no danger, what-so-ever!"

One of his brothers rips the paper from my hand, the other two have me on the ground, face down, before I realize what they've done. I don't see Peter or my sister anywhere and hear the kids crying somewhere in the house.

"You did just what Peter said you would, foolish woman!" one of them says as my hands are zip-tied behind my back.

"You need to let me go!" I scream and find my sister running into the kitchen where I've come in.

"Let her go!" she shouts just before Peter comes in behind her. "Go back to the room and take care of my children. They are crying, Catarina. I will deal with your sister."

"Peter, please!" she shouts.

I see her shaking and looking nowhere near the big sister I know. "I'll be okay, Catarina. I'll explain how things have been handled."

SHE TURNS TO LEAVE, not looking back at me and I know I have to do something to get her out of this hell hole she's managed to get herself into. I'm lifted up and sat on a chair from the dining set, I helped my sister pick out and Cyprian bought.

Peter pours himself a glass of milk then takes a seat too. "The man you brought into our lives has to be dealt with. Simply giving me back the contract and calling off the goons who were told to kill me if I did what it is my right to do, isn't enough. He must learn he can never do such a thing again."

"He knows. We talked. He'll never do anything like this again. I swear it to you, Peter. Please!"

"I can't allow you to marry him," he says as he looks me in the eye. "If you insist on keeping him in your family then mine will never visit again."

"Peter, please. Cyprian had a childhood that had him not learning how to form friendships. He's learning now. With time, you can expect a full apology. Now, it would be nice if you had them untie me. That's a thing he'll hate to see when I go back home."

"Not to worry. You won't be going back there. Not until we are long gone. I'm taking my family and leaving tonight. And you will be here, but not in plain sight."

SOMETHING IS RAN around my mouth then wrapped around my head, once they're done, I see it's duct tape as one of his brothers has a roll of it in his hand. The chair is yanked back and my ankles are bound with the tape too. I'm picked up and my already tied hands are bound with the tape too. Then I'm tossed over one of his brother's shoulders and taken away.

Down the hallway, I'm taken and up an attic staircase. An old sofa sits in the far corner. It seems he's heading for it and then I find, instead of being placed on it, I'm laid out behind it.

Dust moves around me in large puffs of gray. The sunlight bounces off the small particles and then I hear the footsteps move away from me and the sound of the stairs creaking back into place lets me know what their plan is.

They're going to leave me here, hoping I'll never be found. But I know I will be found. My car is parked across the street. Cyprian knew I was coming over here. He'll search every inch of this house, looking for me.

Trying to stay calm, I listen as Catarina asks where I've gone. Then I hear Peter telling her he let me go and they had to hurry up to get on his uncle's private jet to get on their way back home.

A bit of bustling is heard as I suppose she's gathering things and then he shouts about having to leave and with a flurry of commotion, I hear the door shut and lock. The sound of the alarm being set makes a loud dinging sound. Then I can hear the sound of cars starting and leaving the driveway.

My eyes are burning with tears that are threatening me. But I hold myself together as I think about what I can do to set myself free. I'm not a fool, if I can get free, I can call the police and press kidnapping charges on Peter and his brothers.

But I have to get free and get out to my car where my cell phone is. Rolling over to get out from behind the sofa, I find my body stirs up dust and sneezing with my mouth covered hurts like hell.

A small part of me wants to just give up but I can't. I need to get my sister set free from that monster. He's had her away from us and has her thinking he's something he's not.

He's not a good man. He's not a good husband. He's not a good anything and Cyprian was right about that. He could see right through him.

Well, I pray Cyprian still feels that way and decides to come looking for me. And this time when Cyprian wants to deal with him, I'll let him.

Is there a chance in hell this could end well...?

71

CYPRIAN

"She hasn't answered her cell in three hours," I tell the police officer I had come to my office. "I went to her sister's house, the place she was going when she left here. No one's there. Cami's car is parked across the street from the house, it's locked and I could see her purse and phone were lying on the passenger seat. Something's wrong."

"A person has to be missing 24 hours before we'll make a report and start a search. You said her car is at the residence. Have you tried to contact her sister?"

"Of course, I have. And her brother-in-law." I know I can't divulge the fact I threatened Peter and that has me hindered about what all I can say to the officer. So, I weigh my words carefully. "Neither of them are answering their phones. I gave them each a car and those cars are gone. Do you think you can start a search for those cars? They do belong to me."

"I can do that if you want to report them stolen. But you just told me you gave them the cars, so they aren't stolen. Look, Mr. Girard, if you're really worried then maybe you should hire a private investigator. Our hands are tied until tomorrow," he tells me and puts his little pad of paper and pen away.

Giving him a nod, I get up and escort him out of my office. My mind is a mess. I know something has to be wrong. I know Cami didn't go with them anywhere. I went all through that house and no one's there and many of their clothes seem to be missing.

CALLING ASHTON, I think it's time to call in some favors, since the police seem to have their hands tied. "Mr. Girard, are you ready to be picked up?"

"Yes, and do you know anyone who specializes in finding missing people?" I ask him as I grab my jacket and head out of my office. "The police can't do anything about Cami until tomorrow. That's not good enough for me, so I'm taking things into my own hands and I need more than my one set."

"I'll make some calls. Where would you like for people to meet with you?"

"My place. Get all the help you can find, please. I have a feeling Peter is taking his family and leaving the country. I also have a feeling he might be the only one who knows where Cami is."

"On it, sir."

I wish I felt relief that I'm soon to get help but I don't think any relief will come until I have Cami, safe in my arms again.

Hurrying out, I get into the back seat of the BMW and Ashton takes off. He's on the phone and looks at me through the rearview mirror. "I can have my cousin, Franco, run by the airport to check for the cars you gave them."

"Do that. Take me out to the house. I want to pick up the spare key for the Lamborghini, so I can check it out better. Did you know of any private investigators who might be able to help?"

"I have my sister, Lola, working on that. She's going to get back to me. Her ex-husband is a retired cop. There's a chance he knows someone," Ashton tells me.

"I feel an urgency moving within me that I've never felt before. I know she's in real danger, I can feel it." I pull my phone out and try her sister's number again and find it's going straight to voicemail now. So, I call her parents' home.

"HELLO?" her mother answers the phone.

"Mrs. Petit, it's me, Cyprian."

"Ana, call me Ana, Cyprian. What can I do for you this fine morning?" she asks, sounding chipper and I hate to be the one who will ruin her morning but it seems I'm about to do just that.

"Ana, do you have more than one phone number for Catarina? Cami went to their house this morning and now I can't find her. Catarina and Peter have left with their children and most of their clothes are gone."

"Hold on a minute. Let me get Tommy in on this conversation," she tells me then I hear her yelling for her husband to pick up another phone.

"What's going on, Cyprian?" he asks as I hear a clattering sound as he picks up the phone.

"Cami's missing. And to a lesser extent, so is Catarina and the kids. Peter has to have taken them all somewhere. I can't get a hold of any of them. Cami's car is still parked across the street from their house but no one's in it. Their cars are gone and I'm beyond worried."

"Let me try to call her from my cell," Tommy says and I wait to see if she'll answer him. "Catarina, where are you?"

I breathe out a sign of relief that she's answered him and cross my fingers she knows where I can find Cami. "Thank God."

"What do you mean, you're at the airport?" Tommy asks her. "Where is your sister?"

More silence keeps me waiting and holding my body tense. "Please let her be okay."

"Catarina, Cyprian said he went to your house and her car's there but she's not," Tommy says. "And why are you going back to Cape Town?"

I'm thinking that I need to get to the airport, so I call out to

Ashton, "New plan. Take me to the airport. Catarina and Peter are there."

Making a quick turn, Ashton gets on route to the airport. As I hear Tommy ask, "Why would you follow him then?"

"TELL her that Peter has already married that other woman he told her he was considering and that she is already pregnant. He's been married for months," I tell Tommy.

Ana gasps and Tommy says, "Where is Peter right now?"

"Tell her I think Peter's done something with Cami," I say and hope we're getting closer to finding her.

"Okay, good. I have something to tell you and I'm afraid you're going to be shocked. Cyprian just told me that Peter has taken another wife and she's pregnant. He's been married for months. He also thinks Peter has done something with Camilla."

"Tell her, she should get the kids and hide from Peter and his brothers until I get some help to her," I tell Tommy and hope we can get to her and the kids in time.

"You have to stop crying," he tells her. "You have to get a hold of yourself. Get the kids and hide from Peter and his brothers. Cyprian is going to get help to you. Now I need you to think very hard. Where could your sister be?"

The sound of fire trucks come from behind us, making Ashton pull over to the side of the road to let them pass. I watch them take the exit off the highway that is the same exit you take to get to the house I rented for Peter and Catarina. "Follow those trucks, Ashton. I have a terrible feeling."

He does as I say as I hear Tommy say, "Catarina says Camilla has to still be in the house. No one left from the time she saw her there until the time they left. Peter told her that Camilla was going to lock the house up after they left."

My heart starts to thump harder in my chest as we're stopped a ways back on the street their house is on. And I can see smoke billowing out of the windows on the first floor of the house I rented for her sister and brother-in-law.

"TELL CATARINA that the house is on fire. We just followed firetrucks to it. Tell her to hide herself and her kids and I'm about to be sending the authorities to pick up her husband and his brothers from the airport. Once they're all secured then I'll call you, Tommy, so you can tell her where to go. I'll have someone pick them up. Ask her how many of his brothers are there, so I can make sure they all get picked up."

"She says three of them and to please hurry. The jet is being fueled up," Tommy tells me.

"Got it. I'll call you soon." I put the phone on the seat next to me and get out of the car.

Ashton jumps out, grabbing my arm. "Where do you think you're going? They won't let you anywhere near that house."

I didn't have a plan at all until he said that. "You go tell them about Peter and his brothers. I'm going into that house through the back while you have them occupied."

"No!" he shouts at me. "No way!"

I shake off his hand and start walking away. "Cami's in that house. And I searched it all before. Except for one place. I have to go in. Even if I die, I'll die with her. I can't live without her, anyway."

"Cyprian! Don't!" he shouts as he comes up beside me. "Please!"

"Go tell the authorities about Peter and that he and his brothers orchestrated this and if I find Cami inside then they meant to kill her. They have to be stopped before they get out of the country."

With no choice, Ashton runs up to the firemen and policemen at the front of the house. I slip into the neighboring house's backyard and climb over the tall privacy fence. Peeking over the top of it, I see the fire is in the front of the house right now. The back door is ajar and only puffs of smoke are coming out of it.

I must've left the door open, I suppose, when I checked it a while ago. I hurry to get over the fence and make my way to the back door. Just as I slip inside, I hear a man yelling, "Hey, you! Stop!"

But I can't stop...

72

CAMILLA

The sound of firetrucks has my heart pounding harder than I believe it ever has before. The smell of smoke is a major concern and I think the loud sound I heard a little while ago was something blowing up.

Everything is muffled up here, in the attic. I can hear men's voices and the sounds of their radios going off but I can' make out what anyone is saying. The duct tape they used to cover my mouth is wrapped around my head. It has my ears covered too, making it hard to hear a thing.

I need to get my body up off this floor, somehow. There's a window at the other end of the attic. If I can get to that, maybe someone will see me and help me. If I don't manage that, I'm most likely going to die in this place.

Rolling back to the old sofa, I maneuver my body until I'm lying, face-first, on the floor in front of it. My hands are tied behind my back, so I have no use of them. Arching up, I use my hips to move my body closer to the sofa until I can use my chin to help left my body up.

My neck hurts as I put tremendous pressure on it, to leverage my body up as much as I possibly can. I get to my knees and am able to put the top half of my body on the dusty, stinky, old red cloth sofa and get my feet underneath me.

I get up, slowly. My ankles are taped so tightly I can't move them independently. It's hard to balance with my body so bound up but I manage and start hopping across the floor toward the one window up here.

With my first jump, I find myself having to regain my balance again. As I breathe heavily with fear and the effort my body is making, I can smell the smoke more. It seems the front of the house is what's on fire. And that's where the damn window is.

I make another jump and hear the sound of wood splintering. Another jump has me nearly falling over and the smell of smoke is worse and there is more heat on this side of the attic.

Stopping to regain my balance and my bearings, I look around and see wisps of smoke coming up through some of the cracks that are beginning to form as the fire underneath is spreading to the attic.

Suddenly, I change my entire plan. I need to make it to the attic door. Maybe if I can jump up and down on it, I might get it to fall open. That means I'll fall to the floor but if I continue on this path, I could fall through the floor and into the fire.

Making it near the wall, I lean on it for support while I rest a moment and try to gain some strength that's been sapped from me. I close my eyes and picture Cyprian. Just in case I never see him again, I want to remember him just one more time.

His touch, his smell, his smile, his body. I just wish like hell I had listened to him and not come over here alone. He was right and I was wrong and it may have cost me my life.

Tears fall as I shake my head to shake off the feelings of failure. I have yet to try. I have no idea if I'll succeed or not, until I try.

I hop once, twice. I can see the inset of where the attic door is and it seems to be about three more hops away. So, I go for the next one and find my feet going all the way through the floor.

I am falling...

73

CYPRIAN

So the fireman who spotted me can't find me, I lock the kitchen door behind me. It might be a foolish act but I can't let him stop me. "Cami!"

Hopefully, Ashton told the other firemen that someone might be in here. Suddenly, I hear the sound of squealing tires and sirens moving away from the house. I hope that means police officers are heading to the airport to get the bastards who did this.

If the authorities don't take care of them, I will!

THE SMOKE IS GETTING THICKER the further I move into the house. The hallway is in the center of the house. The attic door is on the ceiling of the second floor. Although going up the stairs is a stupid thing to do. I have a gut feeling that Cami is in that attic.

"Cami!" I shout again as I get to the top of the stairs and see the attic door. A horrible cracking sound fills my ears and I look behind me and see red and yellow flames, licking at the bottom of the stairs.

"Fuck!" I scream. "Can't you cut me a break?"

Pulling the attic door open, I find the stairs there and pull them down then climb up. "Cami!"

I pull myself up into the attic and stand up, finding a hole not too far away. Walking over, I see a bed through the hole. That's all I can see is a bed and I have no idea why this hole is here or how long it's been here.

Walking a bit further, I want to make sure I cover every inch of this attic. The smell is awful up here. And I can see the glow of the fire beneath me as I walk closer to the front of the house.

Sparks of yellow light fill the air in front of me and a loud crackling sound makes me step back as half of the attic floor gives away. The flames are huge and it's hot as hell. I step backward, quickly.

Too quickly. I've stepped into the damn hole and now I'm falling through the floor into what, I have no clue.

Have I made a terrible mistake…?

74

CAMILLA

L ying on the floor of another room, I blink as I regain consciousness. The fall had me hitting something and flying through the air and landing head first, knocking me out. For how long, I don't know.

I do know it's hot and smells like fire and brimstone and I hope this isn't hell. I can hear the sound of more wood cracking and roll over to see what's happening as I'm face first, down on the floor.

My body hurts like hell and I think something might just be broken. I'm having a hard time breathing. That could be from too much smoke inhalation or a broken rib. Quite possibly both.

As I roll the rest of the way over, I catch the sight of someone falling through the hole in the ceiling I caused. He bounces on the bed and flies through the air.

I roll as fast as I can to get out of the way as I see Cyprian's face looking frantically at me. "Cami, move!"

IT HURTS to roll but I do it and manage to get out of his way. Like a cat, he springs up after he lands and picks me up. I groan as it hurts so bad and now I am certain I have broken ribs on my right side.

"Baby, there's not time to stop and get you out of this fucking duct tape. You're going to have to hold on, while I throw you over my shoulder and get you out of here," he tells me as he searches the room.

Pulling off the bedspread and the sheet under that, he runs to the bathroom that's attached to the bedroom. I watch as he tries the water in the sink but nothing comes out of it. Not waiting a beat, he opens the toilet lid and plunges the things into it to wet them as much as possible.

He comes toward me with the blanket and wraps it around me like a cocoon. I can't see a thing but know he's wrapped the wet sheet around himself and then I'm tossed over his wide shoulder.

I cry out with the pain in my ribs but he can't hear that with this shit covering my mouth. "Just hold on, baby. I love you. I'm going to get you to safety."

Closing my eyes, I start praying as I know this house in close to being engulfed in flames. And then we're moving and the pain of me being bobbed around has blackness coming.

I can't take it...

75

CYPRIAN

s I get into the second-floor hallway, I see there's no way we're getting out through the stairs. I race to a bedroom at the very back of the house and lay Cami on the bed, so I can open the window.

She lies still, so I pull back the blanket and see she's passed out. Looking around the room for something to at least cut the tape off her mouth, I find nothing and decide to hurry to get her the hell out of here.

I RUN to the window and push it open then push the screen out. It falls to the ground but no one's back here. I see a neighbor in a back-yard, two house over and shout, "Hey! Hey!"

He looks up at me and his eyes go wide. "You need to get the hell out of there!"

"No shit, Sherlock! Can you go tell one of the firemen about me? There's no other way out. I need a ladder and I have a woman here too."

He nods and hauls ass inside his home. With a bit of time, I go and start to pull at the tape, covering her mouth. I find the end of it and begin to unwrap it. I can see it was ran around her head four times, as I unravel it.

I'm gently tugging it away from her skin and hate finding the red welts it's leaving on her face. I kiss it all over. "Cami, wake up."

Her breathing is shallow and she's not waking up. Finally, I hear voices outside the window. "Wait there! We're coming up to you."

I look out the window and see six firemen with a tall ladder and one is climbing up to us. "Thank God!"

I go and pick up Cami, waiting for the man to get to me. As he sees her, he gasps, "Someone wanted to kill her."

"You're right. Can you get her? I can follow you down, on my own," I say as I move her over to lie across his shoulder.

"I have her. Come on," he says and starts down the ladder with her.

I WAIT a second and take in a breath. Relief washes over me as I know she's safe. The bedroom door bursts open as the flames have found me. Moving quickly, I climb out the window and onto the ladder and get out of the burning house.

Once on the ground, I watch a couple of the firemen cut the tape off her wrists and ankles. A couple of paramedics come with a stretcher and put Cami, who's still not awake, on it.

I make it to her side and run my hand over her face. "Cami, wake up."

"We have to check her vital signs out. You can meet us at the emergency room."

I nod then kiss her forehead. "Tell her I'm right behind you, if she wakes up. Tell her, Cyprian said he loves her more than anything in this world."

The woman paramedic gives me a nod and they slide her into the back of the ambulance. Wasting no time, I spot Ashton and wave at him to get to the car. He rushes to me. "I told the police. They were rushing to the airport. I have no idea what else has happened. So, you found her?"

"She was all taped up. I found her in a bedroom but I think she fell there from the attic. She was awake when I found her but me moving her had her fainting. Follow that ambulance." I get into the back of the car and fasten my seatbelt as Ashton gets in and we take off, after the vehicle that has my life in it.

My hands are shaking as I make the call to Cami's parents. "Cyprian?" her father answers.

"That piece of shit had your daughter bound and gagged in the attic of the house. And he must've set some kind of a timed contraption to catch the house on fire. She was nearly killed. I got her out and she's on the way to the hospital right now. I'm right behind her."

"My God!" her father shouts. "What in the hell has happened? Did you talk to her? Is she okay?"

"She was awake when I found her but when I moved her, she fainted. Her mouth was covered with tape. I didn't get a chance to hear her say anything. But I will get back with you as soon as I know anything. The police were sent to get Peter and his brothers. You should call Catarina and find out if she's managed to stay hidden."

"I will. I let you know." He ends the call and I find we're pulling into the emergency room parking lot.

HURRYING to get out and get back to her side, I put my phone in my pocket and find Ashton coming right behind me. I turn back to him. "Can you call that cousin that was going to the airport to check on things and let me know if he knows anything?"

He nods and goes to a small outdoor area to make the call. I get to Cami and see her eyes are open. "Hi," I whisper.

"Hi," she says with a hoarse voice. "Thank you. You're my hero."

"You're my everything. Are you hurt?" I ask her as I run my hand over her red cheek as they hurry to get her inside.

"My ribs are most likely broken." She closes her eyes.

"I didn't do that when I tossed you over my shoulder, did I?" I ask, praying I didn't do that to her.

"No," she opens her eyes and looks at me. "It happened when I fell through the floor of the attic."

We're hustled into a small examining room and a doctor comes straight to her. "Hello, I'm Doctor Bennet."

The paramedics give him their papers as he shines a light in Cami's eyes. I stand beside her and hold her hand while he looks her over and asks her questions. My mind is numb as I think about how close I came to losing her.

Some chattering in the hallway draws my attention as a woman says, "Did you see the breaking news, Jules? There's a situation at the airport."

Listening a lot harder, I hear the other woman say. "I did. It's awful. Some woman and her kids are being held by some men from Africa. The police are trying to negotiate with them for their release but they're at a stand-off."

"Shit!" I hiss, under my breath.

"Why'd you say that?" Cami asks me.

"It's nothing," I kiss her cheek. "I need to make a phone call. Are you going to be okay for a minute or two?'

"We're going to take her to get x-rays," the doctor says. "You can wait in here for us to bring her back, if you'd like."

I nod and give her hand a squeeze. "I'll be here."

SHE WATCHES me as I walk out of the room and I find her looking at me like she knows I'm not being truthful with her. She can be mad at me later. Right now, she needs to worry about nothing, except getting herself taken care of.

"Hello, Papa, I need a diversion sent to the airport. Get together a large group of the escorts and get them headed that way. I'll get in contact with you in just a bit."

"Is this about that hostage situation? Do you know those people? They haven't released any names yet," he says.

"I know who it is. It's mostly my fault it has come to this. So, I need to do what I can to fix it." I find Ashton outside and go over to him, "Bye, Papa."

"I found out all about it. More than the news people know. I have two of my cousins who went to go find them. What they came upon was the beginning of the whole thing. Catarina and the kids were being pulled out of one of the ladies' rooms by Peter and three other men. I was able to send them pictures I took of them, secretly. I had a feeling I'd need some pictures of them."

"Okay, you were right. I know that now and if you'd like to know, I will always follow your advice from now on, Ashton. But you have to admit, ignoring your advice about Cami was a good thing."

"Anyway," he says as he takes a seat. "The men have Catarina and the kids holed up in another restroom. They say they have knives and will kill her and the kids if the police don't allow them to get on their private jet and go back to South Africa."

"The news of there being a woman in the house should speed up the process with that situation, I should think," I say as I take a seat too.

"Maybe. What gets me is the fact no one has seen a knife. They have had gone through customs and the x-ray machine and there were no knives found on them. I think they're bluffing. But the cops won't take that risk."

"I think you're right. And you said you have two men there right now?"

"I do," he says with a nod.

"Are they capable of helping me take those men out?"

"If you're talking about fighting, not killing," he says with a wink.

"I am only talking about that. Getting into that restroom and getting them subdued while we get Catarina, Sadie, and Sax out. Then the cops can take care of them."

"Can I help?" he asks with a grin.

"I THINK SO. There's four men and four of us. We should be able to make things happen. And I have a caravan of women heading that way.

They can be between us and the police. We can look like a group of people who know nothing is going on and then only us men will swoop into the restroom and take out the trash," I say and he nods in approval.

"I think that might work. Make it happen, Cyprian."

Can this really work…?

76

CAMILLA

"**W**hat do you mean, you're going to go home to get me some comfy clothes to wear?" I ask Cyprian who's making all kinds of excuses to leave me here in the hospital.

I was admitted for the broken ribs, I knew I had, and so they can watch me for 24 hours to be sure I'm going to be fine. And he's acting shady as shit.

"That hospital gown looks so uncomfortable. I'll bring back a cozy pajama set and pick up your toiletries. I want you to feel completely comfortable, Cami. It won't take long. I promise."

"Just tell me the real deal, Cyprian."

A KNOCK at the door has us looking to see who has come and I see three uniformed police coming into my room. "Hello, Camilla Petit. We have to get your statement."

Giving Cyprian a look, I say, "Go get the stuff while I tell them what happened to me and please hurry back to me. I miss you already."

With a kiss to my cheek, he's gone in a flash and I just know he's up to something and he doesn't want me to know a thing about it. One of the officers asks me, "How are you dealing with the news, miss?"

Cocking my head to the side, I ask, "Which part?"

The other officer looks sad as he says, "You know, your sister and her kids being held by her husband and his brothers?"

"Oh that news," I say like I knew all about that. But I had no idea. And now I know what Cyprian is going to do.

Play hero again...

77

CYPRIAN

About fifteen women meet us at a lobby near to where the situation is occurring. The airport is trying to keep it under control by moving people around the area that's been contained.

I have two of the women going to take the attention of the two cops guarding the area we need to break into. We all act as if we're a group of travelers and kind of a bumbling bunch.

We men have donned crappy leisure suits, fake mustaches, and old hats to disguise us all. Thanks to Ashton's extensive collection of seventies-wear, it was easy to make the changes.

Ashton, his cousins and I lean on various poles, waiting to see if the girls can get the cops to leave their posts. The situation is a calm one. There's no brandishing of weapons. No type of communication is going on at all between the cops and the people inside that restroom.

The cops have no choice but wait it out, I guess. But we don't!

. . .

I NOTICE the complacency the officers have. Most are looking anywhere but at the opening of the bathroom. There's no door, all we have to do is slip in.

I see the officers walking away with the women decoys and gesture for us to get on the move. Being quiet but I have the women talking amongst themselves, seeming distracted. While the other men and I trail along the outer area of them. Just as we get to the bathroom, one of the officers looks up. "Hey, you're not supposed to be in this area!"

"Let's go," I whisper and just like I told them to, the women bunch up, so we're not seen.

We get into the restroom to find everyone just sitting on the floor. The element of surprise is on our side and I yank up one of the men and wrap a zip tie around his wrists before he knows what's happened.

Ashton takes another and has to deliver a swift blow to the chin that sends the smaller man to the ground where one of his cousins makes short work of tying his hands behind his back.

Peter is eyeing me as he gets in front of Catarina and her children. His one free brother joins him and I look into Catarina's teal blue eyes and smile. "You ready to be free of this bastard?"

She nods and when he looks back to see her, I slam my fist into his stomach as the others grab the one brother left and bond his hands. I step back and open my arms as Peter regains his composure and glares at me. "You have ruined my life."

"You did that to yourself," I tell him. "Did you tell your wife how you tied up her sister and left her to burn to death in your home?"

Catarina goes pale "Is she alright?"

Peter spins around to look at her. "Do not ever speak to this man."

He PULLS his hand back to slap her and before I can do a thing, Catarina has slapped the shit out of the man. He falls back with the hard hit and then she's on top of him, beating the hell out of him. "You fucking bastard! I'll kill you!"

I look past them and see their children hiding their eyes. Then I walk over and lift Catarina off her husband. "There you go guys, tie his hands and let's take them to the cops."

Catarina's cries have me holding her. "Hush now. Your children are watching."

She pulls it together, stifling her sobs. "Later, though, I will wail like a banshee."

"That's cool," I say and let her go, so I can pick up Sax and hand him to her then I take Sadie and carry her out.

As we leave the restroom, the look of shock that fills the police officers' faces is comical. "How did you get in there?" one of them asks us.

Ashton fields that question. "We had to use the restroom and found these men holding this woman and kids in there. Why do you ask?"

"Because we've been on top of the situation, that's why," the officer says as he looks us all over.

Ashton shrugs his shoulders. "Don't know what to tell you. Here you go, though." He gently nudges the man he's holding toward the speechless cop and we all do the same.

"If you'll excuse us, we have a plane to catch," Ashton says.

"I'll catch up with you. No names, okay?" I ask her to make sure she gets what we're doing.

WITH A NOD FROM HER, we leave. Making a hasty retreat before one of the officers starts thinking and realizes we should be kept for questioning.

Once we're back in my car, I call my father to get the girls out of the airport and back to where ever it is they came from. After a quick drop off of his cousins at their cars, I change back into my original clothes in the back of the car and find we're back at the hospital, thanks again to Ashton and his knowledge of shortcuts.

With a bag his wife made up with toiletries and a set of PJ's for Cami, I get out and go inside to find Cami is finished with her statement to the police and I meet them on their way out. "Done already?" I ask them as I step back, so they can get out of her room.

"Yes, it's pretty cut and dry. Take good care of her. She's a real sweetie," one of them says.

"I will," I say and sweep into the room to find her frowning at me. I hold my finger to my lips to let her know to remain quiet. After a moment, I look back out the door to make sure the cops have left.

"I know about Catarina and the kids," she says as she looks so deep into my eyes, I think she can see my soul.

"No need to worry, baby. That's handled." I take a seat on the edge of her bed and push her hair back. "I'm going to take care of everything."

"Cyprian," she says but I stop her with a kiss.

When I end it, I look at her. "I love you. I love you so much, I'd do anything for you. I know I've done things that started this chain of events. The main thing is you all are safe. Catarina will never have to worry about that man or losing her kids again. And I hope she's learned something about life from this. I'm going to get her the best lawyers, so she can get a divorce and gain custody of the kids. Peter will be rotting away in prison. I'll make sure of that too."

"You seem so sure of everything, Cyprian," she says, sounding skeptical.

"I hear doubt in your voice, Camilla Petit." I kiss her cheek and get up to open the curtains and let the sunlight stream into her hospital room. "Never doubt me or my commitment to you."

"Well, you did come into a burning house for me," she says as she looks at me. "So, tell me how my sister's ordeal ended."

Clicking on the television, I let her hear it from the news reporter. "It's on every local station."

She listens as the reporter says, "It seems the men never had knives, Steve. The officer in charge told us a group of women roamed in between them and the restroom where the men were holding the hostages. There must've been some men with the large group and they slipped into the restrooms to relieve themselves. That's when they found the situation and hastily took care of the men, even using zip-ties to bind their hands. Once they handed over the men to police, the heroes, simply disappeared."

"How?" she asks me. "How did you manage that?"

"Me?" I ask with a high voice. "What makes you think I had anything to do with that?"

"You will tell me every last detail, Cyprian Girard. But after we get home." She holds out her hand and I take it then she pulls me close and kisses me with a soft sweet kiss. "You are going to make a wonderful husband and father if you can manage to not help create such situations in the first place."

"I'll take that. So, when do you think you'll see fit to marry me?" I ask her as I sit on the edge of her bed.

"I'm going to be laid up for a while." She frowns, making me feel sorry for her.

"I'll see what I can do for you, baby. A home wedding, perhaps? In our bedroom?"

"Guess what, Romeo," she says. "Now, I'm off limits for six weeks while my ribs heal.

"And I will be every bit as good to you as you were to me when I was laid up and out of sexual commission. It's what couples do for one another.

As I look at her and think about how close we came to not having this conversation, I have to lay my head on hers and thank the lord above for her.

How will I ever repay him...?

78

CAMILLA

"I like blue," I tell Catarina as she sits on the side of my bed, looking through a wedding planning magazine.

"But pale peach is so in." She flips the page and squeals. "No, wait! Look at this." She shows me a deep red wedding gown. "Crimson!"

"No, I'm not about to let you get a dress that looks as if I'm marrying Satan! Let me see the damn magazine. You can make your own wedding plans with the handsome detective you met while you were dealing with the hoopla of Peter."

"Do you think he and I will really get that far? He's so handsome and protective and I think I love him already," she gushes. "He came into that little room and I found his soft green eyes looking at me with such compassion, my heart melted. Then he took Sax and held him and made him feel better. He was such a take charge kind of man. And I love that. We've been inseparable since that day, three weeks ago."

"I know. And I know you're probably going to leave us soon and move in with him. I see the writing on the wall," I say as she smiles.

"If he asks, I sure will. That lawyer, Cyprian got me, is making miracles happen with the divorce and custody hearings. I'll be a free woman in no time."

"Then the detective will take you back into marital custody, I expect."

She gets up and dances around the bedroom. "Oh, I hope so."

Cyprian comes in with Sax in his arms. "Someone has poopie pants, Mommy."

"Of course he does," Catarina says as she takes her son and leaves us alone in our bedroom.

"Thanks again for all you've done, Cyprian," I tell him, the way I do three or four times each day. "She's never looked happier. Even though I do believe she needs to take a breather in the relationship department."

"Not everyone needs the same things in life. Some wait forever between relationships and some hop right back onto that horse. Your sister seems to like the presence of a dominating man in her life. And I like the new one. He's not a bad guy at all."

"I'm glad to hear you recommend him," I say as I laugh then stop as it still hurts my healing ribs to laugh.

"Have you done any of your classwork online today, baby?" he asks me as he picks up my laptop that's sat at my desk all day without me turning it on.

"I have not. Do you care to help a poor lass?" I say as he comes to sit on the bed next to me and props the laptop on a pillow.

"I will help my lady educate herself, so she can become a mind-blowingly smart scientist." He opens it and starts it up as I gaze at him.

"What would I ever do without you?"

"You will never find that out. I will always be here for you. Now which class would you like to tackle first?"

I point at the class on the desk top and it comes up as I touch the screen. "You know what color wedding dress Catarina said I should get?"

"No," he says as he taps the screen to open my next assignment. "Was it awful or what?"

"It was crimson. A deep red. Like one would wear to marry the devil," I say as I point at the magazine on the bed.

He picks it up and thumbs through it. "I still can't believe you are so against a white wedding dress."

"I want to stand out. Everyone wears white. I want to be different. You only get married once, right? I don't want our wedding pictures to look just like all the others."

Watching him look through the magazine, I find him stopping on a page and looking back and forth at me and the page. "I think you'd look amazing in this one."

When he turns it around for me to see, I see the pale blue dress I had liked and my sister had nixed. "Great minds think alike. I had liked that one too. Catarina didn't like it."

"Well, this isn't for her to like or dislike. This is for you, my sweet lady. That day is about you," he says then runs his hand over my cheek.

"And you," I say as I push his light brown hair back. "Us."

"Us," he echoes. "I still can't believe so many years passed me by, leaving me thinking I wanted to live alone, living a decadent life with no worries, ties, or real people in it."

"THEN YOU DECIDED to stop in at a little store and bother the cashier."

"Bother?" he asks. "I wouldn't say that word."

"I would," I say then kiss his cheek. "Come on, let's get this work done then you can give your lady a sponge bath. We can discuss the honeymoon plans."

"Bora Bora?" he asks as he's pushing for that as a honeymoon destination.

"France," I say as I'm pushing that destination. "And here's the kicker, Cyprian. "I'm thinking about a destination wedding. My family would love to visit the place where my grandparents and father came from. Your father's roots are there too. Perhaps he could delve into them a bit."

"You'd like nothing more than to teach my parents how to be a part of a family, isn't that right?" he asks.

"So," I say as I push a button on the screen and select my answer to the question.

"So, you might be disappointed," he says. "They're set in their ways."

"As were you," I say and give him a smile. "Give me time. You'll see."

And he will too...

BOOK 11: THE ALTERING

A Bad Boy Billionaire Romance

By Michelle Love

79

CYPRIAN

"Every man needs a bachelor party, Cyprian," my father tells me as I ride with him to enjoy a nice meal out as a single man. My father has been pushing for a real bachelor party for weeks now. I've insisted I don't want one.

I've had enough partying to last a lifetime!

"Papa, I know you think that's a thing I should have but I've told you a hundred times, I don't want one. Let's just enjoy a nice meal together on the last night I'll be a single man and let that be that."

I watch his foot begin to tap as we ride in the back of his limousine. His finger starts tapping his leg and I see sweat begin to bead on his forehead. His obvious nerves are making me nervous. I'm sure he's got something up his sleeve.

The car pulls to a stop at an old warehouse and I find my father looking more than a bit sheepish. "Here we are, son."

The driver gets out and opens my door. A blindfold is in his hand and I turn to find my father getting out too. "Papa, what's going on?"

"Just go with it, Cyprian," he says as he chuckles. "It's going to be fun. I promise."

Taking my phone out of my pocket, I attempt to call Cami but I find my father has it in his hand and tosses it back into the car then shuts the door. "Papa!"

"Come now, Cyprian. The guests are waiting." He takes me by the shoulders and turns me around then the driver places the blindfold over my eyes.

"Papa, I don't like this!"

"Come now, Cyprian. Be a good sport, won't you?" he asks as he leads me away from the car and into, what's certain to be, a den of iniquity.

The squeaking sound of a door opening has me feeling like I should rip off the blindfold and bolt away from my father. But I can't seem to make myself do that. Even though I know I should!

CHEERS RING out and music begins to play as we walk into a cool room. Air is forced out of vents and it makes a slight breeze run over my face as we go deeper into the room.

We stop as my father directs me, "Here we have four women..."

"No, Papa!"

"Hush, Cyprian. It's a game. That's all," he says. "Okay, here we have four women. You are to touch only their hands. I want you to pick the one who stirs something inside of you when you touch her."

"There's only one who stirs anything inside of me. She's out with her sister and mother for her bachelorette dinner. So, I will touch them all and you will see, I'm telling the truth when I say Camilla Petit is the only woman who does anything for me."

"Yes, yes," he says, hurrying me along. "Come now. Here's the first set of hands. Hold them, Cyprian. Tell us what you feel."

I take the hands which are extended to me and hold them in a loose grip. "Nothing stirs me. Sorry."

"Here, try the next set," he says as he takes me and moves me over a step.

I stop myself from gasping as I take the hands and feel their shape is recognizable. But nothing inside me lights up. Running my thumbs over the palms the woman whose hands I have in mine, I find them familiar. "These hands remind me of someone's but they're not hers."

"That someone being who, son?" my father asks with a slight chuckle to his deep voice.

"Cami's. But I know it's not her. Not only is she not here, the touch of her hands always moves me. Those hands didn't move me at all. No offense," I say as I nod in the direction of the woman. "They're lovely hands."

I hear a giggle and think I recognize it but the music is so loud it's hard to say for sure. My father moves me over a step. "This young lady is next."

Stepping over, I find my hands are taken quickly and I know in an instant, these hands hold no attraction for me. "I don't feel a thing. Next," I say.

"Last set, son," Papa says.

"I'm sorry ladies. Only one holds my heart in the palm of her hands and I can feel it there every time I hold her hands."

Moving my hands to find the next pair of them, I find them nowhere. Then the slightest touch of a fingertip sends lightning through me. I fight the urge to pull off the blindfold as her hands take hold of mine and my cock twitches.

Please let this be Cami and not someone else!

HOLDING back the real question I want to ask, I say, "Hmm, there is a bit of something here."

Her thumbs rub the tops of my hands as mine rub her palms. My cock grows as I move my hands up her arms and find spiral curls, soft as silk. I twirl one of the curls with my finger and take in her scent.

"What do you have to say about this one, Cyprian?" Papa asks me. "Is she to your liking?"

"I believe she is," I say and pull her into my arms, certain it's Cami I'm holding. "Care to dance?"

I feel her nod her answer and sweep her away with me to dance.

Holding her close, I spin around with her to the fast music and know it's her as our bodies are very familiar with each other.

Her taught nipples press against my chest, sending my cock into a full-on erection and my need for her is a necessity. She moves her body to grind herself on my dick and her lips press the place just behind my ear.

"Perhaps we should find somewhere private to go and take care of your little problem," she says.

I stop and let her go. That's not Cami's voice!

JUST AS I'M about to take off the blindfold, her hands grab mine. "Don't," I shout.

She pulls me back to her with a whisper, "Come on. It's your last night as a free man."

Her voice is much too high to be Cami's, I've made a mistake. "It's been a while since I was a free man. I'm sorry. I can't do this. It's not right."

Pulling away from her, I find she won't let my hand go. "Stay."

Shaking my head, I say, "No. You would never understand. You're an escort, I'm sure. You don't know what it means to love and be loved. I know I never want to be with anyone other than the woman I will marry tomorrow. It's nothing against you. I'm sure you're very nice."

"You felt something when we touched," she says with such a high voice it seems unnatural. "Admit it."

"Cami?" I ask as I jerk my hand out of hers and pull the blindfold off.

Her sweet smile is what I find and I growl as I take her hand again and pull her off the dancefloor as she says, "You don't seem very surprised."

Sitting on a chair at an empty table, I pull her to sit on my lap. She strokes my cheek as I look around and see my father yapping it up with her sister and her mother. "I see what you did there. Are you quite happy with yourself?"

She nods and kisses me. "You do love me."

"I do," I tell her then kiss her.

Our mouths mingle, letting our tongues do the talking. When we end the kiss, we're both panting a bit. "Tomorrow, you and I will really become one. Are you ready for that, Cyprian?"

"More than you can imagine," I say as I scout the room for the exit. "Are you ready to get out of here?"

"CYPRIAN, your father put a great deal of work into planning this. It would be rude to leave. And I'm here with you, so all is well. Come on, let's dance and drink and eat and live it up. It's our very last date, you know." Climbing off my lap, she gets up and takes me back out onto the dancefloor full of people I don't know as my father has managed to fill a room with strangers.

"Our very own party in Paris," I say as we dance around the floor.

"And there's more surprises for you. You see, some of these people are your family. Distant relatives I managed to find when I looked for people in France you and your father might be related to. You'll be discovering a family while you're here," she tells me with a wink.

"You managed to hide all that?" I ask. "What else do you have up your sleeve, naughty wench?"

"A lot. So, get prepared, Cyprian. Your small world is about to open up."

Is that really a good thing...?

80

CAMILLA

H e really loves me!
     I never should've doubted that but sometimes a woman just has to know. Cyprian has had so many women in his life I was unsure if he really felt as strongly about me as he has claimed to.

He knew the moment he touched my hand it was me. I was worried, I have to admit. He lingered on my sister's hands longer than I thought he would. It had me thinking my idea was going to backfire on me and put me in an awful mood.

Retiring from the busy and boisterous dancefloor, I lead Cyprian to meet his never before known, great aunt and great uncle. "Here's your surprise family, Cyprian."

As they all share hugs and exchange hello's, I fall back a bit and gesture to his father to come and join his son in this happy moment. I scan the room to find Cyprian's mother and catch her eye and wave her over too.

It's such an odd way his parents are. In no way, a couple, yet they share something that makes them a part of one another. I hope to get them to see they mean more to each other than either of them realize.

"You're aunt and uncle, Corbin. These are your father's siblings who moved here after a few years in America," I tell him as he approaches us.

He blinks a few times as he looks at them, talking with his son. "How'd you find them? I knew about them. They moved long before I was born. My father told me about them."

"You can find everything on the internet," I tell him as I give him a gentle nudge. "Go and introduce yourself to your family."

With a nod, he moves in to talk to a family he'd heard of but never laid eyes on. I smile as I watch them all talking so easy and free. Like they've always known one another.

CoCo COMES up to me and whispers, "Who are these people?"

"These people are related to Corbin and Cyprian. I found them and invited them here tonight and to the wedding tomorrow. I've found some people you might like to get reacquainted with too. I'll bring Cyprian to you all as soon as he gets through catching up with this part of his long-lost family." I take her hand and pull her along with me. "I know your parents passed away a good while back."

"I was sixteen when they died in a wreck. I lived with my grandparents for only a year before going to work in a strip club. They never knew what it was I was doing. I told them I was waitressing," she tells me.

"I heard," I tell her, earning a surprised expression from her.

"How?"

I merely point to a small table in the back. "They told me."

"That cannot be my grandparents," she says with a hushed voice. "I don't even recognize them. It's been forever. Quite frankly, I thought they were most likely dead."

"Nope, alive and sitting right there, waiting to see you and meet their great-grandson for the first time ever," I tell her as I pull her along with me to meet them.

"Wait!" she says as she stops and gives me a terrified look. "Did you tell them what I really am?"

With a nod, I say, "I told them the truth. You're a very wealthy woman, who owns an exclusive club in Los Angeles. They were more than proud to hear you'd done so well with yourself."

"You LEFT out the fact it's a strip club?" she asks as she holds her hand to her throat.

"I did. I saw no reason to get too deeply into what it is you do. You own an established club. You should be proud of yourself for that accomplishment."

"It was given to me. I didn't," she says before I stop her.

"You were given it by the man you gave a child too. And you managed it and made it what it is. You did that. All by yourself. Now, go and talk with the people who helped bring you into the world, Coco. Or should I call you, Delia?"

A blush covers her cheeks. "They told you?"

"They did. And they're waiting to see you, so go and get reacquainted." I give her a push to get her going and watch her go to her family. One she left behind so long ago, it seems impossible.

With Cyprian and his parents on the right track, I go to see what my family thinks about all this. Joining my mother, father, sister, and brother at a table, I ask, "So, what do you think?"

"I think your fiancé almost picked me," Catarina says with a laugh.

"I too was afraid that was about to happen," I agree. "I was shaking in my boots."

Taking a seat between my brother and sister, I find my brother ogling a lovely young lady. "Do you think she'd say yes if I asked her to dance?"

"I bet she would. But just so you know, I'm sure most of these women and maybe some of the men too, are paid escorts. So, don't go thinking you've really hit it off with her. She's paid to hit it off with you if you know what I mean."

His brows raise and he smiles. "Cool!" Then he's up and going toward the young woman.

. . .

"MERCY, I hope he doesn't get himself into trouble," my mother says as she watches her baby boy slip his arm around a prostitute's waist, ushering her out to the dancefloor.

"At least he's a proper age to handle such things," I say as I look around and can't distinguish between who is paid to be here and who is not.

Mixing with Cyprian's family has mine in a place they seem to be a bit uncomfortable in. A place I had planned to keep them out of. But as time went on and I had it in my head to make us into a real family, it became apparent, mine would have to dabble a bit into their world, as they were expected to dabble in ours.

Marriage is a delicate dance where things on both sides have to be meshed into place to form the new family that will be the new couple's. Cyprian and I are on the cusp of making a brand new family to add to both sides of ours.

Are we really going to be able to pull this off...?

81

CYPRIAN

"An angel is what you are," I tell Cami as I lie her down on the downy feathered mattress in our hotel room. "Finding some of my missing family on both sides. I never knew what it was like to know anyone more than my mother and father. It feels amazing. And I have you to thank for that."

Pushing her dark red dress off her shoulders, I pull it all the way off and toss it over my shoulder. The red bra and panty set are all that's between her and me as I've already ditched my clothing as soon as we walked through the door.

Her fingertip runs up my stomach. "So, you like knowing that you have more than a couple of people in the world?"

"I do." I kiss her forehead. "And now, you and I will make more people."

She giggles as I slip her bra off. Her arms go around my neck and she pulls me to her, taking my mouth with a hot, lust-filled kiss. "You had me worried for a moment when you held my sister's hands."

"THEY WERE similar in shape to yours, my only love," I tell her then kiss her again. "But only your touch ignites a fire."

She moans as I run my tongue around her nipple then suck it, gently. Her hands running through my hair, have me sucking harder. I run my hand over her other bare breast and feel my insides turning into molten lava.

Before I know it, the animal in me has been set free and I'm all over her. Ripping her panties off, I throw them toward where I thought I saw a trash can. I move my body down hers until I feel the heat from her, taunting me to see if I can manage to get her even hotter.

Pressing her bent knees to the bed, I spread her wide for me and stop a moment to appreciate the beauty she is. "Cyprian, you have my heart, you know."

"And you have mine," I say then lean over to taste her sweet spot. Her groan makes me growl and it sends her body into a small quiver.

"Yes," she hisses as she tangles her hands into my hair. "Kiss me."

Using my tongue, I run it up and down the recesses that beg for attention. She keeps trying to pull her legs up but I hold them down, keeping her wide open for me.

Her bud is swollen and ripening as I look at it. Her hips move up, lifting her body up to meet my lips. I give it a small kiss then watch her as she moves her hands out of my hair, to play with her tits.

Small kisses I pepper her with until she's gyrating, needing more. Once my tongue moves over the now very swollen pearl, I lick it and find myself needing more than a mere taste of the fruit.

Sucking it into my mouth, I roll my tongue around it, kissing her intimately and deep. Her body is racked with pleasure as she growls, moans, groans, and screeches at times. I keep kissing her until her body arches and she cries out with a climax.

With her sweet juices released, I move my mouth to taste what she's released for me and find myself frantically licking her to get every last drop. Once I feel her insides slowing the squeezing they were doing, I move up her body and deliver a kiss to her, letting her taste herself on my tongue. Her kiss is ravenous and her legs wrap around me as she lifts her body up to mine.

I force her back down and thrust myself into her hot, wet, depths of pure bliss. I moan as I fill her and feel her body close in around me. With a soft stroke, I make short pumps until I feel her quivering again and releasing more juices with another orgasm, giving me more lubrication to work with.

Her body is completely aroused as she begs for more. Her nails move up my back and sting my skin as they cut into it. Taking her hands, I hold them over her head and pull my mouth off hers to look into the deep blue pools of her eyes.

Hunger fills them as she arches up to meet my thrusts. Her lips curve into half a smile. "This will be the last time you take Camilla Petit, Cyprian."

MY HEART FILLS with the knowledge that at this time tomorrow, she'll be my wife. Mine!

"Then I better make it count, huh?" I watch her as I swirl a little and her eyes close with how good it feels.

"Cyprian, how wonderful it is to know you and I will be together forever."

"Forever," I echo as I grind into her until her body is shaking with another orgasm. "Open your eyes, Cami. Let me see you when your body releases for me."

Stormy eyes open as she looks at me. I can feel her insides pulling at me and her eyes see into me. I feel as if she's an extension of myself. My body spasms as she takes me with her.

Our eyes speak to each other. No words need to be said. It's all in those eyes. The love, lust, need, all of it resides in our eyes. If we lost the ability to speak, we'd still know what it is we do for one another.

Lying on top of her, I lean a bit to one side to distribute my weight. Letting her hands go, I stroke her stomach as we catch our breaths. The sounds of two people trying to regain composure after giving all they had to the other, fill the hotel bedroom.

"We will be happy, won't we?" she asks.

"I'll make sure of it," I tell her then kiss her warm cheek.

And I will too...

82

CAMILLA

"Why are my legs shaking?" I ask my sister as I get up after having my hair and makeup done.

"You're nervous," she says like it's so normal I should already know that.

"But I have nothing to be nervous about. I love him, he loves me. We want the same things. Why am I shaking?"

"Here," she says as she hands me a small shot glass. "You need this."

"I don't want to be slurring my vows, Catarina," I say as I try to hand it back to her.

"You won't. Just take it down. It'll calm you. And you also don't want to stutter out your vows, either," she says with a giggle.

She's right, so I take the drink and feel the burn all the way down to my tummy. "Ow!"

"Burns, doesn't it?" she asks as the ladies, helping me to dress, giggle.

Stepping into the middle of the puddle of gossamer, silk, and satin, I'm perfectly still as the two women pull it up and start the process of binding it up in the back.

The light blue is just a bit off from the traditional white wedding dress. My deep blue heels accent it perfectly, but who really cares, as no one will most likely ever see them under the full length and very poufy dress.

Catarina picks up a necklace off the vanity and I ask, "That's not something you wore to your wedding, is it? No offense, but that marriage was a bust. I don't need anything jinxing my marriage to Cyprian."

With a scowl on her face, she shakes her head. "No! Of course, not. This was our great-great-grandmother on our father's side. I got it from his sister, Aunt Dahlia. She said you could keep it, to hand down to your oldest daughter."

With the dress tied up in the back, securing me from having it fall away from my body during the ceremony, I turn, so Catarina can put the necklace on me. "So, this is my something old." The other women are finished and silently leave the room.

"It is," she says and lays the gold necklace, with a set of two hearts as the pendant, on my bare chest. It ends right before my gown begins and adds to the look, perfectly.

"I love it. And what a nice story I'll have to tell my daughter someday about how it came to be hers." I gaze in the mirror and think about how lucky I am.

WITH MY HAIR pulled into an updo that would rival the goddesses of Rome, I find Catarina pushing me to sit in the chair again as she reaches into a bag she brought and pulls out a sparkling tiara. "Here's your something new. Cyprian gave it to me to give to you. He wants his princess to wear her crown."

Taking it from her, I look it over and wonder out loud, "Do you suppose these diamonds are real?"

She takes the box it came in, out of the bag and the name on the box, Tiffany & Co. tells me it's very real. "I'd say so," Catarina says then puts the box back and comes to place the tiara on my head."

We both look at my reflection and she wraps her arms around me as I stroke her arm. "Thank you for being here for me."

"You'd have a hell of a time keeping me out of your wedding, baby sister." She pulls off her bracelet, a gold band with a grape vine etched into the metal. "And this is your something borrowed. You're wearing your something blue, so our bases are all covered."

"Great," I say. "So, if everything is so perfect, why am I still quaking and shaking with nerves?"

With a shrug, she says, "You need more of the hard stuff. Come on, I'll do another shot with you."

I don't argue this time as I think about walking down the aisle on my poor father's arm, jittering like a coked-up monkey. Down the hatch, the hot liquid goes and I still feel like I'm freaking out.

Maybe one more will help...

83

CYPRIAN

A knock at the door to my dressing room has my father going to open it. "Cyprian!" Cami cries out as she literally spills into the room. "There you are!"

"Cami?" I ask as I get up and have to take her in my arms as she's stumbling along and bound to fall. "How much have you had to drink?"

"Too much. And I can't do it, Cyprian," she slurs as she holds onto me for dear life. "I can't walk down that aisle."

"Not like this you can't," I say. "Bread and coffee, mother, please."

My mother heads out and I find my father frowning. "Poor girl." He helps me get her to a chair then looks into her eyes. "Do you not wish to marry? It's okay. You know I'm not about marriage. It's okay to change your mind."

"No!" she says then her eyes roll up in her head, it falls back and hangs to one side.

"Cami!" I smack her cheek lightly, then a bit harder when that doesn't wake her up. "Not today. Of all days, not this one!"

"She's not ready, Cyprian. She might never be," Papa tells me. "Look what's happened. She was so nervous, she got drunk. It's a subconscious sign that says she doesn't want a marriage. Though she seems traditional, she's not. Just look at her. How sad. You won't hold her to a marriage, will you, son. How tragic that would be."

"Papa, are you crazy?" I ask him as I continue to pat her on the cheek. "Of course, I'm holding her to it! I've waited patiently for nearly a year. She just drank to calm her nerves. Hell, I have them too. I think it's completely natural to have them. We're about to make huge commitments in front of our families and the pressure is high."

My mother comes back in and sighs as she sees the state my fiancé is in. "Oh no! It's too much for her. I didn't see this coming. I thought she really wanted this wedding."

"She does," I say as I take the cup of coffee from Mother and set it on the table. "She's not a huge drinker. I'm sure whatever she was drinking was stout. It's not a big deal. She'll wake up and be ready to go. I know she will."

"I'll get a wet cloth to see if that doesn't bring her around," Mother says as she leaves us again.

As she opens the door, I see Catarina and she looks relieved. "Good, she's in here. I lost her when I had to leave her, so I could use the bathroom. What did you do to her, Cyprian?"

"I think I should be asking you that all-important question, Catarina. She was entrusted to you. What happened?" I ask her as she looks at Cami and pokes at her.

"She was shaky. I gave her a shot or two or three. Maybe a little more than that." She tugs at Cami's arm. "Man, she's out!"

"I know that," I say with an irritated tone. "Now what will we do?"

"Um, uh, man, I don't know." Catarina puts her hand to one side of her mouth like she's telling me a secret. "You see, I had the same amount of shots she did."

"I can smell that and see it. Catarina, shame on you," I reprimand her then hand her the cup of coffee that will do no good for Cami as she's passed out.

"I'll go see how long the priest will be able to wait," Papa says, then leaves us.

"I'm sorry, Cyprian," Catarina begins to wail. "I really am. I've ruined your wedding. It's all my fault!"

"Don't cry," I say as I try to soothe her. "You'll ruin your makeup and you're her maid of honor. She'll wake up soon. She'll feel like hell but we'll get the vows said and be married and then I'll take her to our hotel room and she'll sleep it off."

"But now she has to feel like shit at her only wedding. I mean I hope it's her only wedding."

"I hope so too," I say and find a magazine to fan Cami with. "Baby, wake up, please."

Settling into a pool of self-pity, Catarina takes the coffee and goes to sit down in a nearby chair. "Perhaps I did this inadvertently. Maybe I'm jealous that she found true love. The likes of which I've never known. First my marriage to Peter, then the thing with the cop, didn't work out. I can't find love to save my life and Camilla just happened to find a man, who walked into the store she worked at and they fell in love. Why can't that happen for me?"

"It's not as if we didn't have our trials. It wasn't always so perfect. Nowhere near. And you'll find love. Perhaps you should stop looking to get it from overbearing men, though. You see, you're better than that. You're smarter than the kind of women who need men like that. You should look for nice men. I just met a cousin last night. He kept looking your way. You didn't even notice him, though."

"He did?" she asks as she wipes the tears from underneath her eyes, smudging her mascara.

"He did. He's a nice guy. That's probably why you didn't notice him. The man you were hanging all over was someone who was paid to be there. A gigolo."

"Crap," she says as she puts the coffee down on the table in front of her. "I thought he liked me."

"He was paid to like you," I tell her. "That's how I grew up. With a bunch of women who were paid to like me. Paid to let me do anything I wanted with and to them."

"That's terrible. So, this cousin, is he handsome?" she asks as she gets up and looks in the mirror. "Damn it, my makeup!"

Taking a tissue, I dab at the black smudges under her teal colored eyes. "I can fix this. I guess you could say he's handsome. I didn't think he was ugly. I can make sure you two meet after the wedding if you want."

"Should I? He lives in France, after all," she says as she looks into my eyes.

"He's just visiting," I tell her. "He lives in New York. He's an investment counselor there. Funny, huh? He's in the same line of work I am. I'm thinking about seeing if he'd like to come to work for me."

"Introduce me. If we hit it off, then offer him a position." She smiles and gives me a hug. "You're going to make an excellent brother-in-law, Cyprian."

"If we can get my bride to wake up to make me one," I say as my mother walks back in.

She goes to Cami and presses the cloth to her forehead. "Camilla, wake up."

Cami's eyes flutter open and she grabs my mother by the wrist. "Can I call you mom?"

Mother smiles then laughs. "If you'll wake up and marry my son, you can."

"K, Mom," Cami says then lifts her head up and looks at Catarina. "You've been crying."

"I got you drunk. I'm sorry," her sister says then makes her way to her. "Are you ready to get married now? Can you walk?"

I HURRY to help Cami get up and find she has to lean, heavily on me. "Your father will have his work cut out for him, bringing her down the aisle to me."

"I'll go and get him," Catarina says as she wobbles toward the door.

"Allow me to," Mother says then pats Catarina on the back. "You take some more of that coffee and give some to your sister."

I watch my mother, a woman I've never seen have a motherly instinct in her life, do things a normal mother would do. "Mother, thank you."

She looks over her shoulder at me with a smile. "You're welcome, son."

Looking at the woman, who hopefully will become my wife very soon, I feel overwhelmed by my love for her. She's managed to transform not only myself but my mother and father, to some extent. "You are a miracle worker."

Her sleepy smile makes me laugh as her eyes droop a bit and she hiccups. "You are a miracle, my love."

The door opens and in comes her father, looking sternly at Catarina. "Did Coco tell on me?" Catarina asks him.

He nods and shakes his finger at her. "You're supposed to be the big sister. You're supposed to take care of Camilla. This is her special day."

"I'm sorry," she begins to cry again.

"No need to cry. It's all going to be fine," I say as I take Cami to her father. "Brace yourself, she's kind of like a jellyfish."

"Bye, bye," Cami says as her father takes her from me.

"I'll see you soon." I watch them hurry away with her to freshen her up and I go out to get the show on the road.

My father meets us in the hallway. "The priest is available for another hour but that's all."

"She's awake. Her father has her. We can go and wait for her to make her walk down the aisle." I take my mother's arm and lead my parents to the church where I will make my vows to Cami, making her and I a thing I never thought I'd be a part of, a married couple.

Is it possible to really live happily ever after...?

84

CAMILLA

"Just take a whiff of this," my mother tells me then puts something under my nose that sends a wave of heat through me as I take in the scent of acidic odor.

"Yuk!" I shout as I accidentally take another big sniff. "What is that?"

"Smelling salts," she tells me." I always carry them with me."

"I'm not even going to ask you why that is," I say. "I'm just glad you do. My head is nearly clear now."

"Great," Papa says. "Then let's get this thing going. Catarina get your butt out there to let them know we're ready to go."

"Yes, Papa," she says as she grabs her bouquet of flowers. "And I'm sorry, Camilla."

I give her a nod and let my mother pull the veil over my face. "Time to go, baby girl."

"The nerves are gone," I say, mostly to myself as I'm surprised I feel only happiness, not nervous at all.

I hear the music start up and take my father's arm. "You look gorgeous."

"And you look handsome in your fancy tux, Papa."

Mother goes out before us, going to take her seat. "I love you, Camilla. See you out there."

"I love you, too."

GOING ALONG WITH MY FATHER, he pats my hand as he says, "You and Cyprian can have a long and happy life together, just like your mother and I have. Things will come along to threaten your happiness but all can be overcome. Love is like a river, it has deep spots, where you can lounge in the luxury of it and shallow spots where it becomes rough as stones crop up to make the water treacherous. Cling to one another during those times. That's when you need to gather strength from each other. Don't turn your back on him if he's having a rough patch in his life and remind him to do the same for you when you find yourself having trouble. Never go to bed angry and don't say things you can't take back. Words can scar just like physical injuries."

Tears have sprung up in my eyes, making it difficult to see where I'm walking. "That's some good advice, Papa."

"I hope so," he says. "It comes from the heart, mon canard."

The music stops as we approach the entry to the main church. The wedding march starts and my heart starts banging like a drum in my chest. My father takes a step and I go with him. Wishing like hell the tears were gone, so I could see my handsome man, waiting for me at the end of the red carpeted path that's leading me to my future.

85

CYPRIAN

The ice blue dress looks fantastic on her. The veil has her hidden from me and it has my heart shuddering as she comes to me. Today she will become mine. She will carry my name and she will give me children who will carry that name into the future.

My life will not be the empty shell it was. I will live on through my children. The future is so different from what I thought it would be.

I thought I'd be a man like my father. Living, merely to make money and party with women who'd let me do anything I wanted to with them. Instead, I'm going to live a life with a woman who tests me on occasion. And fills me with wonder always.

I doubt boredom will ever come into play in our lives. If it does, for some reason, I'll make sure to show it to the door. She and I will make our marriage a happy one.

The closer she gets to me the better I can see her under the light blue veil. Her eyes glisten with tears but the smile plastered on her sweet face tells me they're happy tears.

Her father places her hand in mine as he says, "Take good care of my baby, Cyprian. I'm trusting you."

"I will, sir. I promise." I turn us to look at the man who will say the words to make us one.

I expected to find her hand shaking but she's calm. Her hand is cool and as always, it leaves my pulse nearly racing with just her touch. I don't know if it will always give me this reaction and I don't care. At least I've been able to feel this for a while. It's amazing and the memory alone is better than never feeling it at all.

Her voice is smooth as she repeats the words the priest asks her to. I get to hear that voice every day for the rest of my life. I get to hear her cry, laugh, pant with desire, and the delivery of our children. I get to hear it all!

I REPEAT the words he asks me to and watch her smile as I vow to love, honor, and cherish her. I already do, but these words cement the fact I always will. She is my world. My everything!

I'D BE A LESSER man without her. I know that now. I know so many things I never knew until I met her. And to think how I was set to give this woman a piece of my mind when I heard her talking about me that night.

It seems like a lifetime ago. I stood and listened as she talked about me, without knowing I was listening. Thinking I was a man, I was not.

I suppose I was a bit on the perverted side. I certainly saw sex in a way that was unhealthy. Cami has taught me what it's supposed to be about. It's not an act, the way I had always thought of it. It's so much more than that. With the others, it was an act. With Cami, it's a reality that deepens our connection each and every time our bodies come together to worship the other's.

She is my goddess. My hope. My eternity. And with the last words said between us, she is now my wife and I am her husband. Pushing her veil back, I look at her and mouth, 'I love you.' She mouths it back to me. When our mouths meet to seal the deal, it sends an explosion of stars into my head.

This is it. We're married. To death do us part.

My God, can this be real...

86

CAMILLA

The sound of rain, falling outside the window of our bedroom, has me thinking about how this whole thing began. Cyprian, lies next to me, his arm thrown over me as he makes little snoring sounds.

We've been back home for a week. Looking at the rings on my finger, still gives me the chills. I am the wife of a billionaire, who I love more than I knew was possible.

I talked so much shit about this man before I even knew him. To think of how I thought about him and to see how this ended with me married to the man I once thought of as a pervert, has me smiling.

Life isn't a thing you can plan. Things pop up that you never expected. Did I expect the man who had his driver come in for condoms every Friday and Saturday night to end up being the man I'd share my life with?

Hell, no!

AM I GLAD THAT HAPPENED?

Hell, yes!

. . .

HIS LIGHT BROWN hair has fallen across his face, so I push it back. I love gazing at him while he sleeps. He's beautiful.

I PICK out things about him I hope our kids will have. His nose will be a thing I'll want all our sons to have. It's perfect. His lips are just the right amount of pouty and I think our daughters would look pretty with them. His eyelashes are thicker than mine, so I hope our girls will get them. And his muscles are a thing I hope the boys get.

His temper is more even than mine is, I hope they all get that. A family only has room for one hothead!

HE STIRS and catches me looking at him. A sleepy smile moves over his lips. "What are you doing, Cami?"

"Nothing," I say as I stroke his hair. "Go back to sleep and let me keep looking at you."

A deep chuckle makes his body shake and vibrate mine. "Okay." His light brown eyes close and he snuggles his face into my neck, tickling it a bit.

My giggle has him tightening his arm around me and kissing my neck. His kisses are light at first then he's making longer kisses and sucking at my neck a bit, making me moan.

In between my legs goes wet. I turn my body to press up against him. His pulsing male organ touches me, coaxing me to run one leg over his hip, so I can settle into him better.

His mouth keeps moving until his lips touch mine. I snake my arm around his neck as I grind my body to his, making his cock grow by leaps and bounds. Moving over me, he pulls his mouth off mine to watch my expression as he moves his erection into me.

"Yes, there it is," he says as I moan with how good he feels inside of me. "You glow, baby. When I'm in you, you physically glow."

Shying away, as he watches me too intensely, I find his mouth back on mine as he starts moving with a long, slow rhythm. Our bodies move together like waves in the ocean.

The way his hands move over my shoulders and down my arms, sends chills through me, making bumps appear all over my skin. His hands take mine and he holds them over my head in one of his hands.

I hear the sound of him opening the drawer of the nightstand next to him and feel the soft velvet covered cuffs go around my wrists as he cuffs me to the headboard. "You have the right to remain silent," he whispers to me as he takes his mouth away from mine."

I moan a bit as he moves his body in a way that leaves mine begging for more. "Oh, baby."

"Shh," he shushes me. "You have the right to remain sexy as hell."

I smile a little as he gives me a hard thrust. "Uh!"

"You have the right to scream when I make you see the lights of Heaven," he says then licks up one side of my neck.

I squirm as it tickles. "Baby!"

MOVING HIS BODY OFF MINE, he leaves me panting as he picks me up and turns me over on my knees, replacing my cuffed hands on the headboard. His hands all over my ass, have me shaking.

"Ask me for it," he says as he rubs one particular area on my right cheek.

"Please," I moan as I ache to feel his hand come down on it.

A swift pop and my ass tingles with the action. "You like?"

"Yes," I moan as I heat inside even more. "Again."

Another lands on me and I yelp as it sends sparks of pure energy through me. "You want more?"

"More," I beg. "Give me more."

Again, and again he spanks me until I shout, "Lemon!" My body is quivering and I'm near tears as he stops his assault and kisses my ass all over.

Soft kisses followed by licks and little nips and sucks have me begging him to get inside of me. He growls as he complies, "My wife likes it when I fuck her, huh?"

"She does," I moan. "Please, Cyprian. Don't make me wait any longer, I'm about to explode."

His first thrust sends the air out of my lungs as he says, "You wait until I say you can release."

I groan with how hard that'll be. "Oh, please."

He pulls all the way out. "If you can't."

I stop him. "I can. Please, Cyprian. I'll wait until you say."

"Good girl," he says then moves back into me with another hard thrust.

My ass is a flurry of sensations as his body beats it with every hard stroke. I grunt to hold the orgasm at bay. "Cyprian, God!"

"Wait for me," he says between clenched teeth.

The wave builds and threatens to cascade over the edge without his command and it takes all I have in me not to let it go. I hold it back, gritting my teeth as he slams into me.

I can't control the shuddering my body starts and a sweat breaks out, covering me. It makes our bodies slip against the other's and he begins to moan. His cock jerks once inside me then he shouts, "Give it to me, baby!"

Shattering into a million pieces, I let my orgasm go free and find my head nearly exploding with the amount of adrenaline that goes skyrocketing through my body.

Tremors of pure bliss go through me and I feel his body trembling too. "God, that was amazing!"

His lips land on my back. "You did good, baby."

MY HANDS ARE UNCUFFED as he leans over me, keeping our bodies together. He's still stiff inside of me and I'm not sure he's ready to stop. He rubs my shoulders as I put my hands on the bed to keep my body up.

After a few moments of massaging my shoulders, he pulls out of me and I fall to the bed in an exhausted and spent heap. Rolling me over, he picks me up to face him. I see his cock is not nearly ready to stop the party and smile. "Insatiable."

He nods and takes my arms, wrapping them around his neck. "Wrap those pretty legs around me and let me bury myself in your hot underworld."

I giggle a little and do as he says, finding it burning a bit as he slides back into me. "Did you put some of that jelly stuff on you?"

"I did," he says as a warmth spreads through me. "The bottle had the words, 'sure to please' on it. Is it pleasing you?"

The warmth is beyond amazing and has me rocking my body to get him to move even faster. "Yes, it is pleasing me. Oh, God, Cyprian!"

He laughs as I wiggle on him. "It seems to be working."

"It is!" I say as I gyrate. "I need it harder. Faster and harder."

He lays me on the bed, so he can do what I need him to. "Better?" he asks as he slams into me deeper.

The warm feeling hits a place so far inside me, I arch up to try to get him even deeper. "I don't know how you got that stuff on you so fast but I'm damn glad you did. Fuck me hard, Cyprian."

The way his mouth quirks up into a half smile tells me he likes it when I get nasty with him. "Your wish is my command."

He takes me like he owns me. Which he pretty much does. I have no need to experience any other man. Cyprian leaves no fantasy unfulfilled!

THE HEAT GETS SO INTENSE, it sends me into a hard orgasm, making me shriek like I'm being murdered. His mouth shuts me up as he kisses me and doesn't stop pounding me until I'm a pool of jelly and he finds his own end.

As my body still quivers, he moves us up on the bed, still on top of me. I find exhaustion creeping up on me fast and feel the steady comfort of his heart pounding against my chest as the darkness closes in on me.

Is it too much to hope this never ends...?

87

CYPRIAN

"Look what I found today," I tell Cami as I tug her to come with me to look at a rare find.

I push open the door to the bedroom across the hall from ours and she gasps as she sees what I've purchased. "A baby bed?"

"Yes, isn't it the most beautiful thing you've ever seen?" I take her to touch the cherry wood bed I found at a shop in town. "I had to get it. I've never seen anything like it. Look at the ornate carvings. It's gorgeous."

"It is but I'm not even pregnant yet. It might jinx us. It has been months since I stopped taking birth control and nothing's happened yet," she says as she runs her hand over the smooth polished wood.

"The gynecologist told you it could take up to a year for your system to get back in order. It will happen. I'll make sure of that," I say as I chuckle and grab her up in my arms, making her face me.

Her smile is a bit on the sad side and I find it makes my heart hurt. "In three months, it will have been an entire year since I've been off birth control."

"I'm not worried a bit about it. It will happen. Maybe I need to stand you on your head to make it take." I laugh and spin her around. "I'll do whatever it takes to plant my seed, baby!"

"I know that. It's just that I'm getting worried," she says as she frowns.

"Baby, don't be. We have enough money to do whatever we have to, in order to have a baby. I'm not worried. You don't need to be either." I take her hand and take her out of the room that I thought she'd be much happier about.

Now I can see this is weighing on her and I hate that. Then it hits me like a brick.

Is this what I get for years of living like a sexual deviant?

88

CAMILLA

The truth is weighing me down as Cyprian looks at me with a bit of worry in his eyes. "Cami, what if this is how I am to be punished for how I've lived?"

"Don't be silly. That's not how things work, Cyprian." I tap the place next to me on our bed. "I should be honest with you."

He sits down and looks at me with furrowed brows. "Honest?"

With a nod, I proceed. "You see, the first guy I was in a relationship with, wanted me to have his baby. I was seventeen and as stupid as they come."

"Oh, my God, Cami!" He looks at me with wide eyes. "You had a baby and gave it up for adoption. We can go get it. I'll pay the family you gave it to any amount they want to get it back. Was it a boy or a girl?'

Shaking my head the entire time he's talking, I finally get to say, "No, it's not that."

"Don't tell me you had a..."

I stop him before he even says it. "No, not that either. I got pregnant. I got pregnant three times and I lost it by the third month every single time."

He bites his lip then shakes his head. "You were a kid, Cami."

"I know that." The guilt in me climbs all the way to the surface. "I hate like hell admitting this shit. You have no idea how much I hate to admit I did such a stupid thing."

"It was stupid. But thank goodness you weren't stuck with a bad decision," he says as he rubs my shoulders.

"Here it goes. I'm just going to put the past out there. I never intended to talk about the stupid shit I did but I need you to see that we may never have our own children, Cyprian."

"What else did you do?" He looks at me with a puzzled expression.

"I like the way you look at me now. I like the way you see me as an educated woman with her head on straight. If you know this about me, I'm kind of afraid you'll never see me in quite the same way," I tell him.

HE JUST SHAKES HIS HEAD. "You are who you are now to me, Cami. Nothing from your past can change that."

"I think you're wrong but you married my ass, so you're stuck with me and that means the idiot I was way back in my younger years. So, here it goes. After the first guy and the three miscarriages, he broke up with me. A little while later I met another guy and you won't believe what I did."

"You wanted to get pregnant, huh?" he asks as he gives me an odd look. "How old were you then?"

"Nineteen. So, the thing is, I lied to that guy and told him I was using birth control. I was trying to get pregnant on purpose and I had four more miscarriages. He didn't know anything about the first ones I had but the fourth one happened while we were sleeping together. It was a blood bath and I had to ask him to take me to the hospital."

"All ended before that third month?" he asks as he seems to be calculating things in his head.

"They did."

"You dated one more man. Did you do that with him too?" he asks as he tries hard not to look judgmental.

"No, not with him. I was getting smarter by that time. I was twenty-one and full into college and looking at other things in life. But I always had a little thing going on, inside of me that told me I might not ever have kids."

"Is this something you've told your gynecologist, Cami?"

"I have. I swore her to secrecy. I've hidden this from you and now I'm beginning to feel like you should've known this before you married me." I look down as I feel the guilt overwhelming me.

His finger touches my chin and I find him smiling at me. "Camilla Girard. I would've married you anyway. I love you. I love all of you. And just to be sure about everything if we have no pregnancies after a year, like the doctor told you, then I'll get my sperm checked out too. This isn't all on your shoulders alone, baby."

"AND IF WE NEVER HAVE KIDS?" I ask him as I know this man wants kids like crazy. He's always looking at baby pictures on the internet and looking up names for kids and I know this is a definite goal for him.

"We will have kids. There's more than one way to skin a cat," he says, earning a frown from me. "Okay, skin a cat is kind of gross. But you know what I mean. There're all kinds of ways to have babies nowadays. You're a freaking scientist. You know this!"

"Test tube babies aren't my idea of what God wanted. Maybe the almighty knows I'd be a shitty mother," I say then look away.

Again, he pulls my face to look at him. "We both know you wouldn't be a shitty mother. But we can put this to rest for a while and let time take care of the hormones and then we'll take this thing, head-on."

"I can't believe you aren't pissed at me for withholding this information from you, Cyprian."

"I don't know why. I adore you. I'd have married you with anything in your past, short of being a secret ax murderer," he says with a laugh.

"I don't know what I did to deserve you, but I'm damn glad I have you. You have to be the best husband in the world," I tell him and pull him to me and kiss him.

"It's only because of you that I am who I am today. With you at my side, I can achieve anything. Anything at all, Cami. Don't worry. We'll see our dreams come true. Just you watch."

Is it bad that I don't believe him...?

89

CYPRIAN

A m I pushing Cami to do something she doesn't want to do? The months have passed with nothing happening. She's been off the birth control for a year and a half and she's not even had a missed period by even a few days.

She wants to give it more time but I think it's been long enough. I pushed to see a specialist and now we're both being tested to see who is at fault here.

I pray it's me. That sounds weird, I know. But she's just so positive it's her that I'd like nothing more than to take that monkey off her back. We've been called in to hear the results and I have her hand in mine, praying it's me and not her with the problem.

"I have the test results right here, Mr. and Mrs. Girard," the doctor says as he pulls his reading glasses up and plants them on his face.

Cami's hand starts shaking and she closes her eyes. "Who is it, doc? Who's stopping us from having what we so desperately want?"

"I'm not sure how to tell you two, this. You seem very worried about this and you've only been married a short time. Things can change with time. Stresses can be relieved and things might come around," he says.

. . .

"Go AHEAD and tell us the news. We'll deal with it. We're good at dealing with what's beyond our control, doc. We'll be fine, no matter what the news is." I tell him and hold Cami's hand tighter as I lose any hope that it's me with the problem. It's obvious the doctor sees her nerves and knows she's going to be upset with the news.

I brace myself for the tears she's about to shed as the doctor pulls the paper with the test results out of the large manila envelope. "Cyprian's sperm count is low. That's the reason you aren't getting pregnant, Mrs. Girard. Your results are normal. That's why your menses have all been normal. You are fertile. Now, if you can carry a fetus past the third term isn't a thing I can tell you. You'll have to get pregnant to see what happens then. We can always use donated sperm to make your wife pregnant, Mr. Girard," he ends his devastating words as he looks at me.

"No," I say before he says another word about putting another man's sperm into my wife's body. "Hell, no!"

What the fuck just happened here...?

BOOK 12: THE EVOLUTION

A Bad Boy Billionaire Romance

By Michelle Love

90

CAMILLA

eavy breathing is all I hear as Cyprian has an apparent attack of anxiety. "Ashton, you should pull over. Cyprian needs some fresh air, I think," I call out to the driver as we're on our way home from the fertility specialist's office.

His eyes are wide as he looks at me with panic. "What's wrong with me?"

"You're freaking out," I tell him. "Put your head between our knees and stop breathing so fast."

"No, I mean, what's wrong with me? Why can't I make babies?"

Shaking my head, I answer, "I don't know. You said, yourself, there's more than one way to skin a cat, Cyprian. You don't need to worry. Just remember the things you told me about this."

"I shouldn't have prayed for it to be me," he gasps out.

I find myself surprised he did that. The car pulls to a stop in the parking lot of the convenience store we met in. I get out of the car and help Cyprian out, with Ashton's help.

"Can you go inside and get him a cold fountain drink? Anything with sugar." I take my husband's hands and hold them between us as he looks up at the evening sky and I see the tale-tale sign of tears.

"I thought I could take this burden but I can't, Cami. I can't take it!"

Hugging him, I try my best to console him. "Cyprian, it's going to be fine. It will be. I promise."

Ashton comes back with the drink and I hold the straw to Cyprian's lips. He takes a sip and then another as he watches me. "I don't deserve you," he mumbles.

With his breathing, back under control, we get back into the car and Ashton takes his place at the wheel. "I'll get you two home."

"Thank you," I say as I run my hand over Cyprian's leg. "I'm going to do my homework on this. We will have our own kids. I'll do all I can to make sure you get some kids running around the house before you know it."

Resting his head on the back of the seat, he looks at me with so much sorrow in his light brown eyes. "Cami, if you want to divorce me, I'll understand, completely."

"What?" I gasp as he's insane for even saying such a thing. "I married you out of love. I'll take all of you. Imperfections and all. Don't ever say that again."

"You'll make a great mother," he says then looks away. "You should have kids."

"And we will. No matter what, Cyprian, we will." I run my hand over his cheek and he looks back at me.

"Not with a sperm donor! We won't use a sperm donor," he says as he shakes his head back and forth, rapidly.

"Okay, we'll leave that way out of our minds." I pat his hand to reassure him. "I don't want to have a baby with anyone but you, anyway. I dream of seeing versions of you and I running around. Not me and someone else. Don't worry."

As we pull to a stop in front of the house, he looks at me and asks, "Did you ever think in a million years I'd have a low sperm count?"

. . .

SHAKING MY HEAD, I answer, "I did not ever think that. Not with your virility. But I will research my heart out to find out what can be done to help you bring that count up."

Walking into the house, I find him scooping me up into his arms and carrying me upstairs. "Let's just keeping doing it until we can't anymore."

Laughing, I say, "Put me down, Romeo. I really do need to do my research on this before we do anything else. We already have sex multiple times on a daily basis, already."

"I know." He puts me down, his head hanging low and making me feel worse than if it was me who was the problem with our infertility.

"Come on," I say as I pull him along with me to the bar. "Let's have a drink and I'll get out my laptop and we can peruse the plethora of information we're sure to find on this subject. You aren't the only man this happens to."

Lagging back, he makes it difficult to get him where I want him, relaxing in a comfy chair and sipping on some Cognac. "The specialist said stress might be the cause since I'm so busy with work. Maybe I should step down from the CEO position."

GOING TO THE BAR, I settle him in a chair and put his feet up on the ottoman then go and make him a drink. "I think you might think about getting yourself another assistant and letting others help you more but leaving the position of the company your father worked hard for isn't a thing you should do. You love your work."

"I love you more," he says as I hand him the glass. He pulls me down on his lap and leans his forehead against mine. "Stress has always been a factor in my weekday life. That's why we partied so hard on the weekends. To get rid of that. Do you think the way I've stopped doing that is what has me like this? Impotent."

"Okay," I say as I pull my head back to look at him. "You are not impotent. You, merely have a low sperm count. There can be many contributing factors to that. And if you think I'll ever allow you to go back to that party scene, you're sorely mistaken. Those days are behind you, husband!"

"Got it, wife!" he says with a chuckle. The sound is good to hear coming from him after his reaction to the news. "So, grab your laptop and let's do some brainstorming."

He seems to be getting into a better frame of mind, so I climb off his lap and go to my office to get my computer. As I leave the room, I hear his cell ring and he moans then answers it.

I must be one of his parents asking how the visit went with the specialist. Boy, won't they be surprised by the news he has for them? I know I was flabbergasted by it!

Could children be the one thing we won't get...?

CYPRIAN

"It's me, not Cami, Papa. Can you believe that?" I ask as I'm still not processing the information. "I prayed for it to be me and I feel like an idiot for doing that."

"Your prayers didn't make a miracle happen, son. What did the man say was the reason why?"

"He didn't know for sure. There can be many reasons," I tell him then sip my drink. "One thing's for sure, I have some life changes I have to make. Less stress is one of them."

"Yes, the stress of working the way we do, or I did, is a thing that can get to a man. Maybe you should take some more time off," he offers me. "I could step in for a while longer."

"You've already done that so Cami and I could have a month-long honeymoon not that long ago. And with all that relaxation, it still didn't change a thing. I don't know what will help."

The door to the bar swings open and in comes Cami, "I think I've found something, Cyprian! We need to have less sex!"

"God, no!" I shout. "Papa, I have to go. Cami's lost her mind!"

Tossing the phone on the chair next to me, I look at Cami and find her looking back at me with pure joy in her deep blue eyes.

"Seriously, Cyprian. I think the problem is that we have too much sex."

"Baby, sugar, honey," I say as I pull her back to sit on my lap. "Babies are made by having sex."

"I AM A SCIENTIST," she says as she frowns at me. "I'm well-aware of how babies are made. But look at this article I found." She turns the laptop toward me and I see a picture of a man with a large X over his genitalia. "It says here that when a man ejaculates too much and too often, it can lower his sperm count. Baby, you ejaculate, on average, five to six times a day."

"And you're saying that's too much?" I ask because I don't think it is.

"It is," she lets me know.

"And you never felt the need to let me know this until now?" I ask her as my cheeks heat with embarrassment.

"Well, I didn't actually have a problem with it. It's nice how many times you can make me come unglued in a twenty-four-hour period. Up until now, it hasn't been a problem, it's been a very big benefit." She bites her lower lip and looks into my eyes with a sultry gaze.

"So, you'd like to start this thing with less sex?" I ask her as this makes no sense to me. One doesn't have babies by having less sex. That's just crazy!

"I THINK we should start there and add in some more things. Get rid of your tight underwear. You can wear loose boxers instead of those tight ones." She points at another thing on her computer screen. "Your rock-hard body is made by exercising pretty excessively every day. If you read this, you'll see that can be a problem too."

"Whoa, hold on!" I shout as she's trying to take too much away at one time. "You think I can stop having sex and stop my daily routine too? I can't do that! You see, I don't ever show anyone any pictures of myself before I turned eighteen and started working out. I was chubby. I don't want that to happen to me again. It takes the working out to keep me fit."

With a laugh, she says, "You're more than just fit. You're buff. You're built like a gladiator, Cyprian. I'm not saying you can't do some moderate exercise but all that you're doing now needs to slow way down if you want to have kids, that is."

"You know I do," I say as I sigh. "But this isn't going to work. Without sex and exercise, my stress level will climb to new heights. That's what I do to help with the stress of my job. I'll have to turn to drinking, I guess."

She points to another part of the article. "Nope. That's another thing you'll have to cut out."

"No way! Damn it!" A pout forms on my lips and I have a feeling it's going to be on them a lot if I decide to do this.

"If the shoe was on the other foot, I'd be looking at getting fertility treatments that could lead to having multiple babies all at one time. But I'd do it. I'd have to have hormone shots and extensive treatments that would make me irritable and easy to get upset. But I'd do it."

"Saint," I say as I shake my head. "I'm not one of those. I don't know about any of this. You're talking about upsetting my entire life-style. You see, Cami, I get up and I go to the gym I've built here and workout. Then I shower and get ready for work."

"I'm aware of that. I do live with you," she says with a smile.

"Okay, then you know my life is a mess of things that I'll need to stop if we're to have a baby."

"It is," she says then climbs off my lap. "Look, I need to go see the chef about the Thanksgiving menu. It's in two weeks and I want our first ever Thanksgiving to be a hit since both of our families are going to be here. I'll leave my computer for you to read about your situation. If it's not a thing you want to do, then I'll understand."

I watch her walk out the door and wonder if she really will understand if I can't do everything it says I should. I want kids, I do but giving up every damn thing that makes my life worthwhile seems too much to ask a man to do.

Looking up, I have to ask, "Why, Lord?"

When I look back at the computer screen, it flashes and I set it down, worried I might have done something to it. The screen goes black then I see it come back on.

My heart stops as the image of a tiny baby fills the screen. It's all wet with the icky stuff that it's born with, covering it's little, wrinkly, red body. And in the background, are the parents. Smiles and tears on their faces tell more than words ever can.

Closing the computer, I set it on the table next to me then get up. To the little wet-bar, I go to pour the remainder of my Cognac down the drain. I want a baby more than anything. More than sex, more than being built like a brick shit-house, more than booze. I want a baby that looks like me and Cami more than I've ever wanted anything, other than the kid's mother.

The traces of the amber liquor roll in a circular fashion around the tiny drain and I have to wonder if this will be enough.

Will I see the day when my wife's tummy is swollen with my child...?

92

CAMILLA

"The aromas in this place are amazing!" Catarina tells me as she brings the kids and comes inside. "It's been a while since I've been here. Is Cyprian's cousin, Jasper coming today too?"

"He's here," I tell her as I take her coat and she picks up the kids' coats as they've shucked them off and ran to find the rest of the family. "But you'll have to go easy with him, Catarina. He's not like the forceful men you've left in your past. He's not that caveman who'll toss you over his shoulder and take you to his cave. You can't expect that from him."

"We've been on a handful of dates since you're wedding, nearly a year ago. He's just not making any effort," she whispers as we make our way into the formal living room where everyone has congregated to wait for the Thanksgiving meal to be served.

"Perhaps you should meet him half-way," I say as she's not once gone to see him in New York.

"That's not my style." She tosses her hair back and pouts.

. . .

"YOUR STYLE MADE need to change if you want a nice man in your life." I push the door open and find everyone talking and laughing. Everyone except Cyprian. He sits on one of the sofas with a glass of coconut milk in his hand, a blank expression lets me know, he's nearing his breaking point with the celibacy, no exercise, and no alcohol.

Nudging my sister toward the smiling man whose eyes lit up as soon as Jasper saw her, I make my way to see if I can't bring a smile to my husband's face. Taking the place beside him, he looks at me. "Looks like everyone's made it. I'll go tell the kitchen staff we're ready to eat."

"I'll come with you," I say as I get up and take his hand.

After we leave the room and walk a little ways down the hall, I wrap my arm around him and pull him with me onto one of the many patios outside the house. The air is brisk and cold. "What are you doing?"

"I want to ask you something," I say as I press up against him, pushing him against the wall. "I want to ask you if we could possibly make love tonight. It's been two whole weeks."

He stammers as his eyes search mine. "Are you being serious? I thought you said we'd have to wait until Christmas?"

"I know I did. But you look like you could use a little reprieve from your sexual exile. We can get back to the celibacy thing tomorrow. Then we can have some Christmas fun in a month from now."

"A month," he says as he wraps his arms around me. "My God, it sounds so long. So far away."

"SO, IS THAT A YES FOR TONIGHT?" I ask as he looks past me and out at the scene behind me.

"We should wait. I really want this. I can wait," he says then lets me go.

With a nod, I go back inside with him following me. I can't wait, though and I will get him to give in later. He needs this. He needs to get a break from this.

93

CYPRIAN

"I shouldn't have eaten that much," I say as I can feel the bulge in my stomach. Normally, if I was still exercising, my stomach would be much too tight to show anything I ate. But my body is already beginning to look softer.

Cami sits next to me on the sofa in front of the fireplace. Everyone has left after the Thanksgiving dinner, leaving us all alone. My body goes tense as she pushes my sweater up, running her hand over my stomach. Her lips touch my neck as she coos, "I need you, baby."

"Aw, you're not playing fair," I whine at her as my cock stirs. I haven't allowed it to even move this much and she's going to make this so hard not to do.

"I know I'm not. I want you. I ache for you," she says with a low groan. "I don't care if we don't get pregnant. I want you. Please, Cyprian. Please take me to Heaven like you've always done. Kids will come to us or they won't. I need you." Her mouth feels like hot lava as she sucks on my neck.

"Cami," I moan as her mouth moves around then she's on my lap, straddling me and putting her mouth on mine.

It's been two weeks since I've tasted my wife's kiss. My hands move to take her by the shoulders and pull her off me. Instead, one goes to hold the back of her neck as the other runs up her spine.

My mouth won't let me stop. My cock grows as she moves on my lap, enticing me to give into her. Though my head is telling me I shouldn't be doing this, my heart and lower regions are telling me they won't let me stop.

Her mouth leaves mine and she looks into my eyes. "In front of the fireplace would be very romantic, don't you think?"

I can only nod as she gets off me and tosses a soft throw on the carpeted floor right in front of the fireplace. The warmth of it flushes my skin as she pulls my sweater off. Her hands move over my not so hard abs.

I push her dress off her shoulders, kissing one of them as her creamy flesh begs me to. Soft kisses I trail up to her neck as she undoes my pants and they fall down my legs to the floor.

Kissing her earlobe, I whisper, "I love you, baby."

Her mouth moves down my chest as she moves down my body, ridding me of the boxers and kissing the tip of my very erect dick. "I love you," she says, making her lips graze the tip of the organ that is pulsing with the blood that's leaving every part of my body to fill it up with what's about to happen next.

Moving her to the blanket, I take off her bra, stopping to admire the tits I have dreams about. Massaging them, I find her moving her hands with mine. "You're beautiful." I leave a kiss on one nipple.

"So are you," she says as she pulls her hips up. "These panties are bothersome. Would you be so kind as to remove them?"

As I do as she's asked, moving down her curvy body and pulling her panties off. My face hovers near her sex. The heat from it warms my lips. I could just get her off and keep my sperm to myself. "How about we change things up?"

With a kiss to her clit, I find her hands on my shoulders. "How about we don't?" She pulls at me to come to her and I can't seem to tell her, no.

Instead, I trail kisses up her stomach and stop at her throat. "You want me inside of you, don't you?"

She shakes her head. "No, Cyprian. I need you inside of me. I crave you. I want to feel that smooth skin slide into my wet depths."

"Damn it," I groan as her words have me even harder. "Baby, are you sure?"

"Please, Cyprian." Her lips press against the hollow of my throat. "Show me how much you love me. I've missed you, even though I've seen you every day, I've missed your touch."

"As I've missed yours," I say as I move my cock to her entrance and shiver as the tip touches the outer edge of her sweet, sweet canal.

She arches up to me and I find myself moving up. "Please."

I can't stop myself. I have to feel her. Slowly, I ease into her and our combined moans fill the air. "Yes!"

Her satin skin runs all around me. Her heat is felt all the way to the tip of my toes. "Please don't hate me later for this, Cami."

"I could never hate you, Cyprian," she says as she takes my face between her palms. "If a child never comes to us, I still will never hate you. You and I are one in the same. Now let's put this nonsense behind us and be the man and wife we were before we let this get in our way. I love you and I want to show you. And I need you to show me how you feel about me."

With one easy, long stroke, I say, "Words cannot express how much I love you. So, allow me to show you just how much I cherish you." Her lips taste like lemon pie, she smells like sage, rosemary, and thyme. She feels like and angel in my arms and I'm ready to show her what she means to me.

Children or no children, I have a wife who loves me so much, she'd forgo children just to feel my touch. I can't see that as a bad thing.

But will I be the one who regrets this night...?

94

CAMILLA

His hands are soft as they roam over my skin. His lips graze along my collarbone, sending a slow heat all through me. I don't recall a time I've felt quite like this. I'm not exactly horny. It's more of a need to be with him. It's odd but I'm thankful he's given into me.

My body arches up to his as he makes a near exit. I can't seem to get enough of him. His back is rippling as I move my hands all over it, relishing how his muscles feel.

He's complained about them becoming less defined in the two weeks he's limited his exercise regimen. I feel a slight difference but he's still a total hard-body. His commitment to raising his sperm count has been astonishing.

I know it's only been two weeks but he's amazed me. Not only did he limit his exercise, a thing he dearly loves doing, but he's stayed celibate. No alcohol has passed his lips and he's ingested only food that he found out raises sperm counts. His determination to have children is inspiring.

. . .

I DIDN'T THINK he'd go this far. It's nowhere near as much as a woman would have to do to try to overcome infertility but it's a hell of a lot for a man to do. Cyprian will be an excellent father, of that I have no doubt.

"I love you, Cami." His lips move along my neck then his hands move through my hair and he inhales. "You smell like home."

Breathing him in too, I whisper, "You smell like I could seek sanctuary in your arms forever."

His movements have my body flowing with his. A perfect slow dance that joins us. I don't recall it ever being like this. So, easy yet deeper than any other time before.

My eyes catch his as he moves from kissing one side of my neck to kiss the other. He stops and we look at one another. I caress his cheek as I feel the tremors, signaling the onset of my climax.

He feels it too and kisses my cheek. "Come for me."

Grabbing his shoulders, I wrap my legs around his waist and hold him as close to me as I can as my body explodes around him. "God! Yes!" My jaw is clenched as I grind my body against his until his eyes close and he goes stiff.

His heat rips through me, going like a missile into my soul. I feel the pulsing all through my body as it releases. Our hearts pound as he lies on top of me. Like two drums, beating out a rhythm, the sounds fill my ears.

I open my eyes as his lips touch mine. "I love you, Camilla Girard," his lips move over mine with his words.

"I love you, Cyprian." I feel a tear fall and have no idea why. It must be the beauty of what we've just done. I have to say it was the most beautiful thing I've ever felt.

Holding me until there is nothing left, Cyprian kisses me until the last bit of ecstasy has ebbed. I feel safe in his arms. I feel loved, and needed.

And I pray we didn't mess things up...

95

CYPRIAN

A month has passed since I've touched my wife. My insides are on fire for her. It's Christmas and we're on our way to bed just as soon as we exchange the last two gifts we got each other.

I am primed and ready for action. With a month of baby juice stewing away inside of me, I foresee no problems with my sperm count. I took a little test I found and it came up with a great number.

It seems I'm very fertile right now and Cami's about to be the recipient of a load of the stuff. I hope her eggs are ready to hatch!

HER GIFT IS the test I took earlier today. I know it sounds kind of nasty and a bit on the gross side. But I put it in a see-through plastic baggie, I placed it in a box and gift-wrapped it for her. Her hands won't get dirty until later!

"Here's mine, Cyprian," Cami says as she comes into the sitting room upstairs where I've been waiting for her.

"Where'd you go for so long, Cami?" I ask as she walks up to me and I pull her to sit on my lap.

"I made a quick phone call to Santa and got a last-minute

Christmas present for you. It took him a few minutes to get it to me but he made it," she tells me with a giggle.

She's holding a box that looks like it might have a bracelet in it. It's long and slender, wrapped in red paper with a black bow. I'm not a man who wears jewelry, so I'll have to act like I like the thing.

"You open yours first," I tell her as I pick up the box off the table next to me.

She places her gift on the table and takes mine. "What could this be?" Pulling the bow off the box, she pulls the lid off it and sees the mound of blue tissue paper covering the baggie with the test results in it. "Cyprian, what's this?"

"PICK it up and see what it is," I say as I watch her face, intensely.

My stomach feels tight as I wait for her to see that I'm loaded with little swimmers. She picks up the baggie with two fingers as she looks at the device inside of it. "What the heck is this thing?"

"Do you see those numbers on the little opening at the end of the stick?" I ask her.

She nods. "And what do they mean?"

"That I've managed to build up my sperm. You have an excellent chance at getting pregnant tonight," I say then kiss her cheek. "What do you think about that?"

"I think that's going to be quite impossible," she says with a frown. "I can't get pregnant tonight. Sorry, Cyprian. Christmas will not be the night we conceive our first child."

"AND JUST HOW do you know this, Cami?" I ask as she's not that damn aware of her body to know this won't work tonight.

"I just do," she says with a shrug. "Trust me."

"Are you saying you want to wait a while longer before we have sex?" I ask. "Because I'm about to explode, baby."

"We can definitely have sex." She runs her arms around my neck and kisses me long and hard, with a side of wanting as her tongue does a number on mine and my cock springs to attention.

I get up, cradling her in my arms and carry her to the door. Her mouth leaves mine and she looks puzzled. "I'm taking you to our bed, Cami. What's that look for?"

"We can't yet. You still have to open my gift. Put me down, so you can do that. Then we can go to our bed and you and I can devour one another until the early morning light sends us to sleep."

Oh, yeah. The stupid bracelet I'm going to have to pretend to like!

"OKAY," I say as I put her down and she walks over to pick it up. "Let me have it."

She turns to look at me with the box in her hand. "You don't sound excited about seeing what I'm giving you."

"Sure, I am. I just have loving you on my mind and I'm more than ready to get to that." I gesture to the hard-on that has my pajama bottoms stretched to their limits.

"I see that." Her eyes go to my cock and brighten. "But I want you to open your present first. Then we can get to that business."

Wiggling my finger at her, I say, "Bring it to me, baby."

HER FINGERS PLAY with the belt of her red robe and she pulls it, letting her robe fall open, revealing a very sexy, red, barely-there negligee she's been hiding underneath it. Stepping forward, she holds out the gift to me then runs her hands up her body and bites her lip. "I can barely wait."

Taking the box, I pull her into my arms, nuzzling her neck, I whisper, "I think this little gift can wait until I've tasted you."

Before my lips touch hers, she twists her head to stop me. "Open it, please."

With a sigh, I let her go, so I can get the gift out of the way, so we can get to the good stuff. "Okay, have it your way. Just know I'm about to fall apart here."

"I know you are," she says as she watches my hands untie the bow and pull the top off the box.

I freeze as I see what's inside. "Cami!"

"Yes," she says as I pull the clear baggie out of the box.

"Cami!" I say again as my mind is going foggy. "It's a plus sign! It's a plus sign!"

"It is," she says with a giggle. "Looks like we conceived on Thanksgiving night. See, I told you we couldn't conceive our first born on Christmas night. Sorry about that."

Putting the pregnancy test down on the table, I pull her into my arms and pick her up. "You little minx! How long have you known?"

"I was two weeks late and I just took the test a few minutes ago. That's why I took so long to get back to you. So, what do you think about this news?" Her smile is the widest I've ever seen.

"I think I'm the happiest I've ever been except for that day in Paris when you said the words, 'I do.' And how do you feel, Mrs. Girard?"

"I feel amazing," she says as I whisk her out of the sitting room, taking her to our bedroom to celebrate the pregnancy and the end of my celibacy.

"Don't worry, I'll be gentle with you," I say as I lie her on the bed.

"Don't you dare," she says with a growl. "Cuff me up and fuck me like you own my ass."

My cock nearly splits my PJ's open as it surges with her sexy attitude. But I remember all too well that getting pregnant was never her issue. Staying that way was.

"No cuffs, no fucking, nothing but sweet and easy lovemaking for you, my dear wife. You'll be pampered, spoiled beyond belief, and handled like the treasure you are." Dropping my clothes to the floor, I ease onto the bed, pulling her clothes off her and watching her smile like the devil.

"What did I ever do to deserve you?" she asks me like she has no clue.

"You made me who I am today, Cami. You took a selfish playboy and made him into a man you can trust with not only your life but the one you carry, as well. You hold us inside of you and I will always protect us." Taking her lips, I deliver a sweet kiss to her to let her know, without a doubt, that I cherish her.

I wonder if she can really make it full term this time...

96

CAMILLA

"I wish you'd stop looking at me, Cyprian," I whine as he paces next to the bed and can't keep his eyes off me as my oby-gyn examines me.

I've made it to the third month of pregnancy. But when I woke up this morning I was cramping only a bit but it was enough to get me to tell Cyprian what I was feeling.

The man flew out of bed and called my doctor to get her over here right away. She came, complete with a portable sonogram machine she's about to check me out with.

"She's not effacing," she says as she stops the internal exam. "Now to see if everything looks good on the inside."

CYPRIAN STOPS his incessant pacing and looks at the monitor. It takes forever to find the tiny baby but she finally does and we see it move a bit as she mashes my belly with the wand. He points to the little spot. "There he is!"

"At this point, all fetuses are female," the doctor corrects him. "It'll be a while before we know if she'll stay a girl or become a boy."

"But the baby is okay," he says. "That's the main thing." He kisses the top of my head and sighs. "I wish we could keep her hooked up to this thing so we could watch the baby's every move."

She laughs but I don't, knowing full well he really would just sit and stare at the machine if that was a possibility. "What should I do to try to make sure I keep this baby?" I ask her as I'm nervous about losing it.

Putting away the machine, she looks at me with a grim face. "Stay off your feet this next month. Let's see what happens. Can you do that?"

"She can and will," Cyprian answers for me.

"I do work," I say as I took a job a couple of months ago, at a lab.

"Not anymore," Cyprian says, quickly. "I'll make the call. You can go back to work after the baby is born. If that's something you want to do."

"I don't want to leave my job right now," I let him know but I'm met with two shaking heads.

MY DOCTOR IS the first to say something to me about it, "You told me you were doing work with infectious diseases. That's not a good thing to be doing when you're pregnant, Camilla. And the time on your feet is another bad idea if you want to hang onto this baby,"

"Which I do," I say as I know she's right. "Okay, Cyprian, I'll stay in bed."

He claps like he's so happy he gets to wait on me hand and foot. "Perfect! I'll ask my father to cover for me at work and be right by your side. Day and night."

"You have a great husband here, Camilla. I can't say I've seen many like him. Let him take care of you. He seems to be itching to do that," my doctor says as she gathers her things to leave.

Cyprian helps her to the bedroom door. "Don't worry about her. I've got it all under control."

"I can see that," she says then looks at me. "I'll call to make another house call at the end of the month. If you experience any discomfort or spotting, call me."

"We will," Cyprian tells her then closes the door behind them as he carries the heavy machine out for her.

I lie in bed and wonder what the hell happened to my life. Suddenly, I feel trapped. The room looks like it has bars on the windows, keeping me here, where it's supposedly safe.

Only I know there is no safety anywhere within these walls. I could lose the baby, no matter what I do. And I don't know how Cyprian will handle it if that does happen.

Can he take life with me if this is a big part of it, losing pregnancies...?

97

CYPRIAN

As I run the water over her head, I smell the coconut scent of the shampoo as I rinse her hair. Her tummy is swollen with our baby. She's held on for eight months but it hasn't been easy.

Restricted to complete bed rest has Cami an irritable wreck. "Ow! You pulled my hair!"

"Sorry, baby. I didn't mean to." My hand was nowhere near her hair but she snaps about things all the time.

I can't blame her. She's overweight with not being able to move around hardly at all. She complains about feeling like a beached whale and her body aches all the time.

The things I went through to make sure I had plenty of good swimmers can't compare to what she's having to go through to bring our son into the world. She cries more often than I think she should. She tells me over and over how she never wants to go through this again.

I feel awful about what she's going through and have promised her he can be our only child if that's what she wants. I want more but I would never ask her to go through this again.

It's horrible for her and the worst part hasn't even come yet. The birth process isn't expected to be easy. Her doctor has cautioned us that a Cesarean is most likely going to be necessary as she has very little muscle to help her push the baby out with.

"JUST GET me out of the tub. I'm getting cold," she says as I finish rinsing her hair.

"If I don't put in some conditioner your hair will go wild, baby," I tell her as I make an attempt to finish the job of bathing her.

"Like I give a fuck about that!" she shouts at me. "Just get me the fuck out of this freezing water!"

"Okay, baby," I say as I grab a towel for her then help her to get up out of the anything but freezing water. I've kept adding in hot water to be sure it didn't get cold but she seems to get cold so easily. I assume it's from poor blood circulation.

I watch her legs tremble as she steps over the side of the bathtub. Her nails dig into my shoulder as she braces herself. When she takes in a sharp breath, I know she's having a contraction.

We freeze as it happens and her eyes close as she breathes in and out, slowly. "Stay in there, Colton. Please, stay in there for a little while longer for Mommy," she whispers.

Wrapping the towel around her, I pick her up and carry her to the bed. "It's going to be okay, Cami." I prop her feet up on a pillow to raise them like the doctor told us to do.

The poor thing can't move hardly at all without contractions starting. I massage her stomach then feel her body begin to shake and cover her up. "I'll go get a towel to wrap around your wet hair. I'll be right back."

"CYPRIAN," she says as I walk away. "I'm sorry I'm being such a bitch. Thank you for everything."

With a nod, I say, "You're welcome and I'd never call you a bitch." I leave to go to the bathroom and hear her moan.

Looking over my shoulder, I see her rubbing her stomach. She's having another contraction, so I hurry to get the towel. The woman lying in our bed is nearly unrecognizable. It's hard to take that I wanted a baby so bad I'd do this to her.

When I come back into the room, I find her eyes red-rimmed from crying. "Cyprian, they won't stop. I'm having one after another."

"Well, we know those aren't the right kinds of contractions. Remember what your doctor said?" I pick up my cell and call the doc to get her to come over here. "She'll come and give you a shot and they'll stop."

Her hand grips my arm as she grits her teeth. "Tell her to hurry." Red fills her face as she stops breathing with the pain.

"Breathe, Cami," I say then blow in her face, so she has to take in a breath. "Hi, it's me again. I need you to come to our place. Cami's having those Braxton-Hicks contractions again." I end the call. Her doctor knows this drill well since she's done it at least once a month and sometimes twice.

"Ow!" she yells then the red fades as she looks at me. "I want this to be over."

"I know, baby," I say as she settles back. "I do too. He's only a month away from being fully developed. Only one more month."

"I can't do it that much longer. I can't." She shakes her head then stops and her face goes red again.

She has a death grip on me as the pain has her breaking into a sweat. I take a seat on the edge of the bed and let her squeeze one hand while I run my other hand over her damp forehead. "I love you, Cami. If I could take this pain upon myself, I surely would."

The pain leaves her and she looks at me with sorrow-filled eyes. The dark blue they were has faded to a pale shade. "I know you would." She bites her lip and looks away. "I'm a useless wife. I wouldn't blame you if you left me."

The tears start flowing and I kiss them away, the best I can. "Stop saying things like that. I'd never leave you. You are my heart, my soul, my life."

The tears continue and sobs begin as she loses all control. "I hate who I've become!"

Hugging her, I can feel her body tense up with another pain and I rub her shoulders as I hum into her ear. "Everything is fine. Everything will be alright soon, baby."

She groans with the pain and I find my heart hurting so much, I think it might break free from my chest. As God as my witness, I will never do this to her again!

Is there a chance in hell she will ever forgive me for doing this to her...?

98

CAMILLA

The sirens stop as the ambulance pulls into the ER parking lot. "We've made it, baby!" Cyprian says as the paramedics hop out the back of the ambulance they put me in only half an hour ago.

"We have," I say with relief. "I thought I was going to have this baby in here."

THEY TAKE the gurney out and I find myself being moved into the hospital at top speed. I have no idea what the rush is now. They started an IV and I have some morphine coursing around in my veins, bringing me more relief than I've had since I can recall.

Cyprian is right next to me, holding my hand and running along with the two men who came to get me. I see my doctor coming into the hallway with blue scrubs on. She gives Cyprian a serious look. "Get inside and let the nurse scrub you up. We're going to have to do the C-Section."

"What? Why?" he asks as I watch one of the paramedics hand over my chart.

He looks at my husband and says, "We lost the baby's heartbeat about ten minutes ago."

The morphine is suddenly gone in an instant as I shriek, "No!"

"Just stay calm, Camilla," my doctor directs me. "This happens, I just need to get you into surgery and get this baby out of you."

Cyprian is frozen as he looks at me. Then he bolts to my side and kisses me hard on the mouth. "I'll be with you. I'll be there for him when they take him out. Don't worry."

"I have to worry!" I shout then find them moving me into a dimly lit room and a mask is placed over my face. The last thing I see is Cyprian and he's smiling at me.

The darkness closes in on me and I want to cry but can't manage to do it.

Is this how it will end for us...?

99

CYPRIAN

His body is blue as they pull him from Cami's stomach. The cord is wrapped around his little neck and he's not moving. I want to fall down on my knees and beg God to take me instead but I have to stay strong for my wife.

"Is HE?" I manage to get out.

A nurse takes me by the shoulders and sits me in a chair. "Wait here, Mr. Girard. We don't know anything yet."

I can't take my eyes off the little blue baby as they painstakingly unwrap the cord wound around his neck and shoulders. I don't know how he managed to get himself all wrapped up like that.

They all handle him so roughly, yet his body is limp in their hands. The last bit of umbilical cord is taken away then the doctor hands him off to the pediatrician and his staff.

Unable to get up as I feel weaker than I ever have. I watch as they take him to the waiting clear bassinet with the large light above it and start doing things to my son.

The pediatrician turns to look at me. "Come here and call to him, Mr. Girard."

I get up and go to find my baby boy still blue and unmoving. Taking his tiny hand with one finger, I say, "Hey there, Colton. This is your daddy. I'd love it if you'd wake up for me. You see, your mommy and I have a bet going about the color of your eyes. I say they're going to be blue and she says they're going to be brown. If you could open them then I could tell your mommy she was wrong and I'm right."

The slightest feeling of his hand gripping my finger has me looking at the doctor. His stethoscope is on Colton's tiny chest. "I hear something. Keep talking."

"Colton, your mommy would really like to wake up and find your sweet face looking back at her. If you could just come on home to us, we promise to love you forever and ever. Just come on and take a breath, buddy. Daddy's here. I'll always be here for you, my little man."

With an eerie coughing sound, I step back as the doctor puts something in my son's mouth to suck stuff out of his throat then he picks him up and I hear his tiny cry. "Come on, Colton!" the doctor says as she jostles the tiny kid around.

"Colton, come on," I say, then hear the whole room full of nurses and doctors calling my son's name.

"Colton! Come on, Colton!"

His cries grow louder and I'm amazed to see the blue of his skin turn to red then fade into pink. His arms are flailing and his body is arching as the doctor lies him back down and a nurse hands me a pair of scissors. "Time to cut the cord, Daddy."

I HAVE to wipe the tears out of my eyes to see well enough to do such a thing and cut my son's cord. Before I know it, they have him all bundled up and he's handed to me.

Holding him and watching him breath is like a miracle to me and I kiss his forehead. "Daddy loves you, son. Daddy loves you so much. Thank you for coming back to us. Thank you." His eyes open just a bit as he seems to be looking for me. "Blue! I knew it."

I turn to look as the doors to the OR open and a man comes in with a bag of blood. "I'll need at least two more. Have them ready," Cami's doctor tells the man who puts the bag up on the IV stand and leaves as the nurses get it going into her IV.

Carrying the baby with me, I go back to Cami's side and see her looking paler than I've ever seen her. "She's lost a lot of blood?"

"Yes, she has. She was anemic already. I knew I would have to give her more blood. I had her sign papers on it the other day when I was doing her last check up."

"You sure did a number on your mommy, little buddy," I whisper to him and find a nurse tapping my shoulder.

"I'm sorry. We need him back for a little while," she tells me.

Reluctantly, I hand him to her, kissing his little head before he leaves my arms. I watch her carry my son away and know in my heart he will be the only child I ever see born.

I could never ask Cami to do this again. Taking her hand, I find it limp and wonder if she'll ever really be the same person she was before.

Who can come back after all this...?

100

CAMILLA

C yprian stands close to Colton as he blows the candles out on his third birthday cake. I watch them as they laugh and my heart fills with something completely unexpected. I want another baby!

MY HUSBAND IS dead-set against another baby. I get it. I do. And I was too, at first. But with Colton being three now, I can see he needs brothers and sisters and I feel the need for more kids too.

Cyprian sets our son free to go play with his cousins. Catarina makes her way to me with her new daughter in her arms. Maybe that's why I want another baby. A girl would be nice.

"Jasper asked if we could take Colton with us for the night. He has a present for him at home he forgot to bring," she says as she gets to me.

Plucking the baby out of her arms, I say, "That actually sounds perfect to me. You see, I want to have a serious talk with my husband and having Colton gone for the night would be great."

With a plan forming in my head, I run up to the bedroom to get rid of the drawer full of condoms Cyprian has kept filled these last three years. He's vowed never to plant his seed in me again. But I'm not having any of that nonsense!

101

CYPRIAN

"Have you gone insane?" I ask my wife as she sits on the bed in a cute little nighty asking me to get her pregnant.

"How is a wife asking her husband for another child considered insane?" she asks me with a pouty bottom lip.

"Um, did you forget the hell you went through?" I ask her as she clearly has. "Let me remind you."

"No," she says as she holds up her hand. "I don't want to be reminded. This will a brand new experience. No worrying about anything. We simply stop using protection and if it happens it was meant to be. That's it. No pressure at all."

"Except the pressure put on me. You see, I'm not proud it was me who made you go through all of that." I sit on the bed next to her and stroke her pink cheek. "It hurt me, baby."

"I GOT OVER IT," she says. "Please, Cyprian. Please."

"Begging won't help. I remember it all too well." I get up and go to the nightstand to get out a condom. "But I will satisfy that need you have." Opening the drawer, I find it empty. "Cami!"

"I threw them out." She pulls the thin spaghetti strap off one shoulder and rolls it, seductively.

"You shouldn't have done that without talking to me first. I'm telling you, I don't want to see you like that ever again. I felt terrible the whole time."

The other strap is pushed down and her tits pop free as the silky thing falls to her waist. "Please, Cyprian. Let's just forgo the condoms. I'd love to feel your silky skin inside of me again."

"DAMN IT!" I shout as my cock springs to life with her words.

"Don't you want to feel me again?" she asks as she bites her bottom lip and looks all cute and sexy.

Her hands move like stealthy spies as her eyes hold mine. The deep blue back to them. It took months for the color to come back to them. It took a solid year for her body to come back to what it was before the hard pregnancy and she wants to go back to that hell?

My pajama bottoms pool at my ankles as her hand moves over my cock. "Cami," I moan as she strokes me.

She stands up and her nighty falls all the way off. "Cyprian," she moans back at me.

Moving slowly down my body until she's on her knees in front of me, I tense as her mouth moves over my cock and her fingers tickle my balls. "Baby. Don't make me do this to you."

She moans as she takes me into her mouth and runs her tongue along the underside of my throbbing dick. I'm putty in her hands before I know it. Just before I pour myself down her throat, I pick her up and toss her onto the bed.

A growl fills the air as I turn animal and find myself feeling lusty and hot for her. "You just remember, you asked for this."

"I will," she says as she holds out her arms. "Come to me, baby."

So, I do as she says and thrust my unsheathed sword into her and hope I don't kill her this time around...

The End

ABOUT THE AUTHOR

Mrs. Love writes about smart, sexy women and the hot alpha billionaires who love them. She has found her own happily ever after with her dream husband and adorable 6 and 2 year old kids. Currently, Michelle is hard at work on the next book in the series, and trying to stay off the Internet.

"Thank you for supporting an indie author. Anything you can do, whether it be writing a review, or even simply telling a fellow reader that you enjoyed this. Thanks

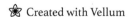 Created with Vellum

CPSIA information can be obtained
at www.ICGtesting.com
Printed in the USA
BVHW040138280221
601119BV00038B/464